To Louisie
Hay

oo 9

One
Chrysanthemum

One Chrysanthemum

Joan Itoh Burk

BRINDLE
& GLASS

Library and Archives Canada Cataloguing in Publication
information is available from the National Library of Canada.

Cover image: Robert Lemay

Brindle & Glass is pleased to thank the Canada Council for
the Arts and the Alberta Foundation for the Arts for their
contributions to our publishing program.

Brindle & Glass Publishing
www.brindleandglass.com

1 2 3 4 5 09 08 07 06

PRINTED AND BOUND IN CANADA

In loving memory of
Madame Chiye Hachisuka

Dear "Auntie" Chiye

ONE
Autumn 1965

*T*he wind danced a garbage can down a dark Tokyo street, threw it into the air and sent it crashing against a garden wall. The noise pulled Misako from a drugged sleep and propelled her out into the night to fly with the leaves. 'Round and 'round she whirled, over a crowd of strange people. They were waving and calling up at her, their rasping voices telling her something about Hideo, something she didn't want to hear. Misako clasped her hands tightly over her ears and gave herself to the wind. She spun over their heads, off into the inky darkness.

The wind dropped Misako onto the muddy edge of a raging river. Dark waters lapped against her body and the rain beat down on her head. She felt the veins in her head swell and a wave of nausea swept through her body.

Misako's hand shot out from under the quilt and found the lamp switch. The white ceiling floated into focus. Panting with fear, she sat up and looked around the room. Everything was dry and familiar. The storm was raging outside; rain beat hard on the tile roof and a clump of bamboo knocked against the bedroom's wooden shutters. She fell back on her pillow and tried to separate dream from reality.

The storm was real. There had been typhoon warnings throughout the day. Neither Misako nor her mother-in-law had been surprised when Hideo called to say he would spend the night at the office. Most Tokyo offices turned into makeshift hotels during storms or strikes by the National Railway. Misako wasn't sure if it was a precaution against arriving late for work the next morning or merely an excuse for all-night mahjong games. Hideo's mother thought it noble of her son to devote so much time to his job. She praised him every time he came home late, which had been happening more and more often.

The two women ate dinner and watched television. The evening passed normally until Misako had a vision. It happened a little after eleven. She was taking the futon quilt out of the bedroom closet when her eyes filled with a vision of her husband and a young woman. They were in a dimly lit red and black room, naked, their bodies entwined on a western-style bed.

1

Hideo was moaning and thrusting against the strange woman's body.

Misako fell to her knees, shocked by what she had seen. The quilt lying on the tatami floor in front of her had become part of the hot, filmy room of her vision. Her innocuous pink wedding futon had become an extension of the lovers' pulsing mattress.

The vision lasted mere seconds but Misako's mind took in every detail. She saw the half-empty whiskey bottle on the table next to the bed. Even the black mole on Hideo's left shoulder was clear. The woman's legs were wrapped around his back. Misako felt sick. Desperate to forget what she had seen, she took two sleeping pills. The last thing she remembered before falling into a deep sleep were the broad, ugly feet of the woman.

Two strikes of the clock in the downstairs hallway joined the noise of the storm. Misako lay in bed trying to muffle the sound of her crying, afraid that her mother-in-law would hear her sobs through the thin wall. She hadn't seen things in a long time. Her mother used to say she had visions because of an overactive imagination. The trouble with that theory was that the visions usually proved true. But saying that made her mother angry. If Misako insisted, she was accused of lying.

As a child, Misako had struggled to control the phenomenon by closing her eyes tightly and thinking of something else. Her mother said multiplication exercises would sweep her mind of such nonsense. Two times two is four. Four times four is sixteen. Eight times eight is sixty-four. By her teen years, Misako had become so skilled at using the technique that she could make a vision evaporate the instant it started. The exercise became so automatic that she wasn't aware of anything more than a sudden need to think of multiplication exercises. But lately, it didn't always work. Her buried secret was beginning to surface. It was subtle at first, a vague awareness that she knew what was about to happen, going to the kitchen door to greet a friend who was just approaching the house, or knowing who was calling when the telephone rang, before she'd even answered it.

Then there was the agitation she felt one afternoon when she walked past the home of an elderly neighbour. The feeling of distress was so compelling that Misako opened the gate and walked directly to the back garden where she found the frail old woman lying on the ground in pain. Her neighbour had fallen and broken her hip. Everyone said how fortunate it was that Misako had heard the woman's cry for help. The reality was that no one passing the front gate could have heard the old woman's feeble cry from the far end of the garden. But Misako wanted to believe that she had.

Denial had come easily until the horrendous vision of Hideo and the strange woman. So this was the reason for his recent indifference toward her.

"Damn Hideo!"

The words slipped out. She clapped her hand over her mouth. The noise of the storm suddenly seemed comforting. Mother Imai couldn't have heard her even if she was listening. "Damn Hideo," she whispered into her hand. As much as she hated the thought of having visions again, Misako had no doubt that everything that she had seen was true. Hideo had not been in the office but in a love hotel with some woman. How could he make love to a woman with such ugly feet? Misako had always been vain about her own slender feet.

The gentle patter on the roof sang of the storm's retreat. Snoring came from the next room. It was near dawn and the priest at the nearby temple would be preparing to sound the morning bell. Trying not to disturb her mother-in-law, Misako slid the bedroom door open and crept down the stairs to the bathroom.

The floor tiles were cold but the water in the covered tub was still warm. Misako took off her sleeping kimono and knelt before the low-set mirror to pin up her thick, shoulder-length hair. Large, red-rimmed eyes looked back from her small oval face. That was another thing Misako disliked about herself; her eyes were more deeply set than those of most Japanese. A teacher in high school once told her she could pass for a Filipino. That annoyed her. She didn't want to pass for anything other than a Japanese.

Misako gathered her hair at the back of her neck and dipped a small wooden bucket into the water. She threw it over her shoulders and felt the warmth pass over her chilled body.

A block away, a monk in a black oilskin cape walked across a temple courtyard. The rain bounced as it struck the ground around him. He climbed the narrow ladder to the covered tower and stood before the large bronze bell. With a jerk of his head, the priest threw back the hood of his cape, exposing a bald head. He gently touched the log that hung before the bell and checked his wristwatch. One minute to go. The priest bowed his head and began to pray.

Misako sat on a small wooden stool and washed her body with a rough cloth. As she scrubbed her arms and shoulders, streams of soapy water ran between her small breasts and down her thighs.

It was time. The monk swung the log against the bell to announce the new day. The mournful call cut through the grey, rainy morning and slid across the garden.

Misako lifted her head and smiled. As long as she could remember, this was the sound she had loved better than any other. This was the music that soothed her pain and brought her peace. She closed her eyes and listened to the ringing of the bell. The pleasure lasted until she began to soap her feet. It was then that she remembered the woman in the vision.

TWO

*A*t the same time that Misako sat surrounded by warm water and self-pity, her grandfather was meditating in his Buddhist temple in the northern prefecture of Niigata. No rain fell on the small city of Shibata as a young monk swung a log against a massive bell to announce the dawn. The sound travelled through the morning air and into the wooden houses to tap at the consciousness of the slumbering citizens.

The bell's mighty moan reached the elderly priest's room but not his ears. During meditation, nothing penetrated the sealed-off chamber of his mind. He was not aware that the morning light fell like a luminous ribbon through the small, high window. He didn't see it creep across the yellowed *tatami* floor to slowly infuse the room with a ghostly glow.

The old priest sat cross-legged, his hands folded on his lap, thumbs pressed together. His tawny bald head protruded from several layers of black kimono, like an ancient ivory turtle stretching a scrawny neck outside its dark shell. He sat, his eyes closed, before an alcove that displayed a box wrapped in white silk and a worn scroll picturing a Buddha sitting on a faded-blue cloud. When the sound of the bell died away, the figure of the priest seemed a lifeless form in a sepia photograph. Minutes passed before he opened his eyes and unfolded his hands. The decision had been made.

"Are there no special privileges in old age?" The whispered question floated in the emptiness of the room as if to argue a case to the spirits of his priestly ancestors. Solemn photographs of his long-dead parents silently stared down from their places, high on the age-worn wall.

For several weeks, he had kept a box of human ashes in his room. That alone was considered peculiar behaviour and the other two priests at the temple discussed it in hushed tones. Only yesterday his assistant, Teishin, had rubbed his chubby hands, pleading for the ashes to be placed in the back altar room.

"Another couple of days," the old man said. "I want to keep the box here and think about it. Just for another couple of days."

"But what more can possibly be done?" the assistant asked in a tone of exasperation. "The cremation and prayers were carried out respectfully. What more is to be done for unknown remains?"

"Yes, yes, you are right," the old priest said, waving his hand in dismissal.

The box of human remains had come to the temple after the great storm of August 1964, when torrential winds and rain pounded the area. There had been floods, mudslides and many deaths. Shibata's swollen Black River had spat out dozens of baby streams, digging into the land as they ran from the banks, growing fat with the weakened earth. The mud and water swept overland, smothering ripened rice fields, crumbling paved roads, carrying away automobiles and invading homes.

The path of destruction made its way from the river and into part of the city, through the museum compound that was once the villa of the former feudal lords of the Shibata clan, known as Shimizuen. Over a period of more than three hundred years, the grand house and Kyoto-style garden had experienced glory, war, earthquakes, neglect, abandonment and meticulous renovation. The storm of 1964 brought devastation once again, covering everything with a blanket of sludge

Two days after the storm, the wind still keened softly through the villa's shattered roof. Mr. Saito, the museum's present director and an engineer stood on the veranda surveying the damage. It was an appalling setback after so many years of restoration work.

The tenacious bamboo rode out the great storm of 1964, but the winds toppled two ancient pine trees into the garden's pond. The director surveyed the wreckage while an engineer wrote notes on a clipboard. The cleanup would have to begin with the seething mudhole that had once been a pristine pond.

The pond was fed by a five-foot-wide stream that ran along the garden's south wall. Fresh water from the well-banked stream was piped into the pond. During the garden's modern restoration, a pipe system had been installed so that the stream would feed the pond as a gentle waterfall, trickling down several carefully placed rocks. After the storm, the plan was to pump out the muddy water to the point where the debris could be removed without injuring any of the valuable fish that might have survived. Some of the mud that had covered the garden could be shovelled back into the pond and allowed to settle before the pond water was slowly replenished. As for what was to be done about the sad state of the grasses and moss, the master gardener who was overseeing the garden's reconstruction would have to come again from Kyoto for a consultation.

Mud oozed over the top of the director's rubber boots as he picked his way around the garden, climbing over fallen trees and stopping to watch a worker deposit a dead, prized red koi into a large plastic bag. The pond had thrown up a surprising amount of debris—beer bottles, pop cans, an old straw sandal, a piece of rough wood that must have once been a small boat.

"Save that wood and the footwear," the director ordered. "Throw the trash away but save anything of possible historic value. If you are not sure, ask. And I want to know how many dead carp are found."

A week later, the bulging accordion hose of a water pump began to pull some of the sludge out of the pond. A large wire net barrier was erected to keep the surviving carp away from the shallow end of the pond, where the pump was. Every two hours, the pump was stopped and the operation inspected to see what progress was being made.

During one of these exercises, a mud-stained worker approached the director with something wrapped in a piece of muddy cloth. "Sir, I thought you should be the first to see this."

The director removed his dirty glove and accepted the object. Inside the towel lay a mud-smeared human skull. "Where did you find this?" he asked.

"Under the stone bridge. The water is down below knee level there. I shovelled it out thinking it was a dead fish."

Saito held the muddy skull up and turned it around in his hand. "Interesting. Dig around that area carefully. There could be more of this fellow," he said with a note of excitement. For some time he had been striving towards having the Niigata prefectural government declare Shimizuen as an important cultural property. If this skull had historical significance, it could help his cause.

"Such a find is not surprising," he said, "considering the war and revolution this garden has witnessed."

News of the discovery quickly travelled around the garden, lightening the mood of the clean-up crew. Their tea break was more animated than usual. The director assigned a second man to help dig near the bridge and he personally examined every shovelful of mud that they pulled up. By the end of the day a pile of human bones lay on a straw mat at the edge of the pond. The excitement the discovery generated considerably slowed the cleanup work.

"I think we have all there is now," the director told the workers.

"Those bones look small for a man," a worker remarked.

"People were smaller in the old days," another worker offered. "Maybe being buried in mud so long made the bones shrink."

"Museum business," the director told them. "The experts will give us the answers in time. This fellow probably waited many years to be discovered. Another few days won't matter to him." Everyone laughed and went home to tell their families the day's news.

In spite of the director's excitement about the discovery, he felt uneasy feelings as he left for home that evening. It was all very well to come across historic materials on the site, but there had been rumours in the past about a young girl haunting this garden. He didn't want the whispers resurrected. Advocates of formal tea ceremonies regularly met in the tea house. The revenue was an important source of income for the museum's upkeep. It wouldn't do if gossip led people to think of the garden as anything but serene.

Within a couple of days the bones had been washed, dried and laid out in their correct anatomical positions on a table in the museum's storehouse. They made up the better part of a human skeleton, but part of one leg and a number of small bones were still missing. The local newspaper carried a rather small item about the bones, but the ruined rice fields and local deaths from landslides were more important. Many of the farmers were devastated by the realization that it would be several years before they would be able to plant their rice fields again.

"The skeleton is museum business," the director said. "When there is time, we will bring in an expert in to analyse the bones."

A month later, in September 1964, Dr. Noguchi, the top orthopaedic surgeon at Niigata's University Hospital drove to Shibata on a Saturday afternoon to view the find. He and the director were old friends, and the doctor had come more for a dinner invitation than on official business. After a cup of hot tea at the caretaker's cottage, they strolled over to the museum's storage house.

"I'll be frank," the director said as they entered the room. "I think these might be the remains of a member of the Mizoguchi army, someone who fought defending this property during the revolution. I am hoping you can give me an idea of when this man died."

The doctor wore glasses with spring-loaded frames that allowed the lenses to be lifted up. He walked around the table, flipped up his lenses and bent down to examine the skull.

"No warrior's bones here," he said with a laugh. "More likely a very young lady."

The director wrinkled his forehead and made a small noise in his throat. "Well, that's something I didn't want to hear." He rubbed his chin and added, "Are you sure? The bones must be very old. Couldn't they have shrunk in the water?"

Dr. Noguchi smiled as he picked up the skull for closer examination. "As far as I know, bones might crumble after you are dead but they don't shrink. No, I am sure these are the bones of a young female. The basilar suture is not completely closed. It's hard to say exactly. I think she could have been about fifteen or sixteen, certainly not more than seventeen years old." Then the doctor made a slow *horr*, sound in the back of his throat to express surprise. "*Horr*! How extraordinary."

"What is it?" the director asked.

Dr. Noguchi held the skull on its side and pointed to a small hole on the left side of the cranium. "This is the external auditory canal. We all have it. Without it we couldn't hear. But look—" Turning the skull to expose the right side of the skull, he offered it to the director for inspection.

"There is no hole on this side," the director said with some surprise. "I didn't notice that before. Is that rare?"

"Oh, very rare. You wouldn't have noticed it when the skull was muddy. It could easily be missed if you have never examined a skull before. It's not exactly my field, but I think it happens only in about one out of every million live births, or maybe less. Very rare indeed."

"Then, what would it mean?"

"The obvious explanation is that this girl could only have had hearing in her left ear. The chances are she may not have had an ear at all on the right side of her head. This is a birth defect that is almost always accompanied by abnormalities. Sometimes there is merely a flap of skin in place of an ear. Of course, that is impossible for us to tell now because we have only the skull."

Saito's shoulders slumped again. "Interesting, but it doesn't help in estimating how long she has been dead, does it?"

The doctor pulled a long, audible breath through his clenched teeth. "No. We still only have bones here. There is no flesh left. Even if there was, the rate at which flesh decays from a corpse is dependent on various factors that are impossible to estimate. If there was some clothing, one might be able to give an educated guess. You might go back and see if there was any other material buried in the mud near the skeleton."

"I didn't know it was so complicated. I thought you could tell the age by examining the bones." The director was clearly unhappy with the doctor's findings.

"Sorry," the doctor said as he set the skull in its place and bent down to get a better look at the pelvic bones. "These were the bones of a young, healthy female, except for her lack of a hearing canal on one side of her head. Maybe someone who specializes in forensic anthropology would be able to tell you more. Perhaps one of your museum colleagues in Tokyo can help. They deal with this sort of problem more than I do."

"*Ah so*," the director said, shaking his head with disappointment. "A young girl. I was hoping for something to add to the site's history."

The doctor seemed amused at his friend's concern about the sex of the skeleton. "I'm sorry I can't tell you that these are the remains of a samurai with a sword puncture in the rib cage. Unfortunately, I am positive that these are the bones of a young girl with good teeth and hearing in only one ear. How she got into the pond is the mystery."

The director grunted, smiled weakly and looked at his watch. "Well, let's discuss it over dinner."

The doctor smiled broadly and bowed.

"And Dr. Noguchi, I would appreciate it if these findings are kept confidential. I do have a former classmate in Tokyo who may be able to tell me more. The matter is not settled yet," the director said and sighed. "The storm has caused serious problems for our restoration plans."

"*Hai*, I understand," the doctor said with a serious expression on his face. He was trying to be sympathetic, but he was also beginning to think of hot sake and what he knew would be a very good meal with newly harvested Niigata rice.

❀ ❀ ❀

There was nothing historically significant about the bones. The report from Tokyo shed no new light on their age. Maybe a hundred years old. Maybe only fifty. It was difficult to be certain. The situation was turning out to be a great bother to the museum director. The chief of police discussed it in detail over another grand dinner hosted by Mr. Saito.

"The police are too busy to be concerned with local history," the chief said as his host filled his sake cup. He saw no advantage to pursuing the matter further. "The bones have been in the pond for some time. Starting an investigation at this stage would only fuel the old nonsense about the garden being haunted. Even if it was a murder, the perpetrator would be long dead himself by now. The police are busy. No, it is best to have the bones cremated and put an end to the matter."

Mr. Saito agreed and offered the police chief more sake. At this point he was eager to be rid of the entire matter. It was for this reason that he decided not to mention the skeleton's lack of a hearing canal. What did it matter? The girl was long dead and he didn't want her remains to cause more speculation.

As the senior priest at the nearest temple to the big garden, Misako's grandfather officiated at the private cremation. The director told him the story, minus the ear detail, and asked for his discretion. After some thought, the old priest offered the temple's back altar room as a resting place for the mysterious ashes. There were a few other containers of human remains there, mostly from returned war dead.

The director agreed, and after endowing the temple with a generous offering, left feeling confident that he had made the right arrangements. Now, almost a year after the disastrous flood, the incident could finally be put to rest. The silk-wrapped box of ashes would join several other such receptacles on a dusty shelf, guarded by a variety of broken and discarded religious figures. Once a year during Obon, the Festival for the Dead, a priest would dust the room and decorate the shelves with flowers and food. Prayers for the dead would follow. Incense would burn and the unknown souls would be honoured.

The arrangement had sastified the museum director; it was the old priest who could not let it go. Instead of placing the remains in the back altar room as intended, he set the box in the alcove in his own room. He did not know why he felt reluctant to part with the cremated remains of a total stranger. The only connection he could think of was an incident that happened long ago when Misako was a child.

His face screwed up into a mask of wrinkles as he tried to squeeze a date from his memory . . . nineteen forty-four . . . a hot summer's day. He was returning from an errand when he saw his granddaughter running toward him. She had been playing in the big garden where her friend's father was the caretaker. Now she was crying and shouting.

"Grandfather! Come quickly! A girl has fallen into the big pond. I saw her."

The priest scooped his granddaughter up into his arms and ran. He was out of breath when he reached the entrance. There he found Misako's friend and her father calmly sweeping the path. The father was a war amputee and he had to bend over almost double to manoeuvre the short-handled straw broom over the stone.

"Has the girl been pulled from the pond?" the priest shouted.

The caretaker straightened up and looked confused. A smirk passed across his face when he saw Misako.

"Your granddaughter must be fooling you. She told me too, but how could such a thing happen without my seeing it? Am I blind? I have been working all morning while the two children played. No one has entered the garden. There has been no strange girl here. I'm sure of that."

The priest put Misako squarely on the path before him and squatted down to look into her eyes.

"Did you tell a lie, Misako-*chan*?"

The child hung her head and answered in a small, shaky voice. "No, Grandfather. I saw her fall into the pond, over there." She pointed toward the large rock that formed a narrow bridge.

"The child must be dreaming," the caretaker said. "My daughter was with her and saw nothing. They were drawing pictures near the bamboo grove. Suddenly your granddaughter was shouting that someone had fallen into the pond, but who? There was no one."

"Who fell into the pond, Misako-*chan*?" The priest was trying to be both firm and gentle.

"A girl, a young lady," she answered, rubbing her eyes. The child was clearly upset, and very tired. There were dark circles under her eyes, something her grandfather had never seen before.

"Did you know this young lady?" the priest asked.

Misako shook her head slowly. She looked so pitiful and helpless, with tears streaming down her small face.

"There was no young lady. There was no stranger here, I tell you." The caretaker was adamant. "Your granddaughter must have fallen asleep while she was drawing and dreamed it, or else she saw a ghost."

The priest squatted down in front of the caretaker's daughter. "And you, Sachiko-*chan*, did you see a strange girl in the garden today?"

The child shook her head shyly.

"I see," the embarrassed priest said. "Surely, Misako-*chan* must have been dreaming. I apologize for the disturbance this has caused." He bowed deeply to the father and his small daughter. "Misako-*chan*, you must apologize for causing so much trouble. Go ahead, tell them you are sorry."

Misako's gaze held her grandfather's for a few seconds before she bowed to her little friend and her father. "*Gomen nasai*," she said weakly.

"No harm done," the caretaker said and laughed nervously. "Just a dream. Let's forget it. Misako-*chan*, come and play tomorrow."

That had happened a long time ago and there were other strange incidents that took place when Misako was a child living at his temple. He knew back then that there was something different about his grandchild. He remembered discussing it with his daughter Keiko but there was a war going on, and everyone had been weakened; there was too little food, too little rest. There were much more pressing things to worry about than a child's behaviour.

When the war was over, Misako's widowed mother married a doctor whose wife had died and left him with two small sons. Misako grew up with her new family only blocks away from the temple, in a house attached to a private clinic. The priest forgot about the incident in the garden until a conversation with a Zen monk plucked at the old memories of his granddaughter's childhood.

It happened in the summer of 1963, during a trip to Kyoto. That was when he met the Zen monk named Kensho.

Misako's grandfather had never seen a man that tall, or anyone with such intense, pale eyes. That particular evening was hot and thick with Kyoto's infamous summer humidity. Four priests sat on the *tatami* floor looking out on the temple's garden, trying to catch a hint of a breeze. Two of them cooled themselves with lazy movements of their bamboo fans.

The priest Kensho had everyone's attention. He was talking about strange happenings, and making animated gestures with his bony hands. The word he used was "clairvoyance." This was the first time in his long life that the old country priest had ever been part of a conversation where a big English word was used.

The old priest had never thought of such things before, but now he was hanging onto every word, like a small boy listening to a summer ghost story. Kensho was telling a true story about a man who found a lost child by concentrating on an item of the child's clothing. After some time, the man was able to tell the parents where to look for their son. It happened in the northern island of Hokkaido. The child had wandered off, fallen down

13

a ravine and was injured. In a matter of hours, a search party was able to locate the boy.

"Are such things possible?" the old priest asked cautiously.

"I believe so. It is called clairvoyance." The tall priest broke into a grin as he slowly pronounced the difficult English word again. "Many people believe in this power. I have read that the Russians are carrying out scientific experiments to prove that it really exists."

"Don't take him seriously," one of the other priests mocked, waving his fan at him. "It makes a good story, but his temple is in Kamakura. It is all that foreign influence in Kamakura. Too many foreigners visiting the great statue of the Buddha there."

"You may be right," the tall priest said good-naturedly. "I only hope they can find that fellow if I ever fall down a ravine."

The comment allowed everyone to laugh. Another priest started the conversation down a more conventional path. Misako's grandfather felt a twist of frustration. He wanted to hear more about clairvoyance.

His chance came later that evening when he found Kensho in the garden admiring the moon. He stood beside the giant and told him how interesting he found his story. "I haven't thought about it for years but I think my own granddaughter has that gift. At least she did when she was a child."

"Clairvoyance?" the Zen monk asked in surprise.

"Of course I'm not sure," the old man said, "but she often told us things that she couldn't have known."

"Does this granddaughter of yours still have this gift?"

The old man blushed. "She is married and lives in Tokyo. I don't see her often. She may have grown out of it. It embarrassed her mother, you see."

"That's very interesting," Kensho said, bending down toward the fragile old man. "I think it very rare in Japan for someone to admit to having such a gift. People don't like being different."

"That is so." The old man bowed, blushed and thought that perhaps he was getting into something deeper than he had intended. Misako's experiences had happened many years before. He decided not to pursue the subject further. His daughter, Keiko, would be very upset with him if she found out he had told a stranger such a thing about her daughter.

"Unfortunately, I am feeling my age tonight. It must be the heat. Perhaps we will have a chance to talk again," the old man said sheepishly. "If you will excuse me for tonight."

"Certainly. Perhaps another time." The tall priest bowed and added quickly, "I understand the red maples can be wonderful in your home prefecture of Niigata. Perhaps you will allow me to visit one autumn, and then you can tell me more about this granddaughter of yours. I truly believe that there are people blessed with such sensitivity. I am afraid I find this sort of thing too interesting."

"*Hai, hai,*" the old man said to his empty room. "The leaves are once again changing in Shibata. I think it would be an excellent time for a visit."

His plan was clear now. As soon as arrangements had been made with the priest from Kamakura, he would ask Misako to come up from Tokyo. He wanted to hold a ceremony for the soul of the girl whose bones had been found in very pond where Misako had played as a child. Was it a coincidence? Or did his granddaughter really have the gift?

With great difficulty, he got to his feet. A man of eighty-three had a right to inflict his will on younger people, he thought to himself, even if the · should think him an old fool. Determination had given him new strength. He slid open the *shoji* door and shuffled down the hallway with more energy than he'd had in years.

Warm comforting smells greeted him as he entered the kitchen. His plump assistant, Teishin, stood chopping onions while a pot of soup simmered on the gas burner. The lid on the rice pot gently jiggled. Teishin looked up from his work, surprised to see the master in the kitchen.

The telephone was an antiquated model fixed to the wall. A worn, black address book hung beside it from a nail. Since he disliked using the talking contraption, the old man greeted his assistant and asked that he find the telephone number of the Zen priest from Kamakura and put the call through. Waiting, he sat on the one chair in the temple and folded his arms. The phone had to be cranked by hand and the long-distance call connected by a local operator. Since it was very early, it took time for a sleepy voice to respond and then the priest from Kamakura was on the line. The old man jumped to his feet, took the receiver from his assistant, bowed to the kitchen wall and spoke.

"*Hai*, Kensho-*sama*! Forgive me for calling so early, but I wanted to reach you before you were off on your daily schedule. Thank you once again for your New Year greeting. I trust you are still in good health."

"*Hai, hai, Sensei.* I thank you for your greeting also and I trust you are very well."

"*Hai*," the old priest said. "I hope I did not inconvenience you at this time but something unusual has happened here and I am eager to talk to you. I wonder if you recall our last conversation when you expressed a desire to visit Niigata to see the red maples. I thought you would consider honouring us with a visit soon."

"So very kind," the Zen priest said, thinking back to that meeting in Kyoto. There was something special about this elderly Niigata priest's granddaughter. Ah yes, she had the gift of second sight. "This unusual matter? Is it about your talented granddaughter?"

"Ah, I am flattered that you remembered," the old voice cracked. "I don't want to mislead you, Kensho-*sama*." He was feeling somewhat foolish again. "However, I think you will find it interesting to visit our humble temple."

"I would indeed like that," Kensho said. "Unfortunately, starting next week my schedule will be very busy for a while. I could come tomorrow and stay for a couple of days, but I'm sure that would be too soon for you."

"No, not at all, tomorrow will be splendid." The old voice rang with so much enthusiasm that Teishin turned from the stove, bemused. "Let us know the time of your train and my daughter will meet you at the station. You have to leave the train at Nittsu, the station before Niigata City. Nittsu is about a forty-minute ride from Shibata."

A few more polite sentences and the plan had been set. The gleeful old master turned to his surprised assistant with still more orders.

"Right after breakfast, please telephone my daughter. Tell her to come to the temple this morning. Tell her it is urgent, but not a word about my telephone call to Kamakura. Do you understand?"

Without waiting for Teishin's answer, the master shuffled through the doorway and down the corridor toward his own room. He wanted to think about what he would say to Keiko. He had to convince her to urge Misako to make a trip to Shibata right away. It wasn't going to be easy. His only daughter was bossy and strong-willed, just like her dead mother. She would ask questions and he didn't want to let her in on his plan, not yet. He had to take great care. Maybe he would have to play on her sympathy. Reminding her of his age was always helpful.

And it worked. The request sounded urgent enough for Keiko to arrive at the temple by nine o'clock. The old priest and his daughter sipped tea as he told her how much he wanted to see his only granddaughter.

"I am getting old. I feel it these days. We don't see Misako often and I have to think about how short my time could be."

"You sound like you are getting ready to die," Keiko teased, trying to hide her concern.

"Anyone at my age should be ready to die," he said, feigning annoyance. "I want to see my only granddaughter and I want to see her soon. Please ask her to come tomorrow, if it is possible."

"Tomorrow?" Keiko was shocked. Her father had never talked like this before. She searched his face for a hint of illness. There was none. "I'll call her this evening but I don't understand why it is so urgent. You aren't sick?"

The old man looked at his daughter, pressed his thumbs together like a Buddha, and spoke through a smile. "At this time it is more important for you to be a loyal daughter than a thoughtful mother. You will be a mother for many years more, but your time of having a living father is growing short."

"*Maa!* What a thing to say." Keiko was annoyed and allowed her voice to grow sharp. "I think you are getting very strange in your old age."

"*Hai,* you are absolutely correct. I am getting strange in the head but old age can't be helped." He said this with a small bow and the sweetest smile Keiko had ever seen on her father's face.

THREE

$\mathcal{M}$isako lived with her husband and widowed mother-in-law in a pleasant residential area in Tokyo's Shibuya ward. The home was large by Japanese standards, with an elegant entrance room where guests removed their shoes before entering, stepping into slippers that waited on the highly polished wooden floor.

The best rooms in the house were two eight-mat *tatami* rooms that overlooked a small garden. Each *tatami* mat was a three-foot by six-foot rectangle of tightly woven straw bound in dark brocade. Most of the time, the flower-painted sliding doors that separated the two rooms were open, creating one large uncluttered space. The focus of one room was an alcove made of exquisite wood and displaying a samurai sword. The other room featured a beautiful low wooden table surrounded by silk cushions and a black-lacquered altar cabinet tucked into the corner. With the garden lying just outside the large sliding windows, the space was serene and peaceful. These rooms were mostly used for guests.

The everyday activity took place in the dining room and kitchen area located off another entrance. It was where the family, close friends and tradespeople came and went. The sliding wooden door was fitted with a bell that sang out whenever it was moved. The slightly less impressive wooden floors of the dining room, kitchen and water closet were covered with an assortment of small rugs. The large bathroom at the end of this section of the house was a mass of tiny, white tiles.

Upstairs there were two more eight-*tatami* rooms, used as bedrooms. These rooms and the hallway housed several wooden dressers. Because the rooms had large windows and the futon beds were put away in the closets in the daytime, the upstairs had a feeling of air and space. It was only the downstairs dining room that was crowded, with a western-style table, eight chairs, a china cabinet, telephone stand and a television set. A curtain of dangling wooden beads led to the small kitchen.

Misako was chopping cucumbers in the kitchen while the senior Mrs. Imai sat at the dining-room table watching the evening news. The table was set for three, with rice bowls, plates, chopsticks and glasses all neatly placed on a flower-printed plastic cloth.

It was almost seven o'clock and the new electric rice cooker blinked a red eye signalling that it was keeping the contents warm. Hot water simmered on the gas stove and a bowl of vegetable pickles waited on the counter. The voice from the television sounded as if it was filtered through a long, narrow tunnel. The talk about cleaning up Tokyo after the night's storm hardly penetrated Misako's thoughts. She was thinking how stupid it all was. Here she was fixing three individual salads and grilling three fish when she knew that Hideo would not be home for dinner again. She had known it all afternoon. There would be another telephone call, another excuse.

Automatically, she turned over the fish on the wire grill with chopsticks. A puff of fragrant smoke rushed up to the fan over the stove. Why had she bought food for three today? Why couldn't she have told her mother-in-law that Hideo wouldn't be home for dinner? The trouble was that the senior Mrs. Imai would have demanded to know how she was so sure. Misako felt the old frustration of not being able to explain something she didn't understand herself.

As the news signed off, the telephone rang. Misako sighed and turned down the flame on the stove as her mother-in-law reached from her chair to answer the phone.

"Oh, too bad, Hideo. How disappointing! Misako is cooking such nice fish. It smells delicious. What a pity you have to work late again. Poor you. You must be tired after staying at the office last night. It couldn't have been comfortable."

Misako calmly picked up two of the salads from the counter, carried them through the beaded curtains and set them down on the table. Outwardly everything was slow and calm but inside she felt a mounting rage. Carefully, she put one salad down, then the other. Don't frown, don't show emotion. Pick up Hideo's chopsticks, his glass and plate. Carry them back to the kitchen, parting the jangling wooden beads. Things seemed to float in slow motion while the room's atmosphere gradually took on a pinkish hue. Out of the older woman's view, Misako held onto the edge of the counter and wrestled with her anger. She could hear her mother-in-law saying, "I'll tell Misako. She's too busy to talk to you now. Don't work too hard."

Damn Hideo! This was too much! He was rarely home for dinner, and after last night's vision, she no longer believed he was working late. Now she didn't want to have dinner with his mother. It would be hard to act normally when so much was boiling up inside her. Misako wanted to go to her room and be alone. It took too much effort to pretend there wasn't a serious problem, but she had no choice. Oh, it would be so good to be able to scream about the woman with the broad feet, to tell her mother-in-law what kind of work her precious son was really doing tonight.

A slapstick routine on television got her through the meal; the older woman laughed so much that she had no time for conversation. The television was always on while they ate. Misako was used to pretending that she was watching. Tonight, she was thinking how women who didn't marry first or only sons were lucky. They didn't have to share a house with their mothers-in-law. How different it would be if this was her own house. She would have even preferred a small apartment.

Misako bit down on her lip, resenting the fact that Hideo's father had been a second son. Her mother-in-law had never had to pay her dues. As the bride of a prosperous Tokyo family, her mother-in-law had run the house with the help of maids, and that was before the war. Now it was 1965! Misako wondered what right this woman had to treat her like a servant.

Mother Imai didn't particularly enjoy living with her son's wife either. At fifty-nine years of age, Hideo's mother was still nice-looking and aware that she had fewer wrinkles on her face than most of her friends. She was somewhat overweight but her salt-and-pepper hair was short and thick with a wave that pulled away from her forehead in a most becoming way. She liked to think of herself as handsome and high-spirited. She thought of Misako as secretive with big, brooding eyes. There was something about Hideo's wife that was hidden. Sometimes the older woman caught an expression on Misako's face that made her uncomfortable. She couldn't guess what her daughter-in-law was thinking, and that made it like having a stranger in the house.

Since the death of her husband, and with her son's bride taking care of the house, Mother Imai had lots of free time and often felt bored. There were friends and a younger sister to visit and her twice-a-month classical singing lesson that she had with a retired, *samisen*-playing geisha. Other than that, the television was her best companion. Her happiest moments were spent in front of it watching *rakugo*, a traditional stylized way of reciting humourous stories. She used to perform it herself, sitting on a cushion with a fan placed on the floor before her. There was a time when people had praised her talent. Certainly, her husband enjoyed her performances, but she hadn't done it in years. She wouldn't consider performing in front of Misako.

To the senior Mrs. Imai, her daughter-in-law was much too serious. Deep in her heart, she felt that her beloved old home had become gloomy ever since her son's bride moved in. It was only the hope of a grand-child that kept her from telling Misako how she really felt. Surely things would liven up around the house when a baby arrived, but that was taking a long time.

At ten minutes after nine, Misako suddenly knew that her own mother was about to call. She put down her knitting and waited. Mother Imai was involved with a sad drama, making little clucking sounds to express her pity for the orphan in the story. Misako had the phone in her hand after the first ring.

"Is anything wrong?" she asked after barely saying hello.

"No," Keiko said. "It's just that Grandfather asked me to have you come visit for a few days. It seems important to him."

"Well, did he tell you why?"

"Not exactly. He said he hasn't seen you for a long time and he is getting old."

"That's funny, isn't it?" Misako sounded amused. "He's not usually so sentimental."

"I know. It seemed odd to me too, but he called me over to the temple this morning and gave me orders. I suppose he is feeling old. If it's conven-ient, I wish you would come. It's been a while since you were here."

"When does he want me to visit?"

"Well, right away. Tomorrow."

"Tomorrow?" Misako's voice rang with so much surprise that it took her mother-in-law's attention away from the television screen.

"If it's not possible he'll understand, but if you have the time, why not humour him? I'm worried about him, Misako. He's been acting strange lately."

"What do you mean?" Misako didn't repeat the word "strange," as she knew it would make Mother Imai ask questions.

"Oh, nothing. I won't go into it on the phone. I'll tell you when you come."

Misako hesitated a moment. There wasn't any reason to stay in Tokyo. Certainly her husband wasn't likely to miss her. Getting away for a few days was exactly what she needed. "I'll come tomorrow."

21

"I know it's sudden," Keiko told her daughter. "If you put Hideo on the phone, I will explain it to him."

"He's working late tonight but I know he'll agree."

"Well then, let me speak to his mother. Anyway it would be rude to call without asking to speak to her."

"*Moshi-moshi,* hello," Mother Imai said into the phone. After the usual polite greetings, the plan quickly took shape between the two older women. Misako would visit Niigata for a few days and there was no reason why she shouldn't leave the next day. Trains left Tokyo every few hours and tickets were not difficult to get this time of year. Hideo's mother was most agreeable. Certainly, she could do without Misako's help for a few days. What else did she have to keep her busy? Ha, ha, ha.

Mother Imai was elated. It would be nice to be with her son without Misako listening to every word they said. They could make jokes together again, as in the old days. And then there were serious matters she wanted to talk to Hideo about in private. Her mind raced as she chatted with Misako's mother. She would remind her son how lonely she had been since Papa died and, most of all, how eager she was to have a grandchild. What were they waiting for? Misako was twenty-nine years old, almost thirty. They had been married five years and still no baby.

"Then it's all arranged. I'll tell Misako the plan," she said sweetly. Misako, however, insisted on talking to her mother again. She felt excited as she talked about the trip. The happy tone of her voice annoyed Mother Imai.

Spoiled brat! she thought, pretending to be absorbed with her television story. Misako never sounds that happy around this house. Let her go back to Niigata. I'll be glad not to have to look at her sour face for a couple of days. Once and for all, I'm going to tell Hideo how I feel. Why couldn't he have married a cheerful girl who had babies? Love marriage, indeed.

When Hideo finally got home, it was after two in the morning. Smelling of sardines and stale beer, he stumbled up the narrow stairs to the bedroom. Misako pulled the quilt over her head and pretended to be asleep. She knew her mother-in-law would have heard Hideo and she guessed that the older woman was standing against the wall that separated their bedrooms. The nightlight was on and Hideo could see that his futon was made up but placed some distance from his wife's. Even in his drunken state he knew it meant she was angry with him.

"Who cares," he mumbled as he threw his suit jacket in the corner and dropped the rest of his clothes on the floor. He fell into bed in his underwear. Misako held her breath. In a matter of minutes, the room was filled with the sound of drunken snores. Misako thought she caught the faint scent of perfume. There was a very soft movement beyond the wall. Misako got up quietly to put out the nightlight. Tomorrow night I'll sleep in my old room, she thought, away from all this.

The next morning Hideo demonstrated his amazing ability to look fresh and handsome no matter how late he had come home the night before, or how drunk. He seemed to bounce down the stairs and entered the dining room adjusting the starched cuffs of his gleaming white shirt. He sat down at his place and greeted his mother, who was watching 'Good Morning Japan' on the television set.

"You must be tired this morning," Mother Imai offered and then let her eyes travel back to the set.

Misako came through the beaded curtains carrying breakfast on a tray. "Morning," she said and put down bowls of soup and rice.

"Morning," Hideo offered grudgingly.

"Misako has to leave for Niigata today," Mother Imai threw over her shoulder. She didn't want to miss a second of the news.

"My grandfather wants me to visit his temple so I thought I would go to Shibata for a few days. My mother called about it last night."

Hideo grunted and picked up the morning paper.

"It's true," said Mother Imai, her eyes darting from son to television, "Mrs. Ichimura and I both think it will do Misako good to go home for a few days." The words "go home" were not missed by Misako.

"*Ah so,*" Hideo said indifferently.

"You don't mind my going, do you?"

"*Dozo,*" he said from behind the open newspaper. "Please do."

"I'll be back in a few days."

"Ummm," Hideo sipped his tea loudly.

"This soup isn't very hot," Mother Imai complained. "Could you heat it up for me, please, Misako?"

"Oh, sorry. How is your soup, Hideo?"

"I have no time to eat this morning. I just want tea."

"It will only take a minute," she said and put both bowls on a tray. From the kitchen she could hear Mother Imai lecturing Hideo about going without breakfast. Before the soup was warmed, she heard Hideo calling out goodbye. She rushed to the side entrance where he was putting on his shoes.

"I thought we could have time to talk before you go to work."

"Not now," he said, obviously annoyed. "I have to be at the office early. I have a job, you know." He grabbed his briefcase and rushed out the door. The force he used to open the sliding door set the bell on the roller jingling.

"Damn him!" she said and then realized that Mother Imai might hear. She went back to the kitchen. The soup was boiling over.

It wasn't until she was upstairs packing that she began to calm down. Folding her sweaters and skirts and putting them into the suitcase made her feel like she was going on vacation. It would be easier at home with her mother and stepfather. Let his mother decide what to make him for dinner. Let her wait up for him tonight. The thought of Mother Imai sitting up, waiting in her sleeping kimono, made Misako laugh out loud. Two hours later she left the house feeling like a bird let out of its cage. Mother Imai seemed in good spirits as she saw her off at the kitchen door, sending regards and a gift of boxed rice crackers to the family in Niigata. She didn't linger or prolong the goodbye. As soon as the door closed behind Misako, Mother Imai hurried back to the television set. It was five minutes past the start of her favourite morning quiz show.

❀ ❀ ❀

The reason for Hideo's indifference to his wife was twenty-four-year-old Fumiko Hara, a young woman who preferred to think of herself as voluptuous rather than plump. "Voluptuous" was one of the useful English words she had learned back in the Tokyo Junior College where she graduated as an English major. At five feet six inches and 145 pounds, she was taller and had more womanly curves than any of her friends. But once she discovered sex that stopped being a problem for Fumiko. The truth was that she was proud that her bust was so full; she had to buy her C-cup brassieres in a special shop that catered mainly to foreign women. Like many other young people of her generation, she was infatuated with all things foreign, especially anything American.

"Sexy" was the word men used to describe her, and many found her appealing. Even during her teen years, Fumiko had to put up with their remarks about her bust. Sometimes gawking boys tried to touch her breasts in the crowded subway. Her teen years were spent wearing baggy shirts, studying English and going to American movies.

After graduating from college, Fumiko met a Jewish-American journalist and had her first affair. Of course the affair was kept a secret from her family. She became very good at making up excuses for staying out late. When the journalist left Japan a year and a half later, Fumiko's knowledge of both English and sex had greatly improved.

She and Hideo started their affair in June. Contrary to what Misako suspected, Fumiko did not work in a bar but in a travel agency in the same Muromachi area where Hideo's office was located. They had met when he went to inquire about a company outing that his company was planning. From the very beginning, there was a magnetic pull between them. Fumiko had thought she preferred foreign men but Hideo captivated her at first sight. She thought him very handsome, tall and well dressed. She was charmed by his smile that flashed straight white teeth. He was wild about her bright red sweater. Hideo returned to the agency the next day—for more information, or so he said. That was the first time they went to a coffeehouse together.

Everything about Fumiko excited Hideo. He was crazy about her full red lips and the way her shining black hair hung in a thick, loose rope down her back. She was so different from his delicately pretty wife. He thought Fumiko was sexy and fun. From the first time they met, he had an urge to put his hands up her sweater to see if those wonderful, full bumps were real. He had never had sex with a woman with real, American-movie-star-standard breasts. Thinking about them became an obsession. When he found himself absentmindedly doodling women's breasts on his desk blotter, he decided to ask her to dinner.

They met after work on a rainy evening and he suggested they go to his favourite sushi shop near Akasaka. Getting into the taxi, her breast pressed against his arm for a second and his heart jumped in his chest. Hideo was no innocent when it came to sex; still, this seemingly accidental thrill was a new experience.

At dinner Fumiko didn't sip at the tiny cups of hot sake like the other girls he knew; she tossed it down at the same rate he did. At nine o'clock they left the restaurant in a jovial mood. Fumiko put her coat on and excused herself to go to the washroom while Hideo took care of the bill. When they got outside, it had stopped raining. Hideo tossed his coat over his right shoulder and took her hand. They started down the street, still making jokes and laughing. Suddenly Fumiko let out a little-girl cry of joy, pulling him over to a toyshop window. There was nothing special that he could see in the window; there didn't even seem to be anyone inside the shop.

They were standing in the entrance with their faces against the glass when she thrust his hand into the opening of her coat. An electric shock travelled through his body the instant he felt the firm, bare breast in his hand. She had unbuttoned her blouse in the washroom and removed her brassiere. People passed on the street behind them as she pressed his hand against the delicious fullness. For a few seconds he stood stunned in secret ecstasy. It was like nothing he had ever experienced before. He had to take his hand away and drape his coat down over his arm to hide the swelling in his trousers.

Fumiko clutched her coat closed, smiled and looked into Hideo's eyes. Without saying a word, he took her arm and hurried her toward the blinking lights of a hotel on the corner. As the door of the red and black room closed behind them, they almost ripped each other's clothes off. Later he told her that he had never wanted any woman so badly and that all other sexual experiences were nothing compared to this. Even the memory of the tender lovemaking he shared with Misako paled. From that night on, Fumiko and Hideo became regular customers at the Red Cherry Akasaka Love Hotel.

FOUR

*T*he train from Tokyo to Niigata ran past a seemingly endless jumble of drab city buildings and houses, past suburban communities and, finally, the small farms that lent some sense of order to the landscape. It was harvest time and farmers were out in the October sun cutting neat, muddy wounds in the rice fields.

Misako watched from the train window; it seemed that this stretch of land between Tokyo and Niigata was like a vast tennis court on which so much of her life had been bounced back and forth. Through the years, she had ridden this train in all seasons, in all weather and with many different emotions. Going to Tokyo to take the entrance examination for university stood out in her mind; that was a nervous, frighteningly long ride. Then there were the times she went home from school for vacations and holidays, and the sad trip she had taken to attend her grandmother's funeral. Later, there were frantic trips back and forth when her wedding plans were taking shape. And now this, a kind of escape, fleeing from the problems of married life.

Although it was a puzzling request, Misako was pleased that her grandfather had insisted she visit. So many of her childhood memories revolved around him. How patiently he had taught her to write beautiful Chinese characters when she was a small child. After her mother married Dr. Ichimura, Misako had continued attending the classes he gave at the temple. It was a skill that she still enjoyed; even Mother Imai had praised her ability and hung an example of Misako's calligraphy on the dining room wall. Misako smiled at the thought of her grandfather and settled back into her seat.

The train plunged through the longest tunnel on the route and everything was suddenly dark. They were in the mountain range now, nearing the hot spring resort of Minakami. The subterranean atmosphere caused some discomfort for passengers who were not used to the two-minute tunnel passing. A few people began to cough and shift in their seats. Misako sensed the discomfort in the car and it stirred another old memory, the memory of her first trip to Niigata. That was almost a quarter of a century

27

ago but she could clearly picture herself as a small child, snuggled under her mother's arm, sitting on the floor with a sea of strangers crushing in all around them.

The recollection, complete with unpleasant smells and loud noises, had been etched on her mind by her mother's words, her retelling of the long ago train journey: "We didn't always live in Niigata, you know, Misako-*chan*. Grandfather's sister married and moved to Tokyo. It was she, my aunt, who helped arrange the marriage between your father and me. I went to live in Tokyo as a bride and you were born there in the city. Unfortunately, your father had to become a soldier and went away to war when you were only three years old. When the warnings came that the Americans could bomb Tokyo, we went to stay with grandfather and grandmother in Niigata. It was getting there that was the difficult part. There were so few trains available because of the war. Everyone with a relative living in the country wanted to get out of the city. So many people and bundles. There was only one good thing about that terrible trip and that was you, Misako-*chan*. You were such a good child and hardly ever cried. It made mother feel brave too."

As a child, Misako had often begged to hear the story. Even now Misako's tensions disappeared as she remembered her mother's words. She fell asleep, missing the beautiful mountain scenery she always looked forward to on the journey.

❀ ❀ ❀

The temple buzzed with activity. Preparations were under way for the visit of the Zen priest from Kamakura. The old master's assistant, Teishin, dashed around, occasionally wiping his sweating pink cheeks. He was airing bedding and beating out the dust with a torn rag attached to the end of a small bamboo stick. He worked in a high state of excitement, smiling and singing little bits of folk songs. This morning Teishin was in his element; he loved to be around people and enjoyed the rare occasions when the temple entertained guests.

It was this happy personality that had endeared the master's assistant to the congregation. Having Teishin come to their homes to chant sutras for their dead relatives was never dreary as he always ended the visit with a joke or a bit of gossip over a cup of tea. They called him *Waka-Sensei*, Young Teacher, even though he was almost forty years old and had been at the temple for fifteen years. What most people didn't understand was that his smiles hid a dark, painful insecurity. His greatest fear was death— not his own, but that of the old master.

Teishin had never dreamed of being anything other than a humble priest. He had no grand aspirations. Yet his formal title was now *fuku-jushoku*, which meant he would become the head priest when the old master formally stepped aside. Teishin never expected or wanted this when he took his vows of priesthood. It was fate that had taken him to a temple that had no proper heir, no living son or grandson to carry on. The old master had followed his father into the priesthood.

As the years passed and Teishin proved himself a likable, devout priest, the temple's elders insisted that he be formally adopted into the Tanaka family and declared the heir to the ageing head priest. It was a perfectly sensible plan but the old man was a great procrastinator. In spite of all the nagging, it wasn't until 1962, the year his wife died, that the old priest formally registered Teishin-*san* as his *fuku-jushoku* with the mother temple. That was the day that Teishin had his first serious nervous hunger attack. Although he had been already carrying more than his own work load at the temple, the weight and implications of the new title depressed and frightened him. It made him feel insecure and hollow inside. How could he, a country bumpkin, take the place of the master he so revered? The next step, he knew, would be the congregation insisting that he take a wife. They would want their priest to be a family man. They would want his wife to do the womanly work that now was mostly done by volunteers from the congregation.

When he thought about all this, he was seized with an uncontrollable urge to eat something sweet. He had always loved food but this new craving seized him almost every night. It was the only way he could calm down enough to fall asleep. Because of it, he started to hoard sweet cakes in the sleeve of his kimono. The more the old man slowed down and the elders began to talk about the need for their priest to have a wife, the more sweets Teishin craved. When a new junior priest joined the temple, Teishin thought that the pressure would lessen. The new priest did lighten the work, but Teishin still insisted on being in charge of the kitchen. He didn't want anyone in the congregation to think that their priests didn't eat well because there was no "wife" to cook their meals.

The youngest man, whose priestly name was Konein, had now been at the temple for two and a half years. A slightly built youth, he suffered from a severe case of acne that had deeply affected his personality. The unsightly red eruptions on his face kept his inner self so tightly contained that no one could get him to say more than a few words at a time. Although this characteristic was sometimes maddening, it in no way hindered his ability to work hard. Moreover, he possessed a quality that the old master valued highly; no matter what he was asked to do, Konein never complained. When people commented negatively about the young priest's silent nature, the old master would joke that Teishin-*san* talked enough in the temple for ten priests.

When he had free time, Konein's reclusive nature sent him to the large rock at the back of the temple. This was his place of solitude. There he would puff on cigarette after cigarette, holding them between his thumb and forefinger, pinching until there was nothing left but a tiny stub.

Blowing smoke rings was his private amusement and he was able to puff out all kinds of interesting shapes. After each blow, he would screw up his small eyes and watch his creation float toward the great, distant pines. The impermanence of the exercise pleased him. He was happy washing bowls that would be full of rice again. He raked the garden, pleased that the leaves would soon recarpet the ground. This morning he helped prepare the temple for the guest by scrubbing the toilets and washing the tiles in the bathroom. Then he solemnly pushed a damp cloth up and down every wooden floor in the temple, knowing they would be dusty again in a few days.

"It is my pleasure," he once said to Teishin in a rare splurge of words, "to tend to the small things that must be done. I wish to be a mere foot soldier for the Lord Buddha."

The old priest clipped a red camellia from the temple garden and put it in an unglazed vase. Next he went to the storage closest and took out a scroll to place in the guestroom's alcove, along with the camellia. The scroll was an old one, decorated with a Zen poem written in beautifully flowing calligraphy:

> *Myself of long ago*
> *In nature nonexistent*
> *Nowhere to go when dead*
> *Nothing at all.*

He read it aloud and frowned. He wasn't sure he understood or even liked the poem. Still it was one of the temple's treasures and the old man felt it was the correct adornment for the Zen priest's room.

When Teishin opened the temple gates early that morning, he met a member of the Old People's Society passing on the street. He had been responsible for forming the society and never missed a chance to encourage the elderly to participate in temple functions. Characteristically, Teishin smiled, bowed and excitedly told the old woman about the esteemed guest they expected from Kamakura.

By nine o'clock the news reached the old master's daughter Keiko through a nurse at the clinic. She immediately put down her work and drove over to the temple to see what her father was up to today. She found him outside, sweeping the temple steps.

"What is this I hear about an esteemed guest coming from a Zen temple in Kamakura?" she asked.

"All guests are esteemed," the old man answered, adding, "Where did you hear it?"

"From a nurse at the clinic." Keiko's voice rang with annoyance.

Her father didn't seem to notice and went back to his sweeping. "No doubt Teishin-*san* has been wagging his tongue. I think he talks too much."

"And you too little. Why am I the last to know what is going on at this temple?"

The old man grinned and continued to sweep as he spoke. "The guest is a priest I know coming to pay respects to an old man. Do I have to inform the whole community on such matters?"

"I am not the whole community. I am the daughter who worries about her father and attends to many affairs at this temple. I am the one you asked to call your granddaughter and have her come all the way from Tokyo on short notice. Now I find you are planning to have a priest visit from Kamakura. How can you spend time with Misako when you will be entertaining a priest?"

The old man looked sheepish as he set the broom against the big wooden door. "I'm so glad you are here, Keiko," he said in a softer, sweeter tone. "I was going to call you and ask you to please meet my guest at the Nittsu train station. He will arrive at one o'clock this afternoon and it would be nicer than having him take a bus so far in a strange area."

"It would be nicer if you'd told me yesterday," Keiko snapped. "I could have asked Misako to be on the same train. Now I have to make two trips. Sometimes I think you don't realize how much I have to do at our clinic."

31

The old man bowed to his daughter. "I'm sorry," he said and turned to go into the temple. As he walked away he mumbled, "Complaints, complaints . . . I hate complaints."

Keiko knew what he was saying; she had heard it all her life. It made her smile. She took the broom and finished sweeping the steps. It was a job she had done a thousand times. Ever since her mother had become ill and died, Keiko had come to take care of some chore almost every day. She enjoyed doing things at the temple.

As irritating as her father had been in recent months, it was a comfort to live close to the temple, to feel part of the family tradition. Three priests or not, it was still the Tanaka family temple and she was the only living true child of her father.

When I'm finished, she thought, I'll order sashimi for their dinner tonight. Teishin-*san*'s cooking is not up to an esteemed guest from Kamakura.

FIVE

*T*he conductor announced the approach of Nagaoka Station. Misako woke from her nap and looked around shyly, slightly embarrassed that people might have seen her with an open mouth or some other undignified sleeping expression. If she had intended to sleep, she would have put a handkerchief over her face. Fortunately the seat next to her was empty and the man sitting across the aisle was engrossed in a comic magazine. She got up and made her way to the restroom. The air in the train had turned thick and yellow with cigarette smoke.

When she came back to her seat, Misako noticed her blue suitcase on the luggage rack. The sight of it softened the anger she felt toward Hideo. That was the case she had bought especially for their honeymoon trip. The memory made her smile. Theirs was a love marriage, not arranged by family. They had met at a friend's home a year after she graduated from college. Through her stepfather's connections, Misako got a job in the office of a pharmaceutical company in Tokyo. It was there that she met and became a friend of a co-worker named Yuri.

Misako met Hideo at Yuri's home one Sunday afternoon. The tennis game the girls had planned was cancelled because of rain. Instead, they hung around Yuri's living room, drinking tea and talking. They were about to go to a movie when Yuri's brother came home with his friend, Hideo. Misako immediately lost interest in leaving. She thought Hideo was as handsome as any movie actor. She blushed when they were introduced.

The four young people spent the rainy afternoon playing mahjong. Yuri's brother complained that it was no challenge, playing with his sister and her girlfriend. Hideo didn't seem to mind. He liked this shy Niigata beauty with the large eyes. By the time the game was finished and they ordered in sushi, Misako was telling herself that she was in love.

Hideo drove her home through the wet Tokyo streets. They parked outside her apartment house and talked for a long time. He touched her cheek and asked her to have dinner with him the following Friday. Misako accepted, knowing that the next time he took her home, they would kiss, just like in the American movies. All week she dreamed of that kiss.

It happened in his car, exactly the way she dreamed it would. Her lips trembled. Her heart raced. She almost fainted with ecstasy. "Moon River!" "Fly Me to the Moon!" Dreams really do come true.

Misako smiled and watched the countryside flash by. Their falling in love had been the most exciting time in her life. It could have been a movie love story. Hideo was handsome and charming, with an excellent future in his uncle's company. Her practical mother had reservations about the match, which she discussed with her husband. Dr. Ichimura listened to his wife's fears and smiled. "Too handsome can hardly be a reason to disapprove of a possible son-in-law," he told her.

Hideo's family had wanted a traditional Shinto wedding and Misako's grandfather wanted her married in a Buddhist temple. Misako insisted on a church wedding in a white Western-style wedding dress with a veil. That was the new fashionable way to be married, even for non-Christians. The modern bride could bow to tradition by changing into an elaborate Japanese kimono during the reception. It was like having your cake and eating it too. She had lived the dream of her post-war generation. It was the happy-ever-after that wasn't so easy.

Beads of rain slid down the train window. The world outside was a grey, melancholy mist. The temperature was dropping. Slipping out of her shoes, Misako stood on the seat to take the suitcase down. Her sweater lay on top of the other folded clothes, as expected. What was not expected was a pair of black *zori* wrapped in clear plastic. The sandals were tucked into the side and half-exposed. Misako had no memory of packing the *zori* and had no reason to want them on this trip. With no formal occasion, she only packed casual Western clothes. Black *zori* were worn exclusively with mourning kimono. The sight of them shocked and puzzled her. Nervously she folded over some other items of clothing and found her black mourning kimono and *obi*. The smooth black silk sash felt ice-cold to her touch.

Stunned, Misako sat down next to the open case. It didn't make sense. How had these unhappy garments found their way into her suitcase? No wonder it was so heavy! Was someone playing a cruel joke? Mother Imai? That didn't seem possible. She had been downstairs watching television all morning.

Misako sat slumped in her seat, frowning and biting her lip. She was sure she had not packed these clothes. Why would she? No one she knew in Shibata had died recently and there wasn't a memorial service planned.

Pangs of fear stabbed her stomach as she closed the suitcase. Sweat broke out on her hairline. She took her handkerchief from her purse and wiped it away. First the vision and now this. Something was happening to her that she didn't understand. For one terrible moment she doubted her own sanity. Perhaps something had happened to Grandfather. But when?

Suddenly she sat up very straight. "Is Grandfather going to die?" The question didn't stay in her head but rushed past her lips. The young man across the aisle put his comic book down and bent forward, eyeing her with curiosity. Embarrassed, Misako turned her face to the window. She pressed her forehead to the cool glass and watched the scenery slide by in smears of blurred colour. Something was wrong. She was being summoned to Niigata for more than a simple visit.

The happiness she felt about going home was marred now and wrapped in worry. She loved returning to Shibata, to the house she had shared with her mother, stepfather and stepbrothers for most of her life. Her mother's second husband, Dr. Ichimura, was "Papa" to her. She had been too young to remember the father that had gone off to war.

The Ichimura family lived in a house attached to a small private hospital that was founded by Dr. Ichimura's late father. The second-generation Dr. Ichimura wanted to specialize in gynaecology and the hospital became a women's hospital. Ironically, his own first wife died of complications from the birth of their second child.

After the accepted mourning time, the doctor's mother began to search for a new wife for her son. She had noticed the priest's widowed daughter at the temple, an attractive and modest young woman. She had a child, but Mrs. Ichimura was looking for a mother for her two grandsons, as well as a wife for her son. Keiko seemed a good choice. Growing up in a temple was not an easy childhood and the doctor's mother wanted a daughter-in-law who was willing to work. She had had enough of spoiled city women with her son's first wife. When the time was right, Dr. Ichimura dutifully attended the arranged dinner meeting and agreed to his mother's choice.

The arrangement turned out well for all concerned. The doctor gained an attractive wife who quickly became a caring mother to his two small sons. His mother had the kind of daughter-in-law she wanted, dutiful, pleasant and hard-working. And Keiko was doing what she was brought up to do, in a happier, richer circumstance than she had ever hoped. Misako gained a father, two brothers, a new grandmother and a lively, bright home that was so unlike the dreary, dark temple. With the new-found security, Misako's annoying visions that so embarrassed her mother happened less and less.

Keiko, wearing a brown tweed suit, waited for Misako on the same platform where she had waited for her father's guest some hours earlier. Her slightly hooked nose and down-slanted eyes always gave her a slightly haughty look. Her father should have prepared her for the Zen priest's unusual appearance, she thought to herself, and saved her some embarrassment. It had given her quite a jolt. He was so very tall that everyone on the station stopped to stare at him. Even she had had a hard time keeping her composure as she looked up into his very pale eyes and gaunt, triangular face.

When Misako stepped from the train, Keiko experienced the second shock of the day. Her daughter looked positively ill, her face pale and drained. Before Keiko could say a word, Misako spat out an excited inquiry, "How is he? Is Grandfather going to die?"

"What nonsense! Your grandfather is very well. He was sweeping the temple steps this morning with the energy of a young man. Die? Where did you get such an idea? Did I give you the impression that Grandfather was ill?"

Misako looked into her mother's eyes and knew she was telling the truth. The relief made her let out a long sigh. "I'm sorry, Mother, it's just that I had a bad dream about Grandfather while I was napping on the train." The lie was necessary.

"It must have been a really bad dream," Keiko said. "Poor you. Don't pay attention to a silly dream. Forget it. Grandfather is fine. He's looking forward to seeing you tomorrow. He looks healthier than you do. Have you lost weight?"

"I don't think so. My appetite is usually good. In fact I feel hungry now."

"Good," Keiko said with relief. "Wait till you see the wonderful Hokkaido hairy crabs I bought for tonight. Papa is looking forward to the three of us having dinner together."

"Wonderful," Misako said and linked her arm with her mother's as they walked. Keiko stiffened slightly but did not pull away. It was difficult adjusting to her daughter's big-city, foreign ways.

"Silly of me to make so much of a dream," Misako said with a bright smile. "Oh Mother, it's good to be home with you and Papa."

"My, such a display of emotion! I thought Tokyo was your home, or did I just dream that you are part of the Imai family now?"

Misako laughed at her mother's words. Still it took a little of the homecoming joy out of her heart. She was no longer in the Ichimura family register and she wasn't always sure if the Imai family were happy about having her in theirs. Unlike the house in Tokyo, the Ichimura home pulsed with contented feelings and Misako didn't want to pollute the atmosphere by thinking about her troubles. Grandfather was certainly well if he was out sweeping the steps. She must have packed the mourning clothes herself. Subconsciously, she must have been worried about her grandfather's health because he suddenly wanted to see her. Maybe whatever made visions possible could also make her forget what she had put in her suitcase. It wasn't the first time that she couldn't understand why she had done something strange.

By ten o'clock that night, all seemed well in Misako's world again. She was in her old room, calm and secure, ignoring the dark thoughts that hovered like shadows in the back of her mind. As she lay in her warm futon she was tempted to think about Hideo and the girl in the red room, but under this roof, a stronger part of her emerged to erase all that. Instead she tried to remember what it was like to be sixteen years old, giggling with her best friend Sachiko. That had been a time when there was nothing more serious to worry about than the next day's lessons. They were comforting thoughts. No sleeping pills tonight. There would be no visions or nightmares. She wasn't going to let anything upset her, not even the great clap of thunder that broke directly overhead at about eleven o'clock. The bang was so loud it sounded as if it was in the room with her. Misako put her head under the quilt and giggled to herself like a schoolgirl.

BOOM! At the sound of thunder Teishin looked up at the dark, heavy beams of the temple's kitchen . He was standing at the sink washing rice for tomorrow's breakfast. "I hope it doesn't rain tomorrow," the priest said out loud and frowned.

The door leading to the courtyard opened and the priest Konein came in, brushing the rain from his kimono sleeves.

"Coming down, is it?" Teishin asked as he placed a heavy lid on the pot.

"Um," Konein grunted and slipped out of his sandals.

"The master will be disappointed if it rains tomorrow. He plans to show his guest around Shibata. Do you think it will rain tomorrow?" Teishin asked with his nose in a great crock of pickles.

"Maybe," the younger priest mumbled.

"Oh, I hope not," Teishin fretted, and popped a bit of cabbage pickle in his mouth. "Not bad," he said with satisfaction. "I made these this morning. Would you like to try some?"

But Konein had already left the kitchen and was walking softly down the corridor where he saw the light on in the master's room. As he passed, he heard muffled voices and knew that the master and the Zen priest were having a quiet conversation.

"We will visit the museum and garden tomorrow," the old priest informed his guest from Kamakura. "There is a long history there. Originally, a Buddhist temple stood on that site, but when the first feudal landlord settled in Shibata three hundred years ago, the land was expropriated and the temple moved."

"Wasn't that the leader of the Shibata Clan, Lord Mizoguchi?" Kensho asked.

"That's correct: Mizoguchi Hidekatsu-*sama*. You surprise me with your knowledge of our small city's history."

Kensho blushed and shook his head. "Forgive my interruption. I confess I did some research last night. Please go on."

"Well," the old man said, "Lord Mizoguchi built his residence and then, according to the records, he summoned a famous gardener from Kyoto to design and build the garden. It was done in the Kyoto style with a large pond made in the shape of the Chinese character *sui* for water."

As he said this, he leaned forward and slowly traced out the character for *sui* with his finger on the *tatami* floor. Then he closed his eyes and contemplated the construction of the garden. The tall priest moved his head in understanding and listened to the rain beating hard on the roof.

They were sitting cross-legged on cushions with a hibachi between them. The white, silk-wrapped box was in the alcove and a thin stream of smoke rose from incense burning in front of the box. The smoke curled up and around the bare light bulb that hung above them, illuminating their shaven heads. Opening his eyes, the old man stared down at his folded hands. His voice came in the staccato pattern of an old-time storyteller.

"During the struggles between the Shogun and Emperor Meiji in 1868, many of the landlords in Niigata backed the Shogun, but not the Mizoguchi Clan. They were loyal to the Emperor and fought the advancing Shogun's army. The fight was fierce, and the castle in Shibata was burned to the ground. Lord Mizoguchi and his samurai retreated to his residence. The situation looked grave until the town's people rallied to help fight the Shogun's troops with spears cut from bamboo reeds. The Shogun's troops fell back. My father was alive at the time and witnessed the victory. He told me the story many times."

Kensho watched the old, watery eyes close again under the unruly white brows. He wanted to ask a question but he was afraid to break the delicate bridge of thought that the old man was struggling to weave across time. Instead, he sat silently and became aware of another sound in the room, something he had not noticed until now. His eyes followed the sound up on the right wall where a rat was moving in the ceiling. Near the source of the noise, high on the wall, two elderly, sombre faces looked down from dark portraits. One was of a priest with heavy eyebrows, the other a woman with a thin face. They were obviously the old man's parents, the couple who lived here a long time ago. This had been the shell that encased their lives, Kensho thought, the place where a young priest could talk about the tumultuous events now being related. Perhaps it had been raining as he whispered the news of the battle. Perhaps a distant ancestor of the rat overhead had been making the same sounds on that night, in that very same ceiling.

"*Hai*," the old man started again, "after the revolution, things were never the same. As you know, the samurai lost their power and many were left to roam the countryside with no masters. The Mizoguchi wealth dwindled. The great garden and house fell into disrepair, passed down to one Mizoguchi relative after another. Eventually, it was sold to a wealthy landowner, whose ancestor had been a retainer to Lord Mizoguchi. It wasn't until after the second world war that the idea of making it into a private museum evolved. Unfortunately, last year, that big typhoon destroyed much of the restoration work that had been started in the 1950s. The winds and flood water damaged the garden and threw bones up from the pond. The ashes from those bones rest there," the old man said, and motioned toward the alcove with his head. The thought of it tired him. He heaved a sigh and closed his eyes again.

The rain seemed loud now and it struck the priest that the old man's sing-song voice and the rain were blending and taking turns, as if part of some clever orchestration. Now the rain was playing its part, but after a minute, the old eyes opened and the priest's solo continued.

"I have asked myself why I hold onto these ashes . . . many times. What could be the basis for the emotion the sight of that box stirs within me? Whatever the reason, I think it has to do with the garden and my own memories. It is a place rich in history and some say it is a haunted place.

In the back of the garden, near the bamboo grove the cold makes one shiver even in the summer. And then," he leaned forward and his voice dropped to a hoarse whisper, "there was that upsetting event that involved my granddaughter."

Another clap of thunder echoed in the night. A flood of rain played a few bars of drum beats on the roof. When it died down, the old priest picked up his narrative, slowly spinning the story of little Misako's experience in the Shibata garden so very long ago. Finally he sighed and added: "Her mother said we should pay no attention to it. She was positive that the child had an overactive imagination."

"And what do you think, *Sensei*?" Kensho asked. "Do you think it was her imagination?"

The old man pursed his lips and thought for a moment. "There was no evidence that anyone fell into the pond. Still, one never knew with young Misako. When I think back now, I have to admit that, as a child, Misako often knew things that couldn't be explained, like the story of the man you told us about in Kyoto."

"I see," the tall priest said slowly.

"I remember," the old man went on, "one spring near the end of the war. It was cold and fuel was impossible to obtain. My wife and I were sitting around the hibachi as someone had made us a gift of a little charcoal. It was about three in the afternoon. Keiko had two cooked sweet potatoes for us to share. We were eating silently when we heard a child's voice coming from the altar room. I can't tell you how shocking it was hearing that little voice chanting a part of the sutra for the dead. All three of us got up to see what was going on. We went to the altar room and there was little Misako, trying to pray as I do at ceremonies for the dead. How could a child remember such words? My daughter, Keiko, became angry, accusing the child of disrespect. The poor child could only respond with terrible sobs. Finally she said that she was praying for her father who had been killed on the battlefield. I tried to calm her and asked her how she could know such a thing. She simply said she saw it. As she entered the temple grounds, she saw her father clearly fall dead, with blood all over his head. Keiko was beside herself and cursed the child's cruel imagination. Still, in time the notice came that my son-in-law had indeed been killed on a battlefield. Maybe it was a coincidence. Then again, maybe it was like the story you told in Kyoto. If it was a coincidence, Misako has had many such coincidences in her childhood."

"How very interesting." Kensho's voice struck a note of admiration. It was hard to control his growing excitement. He was becoming convinced that this old man's granddaughter was indeed a true sensitive.

"*Hai*, I thought you would find it so," the old man said and took a deep breath. "Kensho-*sensei*, I am afraid I have brought you here for rather selfish reasons. I have also arranged for my granddaughter to visit the temple tomorrow. I have a plan that involves both of you; however, I'm afraid I can not explain all the details to you tonight." His face drooped with fatigue.

"Jushoku-*sama*, there is no need to explain tonight. I'm afraid I have overtired you. Be assured that I am happy to be of service to your honourable self in any possible way." Saying this, the younger priest bowed his thanks, stood up and went to the alcove where he knelt again and bowed deeply before the silk-wrapped box. He bowed again to the old master. "Good night," he said softly as he left the room and closed the *shoji* door behind him. As he walked down the corridor, he passed the kitchen. Teishin popped his head around the door.

"Good night," Kensho said, continuing toward his sleeping quarters.

"Good night," Teishin said, and rushed down the hallway to the master's room. He was waiting to lay out the futon and assist the old man's bedtime preparation. Outside, the youngest priest, Konein, swung the log against the temple bell. The sound was muted by the rain.

The room prepared for the priest from Kamakura was shabby, clean and welcoming. The futon was laid out with fresh linen and a small, low desk with a lamp was set before the patched shoji window. Kensho knelt at the desk to make notes in his black book. He closed his eyes at times, straining to recall everything the old master had told him. As he thought and wrote, the temple settled down for the night. He heard the other priests pass his door on the way to their rooms. The light snapped off in the hallway. The rain continued to fall softly against the roof. When he finished writing, he sat in the dark, concentrating, hoping to catch a sense of the past through some fragment of old energy that may still be moving within this venerable space.

❀ ❀ ❀

During the night, the rain clouds passed over Niigata. Countless droplets of water were left clinging to the roofs and trees. When the early morning sun rallied, it sent thin rays of shimmering light to touch the lingering beads of rain. It was a sparkling new day that the old priest and his guest stepped into just after six o'clock.

On his master's instructions, Teishin called the caretaker of Shimizuen garden to announce the visit of the master and his honoured guest. By the time the two priests left the temple, the harried caretaker was frantically raking the entrance to the big garden while his wife boiled water for tea.

The old priest was well rested and in excellent spirits. He walked with his shoulders slightly bent and his hands clasped behind his back. His giant of a friend walked beside him, taking a step and then pausing for the old man to catch up with his three shuffles. Kensho had to bend his head down to hear his companion's soft voice.

"Ah, look at the willow tree over there," the old man said, indicating the direction with a nod of his head. "Still green and fresh. Wonderful tree, the willow. It is the first to green in spring and the last to part with its colour in autumn. Its streaming foliage floats to every breeze, symbolizing a perfect compliance with nature."

Kensho made the appropriate noise of agreement and admiration. This was the first time they had been alone since their talk the evening before and he was eager to learn more about what his host really had on his mind. Now he sensed something important was being presented to him, something delicate that could pass by if he didn't receive it carefully. Deep in his heart, he knew he should be patient, but he was eager to pick up the threads of their last conversation.

"Could it be," he started clumsily, "that Jushoku-*sama* mentions the willow this morning because it is the tree that is associated with ghosts in folktales?" As soon as the words left his mouth he wanted to bite his tongue. His mind screamed, No, fool! Too fast and too stupid!

An awkward silence followed but, to the old man's credit, his short shuffling gait never faltered. His expression was not so controlled and he frowned when he snapped out an answer. "Ghost? Ghosts? Who talked of ghosts? What I said last night has nothing to do with folklore. The ghosts that are said to come out on summer nights to frighten people with their disfigured faces have nothing to do with this matter.

"But then again," he said in a softer tone, "it is natural that you are confused. You must forgive me, as I am trying to talk about something that I don't really understand myself. I call it a spirit because of poor understanding, but it is certainly not related to the scary ghosts of a Kabuki drama."

Kensho rubbed his bald head with embarrassment as he walked on. "I'm sorry for such a foolish remark. I didn't mean to make light of the things you so kindly told me."

"No, no, there is no offence, Kensho-*sensei*." He lifted his head and smiled up at the tall priest, showing his yellow teeth. "I told you about my granddaughter's childhood experience because I cannot dismiss the feeling that there is a connection to the bones found there recently. Your story in Kyoto impressed me greatly. It makes me think such things could be possible. I would hate to think I did her an injustice years ago."

"I'm beginning to understand. I am sorry for being impatient," Kensho said.

They had just crossed a wide avenue and started down a narrow lane. As they walked, the old man chuckled. "It was foolish of me. I shouldn't have spoken about the willow tree in the first place. Willows are never the highlights of an autumn display. Ah, here we are. We turn right here ."

They walked across an old bridge that straddled a narrow, fast-flowing stream. Kensho looked down and saw long grass bending with the flow of the clear water. The wood creaked under his weight. He put out his hand to help the old man step onto a gravel path. A few more steps past a patch of bamboo and they stood before a great wooden gate, crowned by a manicured thatched roof.

The caretaker and his wife greeted them warmly, even though it was hours before the official opening time for the garden. "Welcome, welcome," they said, their faces never hinting at their true feelings. They bowed so low to the priests that it looked as if they were welcoming Lord Mizoguchi himself. Kensho's ears glowed pink. Unlike the old master, he was not born to a temple family and never felt comfortable with the excessive expressions of respect that were sometimes shown to members of the clergy.

The old master sweetly thanked them for accepting their visit at an inconvenient hour. "I wanted my guest to view the garden early, before others arrived." The little old priest's warm smile was melting away the couple's resentment.

"Please, please take your time," the caretaker said. "I have opened the big house for you. The best view of the garden is from the house."

"I'll bring you hot tea," his wife said.

The priests thanked the couple for their kindness and started their walk down the gravel path. A large crow called from one of the tall pine trees.

"Over there," the old man said, indicating the long wall of slender bamboo trees growing to their left, "that is the bamboo that the town's people made spears with when they fought off the Shogun's troops. It is a special variety of thin bamboo that can be very sharp when cut and was planted here to be used as an emergency weapon. You are probably too young to remember that we Japanese were told to plant this same bamboo during the last war, in case we had to fight off the Americans."

"*Ah so*," Kensho said. He was not going to make the mistake of changing the subject again.

"Further past the bamboo and the stream there is a long house where the foot soldiers lived. There, on the right, was Lord Mizoguchi's residence."

"*Ah so*," Kensho said again and they continued on to a second wooden gate, this one with a weathered tile roof.

"Let's stop awhile and view the garden," the old priest said, and led the way through the second gate and onto a path of moss and flat stones.

The house was on the right, completely open with the *shoji* doors of wood and rice paper rolled back, exposing two very large traditional Japanese rooms. The old man climbed up the three rock steps, slipped out of his sandals and settled himself on the *tatami* floor.

"A man of my age cannot pass up a place to rest," he said, smiling and tapping the *tatami* with his right hand. "Come sit here."

Kensho stepped up to the room easily and sat down next to the old man. A soft morning mist crawled over the pond toward them. Bits of it broke away and sent gauzy fingers to touch the muted autumn hues. A great ancient tree bent twisted limbs over the water.

"That small house to the left with the veranda built out over the pond. Is it a tea house?" Kensho asked.

"A moon viewing house, I have been told," the old man chuckled. "Not to say that one couldn't use it as a tea house. The formal tea house is over on the right, toward the back. You can see the roof through the trees there."

"And where . . . ?" Kensho hesitated.

"Were the bones found?" the old priest said, filling in the unfinished sentence. "Straight ahead, somewhere near the bridge. It is not very clear with the mist but you will see it if you walk that way. There is another large rock near the waterfall. In that area."

"You said the skeleton was not complete. Do you think the missing bones are still there?"

"One would think so," the old man said. "That is precisely why I want

44

to hold a memorial service in that area; the service I want you and Misako to take part in.

"Oh, I see." This time Kensho could not keep the surprise out of his voice.

The old man looked out over the water. "I know it is unorthodox," he said, "but that is what I have decided to do. That is the favour I have to ask of you and my granddaughter." He paused and then broke into a smile looking up into his companion's face. "That is, if you and Misako are willing to humour an old man."

The tall priest smiled as well. Of course he would agree. Unusual as it was, Kensho saw no harm in joining his host in praying for a lost soul. And it was an excellent chance to meet a true sensitive. When he answered, he spoke slowly, straining to keep the excitement out of his voice.

"I will be happy to assist you in any way I can."

"Thank you for indulging a foolish old man."

"It is a pleasure to be here with you in this lovely place." Kensho stood up and stepped down into the garden. He was smiling with approval. "I think it a very good plan, considering that parts of the skeleton are still buried there. I look forward to assisting you with the prayers."

"Ah," the old priest said, putting his palms together and bowing his head. "Prayer is prayer. The Lord Buddha can only be pleased that priests of different sects can pray together."

"*Hai*," Kensho agreed with a smile. "When do you plan the ceremony?"

"Monday morning. The day after tomorrow. If you can stay that long."

"And your granddaughter, Misako-*san*. Will she agree?"

The old man smiled. "She will visit the temple today and then we will see. I think she will do it for her grandfather."

Kensho stepped on the garden path. "I had better see the back of the garden. Will you walk with me?"

"No, you go on. I will stay happily waiting for the tea that was promised. Look for the sazanka tree. It is a very old tree and should be getting ready to burst with white blossoms."

"I will," Kensho said as he removed a small black book from his kimono sleeve. "You see, I want to take a few notes," he explained with a grin, before bowing and beginning his stroll in the garden.

Sitting in his meditation position, the old man watched the tall priest move past a large red rock from Sado Island. Suddenly he felt very tired, and sighed. He thought how disapproving Keiko would be when she found out about his scheming. Am I acting like a crazy old man? he asked himself.

The morning air was fresh after the rain. The crow called again from another tall pine. An orange and silver koi jumped in the pond, making a loud slapping sound against the water. The old priest closed his eyes and sighed again. He took several deep breaths and folded his hands in his lap, his thumbs touching. The morning air was fragrant with a scent that hinted of cedar. A small, bright maple leaf floated slowly down on the path before him. Time fell away from Lord Mizoguchi's beautiful garden.

❀ ❀ ❀

Misako experienced the pleasure of waking naturally from an undisturbed sleep. Under her parents' roof all the vibrations flowed positively and lovingly toward her. Mother Imai's disapproval was far off in Tokyo.

"Good morning," Misako said, lazily stretching as she entered the room where her mother was reading the morning newspaper.

Keiko looked up over her glasses. "Did you sleep well?"

"Ummm, very well," Misako grinned.

"Good." Keiko was sitting at the *kotatsu*, a low table that covered a hole cut into the *tatami* floor. A small electric heater had been placed there to warm feet resting on a small shelf above it. A quilt covered the table frame and a proper table top rested on the quilt. The *kotatsu* was a cozy feature of country life that Misako loved and missed. Wrapped in her flannel robe, she lifted the quilt and sat down across from her mother.

"You look like our Misako this morning," Keiko said, "not like that pale, nervous young woman who got off the train yesterday."

"Really, I sleep so well in this house," Misako said, pulling the quilt up to her chin. She looked young and pretty again, the dark marks gone from under her eyes. Her hair was tied back in a blue ribbon. "I wanted to get up early and have breakfast with Papa but I never heard a thing."

"Never mind, you can see him at lunchtime. That tea is hot and I have breakfast ready in the kitchen. Just sit there and enjoy a little service for a change."

"Service," Misako repeated with a yawn. "How nice." Keiko laughed and left the room. Misako looked out into a small sun-filled garden where a large camellia bush showed off waxy, red blooms. She breathed in the fresh cool air and felt the positive energy still lingering from thousands of happy moments past.

She was still smiling when Keiko returned with a tray of steaming soup and rice. They sat across from each other and began to talk. For a while it was as if the last years had not happened. She was the daughter who was eating her mother's home-cooked breakfast, listening to news about her stepbrothers and other small talk. She giggled at Keiko's description of the priest from Kamakura. "He's so tall and pale. And he has strange pale eyes," Keiko said.

"You don't seem to like Grandfather's guest very much."

"Did I give that impression?" Keiko sounded surprised. "I didn't mean to."

"Well, you were not exactly complimentary. Really, Mother, you made him sound like a long, white bean sprout."

"Don't joke," Keiko said, laughing. "I don't dislike him but his appearance makes me uncomfortable. It is the way he stands. He reminds me of a crane. It's a little spooky."

The words were just out of her mouth when Misako stopped laughing. Her shoulders drooped as she put her hand up as if to beg silence from her moth r. She was looking at the telephone.

"Oh no," Keiko moaned. "I've forgotten that you can be spooky too. Don't tell me the telephone is going to ring. Haven't you grown out of that game yet?"

The colour drained from Misako's face. "I don't want to talk to her," she said. "Tell her I'm not here." She flinched when the telephone rang out.

"Don't ask me to lie, Misako. Please. I don't care who is calling. I'm not going to lie. Answer it yourself."

Misako folded her arms like a stubborn child and shook her head. "Then let it ring."

"Answer the phone, Misako!" Keiko was annoyed. "It may be Grandfather trying to contact us. We can't ignore the phone all the time you are here."

The ringing bell was piercing. Misako stood up reluctantly and went to the phone.

"Hello," she said softly.

The voice on the other end of the wire was loud and angry. "I want to know why you didn't tell me Hideo wasn't coming home last night! Do you realize I went to a lot of trouble preparing dinner for *your* husband? You could have saved me the work and worry. All you had to do was tell me Hideo wasn't planning to be home. You knew it before you left."

"But I didn't know," Misako said in her own defence. "Hideo never said a word to me yesterday morning. He didn't even say goodbye. He called it from the entrance. Don't you remember?"

"Don't lie to me! He told you before you came downstairs," Mother Imai screamed into the phone. Keiko looked up. She could hear the voice from where she was sitting. "I just reached Hideo at the office and he clearly said that he told you of his plans before he left the house. Of course he expected you to tell me. That's why he didn't call home last night, and I had gone to a lot of trouble preparing a special dinner for him."

Mother Imai was a large lady given to large emotions. She had been so disappointed that she couldn't concentrate on the television. From about ten to midnight, she had walked around the house talking to herself, going to the door at the least sound from outside. When she went to bed, she couldn't sleep and spent most of the night listening for Hideo's footsteps on the stairs.

When she finally contacted her son at his office that morning, the easiest way for Hideo to calm her wrath was to blame Misako. His mother's hysteria assaulted the telephone so loudly that a couple of his coworkers looked up from their desks and exchanged smiles. It was embarrassing. Hideo would have said anything to cut her off at that moment.

The phone clicked in Misako's ear. Misako in turn slammed the receiver down on the cradle. Her face was flushed with anger. "How dare he tell his mother a lie involving me."

"Come back and sit down," Keiko ordered. "If there is some trouble in the Imai household, you had better tell me about it—now!"

SIX

*T*eishin scratched at the vivid carpet of autumn leaves around the temple gate with a bamboo rake. He was dressed in his everyday faded-black baggy pants and jacket, but his spirits were holiday-high. The rays of sun that filtered through the golden canopy of the giant ginko tree felt like a shower of joy on his skin. "What a beautiful autumn day," he sang as he worked. "What a very beautiful autumn day. The leaves are like bright flowers falling." He was making up new words to a popular folk melody, keeping himself busy while he waited for Misako.

Not the best of days, Misako thought as she rode her bicycle through Shibata's narrow streets, oblivious to the sun and bright autumn leaves. After Mother Imai's ridiculous telephone call, Misako had to confess her suspicions about Hideo's infidelity. Of course, Misako hadn't mentioned her vision of Hideo and the strange girl. There was no use opening up that old hornet's nest. Her mother would never believe it.

"It doesn't sound like your suspicious are well founded," Keiko said. "The best thing you can do is forget it. Even if it is true, it will pass. Men may have weak moments, but they always come back to their family. Don't expect your mother-in-law to take your side. She owes her loyalty to her son and the Imai family. Besides, you have no proof. You don't want to sound like some nagging, jealous wife. Just forget about it. It will pass."

And that was that. Keiko started to talk about the wonderful pears she had bought, and asked Misako to take some to the temple. "Grandfather will love them," she said, and went into the kitchen to wrap the pears.

Misako carried the fruit in the bicycle's basket, along with the special cakes and a bouquet of flowers for her grandmother's grave. Teishin saw her coming. He put down his rake and bowed several times, smiling in her direction. It was obvious that he had been waiting for her. Misako smiled and waved. She had always been fond of him. Dear Teishin-*san*, she thought. He always had the ability to cheer her up. By the time she stopped at the temple gate, Misako was smiling and Teishin was hopping around like a happy child.

Misako didn't meet the priest from Kamakura until later that afternoon.

She and her grandfather were chatting together, drinking tea in the small *tatami* room near the kitchen, when the tall priest awkwardly announced himself and entered the room.

"Ah, Kensho-*san*, come in, come in," the old man called out with a broad smile. "Here is my granddaughter visiting from Tokyo."

"*Ah so*," the priest said, as he knelt down to greet her. Even though her mother had prepared her for his strange appearance, Misako still blushed. She slipped off the cushion she was sitting on and placed her hands together on the *tatami*, touching her forehead to the floor in a formal bow. The few seconds that passed as she hid her face helped her to compose herself.

Kensho returned the formal greeting and offered polite words, as was appropriate for people meeting for the first time. The old priest beamed as he watched. "Relax, both of you," he said, waving his hand and smiling. "Misako, pour our guest tea."

So this was the strange priest who made her mother feel uncomfortable. Misako poured boiling water into the teapot, trying not to look directly at his face.

"Your grandfather told me about you, Misako-*san*," the priest said as he accepted the cup.

"And my mother has told me about you," she smiled, trying to return the compliment. He had the feeling that Keiko hadn't liked him and Misako's words made his ears turn red with embarrassment. "I hope it wasn't all bad," he said.

"Not at all," she lied with a lovely smile, not looking straight at him. "All good. Really." Seeing his distress made her pity him. He was very tall and was obviously shy. She placed the box of cakes before him.

"*Dozo*," she said sweetly. "You must try the cakes I brought from Tokyo. They are Teishin-*san*'s favourite."

"Thank you, I will," he said, and reached for the cakes with a long bony hand.

They began to pass tidbits of information about themselves back and forth. The old priest sat in his usual cross-legged fashion, his thumbs together in his lap. He added comments through his fixed smile, gradually injecting the story of his first meeting with Kensho and how he had first heard about "clairvoyance."

"That's English, you know," he said with a self-satisfied smile." Secretly, he had practiced pronouncing the difficult word.

"Yes, I do know," Misako said, narrowing her eyes first at her grand-father and then in the direction of the priest. They must have discussed this subject quite a lot for her grandfather to learn that long, difficult foreign word.

Kensho read her expression and felt a touch of guilt. "That kind of thing is a hobby with me," he managed to say with a great blush. "I'm interested in such things but I'm afraid I bore people with my stories." He laughed and rubbed his bald head. "I'm surprised you remembered that story. I'm sure it wasn't interesting."

"It was interesting. It was very interesting! Why don't you tell Misako about it?"

"No, no," the priest said, waving his hand in front of his face. Misako-san would be bored."

"Ah, but you are wrong," the old man said. "Misako had a little talent in that direction herself when she was a child. As I told you, she actually knew when her father died. Didn't you, Misako?"

"I don't remember exactly," Misako said, examining her teacup and feeling increasingly uneasy.

"I would very much like to hear about any such experiences you have had, Misako-*san*," the priest said. "I hope you will tell me sometime."

"Perhaps, some time," she said softly. "Won't you have more tea?"

"Yes, please," he said and moved his cup toward her. She poured the cup only half full, hoping he would leave so that she could talk to her grandfather alone. She was beginning to suspect he had called her to Niigata just to meet this priest.

The clock on the wall struck three times. Teishin entered the room for his tea. The sight of the open box of cakes made him laugh and rub his hands together in delight.

"Ah, my favourite cakes from Tokyo. Thank you, thank you, Misako-*san*. You always remember."

"You are welcome," Misako said, glad for his arrival. Suddenly she felt more comfortable. "There is another box there, especially for you."

"Ah, thank you, thank you." He sat down and quickly popped a cake into his mouth. "Delicious," he said, before completely swallowing the treat.

"Where in Tokyo did you buy these wonderful cakes?" Kensho asked.

"Oh, it's a very old shop near Ueno Station. I wouldn't dare visit Niigata without them. Teishin-*san* wouldn't let me through the temple gate."

51

Everyone laughed. The conversation was heading safely toward the demonstrative Teishin, his appetite and his favourite sweets from Tokyo.

The puzzle of the mourning clothes was solved later that afternoon when Misako and her grandfather were alone again. He finally told her about the bones found in Shimizuen garden. He casually revealed his plan to hold a private funeral service at the end of the pond. Without hesitation, he went on to tell her why he wanted the priest from Kamakura to take part in the ceremony. "Because he knows about things like the experience you had in that garden as a child. I want to know if there is any connection between that experience and the bones that were found."

Misako couldn't believe her ears. She hadn't thought about the girl falling into the pond for years and she didn't want to be reminded of it now. "But Grandfather, that was so long ago. I was just a little girl."

"Nevertheless, it did happen. Your mother and I were not very understanding then, but times change. I believe you did see a vision of a girl fall into the pond. I think you are what Kensho-*san* calls that difficult word. Perhaps you have an ability to see what others cannot."

"You seem to remember more about that incident than I do." Misako's voice rang with annoyance.

The old man seemed not to notice her tone. "Facts are facts," he said with his little smile. "At some time, a teenaged girl did fall into that pond. We know that now because a girl's bones were found there. We may not know who she was but it is right to hold a memorial service in the garden where she died. Granted, it is not usual, but this is an unusual situation. Perhaps the bones have a connection to the vision you had there as a child."

"Why now?" Misako protested. "Why after all these years? You didn't believe in my visions, not ever."

"It is true. However, when the bones were found in the pond last year, the memory of your childhood experience started to haunt me. It still haunts me. All I know to do about it is to chant prayers for the soul that may have been trying to cry out through my own granddaughter." The old man shook his head. "I am an ignorant country priest. You and Kensho-*san* have gifts that may help me understand this puzzle."

"But—" Misako began to protest, then stopped. She had never seen her grandfather's eyes so shiny and full of life. The pleading in his voice touched her heart.

"Misako, what harm can a small, private memorial service do?"

"None, I suppose," she said. It all seemed so important to him, and why not make her grandfather happy? "I'll attend your ceremony if you like, but you will have to explain it to Mother. She won't like it, you know."

The old man frowned. "In time, in time." His soft moment had passed. His voice firmed up into a near bark. "Right now I don't want her to know all the details. Don't tell her any more than you have to or she'll just interfere."

"Grandfather, I can't promise to keep it from her."

He pursed his lips like a disappointed child. His expression was so unlike him that Misako giggled.

"Well," she said, "I guess I could try."

"Please do," the old priest said with a small bow and a broad smile. "Now I need some rest. I'm tired." Pushing both hands against the floor, he got up with what looked like a labourious effort. The awkward posture was like that of a small child who had not yet mastered the art of walking. Misako moved quickly to help him. The arm under the layers of his kimono felt like a fragile stick. A wave of affection for this dear old man swept over her.

"Thank you, thank you," he said, patting the hand that supported his elbow. "I can manage now. It is getting up and down that gives me trouble."

"You will have to get down again when you reach your room, unless you are accustomed to resting standing up."

"*Hai, hai*," was his answer, and he let her hold his arm as they walked down the hallway.

When she entered the room, Misako's heart was touched by nostalgia. It had been a long time since she had been in this room. It was like stepping back in time. Nothing seemed to change here. The room was as awesome as she remembered. It smelled of incense and there were still the stern faces of her great-grandparents looking down, watching from high on the wall.

No matter what time of day it was, the room always felt like it belonged to another era. It had only one narrow, horizontal window built high up on the wall opposite the worn sliding *shoji* doors. At that moment, the afternoon sun was shining down through the window, casting an oblong of amber light on the old *tatami*. Thousands of tiny dust specks danced in the one broad ray of sun. Their movements seemed too quick, too gay for this caliginous setting.

Misako went to the closet, took out the dark plaid cotton futon and arranged it on the floor. It was difficult to keep her eyes away from the silk-wrapped box in the alcove. She guessed at the contents and began to understand how important these remains were to her grandfather. Why else would he be keeping the girl's ashes in his room?

"Have a good rest," she said after helping him down and pulling a light quilt over his body. He looked small and tired. The tender feeling she felt for him made her linger, kneeling next to his futon for a moment.

"Thank you, Misako-*chan*." It made her smile to hear him add the *chan* to her name, as he had when she was a child. "You stay with your mother tomorrow and have a nice visit. I want to see you here early Monday morning. Five o'clock, please."

"Monday!" Misako assumed the service he planned would take place the next day. "I'm supposed to go back to Tokyo on Monday."

"What is one day in a lifetime?" he asked looking up at her. "Tomorrow is not a favourable day for a memorial service. Monday is convenient because the garden is closed to the public and we won't have to rush. It wouldn't do to have people around asking questions. Ask your mother for the car, please. We don't want to attract attention on our way over to the garden. There are a lot of old busybodies up and about early in the morning in this town."

"Grandfather, you surprise me."

The old man had already closed his eyes. She closed the door softly and went down the hall to the kitchen.

The flowers she brought for her grandmother's grave were waiting in a bucket of water by the door. Teishin, had left a bamboo vase and clippers for her on the kitchen table. Misako arranged the flowers, slowly, pausing several times to think about her grandfather's plans. It was obvious that he had it all thought out carefully in advance. Of course! If she really did have the ability the tall priest talked about, she would have had a reason to pack her mourning clothes. Maybe subconsciously she had known that she would be attending a memorial service. Misako finished and carefully wrapped up the clippings from the flowers in a newspaper. She felt depressed and helpless at the thought of not being in control of her own mind.

"It's not normal," she mumbled. "It must be some sort of madness."

Entering the graveyard from the rear, Misako made her way past the old pine trees and tombstones, many untidy with remnants of past offerings. Their family gravestone was tall and narrow with the name "Tanaka" carved in flowing characters. Above the name was their decorative plum-blossom family crest.

Teishin had an archaic wooden water pail and a bamboo dipper waiting by the grave. Misako poured water over the tombstone, placed the flowers on the grave and lit sticks of incense. Carefully, she moved the sticks like a fan until a thin stream of fragrant smoke began to rise. It was something she had done hundreds of times, yet now, when she began to pray, she found it hard to concentrate. Her thoughts kept coming back to her grandfather. She pictured the old man as she left him in his room, his wrinkled eyelids closed under the unruly brows. He's getting very old, she thought, as if he was speaking to her grandmother, and I believe he is not as well as he pretends.

Suddenly this thought fell from her mind like a rock thrown from a cliff. There was no need to look around. Kensho had entered the cemetery and Misako's mind at the same time. He interrupted her as surely as if he had tapped her on the shoulder. A surge of resentment made her pretend she was not aware of his presence. What she was doing was rude and it made her shiver.

"Excuse me for disturbing you," he said after a moment, surprised at this rudeness.

Misako turned around and looked up into his face. "You want to talk to me about the ceremony my grandfather plans to take place at Shimizuen, don't you?"

"Yes," he answered, taken aback by her obvious anger.

"And what do you think of the plans?" She looked up into his eyes as she spoke.

Kensho was uncomfortable with her tone. "I respect your grand-father's judgement, he said with a deep bow. "I'm happy to assist in any way he wishes."

"He has told you about my childhood experience in that garden, hasn't he?"

"Yes, he has," he said. "I am sorry that it displeases you."

Misako turned her attention back to the tombstone, speaking again with her back to him. "I was just a child when I had that experience in the garden. It could have been imagination. I'm afraid he is making a fuss over a very vague memory, a little girl's fantasy."

"And do you believe your experience was fantasy?" His voice was calm, very polite.

For a moment, Misako didn't know what to say. She turned to look at him again. Even though he was smiling down on her, his hands behind his back, his head and shoulders bent in that crane-like posture, there was something vulnerable in his bearing.

They were standing on ground covered with fallen pine needles. She blushed and bowed deeply.

"Kensho-*san*, I'm sorry I was rude. It is unforgivable. Sometimes my feelings are so confused." She pushed the pine needles around with the toe of her shoe and plunged her hands into the pockets of her cardigan.

"Misako-*san*, there is nothing to forgive. I understand why you are upset, but since your grandfather is determined, perhaps I can be a help to both of you."

Misako shook her head and sighed. "You probably understand more about these things than anyone I have ever met, still, I don't know how you can help me. It is true that I sometimes have visions. I know that is not normal. I am afraid that what I experience is only my imagination acting up."

"Can you tell me what you remember about the girl in the garden?"

Misako bit her lip and tried to push her mind back through the years. "I remember that my friend and I were drawing pictures by the pond. I looked up and saw a young lady who seemed to appear out of nowhere. She was sitting, no, squatting on the bridge. Something was tied to her back like a baby. Then she leaned forward and tumbled into the pond, head first."

"And your friend, did she see it too?"

"No, she saw nothing."

"Your grandfather thinks there was more to it than a child's imagination."

"Now," Misako laughed. "When I was a child, everyone thought I was telling stories."

"You know that your grandfather told me that you knew when your father died."

"He told you a lot," Misako snapped back.

The priest rubbed his head and flushed. "I'm sorry. You are perfectly right to be annoyed. It is not my place to know such personal things about your life."

Misako bowed her head. "I am sorry. I can't help being touchy about all this. I know you mean well."

"No, it is my fault. I am afraid I am too interested in this sort of thing. Perhaps after the ceremony on Monday your grandfather will be satisfied and that will be the end of it."

Misako moved her toe around in the pine needles again. "I wish it were that simple. You priests find funeral services everyday things, just a day's work. For me, going back to that garden may not be easy. I haven't been there in years and I don't want to rekindle . . . certain feelings."

"You sound afraid," he said, touched by the emotion in her voice.

"Yes! I'm afraid of having more visions. I hate them. They complicated my childhood. I thought I had grown out of them, but recently, they have started again. I'm afraid that being a part of this ceremony could strengthen whatever made me have visions in the first place. I don't want to know things I'm not supposed to know. I just want to be an ordinary person."

The only way the priest could handle the uncomfortable moment was to make a joke. "I too want to be an ordinary person," he said with his grin, "but look at me." He pulled himself up to full height, stretched his long arms out on either side, and crossed his eyes. Misako clapped her hand over her mouth and laughed. He looked so comical. They laughed together for the first time. The priest relaxed and his voice grew tender.

"Misako-*san*. I myself have not yet managed to live a quiet, self-confident existence of my own. Time is a slow but constant teacher. One day you will learn to accept your extraordinary gift and all that you are. It is then that you will be able to contently flow with life."

Misako bowed deeply, turned and walked away slowly. It was the only way she could hide the tears that were filling her eyes. The gangly figure walked behind her on the narrow path. Her bicycle was parked near the gate. She wheeled it onto the street before she turned to say goodbye.

"Thank you, Kensho-*sensei*. I have to go now," she said with a bow.

He returned the bow. "*Sayonara*, Misako-*san*. I hope to see you soon."

"*Sayonara*," she said and got on her bicycle.

He stood watching as she rode away. From the back, her slight figure in the navy-blue skirt and sweater could have belonged to any teenaged girl riding home from school. He stood until she turned the corner and was out of sight before he slowly walked back to the temple in a daze of emotion.

SEVEN

*T*hat night, the priest from Kamakura seemed to have lost his meditation skills. Even when he managed to remove Misako from his thoughts, he couldn't find the empty place that he usually tumbled into at will. Misako's large, innocent eyes hovered on the edge of his consciousness. Any small break in his concentration could send them hurtling toward him like two bright stars travelling across a black sky. Kensho would sigh heavily, close his eyes and try to start again.

Outside, a full autumn moon floated over the temple. The old building was no defence against its light. Moon-glow spilled through the windows and cracks. Kensho stood up and walked about the room. He slid open the *shoji* window and looked out into the garden. It was all shadows and silver. There seemed to be a new dimension to this night, as if the moonlight were playing silent music. The beauty crushed his chest. He knew it was neither the moonlight nor the humble temple garden that was affecting him. He had experienced this wonderful kind of pain before, a very long time ago.

Kensho sat down cross-legged again, where the silver light fell on the yellowed *tatami* floor. He spread his large boney hands, examining them in the eerie glow. These hands were something he could control. He could turn them or fold them together, but emotions were more difficult to direct. Against his better judgement, he could feel the seeds of love and desire deep within himself.

"Misako," he whispered, and winced with the pain of knowing he shouldn't allow himself the luxury of saying her name. Not tonight. Not in the moonlight.

Folding himself into the lotus position, he closed his eyes and tried again to meditate. It took all his powers of concentration to leave the moonlight and inner fire behind. With the two windows of his spirit closed to the physical surroundings, he hurled his will through an endless space, throwing off all thoughts. In the forced emptiness, he felt a well of energy rising from the pit of his stomach, spreading through his body. It reached the top of his head and the tips of his extremities at the same time. When it subsided, he felt everything inside him slowly falling into a large, dark, billowy cloud. For the next hour, the priest from Kamakura sat in the moonlight-drenched room, allowing his silent inner god to heal his wounds.

The son of a small-town teacher, Kensho was born in Hokkaido, the northernmost island of Japan. From the time of his birth, it was apparent that he was not like other babies. At first, his father was terrified that the infant was retarded, which would have been a cruel blow to the schoolteacher, who revered scholastic achievement above all else. For that reason, he was named Daigaku, meaning *higher learning*. When the child began to talk and showed promise, the parents were relieved.

Daigaku's main childhood problem was his height. He was always the tallest in the class and taller than most children in the higher grades as well. People would tell his parents to fatten him up and send him off to be trained as a sumo wrestler, but his father took offence at such suggestions. His mother tried to make him gain weight, but no matter how many bowls of rice or noodles he consumed, the bones still protruded from his chest. He grew embarrassingly tall and pale. His classmates called him Moyashi. Having a nickname that meant *long, white bean sprout* forced him to develop a sense of humour about his appearance. It was the only way to survive.

But why was he different from the other children? The question was always in his heart. He studied his parents carefully and became convinced that he must have been adopted as an infant. He couldn't identify with either his mother or father. It was true that both his parents were thin and slightly taller than most, but not nearly as thin and tall as he was. Neither of them had his pale eyes nor his soft, brown hair.

Only his mother knew the truth, and it wasn't until she was on her deathbed that she told him. It was the summer that he turned twenty years old. She had been ill for some time and Daigaku was sitting on the *tatami* floor next to her futon when she reached out and took his hand, saying that she had to tell him something important. "But first," she said in a shaky voice, "you have to swear that you will never tell anyone."

He quickly guessed it had to do with his birth and blurted out that he already knew that he had been adopted.

"What foolish nonsense," his mother said, her weak voice gaining strength with indignation. "You are our true son, born and conceived in this very room."

Daigaku felt ashamed, begged his mother's forgiveness and vowed to keep her secret. It was then she told him that it was she, herself, who was strange. She was a half-breed, not pure Japanese, and that made him one-fourth a foreigner. She cried as she spoke, begging that no one must know, not even his father. "It is to you now that I pass on this secret of our family shame. Never break your vow of silence on this matter."

Her mother, his grandmother, was a young, small-town geisha when she was sent to nearby Hakodate to work during the busy New Year season. Hakodate is a port city and it was there that she entertained at a party given for the crew from a Russian ship. There was one very tall, gaunt officer who attracted her. He had dark hair and blue eyes. When she served him sake, he smiled shyly. The allure of the invitation from his exotic blue eyes made her giddy. She drank more than usual, threw caution to the wind and secretly gave herself to a strange and wonderful adventure. Until that time, her one sexual contact was negotiated through the head of the geisha house; she had a regular patron back home. He was the one who enjoyed her favours and paid her bills. When the Russian ship was back on the high seas, the young geisha suspected that she might be pregnant. The possibility of the child belonging to a foreigner sent her into a terrible panic.

Her patron was the only son of the owner of the town's best restaurant that employed geisha. The spoiled young man wanted his geisha to break with tradition and marry him. The clever little entertainer calculated that there was a slight chance that it was her young patron that fathered the child. Since she greatly feared a botched abortion, she decided to gamble, tell him she was pregnant and accept the marriage invitation. His father gave in and paid off her debts so she could leave the geisha house.

For months the new bride was constantly frightened, not knowing what kind of a child to expect. It wasn't surprising that such a nervous woman would have her baby prematurely, and she did. It was a fine, healthy baby girl with lots of soft black hair. No one in town knew about the Russian ship and certainly no one ever suspected the geisha's secret. Most people in that town had never seen a foreigner in person. In those days, most country Japanese thought that all foreigners had bright red hair, huge noses and hooves in place of feet.

The mother examined her daughter and recognized subtle traces of her one-time Russian lover. Within a few days she breathed a great sigh of relief because the baby looked perfectly Japanese to the unsuspecting eye. It was not uncommon for people in the north to have lighter skin and almost-round eyes. She was safe. Miraculously, her nervous condition disappeared and the happy couple had six more children. Her training made her a talented hostess and she helped the restaurant prosper. No one suspected the truth about their oldest child, least of all her husband.

It was only when the little girl grew up, married the schoolteacher and had a child of her own that the former geisha realized that her sin was not yet buried. Her first grandchild's eyes were strangely light, like a cat's. The fringe of hair around the little boy's head was soft and brown. It was then that the daughter had to be told, had to be sworn to secrecy and had to vow not to have another child. It was a devastating revelation to the young mother and a terrible promise to have to make. As the grandmother pointed out, there was no way of guessing how the genealogical roulette that takes place at conception would turn out the next time. If a big-nosed, red-haired creature was born to her, the shame would be in the open and fall on the entire family. Worst of all, the schoolteacher would learn that his wife was a half-breed, a love child from a foreign sailor. He would most certainly divorce her. Then there was her baby son to think about. What would his life be like if the story got into the mouths of gossips? There was no choice. Much to his father's chagrin, Daigaku was an only child.

❀ ❀ ❀

The next day, Misako's head was still swimming from the remarkable conversation she'd had with the tall priest. Something important had happened to her in the temple's graveyard and now she didn't feel as burdened with her secret.

She woke up in high spirits, dressed and went to the kitchen to cook breakfast for her parents. It was Sunday and Dr. Ichimura wasn't due to make his hospital rounds until later. Still in his cotton kimono, he sat down at the *kotatsu* and called for tea.

"*Hai, hai,*" Misako said, merrily mimicking a geisha as she came into the room with the steaming cups on a tray.

"I'll be spoiled with two women waiting on me like this," he joked. "I don't get this service when only your mother is around."

"Then enjoy it while you can," she said, and handed him the morning paper before going back to the kitchen. The smell of miso soup and freshly cooked rice filled the house and Misako was enjoying feeling secure and happy in her parents' home.

Just before noon, Mother Imai called again. This time it took Misako by surprise. She had no warning that the telephone was about to ring. Her mother-in-law spoke in an apologetic tone, the high voice tuned to absolute sweetness. She added the endearing *chan* to Misako's name.

"Please forgive me, Misako-*chan*, I was the one who was at fault." Humility wasn't the usual posture for Mother Imai to take with her daughter-in-law but the circumstances called for it. She wanted Misako to come home soon. She'd had dinner alone with Hideo the night before but it hadn't turned out the way she had planned. Hideo wasn't in a talking mood; he especially didn't want to talk about his personal life. He told her that straight out. During most of the meal, he sat silently eating and watching a boxing match on television.

That was another cause of contention between mother and son. Hideo took over the television set and watched mostly sports. Mother Imai missed her favourite shows. Even one evening without her television put her in a bad temper.

Hideo sat in front of the set for hours and made demands, calling for tea and wanting noodles prepared before he went to bed. Mother Imai had forgotten how much there was to do before Misako had come into the family. Now she was insisting that the young couple talk to each other, right now, on the telephone. She wanted life back to normal. Against Hideo's will, she had shoved the phone into his hands.

"I won't be home until Tuesday," Misako told her husband. "Grand-father is well, but he wants me to attend a memorial service with him tomorrow morning."

Hideo responded to Misako's words with a series of *hai* grunts, the little noises of indifference Misako knew so well. She ended the call quickly.

Keiko came into the room just in time to catch the last part of their conversation and wanted to hear all about the memorial service Misako was supposed to attend.

"I think you'd better ask Grandfather yourself," Misako said. "The details are too complicated for me."

"It has to do with the ashes he keeps in his room, doesn't it?"

Misako bit her lip and examined her fingernails.

"Really! I've never heard of anything so strange." Keiko was clearly agitated.

Misako looked at her mother and smiled, "You are the one who said Grandfather is getting peculiar in his old age. You wanted me to humour him, remember? He wants me there early tomorrow morning. And by the way, I'll need to borrow the car. Grandfather said so."

"Well!" Keiko said, and left the room. Misako needed no psychic powers to know that her mother was going to visit the temple today.

That afternoon, Misako decided to take a bicycle ride around the town. She rode up the sunny main street, which was bustling with Sunday shoppers. Passing the Kawanabi Department Store, she turned right toward the temple and, although she hadn't planned it, rode onto Shimizuen garden. When she reached the little bridge that crossed the stream, she got off the bicycle and walked alongside it. The great gate loomed before her. It had been restored since she last visited the garden. She went to the booth and bought a ticket to enter.

Shimizuen garden was more beautiful than she had remembered. The moment she walked through the gates, Misako was glad she had come. There was a group of young girls ahead of her, all dressed in brightly coloured kimonos. Their long silk sleeves fluttered gracefully as they walked. A formal tea ceremony had been held at the tea house and Misako could see more kimono-clad ladies as she went through the second gate.

She took the path on the left side of the pond, away from the tea activity. Tiny red maple leaves made patches of colour on the ground. Elegant pampas grass graced a small peninsula that jutted into the water. A young girl's laughter could be heard from the other side of the pond. Misako walked slowly on the stones set in the moss. The beauty of the surroundings made her feel calm.

There was an opening in the greenery at the rear of the garden, where one could walk between two large camellia trees and enter a small clearing. Misako remembered an old bell tower there. The bell had been removed and melted down during the war but there were paintings of Buddhist angels on the inside of the wooden tower's roof. The angels, she remembered, had pale blue robes and she loved to look at them when she was a child. Now she wanted to see how the paintings had weathered the years. One step past the camellia bushes and she stood frozen. There, leaning against a large rock, was the priest from Kamakura, making notes in a small black book. When he saw her, his face broke into a childlike grin.

"There you are, Misako-*san*. I've been waiting for you."

"Kensho-*sensei*! What a surprise!" she said, putting both hands up to her mouth. "What are you doing here?"

"I'm here on an errand. Your grandfather sent me to find the best spot for the altar tomorrow. Won't you help me?"

"I'll try," she said, reluctantly following him through the bushes and out into the open garden.

"Over there, I think," he said, pointing a long finger. "The altar should be near the spot where the bones were found. I was told it was at the far end of the pond. Near the stone bridge."

Misako blinked, looked at the pond and then back to the priest. "I suppose that's a good place for an altar," she managed to say, meekly, fully aware that her grandfather had firmly set the wheel turning again. There was no choice but to flow with the karma that she herself had started as a child.

"Come on, let's walk over and look more closely." Kensho said and walked ahead.

The tea ceremony had come to an end. People scurried about carrying bundles back and forth over the garden path. Several of them looked toward the end of the pond and were amused at the sight of a young woman in a sweater and slacks walking with a very tall priest. The strange pair seemed to be measuring the ground with their steps.

Misako and the priest chose a small piece of land that curved out gracefully at the water's edge. It was past the stone bridge and to the right of the dry waterfall. At first they judged it to be too small an area but then they reconsidered. It would be large enough for a small altar and three people.

She showed the priest where she remembered drawing pictures of the pond when she was a child. Satisfied that this was the correct location for the service, they strolled over to a bamboo bench close by and sat down. Kensho wrote in his notebook and Misako looked at the garden view, noting the changes that the restoration had accomplished.

But how had the priest known she would come here? When he put his pen and book down, she asked. "How could you know I would be here today? I didn't decide myself until I reached the temple."

The thin face broke into a broad smile. "I couldn't be sure it would work, but I tried to draw you here with hard concentration."

"More jokes?" Misako asked without a smile.

"Not at all. It was an experiment. I really do believe you are a true sensitive. I was testing both our skills."

"I'm not sure I like that," she said looking very uncomfortable.

"Ah, I'm sorry. I'm making you nervous again."

Her eyes widened. "Of course I am nervous when things are happening to me that I don't understand. I hate it."

He stretched his long legs out in front of him and leaned back on the bench. She almost expected him to yawn.

"Have you every thought about your special sensitivity as having something to do with energy? "

"Energy? What kind of energy?"

"Natural energy," he said with a shrug. "You must have seen pictures taken by special cameras that capture different colours coming from a musical instrument being played, or surrounding a person dancing."

"I'm sure I have," she answered, still not sure where he was going with this.

"Putting it simply, being a 'sensitive' may mean being a person who has an especially fine-tuned receiver in his or her brain. One who has the ability to capture and process the energy, or micro-magnetic waves, that bypass most people."

"I'm still not sure I understand what you mean," she said, shaking her head.

"For example," the priest went on, "I concentrated before, trying to send a message calling you to this garden. Your super-antenna picked it up. You weren't aware of what made you come here today, but you came."

"I thought it would be a good idea to see the garden again before tomorrow's ceremony," Misako said.

"That's good, but I have to ask when did you actually decide to come?"

"I'm not sure." Misako was frowning and shaking her head.

"Well, I am sure," Kensho said brightly. "It was when I sat on the ground over there out of sight, concentrated and called you. Of course, I wasn't sure it would work, but your antenna picked it up." As he said this, he put his hands up, wiggling a finger on either side of his bald head.

Misako watched him and giggled. "What a funny way to put it. I never thought about anything even remotely connected to such an idea."

"To be honest," he said, folding his arms across his chest, it is not my theory. I read about it and it makes sense, in a way."

"What got you interested in such things?" she asked.

"Living in Kamakura gives me an opportunity to meet people from all over the world and I am exposed to all sorts of ideas. For a priest, that is not always a good thing. There are times when I feel guilty about my fascination with a subject that is not part of Buddhist thinking. And yet it started with my friendship with an American Buddhist priest. We became friends when he stayed at our temple for several months. He had a lot of knowledge about intuitive thought and said it was a popular subject of conversation at his temple back in California. In our talks, I learned about energy and antennas. He taught me how to try to sharpen my own antenna."

Misako looked over the pond in thought. What he called her antenna was not something she wanted to sharpen. "I wish I could snap my antenna off," she said. "Why complicate your life with visions? I take it you are telling me my visions are a result of my sharp antenna."

"That's a very simple explanation but the right idea."

"But why me? Why should I have an antenna when other people don't?"

Kensho shook his head. "I don't know. My American friend said that before humans evolved to where we are today, everyone had that kind of ability. It could have been a way to communicate or survive. But as language and other skills developed, we lost it. Some say all babies are born with a sixth sense."

"Then why didn't I lose it like everyone else?" Misako asked shrugging her shoulders.

"Again, I can't answer your question, but from what your grandfather told me, you had a most unusual babyhood in that gloomy wartime temple. It is possible that you still live with a heritage of childhood loneliness and the mournful sutras being offered for the war dead. Your natural talents could have developed in such unique surroundings. I have heard that people's sensitivity sharpens when they feel vulnerable and sad."

"And you, have you developed an antenna?"

The question made him laugh. "I confess I have tried, but the results haven't been promising."

"Don't bother," she said. "It's not nice to have visions."

"Perhaps," he said with a twinkle in his eye. "But it can be interesting. Some people feel it is power."

Misako was amazed at his answer. She had never thought of a vision as anything but painful. She folded her hands in front of her face as if she was about to pray and spoke very slowly. "How would you go about developing such a thing?"

Kensho looked past Misako. There were only two moving patches of colour near the tea house now. Most everyone had left the garden.

"First," he said, "you must feel your own energy. Secondly, you must learn to clear your mind to make yourself receptive."

"But how?" she asked.

"Well, my friend taught me to start by pressing my hands together, palm to palm, just like I do when I pray. Try that, but instead of praying, concentrate until you begin to feel your life's energy flowing from one hand to the other."

Misako pressed her palms together and closed her eyes.

"When you feel a slight heat in your hands, you will know it has started. The energy will come from your own centre, around your navel. Do you feel it?"

Misako nodded "yes," and kept her eyes closed.

"Good," the priest was clearly enjoying himself. "Next time, try it when you are alone. Concentrate on the energy. Try not to allow other thoughts into your mind."

"That must be very difficult to do," Misako said, unfolding her hands and opening her eyes.

"It comes slowly. When you become really skilful, you will be able to slowly sink into it, but there is no magic involved."

"Suppose it doesn't work for me?"

Kensho stretched and rubbed his bald head. "Oh, well, then you could try another technique. You can sit comfortably and imagine a very dark night. When there is nothing before your closed eyes, try to picture something. Decide exactly what you want to see and then concentrate until you see it, every detail, colour . . . everything."

"You mean if I want to see, say, a bird or a flower, I should close my eyes and think about it until it appears?"

"Well, I suppose that could be a start, yes, but I don't think I have explained it well enough." He was about to tell her more but Misako already had her eyes closed.

"I want to see a rose, a red rose." Her hands were folded in her lap and she was clearly trying to concentrate. She waited until she could see only darkness and then thought of the last roses she had seen that morning in her mother's garden.

Kensho was amused but he didn't want to speak and spoil her fun. He looked at her face, with the thick dark lashes sweeping against her cheeks. The crushing sensation started in his chest again.

"It's not working," she said with her eyes still closed.

The priest laughed. "You have to be patient. Try drawing the rose in your mind with an imaginary brush." He knew he was talking nonsense but he couldn't resist playing the game. He wanted to take another long look at her sweet face while her eyes were closed.

Two uniformed high school girls came down the path. When they passed the bamboo bench, they giggled at the sight of the tall priest with his long legs straight out, almost covering the width of the path. Misako suddenly opened her eyes.

"Well?" he asked, nodding at the students as they passed. "Did you see the rose?"

"I saw three roses but not as I wanted. These roses were in a vase."

"Good," said the priest in jest. "When you go home, you should look for a vase with three red roses and you must let me know if you find them."

"You are more likely to see them first," she laughed. "They are in Grandfather's room in the temple. I clearly saw them in his room. My mother must have brought them for him today."

Kensho frowned. "Did you know she was going to do that?"

"No, not at all. I concentrated on the last roses she had in the garden this morning. When I saw them just now, they were cut in a vase and in Grandfather's room."

"Then I'm sure that is where I will find them, because you are wonderful."

"Wonderful?" she repeated. "I've never been called that before."

"Then the people around you are blind," he said, and stood up to leave. Misako could only blush with pleasure.

They walked down the path toward the gate. The tea house was empty now; only the schoolgirls who had passed them earlier giggled and ran when they approached. Misako thought it was all so strange. No one had ever told her she was wonderful. No one had ever told her it was wonderful to see things.

"Are you sure you want to go through with the service tomorrow?" Kensho asked as they passed through the first large gate. He was walking with his head and shoulders bent down again.

"Should I be afraid?" she asked. There was no hint of anything but trust in her voice. It was a student's voice asking her teacher a question.

He answered thoughtfully. "I think it will all go well but, if you really saw something terrible as a child, it is possible you could see it again. You may not want that kind of experience."

Misako bit her lip. "No, I wouldn't like that but what can I do? When I saw you choosing the spot for the altar, I realized there is no going back. I can't disappoint Grandfather. Anyway, I'm not afraid now that I know you, *Sensei*. Now that I know you will be there with me."

The sensation of being showered with flower petals came over the priest. Her words made him straighten his body to steady himself against this rush of tenderness.

"Thank you for your confidence," he said with a bow. "We will be there just to pray and prayer is speaking with our hearts; that is always positive." Then he bent his head down again and asked, "Can you go through the morning with no breakfast? Just tea?"

Misako laughed. This priest was always saying unexpected things. "I guess so, why?"

"I find it better in such cases," he said casually. "Body energy gets used up digesting food. We will be fresher without it."

"If you say so," Misako said with a note of amusement. They passed through the outer gate where her bicycle was parked. She looked up at him, eyes brimming with admiration.

"Thank you, *Sensei*. I think this has been an enlightening day for me."

Her words made Kensho's knees feel like they were about to collapse under him. His ears glowed. "Then *sayonara* until tomorrow morning."

"I'll be at the temple early," she said, straddling her bike. "*Sayonara.*"

Kensho walked toward the bridge, passing over it quickly with his long stride. He turned in the direction of the temple and Misako caught up to him.

"Don't forget to look for the roses at the temple," she called as she passed.

"I won't forget." His big face had stretched into a great grin.

Playfully, she doubled back and rode a circle around him as he walked. He put his arm out as if to catch the bicycle but Misako skilfully swerved to avoid it. She sped away, still laughing, turning for one last wave before disappearing around the corner of the intersection. He walked faster, hoping for another glimpse of her at the corner. When he got there she was already out of sight.

What a charming creature, he thought as he crossed the street, his long legs kicking out his kimono skirt before him. Full of a delicious, happy feeling, he smiled and slowed to a stroll. Here, in a public street, it seemed all right to enjoy the fading sunshine of this wonderful day. Once he entered the temple, he would be Kensho, the monk, but for just this little while, Kensho, the man, wanted to relish the tender, rare emotion of love for a woman.

EIGHT

*T*he youngest priest, Konein, smoked his first cigarette of the day under a waning moon. Mentally, he ran through the list of the day's chores. It was longer than usual. Teishin and the priest from Kamakura had been up for some time, preparing for a special memorial service that the master had arranged. Since Teishin was busy, Konein would have to hurry back into the temple and make breakfast. The extra activity meant more work for him and, now that he thought about it, he realized he didn't even know the details.

"Oh well," he said and stamped out the tiny bit of butt that was left. "It's not my place to ask." He looked at his watch again and walked through the darkness toward the bell tower.

Misako was awake, lying on her futon, dreading the coming day. She heard the distant temple bell and thought of it as a moan, lamenting the night's departure. The closer the time came for the memorial service in the garden, the more apprehensive she felt. It wasn't clear in her mind why her grandfather was making this unreasonable request, but she had to admire the way he orchestrated his plan. It was as if she was seeing a new side of him. He had even argued down her mother's objections.

Keiko did indeed go to the temple after learning about the memorial service. She went with fire in her eyes and the last of her roses in her hand. Before she finished the first cup of tea, she let her father know what was on her mind. "What is this I hear about a memorial service you are making Misako attend tomorrow?"

The old man managed to appear casual, not letting on that he had been dreading this inevitable moment of confrontation. "You know about that, do you? Did Misako tell you?"

"No. I overheard her talking to her husband on the telephone. She was explaining why she wasn't returning to Tokyo tomorrow. It seems you had other plans for her, plans you didn't tell me about. Who is this service for?"

The old man shrugged his shoulders. "It is all part of being a priest. The service is for unknown remains and I wanted Misako to attend."

Keiko looked at her father through narrowed eyes. "What unknown remains?" She knew the old fox was not telling her the entire story.

"We priests are here to serve, not to gossip. If some human remains were found in your garden, you wouldn't like it known all over town. Think of all the curious people."

"What are you talking about? Was there a murder?"

"You see!" the old man said, raising his voice and pointing his finger at her. "That is exactly why this is not to be a public matter. Even my own daughter jumps to nonsense conclusions."

"Are you talking about the bones found at Shimizuen last year?" Keiko asked. "The box of ashes you keep in your room?"

"Oh, you know all about that too, do you?"

"Of course, I know about this unnatural obsession of yours."

"Who said it is unnatural? It is my way of showing respect for unknown human remains found in a historical place. The bones have been cremated and now a small memorial service is in order." The old priest's unruly eyebrows moved closer together in a scowl as he bent his body forward and wagged his finger at his grown daughter. "You are blowing this whole thing out of proportion. That is the most unfortunate trait of the human animal, especially the female of the species. Always wanting to exaggerate."

"Why wasn't the service held when the bones were cremated?" she asked without a beat of hesitation.

"It was," he said with a sigh, "but the skeleton wasn't complete. There are still bones from that body in the pond." Oh, how this daughter of his reminded him of her mother! Her nagging was becoming tiresome.

Keiko took a minute to think and sip her tea. She wasn't satisfied with her father's answer, she wasn't going to let him off so easily, not when it involved her own daughter. Misako had enough problems to deal with in Tokyo.

"Tell me, Father. Is this the real reason you wanted Misako to visit?"

The old man looked at his only living child with his little frozen smile. Clearing his throat, he looked down at his folded hands and began his sanitized explanation, but not without a pang of guilt. Keiko noticed that he was suddenly so interested in his own hands that he wasn't looking at her.

"The professor from Niigata University said the remains are of a young person and I thought it would be appropriate to have a young person attend the service."

It was a weak answer and Keiko raised her eyebrows. "There are many young people here in Shibata. What about Konein-*san*? He's younger than Misako is, and a priest as well. Wouldn't it be more appropriate for him to attend?"

"The remains are of a young female, I felt it was appropriate to have Misako attend."

Keiko's voice was heavy with suspicion. "Did you have this in mind when you had me ask Misako to come from Tokyo?"

The old man was in a corner and he knew it. He hadn't felt so irritated in years, not since his wife was alive and they had differences about domestic matters. It had gotten to the point where he was going to have to raise his voice and assert his rank.

"Why? Why do you ask so many questions? Am I not to be allowed to go about temple business in my old age without explaining every detail to my daughter? Perhaps Konein-*san* is needed elsewhere. Perhaps I simply want to share this experience with my grandchild before I die. Why do I have to answer your unreasonable questions? Why?"

It was the first time in years that Keiko had heard her father speak in a harsh tone. There was no use upsetting him more. She bowed and apologized. He waved his hand in the air as if her apology was an annoying cobweb to be brushed away. The little smile returned to his lips. It was clear that their conversation had ended. Keiko left the temple without the satisfaction of knowing exactly what was going on.

That evening Keiko brought the subject up again at the dinner table. Dr. Ichimura couldn't really grasp what all the fuss was about and simply said "That's interesting." Then Misako casually informed her mother that she was planning to wear her mourning kimono to the memorial service for the unknown remains.

"What?" Keiko said, almost choking on her tea. "You mean you brought it with you?"

"Well, yes, but not for that reason. I didn't know I would be attending a memorial service. I'm not sure why I packed it. I must have been worried about Grandfather." Misako sounded confused. Keiko and her husband exchanged a surprised glance.

"*Maa!* How awful," Keiko said. "I sometimes think you and your grandfather are both a little mad."

A little mad indeed, Misako thought as she laid out her kimono undergarments that morning. How quickly things change. Two days ago she was trying to forget a terrible vision. She had never heard of the priest from Kamakura or any of his theories about energy and human antenna. Now she was up before daylight, going without breakfast, following his instructions to prepare for a possible encounter with a ghost from her childhood. Maybe more than a little mad.

At that same moment, two dark figures made their way along Shibata's empty streets. Teishin struggled under a bundle tied to his back. The tall priest carried a large box. They were on their way to set up the altar for the memorial service. The Shimizuen caretaker waited for them at the gate with a flashlight and several great yawns. He was wearing his sleeping kimono, with a padded jacket over it for warmth. The dark sky was just beginning to grow pale with shades of yellow and pink.

"Weird," he grumbled as he saw the priests cross the little bridge. He was put out by this inconvenience and thought the whole idea strange, but he had no thought of puzzling out why it was happening. The director, Mr. Saito, had told him that the priests would be holding some sort of ceremony near the pond. The caretaker only wished it didn't have to be held so early.

Keiko came into Misako's bedroom to help her dress. The kimono had to be pulled up perfectly at the hemline and folded exactly right at the neck to allow a touch of the white undercollar to show. Misako had arranged her hair in a simple, classic style. Keiko finished tying the *obi* sash and stood back to admire her daughter. No matter what the occasion, Keiko always felt proud seeing how beautifully Misako wore kimono, yet she was frowning.

"*Maa!* What a lot of trouble to go through. It isn't necessary or even appropriate to wear kimono. You should just be wearing a dark sweater and skirt. Better still, you should be home in an apron making breakfast for your husband and a couple of babies."

Misako looked over her shoulder at the tied *obi* in the mirror and smiled wistfully. "*Hai*, I would like to be in a sweet home with a couple of babies, but it doesn't look as if that is likely to happen, does it?"

Her mother sighed. "I'll fetch my black *haori* jacket for you. It is really chilly this morning."

❁ ❁ ❁

"Perfect timing," the old master said as Misako drove up to the temple gate. He came down the stairs holding onto Teishin's arm. The tall priest followed carrying the white, silk-wrapped box close to his chest with both hands. Konein ran ahead and opened the car doors, bowing them on their way.

At exactly five minutes past six o'clock, the sedan turned into the Shimizuen parking area. The caretaker, now dressed, waited with his wife. They hurried to assist the old priest out of the car. All five of them stood for a moment bowing their greetings. Misako removed her *haori* coat and started to fold it to leave it in the car.

"I'll take it to the tea house," the caretaker's wife offered. "It may still be cold when you are finished the ceremony. I'll have tea waiting for you there."

The priest removed his *haori* coat as well and gave it to the woman. Everyone bowed again and the master instructed the caretaker. "We are here to hold a service and want complete privacy. Please, do not let anyone disturb us."

When the large gate was closed behind them Misako felt a sealing off of the space. For more than a minute she and the two priests stood silently, composing themselves. It was as if they had stepped onto a tiny island in the middle of a vast sea. Finally, the old man issued his orders in a hoarse whisper. Misako's heart began to race.

"We walk in single file," he said. "I will go first, then Misako, and lastly, you, Kensho-*san*. Misako, you carry the remains." He stepped forward on the gravel. Misako came and stood behind him, accepting the box from the priest with a bow. As she took the box of remains, a sudden chill went through her and she shivered.

Her grandfather saw it and made a clucking sound of disapproval. "Misako! You should be wearing warm underwear under your kimono. Young people don't know how to take care of themselves these days," he complained.

"I'm not cold," she said in a low, embarrassed voice, stealing a glance at Kensho. "I just never held this kind of box before."

"There is nothing to fear," the tall priest said softly. "I'm here with you." Misako moved her head slightly to let him know she understood.

Signalling them with a look and clasping his frail hands through his prayer beads, the old priest started out, walking slowly. Misako and Kensho followed.

Misako became aware of the coolness of the silk on her hands. The contents of the box didn't seem to be well distributed. By the feel, she judged the bits of bone and ashes to be pushed to one side. Gently she tried to move the box to spread the contents more evenly. While doing this, she asked herself why it mattered. Why should I care about these ashes? The answer came in the warm glow that was replacing the first unpleasant, cold sensation. This new feeling was sweet. The kind of affection she might have felt for a younger sister.

The procession paused at the second gate. The garden that spread before them was deathly still. The placidity injected a new tension. The security of sound was gone. No birds flew over their heads, no insects chirped, no fish could be seen moving in the pond. Not a leaf fluttered on an autumn tree. It was like walking into a still-life painting.

With the main house behind them, they followed the path to the back of the garden. The old priest moved slowly past the tea house, past the bamboo bench. The purple brocade that hung from his shoulder made a stunning contrast against the orange, gold and green hues of the garden.

Teishin and Kensho had done their job well. The space was covered with woven straw mats and the altar was a low table covered with white silk. A statue of Buddha shared the altar with two candles in lotus-shaped holders, a few simple flowers and a dish of sweet cakes. A small gong rested on a purple pillow, a wooden mallet by its side. On the other side of the mat, a black and gold lacquered tray held a bronze incense burner.

No one had to instruct Misako; she knew the rituals well. The priests stood at the edge of the mats as she slipped out of her *zori*. Like an actor moving in a Noh play, she slid her white *tabi*-clad feet across the mat, knelt and carefully placed the box on the altar. Bowing deeply, she moved backwards on her knees, making room for the priests to take their places kneeling in front of her.

Kensho helped the old master down. He lit the candles and then, with the candle flame, lit the three incense sticks. One of the incense sticks flared. Kensho put it out by rubbing it between his fingers and then lifted each stick in a gesture of honour, one at a time, before placing them in the censer. He glanced over his shoulder and saw Misako's head bowed over her folded hands. He lightly touched the Master's arm to indicate that everything was ready.

The old man took a deep breath and struck the gong hard with the wooden mallet. The sound flew up to shatter the silence. A startled crow cawed and flew from the top of one pine to another. The priests started the chant. "*Ki myo mu ryo ju nyo rai. Na mo fu ka shi gi ko. Hozobosatsu in ni ji.*" *Crash!* The mallet smashed down again. The voices droned on in what seemed to be one monotone note. Each priest took his breath in a different place, allowing no break in the chain of chant. Incense smoke wavered up and hung in a level haze. Misako gave herself to the hypnotic rhythm, remembering Kensho's words, feeling the warmth in the flow between the palms of her hands. She desired to be a priest with them, to pray and think only for this lonely soul. These remains were connected with the vision she had seen here, years ago. She tried to picture herself as a child, sitting here drawing a picture of the pond.

"We are praying for you," she silently mouthed into her folded hands. "We care. Our prayers are our gifts to you, and our minds and hearts join in honouring you. You are not alone."

In her own untrained way, Misako was sending out all the spiritual force she could muster. She wanted the prayers to fly in celebration of the life that once existed here. Surely the girl must have had a home nearby, a family. They couldn't have known what happened to her. How they must have suffered when she disappeared. Now all that was left were ashes and some bones lost in the pond's mud.

Deep in these thoughts, Misako felt the glow of energy moving up her arms, past her shoulders, up, up to gush and flow down again from the top of her head. It poured over her body like liquid light until the glow started to rise, taking her with it. She seemed to be floating in the cloud of incense, no longer looking at the backs of the priests. She was looking down at the scene from above, hovering like a bird. She could see the top of the altar, the top the priest's bald heads with amazing clarity. She saw an overview of her own head, the tortoise comb she had placed in her hair that morning. She heard the chants.

There was someone on the bridge, a girl kneeling beside a pile of stones. The figure was bent over, placing one stone at a time onto a square of dark material. Everything was happening slowly. Still bent over, the girl wrapped the material around the rocks, squatted, strained and pulled the bundle up on her back. She tied the two ends of material across her shoulders, paused and rolled forward into the water.

A very large splash of water flew into the air. Misako saw the water rippling out into large, dark circles. Little waves lapped up on the rocky shore where their altar stood. There was another large splash, or was it the mallet crashing against the gong again? The chanting stopped. It was the place in the service to rest.

"*Namu Amida Butsu.*" The old priest repeated the holy invocation, rubbing the palms of his hands together. "*Namu Amida Butsu,*" he said again, placing his hands down on the mat and bowed deeply to the altar. "*Namu Amida Butsu,*" he prayed as he bowed lightly to the tall priest beside him.

"*Namu Amida Butsu,*" Kensho repeated, bowing first to the old priest and then turning to bow to Misako, but a sharp discord was struck in the choreography. His bow was not returned; she wasn't reacting to him but staring ahead like a blind person. A tingle of fear went through his heart. He saw that she was in a trance. Every muscle in his body tightened.

Unaware that anything was wrong, the old priest started his chant again. "*Is shin cho rai.*" He hit the gong. Kensho saw that Misako didn't blink, didn't move. He looked closely at her, searching her face for a hint of what was happening. It was her dear, little face but it was different. The heavy eyebrows were the same but the eyes under them looked red-rimmed and distant. Her whole body started to tremble.

The sutra chant kept flowing in and out of Misako's consciousness, building in passion and pace, like the singing at a bunraku play. Her body was down there but she had nothing to do with the life in that body. There seemed to be a dark form moving it, a puppeteer working his hands within her, making her tremble.

The old man realized he was chanting alone. Slowing down, he turned his head, his eyes questioning. Kensho kept his eyes on Misako as he touched the old master on the shoulder.

"Keep chanting! No matter what happens, keep chanting," he said in a firm whisper. His eyes never left Misako's face.

Confused and reluctant, the old priest obeyed. He continued the chant, pronouncing each sound slowly in a quivering voice. He did not turn back to the altar but stared at Misako. As he watched and chanted, he was astonished to see his granddaughter's face working into various expressions of terror. He couldn't believe he was seeing this dear face so distorted, her tongue flopping in and out of her mouth. The old man's growing panic entered his chant, making his voice race faster and faster. His own face fell into the wrinkled mass of a crying baby. Over his quivering words, he heard Kensho calling Misako's name. He couldn't imagine what was happening.

"No, this is wrong! What is happening?" he shouted. When Misako's body started to shake as in a convulsion, he put his hand out to her. A terrible moan came from her throat.

"Misako-*san*, Misako-*san*, Misako-*san*," Kensho cooed tenderly as he softly tapped her cheek with one hand. His other hand was on the old priest's shoulder, trying to keep him calm and at a distance.

Misako pushed his hand away and moaned. A stream of saliva fell from her lips. Tears gushed from her eyes and her hands pulled strands down from the sides of her upswept hair. She screamed and the old man felt his heart bursting in his chest.

"What's happening?" he shouted. His face turned purple. He grabbed at her, shouting her name.

Misako screamed again and her body went limp. The puppet was thrown to the ground. The old man, still kneeling, pushed Kensho aside, lunged forward and fell on top of her. Misako's hovering view of the scene went black. She had fallen into a faint.

The caretaker was having breakfast with his wife when he cocked his head as if to listen to something. "What's that noise? Did you hear someone scream?"

His wife, about to eat a pickled plum, stopped to listen, her chopsticks an inch away from her mouth. "I didn't hear anything. What did it sound like?"

"I'm not sure," he said, holding his hand up for attention. "A scream, maybe a shout."

"There is no one in the garden but the priests and that young woman. Funny business if you ask me," she said before popping the sour plum into her mouth.

"There! I heard something again." The caretaker put down his rice bowl.

"Sometimes you can't tell if noise comes from the garden or the street beyond the bridge. Some children out early maybe," the woman said. "Anyway, if they want something, I already placed their coats and the refreshments in the tea house."

The caretaker poured hot tea over the last grains of rice in his bowl and drank it down. "I hope they don't take too long, those priests. I don't want to spend all day waiting for them to finish. Such bother on our day off. So early this morning. Such bother!"

"They may be here for hours," his wife said. "They brought so many things to set up that altar. I've never seen such a thing outdoors. Who is it for? Funny business, I say."

"That's for sure," the caretaker sneered and took the last cigarette from a crumpled pack of Golden Bat tobacco. "Well, maybe all the praying will bring good luck. Not that the garden needs it, so many people visiting these days. Next weekend the neighbourhood will be complaining again about the tour buses jamming the street." These thoughts still occupied his mind as he made his way outside and started to rake the fallen leaves.

The morning sun was shining, promising a beautiful day. A movement past the inner gate to the big garden caught the caretaker's attention. Removing the cigarette from his lips, he turned his near-sighted eyes and strained in that direction. There was a large, dark object moving quickly toward him. It looked like a great black crow flying low to the ground. Putting down the rake, he moved cautiously with bent knees, squinting to see more clearly. The thing came faster and closer. The blur began to clear. The caretaker could make out the tall priest running with his black robes flapping about his long legs and waving arms. He couldn't make out what the priest was shouting, but he realized that something was terribly wrong.

The neighbourhood doctor's office was over the bridge and up the street. As soon as the caretaker heard the news of the old master's collapse, he ran to fetch help. His wife heard loud talking and came out of the gate-house to see her husband dashing across the bridge.

"What happened? What's wrong?" she called to Kensho, who was leaning against a tree trying to catch his breath.

"It's Jushoku-*sama*. He's passed out. It looks serious. I carried him to the teahouse. Please bring blankets. Hurry!" As soon as he got these words out, he turned and dashed back. The caretaker's wife was slow to comprehend what he had said. Twisting her hands in distress, she cried out "How terrible!" before turning back to the house. She stumbled twice before reaching the door. By the time she managed to gather the blankets and return to the path, the doctor and her husband came running back and passed her. Fumbling with the blankets and mumbling *"taihen"* to herself, she tried to hurry, her wooden clogs banging against the stones set in the path.

They found the old man's body stretched out on the tea house's immaculate *tatami* floor. His head rested on a pillow made from Misako's rolled up silk *haori* kimono coat. Kensho's finger-length *haori* was spread over the body like a blanket. The garment covered the small priest from chin to toe. The empty kimono sleeves of the coat spread out on the floor like large, black wings. The master looked pale and serene, like an ancient seraph about to take flight to some wonderful secret land.

The doctor knelt by the body to examine him. Misako bent her head to her lap and cried softly. The doctor shook his head and took out a clean, white handkerchief to place over the old face. Kensho knelt beside her.

"It looks like a stroke killed him," the doctor said. "I can't be sure, but it looks like a stroke. How did it happen?"

Misako lifted her head to answer but the priest spoke first. "We were having a memorial service in the garden. About halfway through the prayers, Jushoku-*sama*'s face turned purple and he fell over."

"Was he unwell this morning?" the doctor asked.

"No. He seemed very well," the priest said, adding, "Let me introduce myself. I am the priest Kensho visiting from my temple in Kamakura. This is Jushoku-*sama*'s granddaughter, Mrs. Imai, visiting from Tokyo."

Misako bowed and mumbled her name, wiping the tears from her cheeks.

"Ah yes, I know your parents very well. I think I remember you before you married. The years go quickly. Let me see, how old was your grandfather?"

Although Misako knew her grandfather was dead, the past tense "was" struck her with sharp pain. "Eighty-three," she said in a whisper.

"A great loss, great loss," the doctor said, looking down at the body. "Respected in the community."

"Thank you very much," Misako said, bowing her head into her handkerchief.

"This must be a terrible shock for you, Mrs. Imai. You look very pale. We must think of getting you to your parents' home."

"I'll be fine," she told the doctor. "I am sorry to cause you concern."

The caretaker knelt behind the doctor, looking very grave. His wife stood by the door, still holding the blankets. Her mouth had fallen wide open, giving her the expression of a fish. The shock of death, the scene and Misako's appearance was more than she could absorb. She stared at Misako, who looked like she had just come from a battlefield. Not only was her hair in disorder but her face was stained with tears, her eyes were swollen and the collar of her kimono was pulled loose. She didn't look like the same young woman who had entered the garden.

In the back of the caretaker's wife's mind, a seed of pleasure was germinating. It would stay tiny and unnoticed for the next few hours but would burst open later, when people came to hear the story of what happened in the garden. All of Shibata would be having this story with their three o'clock tea. They would shake their heads and cluck their tongues. The caretaker and his wife would suddenly become popular, as everyone would want to hear firsthand what had happened. There would be gifts of sweet cakes and sake at their door before this day was over. The caretaker's wife closed her mouth, put down the blankets and went to kneel beside Misako. She bowed, and in a timid voice offered to help the distraught young woman back to the gatehouse. She would give her hot soup. Misako never even heard the offer.

NINE

*T*eishin was happily chopping vegetables for lunch when the kitchen phone rang. The excited voice of Shimizuen's caretaker told him that his master had collapsed during the service in the garden and was now lying dead in the tea house. The bewildered priest kept saying "What, what?" into the phone. He couldn't believe what his ears heard. His master was dead! Teishin slid to the floor and sat there with his arms limp and his legs splayed out before him. He remained there, staring at nothing for several minutes, and then burst into tears and bawled like a baby.

Soon after receiving the call informing her of her father's death, Keiko and her husband rushed to Shimizuen's garden. Dr. Ichimura immediately took Misako back to the house and put her to bed with a strong sedative. Keiko waited with the priest to accompany the body to the temple. When that unhappy task was over, Keiko ordered the exhausted and shaken Kensho to his room for a rest. He went meekly.

Technically, Teishin was in charge now, but he was in no condition to take on even the most fundamental arrangements. Dry-eyed and business-like, Keiko moved about the temple with great familiarity. This was the home where she had been born and raised. She knew every inch of the building, where things were kept and what her father's wishes were. In a way, it was like the war years when she and her mother worked constantly, running the temple while the priests attended to the endless ceremonies for the fallen.

Konein rang the temple bell announcing the death, one firm hit after another, with little pause. All over Shibata, people stopped what they were doing and wondered who had died. It was almost noon.

By afternoon tea time, the outside wall had been draped in black-and-white striped material and large wreaths of artificial flowers stood on tripods lining the path to the temple's main entrance. A paper sign, inscribed with the characters *mo chu*, announcing "in mourning," had been pasted on the entrance gate.

Women from the congregation moved about the temple, cleaning everything and speaking in hushed tones. Condolence offerings of tea, incense, sweets, fruit and flowers were beginning to arrive.

As Keiko washed her father's body, surprised at how small and delicate he was. She and the funeral director took great care wrapping the old man in his death kimono and laying him down on a freshly covered futon. Later, they would place his body in a coffin. The futon was turned around from its usual sleeping position as corpses are laid out with their heads to the north. This is what old people call the direction of the rat.

Lovingly, she tied a small, age-yellowed sack on a string around his neck. The sack contained the old man's withered umbilical cord, childhood hair, nail clippings and whatever else his own mother had carefully saved in the ancient custom. Along with this, Keiko tucked snapshots of his dead wife and sons into the folds of his kimono. All of this she did with few tears and great love. Her own lips took on the little smile her father had always worn.

During these intense hours, Keiko relived moments of her childhood. She remembered when she had been ill as a child. She couldn't have been more than six years old but she still vividly recalled her father sitting by her futon, wiping her feverish head with a cool cloth. He was young then; his unruly eyebrows were black, the whites of his eyes bright and clear. Keiko had put her small hand out to him in thanks. He had taken it in his own and said: "One day you will have to do the same for me, Keiko-*chan*. Someday I will be weak and you will be strong. I know you will help your mother and me when we are old."

"Oh yes, I will, Father, I will," the little girl promised, her eyes wide and shining with sincerity. She had fallen asleep that night feeling taller and more important than ever before in her young life.

Keiko touched the waxen face and finally allowed her tears to flow. "I will, Father," she whispered, "Oh, I will."

Instead of resting as Keiko had commanded, the priest from Kamakura made his way back to Shimizuen garden and had the caretaker assist him in dismantling the outdoor altar. Together they managed to transport everything back, entering the temple through the back gate.

Then there was the matter of the box of ashes which was now in the home of the caretaker. Kensho went back to fetch the box and covered it in a square of dark cloth to avoid attracting attention on the street.

The back altar room was in reality a tomb, the air heavy with soul dust. The low ceiling was panelled with faded paintings of Buddha and

Buddhist saints. Age-worn birds and flowers decorated the sliding wooden doors. Along two of the walls, shelves held a dusty variety of damaged religious statues and receptacles of various shapes and sizes containing human ashes and other traces of lives long gone. Yellowed photographs of soldiers and sailors covered a large section of one wall, the faces of the parish war dead.

The priest entered the small room and knelt, placing the box on the browned, worn *tatami*. He took a piece of tissue paper from his sleeve and cleaned a spot on the lowest shelf. Carefully, he placed the box of ashes there. It stood out against the gloom of the forgotten. The white silk was too new, too white and too fresh for the surroundings. Still, he was satisfied that this out-of-the-way room was the most inconspicuous place in the temple to keep the unknown ashes.

Keiko knelt to the right of the coffin during the prayers. If anyone had told her that the near aversion she had felt toward the tall priest would melt into something bordering on admiration in just one day, she wouldn't have believed it. Poor Teishin was an emotional wreck, blubbering continuously as the ceremonial plans were being made. It was the outsider from Kamakura who calmly took charge, making sure that the two other priests were able to carry on. Worried about Teishin's state of mind, Keiko was relieved to see how Kensho stayed close to him, discreetly helping him through the evening. Considering the crowds and confusion, the first night's wake was going well.

Mourners moved in and out of the temple, some staying most of the night. At one point, the main altar room was so filled with rows of people sitting on the *tatami* floor that some had to move out into the corridor. Flowers kept arriving and people had to squeeze closer together to make room for yet another fragrant arrangement. Prayers were chanted and incense burned. White handkerchiefs dabbed at eyes and heads shook in shocked disbelief.

A battalion of women wearing aprons moved in and out of the kitchen carrying trays of hot tea and sweet cakes. Others washed dishes and chattered in their Niigata country sing-song tones. Delivery people came to the kitchen door and left more boxes of food and more flowers. There was so much noise and activity in the temple that the rats didn't dare leave their nests all night.

Like a faithful pet, Teishin fell asleep at the foot of his master's coffin in the very early hours of the new day. He didn't mean to sleep there, just to sit a little while by the closed pine box after the other people had gone. Everything had been a haze of confusion ever since the terrible news had reached him that morning. He still moaned with the pain. How could this have happened so suddenly? How could he possibly manage? He wanted to be the one who had died.

The main altar room was warm and redolent with flowers and incense. Teishin sat stroking the coffin as dark thoughts whirled in his head. Like the air in the room, his thoughts were oppressive. Dead! The master was really dead. In despair, he put his head down on the coffin and cried until he fell asleep.

The sedative that Dr. Ichimura gave Misako imprisoned her until almost four o'clock in the morning. She was disoriented when she awoke. She wasn't sure where she was. There seemed to be a big, dark person standing looking down on her. As her eyes adjusted to the room, she realized that the dark figure was her own black kimono. It was on a hanger, hung high on a wall hook. The mourning kimono! "Grandfather!" she called out. The only answer was the steady ticking of the clock in the next room. She sat up in bed and watched the grey shadows settle into familiar objects. Her head pounded as she went to her parents' room. The sliding door was slightly open and she could see that her mother's bed was not laid out. Dr. Ichimura was sleeping on his futon. Misako could tell that it was hastily put down and had not been prepared by her mother. His shirt and jacket were folded in a corner of the room; his socks were left on the floor next to his futon. Her mother must still be at the temple. Misako went back to her room to dress, crying because she knew she had missed the first night of her grandfather's wake. It was obvious that her stepfather had come home only a short time ago.

In fifteen minutes she was washed, and dressed in warm slacks and a sweater. On the way out of the house, she remembered the icy temple floors and went back for an extra pair of socks. Grabbing her mother's jacket from the hook near the kitchen door, she stepped out into the early morning fog. Her bicycle was the only movement on the street until the yellow fog lights of Keiko's car came toward her. Her mother put her head out the car window.

"Misako, you should be in bed. You are suffering from shock. Papa said so. Come home with me now."

"Why did you let me sleep so long?" Misako sounded angry.

"Everyone is gone now. People understood about you not being there. You had a terrible experience."

"Were there many people?" Misako asked, knowing the answer but wanting to hear it for her own comfort.

"Crowded! We will go to the temple together later. Everything is under control. The congregation has been wonderful. Come home and I'll tell you everything."

"No, I can't." Misako put her foot down on the pedal as a sign of determination. "At least I can spend time with Grandfather before the others come back."

"Wait," Keiko pleaded. "I talked to Hideo's mother last evening. Hideo wasn't home but she said they will be here for the funeral on Thursday. I told her you will call today."

"Thank you. I'll see you later." The bicycle jerked and shot down the street. Keiko sighed and drove home slowly through the fog.

The young priest, Konein, was so exhausted that he didn't wake up on time to ring the morning bell. Kensho was aware of it and quietly went out to the courtyard to do the job. He had not slept himself, but he felt a surge of unnatural energy, as if he could go out and run fast. It was on the way to the courtyard that he passed the altar room and found Teishin sleeping with his head on the master's coffin. Teishin looked so innocent, curled up like a child, his plump hand under his round, pink cheek. Kensho watched for a moment, thinking that it wouldn't be easy for this good-natured fellow to take the place of the shrewd old man. Sighing, he gently tapped the sleeper on his shoulder. Teishin looked up with the glazed expression of the blind.

"Come on, Teishin-*san*, I'll help you to your room. You mustn't sleep here. Go to your own bed for some proper rest."

Teishin blinked and stumbled to his feet, holding onto the big man's arm. "Thank you," he said and let himself be led to his room.

The early fog settled around the tall priest like a falling curtain of gauze. He climbed the ladder to the tower and confronted the demanding bell. When he bowed his head to pray, the words tumbled from his lips automatically. His mind gave the words no meaning. His thoughts were still trapped in yesterday's cage. The bursting energy made him feel sick. He felt sick for the old master's sudden death, sick for Misako's suffering and sick with his own guilt. If only he hadn't encouraged Misako to take part in that ceremony. If only! Why didn't he realize the danger? How could he be so stupid? He remembered the unspeakable moments when Misako regained consciousness and found her grandfather dead on the mat next to her. Horrible! Horrible! If only!

Even though the air was cold, the priest's skin was burning. Pulling at the neck of his kimono, he freed his arms and let the layers of garments hang from the sash at his waist. Bare-armed and bare-chested, he stood before the bell with clenched fists. His ribs showed through his skin and his face fell into the grimace of an enraged samurai about to strike with his sword. With an angry roar, he grabbed the rope and let the log swing against the bell, sending it forward with all his might. The sound crashed back as if in defiance. "If only!" he shouted into the darkness. "If only!" Pulling the log back, he let it go, again and again, not waiting the prescribed second and a half to pass between the rings. Each time he did this, a little more of his energy seeped away. The bell responded to the beating with short, loud cries. It wasn't until the sixth ring that his frustration began to ebb enough for the ring to return to the usual mellow song.

Still breathing hard and dripping sweat, he climbed down the ladder and fell to his knees. He pounded the earth with his fists, again and again, crying, "If only! If only!" Something white moved, making him swing around as if to spring at it and cut it down with an imaginary sword. The something was a pair of white socks, Misako's socks. She was standing several yards away holding onto the handlebars of her bicycle, trying to peer through the greyness of the morning.

"Kensho-*sensei*," she called softly, as if not trusting her eyes. "Is that you?"

"Misako-*san*," he answered in a startled voice, quickly jumping up while pulling the layers of kimono back over his bare arms and shoulders. "Are you all right?" he asked trying to hide his embarrassment.

"Yes, but what are you doing? You will catch a cold! It is cold and damp out here." He came close, looked down at her and managed a very painful grin. "Oh, I was doing some exercises after ringing the bell. I didn't expect anyone to see me."

"The bell didn't sound right. You rang it too quickly."

"I know, I'm sorry. I guess nothing is normal, but how are you feeling?" he asked.

"Papa made me miss the first night of grandfather's wake. I was upset when I woke up." Saying this, she turned and wheeled the bicycle toward the kitchen door. The priest walked beside her.

"I'm glad he made you sleep. I've been so worried about you."

She made no comment until she stood before the high step leading up to the kitchen. When she spoke, it was with her head down, as if talking to the ground. "It was like a nightmare, wasn't it? I keep hoping to wake up and find it didn't really happen."

"*Hai*, I understand. If only I hadn't encouraged you to be part of that ceremony. I should have known better." His voice was shaky and filled with regret. "I'm so sorry."

Misako removed her shoes and stepped up. Standing on the foot-high step, facing the tall priest, it was now possible for her to look straight into his pale eyes.

"It was because of my childhood vision that grandfather wanted that ceremony. If it wasn't for me, none of this would have happened." Tears rolled down her face as she spoke. "Now what do you think of this thing you call a gift? All it ever did was cause trouble for me, and now this."

The priest hung his head. "You are not responsible, Misako-*san*. I am the one who is to blame. I should have realized the danger. I should have known better."

Misako saw the pain in his face. "Nothing will bring Grandfather back," she whispered, and began to sob. Her head fell forward and rested on his right shoulder. He stood like a petrified tree, until he slowly moved his arms and held her, tears gushing from his own tightly closed eyes. He couldn't speak for the eternity of a moment. Then she moved away. Kensho stood stunned.

"I am going in now. I am going in to be with my grandfather," she said softly.

He managed a whispered "*Hai*." She turned and walked through the bright kitchen into the gloom of the dark temple. Kensho stayed immobile at the kitchen entrance. When the strength came back to his legs, he stepped up and stood in the kitchen, not knowing what to do. He rubbed his hands together and turned around in a complete circle as if in a state of confusion. The big aluminum kettle reflected the bare light bulb. It blinked at him and brought him back to reality.

"*So da!* I'll make tea," he told the old round wall clock. "That's what I'll do. Misako-*san* is cold and needs a cup of hot tea."

While squatting over the Japanese toilet, built flush to the floor, Mother Imai gave way to a fit of hysteria. It was the sharp stab of pain in her arthritic knee that triggered the outburst of screaming and the pounding of her fists against the wooden door. As usual, she had risen early, wrapped herself in a flowery robe, wanting to take care of the urgent demand of her bladder. Almost more urgent this morning was the need to talk to her son and the desire to know if he had returned home last night. Without calling his name, she slid open the door of his bedroom as quietly as possible. Even in the semi-light, she could see that the room was empty.

"No!" she moaned, leaning her head against the wooden door frame. A wavy lock of hair fell down over her eye. How was she going to let him know Misako's mother called last night with the news of her father's death? Misako was sure to call this morning.

"Poor Misako was with Grandfather at the time of his fatal stroke," Keiko told her on the phone last evening. "I'm afraid she is suffering from shock. My husband gave her a strong sedative and we hope she will sleep until the morning. I know she will want to talk to Hideo as soon as she is able."

Mother Imai's voice came out even higher than usual. "How terrible! I am sorry to hear such news. Hideo will be upset when he hears of it. He's working late tonight. Very important customers in town," she lied. "Certainly he will call Misako in the morning. No need to wake the poor girl when he comes in tonight. I know it will be late. Surely I understand that Misako needs rest after such a shock."

Mother Imai went on and on, sending her condolences and talking about what a fine man the old priest was. Not knowing what else to say, she ended with a promise that of course Hideo and she would attend the funeral. "It is unbelievable that it could have happened so suddenly. Who could have imagined it when Misako left here for Niigata a few days ago?"

The conversation whirled in her head as she crouched in the water closet. The squatting sent piercing pains through her knee. She screamed and banged on the door of the cubicle because her knee pained and because she didn't know if she could reach Hideo before another call came from Niigata. The frustration and humiliation hurt more than her knee.

The worst of the hysteria lasted only a minute but she was still crying as she washed her hands at the small sink outside the toilet door. Her heavy, uninhibited sobs rang through the empty house. The three delicate sprigs of white freesia on the shelf over the sink quivered in their vase. Their movement and the tears made the mirror's reflection dreamlike and unreal.

Seeking comfort, she went into the dining room and snapped on the television set. It was too early for any programs. Coloured patterns and beeping sounds were all the machine could produce at such an early hour. New waves of frustration sent her rushing into the *tatami* living room to open the black lacquered doors of the death box, where Papa's familiar face looked out from the small altar. Kneeling down, she studied the photograph of her deceased husband. His eyes seemed to look over at the other side of the room, over her head. She lit an incense stick and rang the altar's little bell. Dabbing her eyes with a tissue, Mother Imai started to pour out her troubles to the picture of her dead husband.

"Papa, Papa, I am ashamed to say our Hideo is not a good son, not a good son at all. He is no comfort to his mother. I have pleaded with him for almost a year to install a Western toilet so I don't have to crouch down with this bad knee. His mother's pain is of no importance to him. Now this embarrassing situation he has put me in with Misako and her Niigata family. How can I face them? Her grandfather died and I have no way to contact Hideo with the news until the office is open this morning. Misako might call before that. Where does he go all the nights he stays away? I don't believe it is business. Not anymore. He could be in some slut's bed and I think Misako suspects it too. I see big trouble ahead if this continues. Big trouble, Papa. Our family is surely going to lose face."

She spoke quickly, half crying, half talking. The sound of her voice filled the room. No comfort came from the photograph. She stopped talking and just rubbed her hands together as if in prayer, thinking, what shall I do, what shall I do? The dreaded ring of the telephone sounded like an alarm bell. Mother Imai cringed and crept closer to the death box. "If that's Misako, what will I say?"

The phone was ringing, again and again. She put her face close up to the photograph. Her husband's face looked bored, indifferent to her plight. "Misako knows I would be home at this time of the morning. How could I not be home?"

The phone was not going to give up. She wiped her eyes with her hand and pushed back the curl on her forehead. Hoping with every step that the telephone would stop before she reached it, Mrs. Imai forced herself to get up and walk to the dining room. The television was now blaring exercise music. "One-two-three, one-two-three." Two smiling young ladies, dressed in shorts, were bending and twisting on the morning exercise show. "One-two." Mrs. Imai punched the off button and stood before the ringing phone. With a trembling hand she lifted the receiver and said "Hello" in a small voice, trying to sound as if she had been awakened from a sound sleep.

"What lazy bones you are this morning," a laughing male voice came through the earpiece. To her great relief, it was Hideo.

The last thing Hideo felt he needed in his life was a death in his wife's family. He didn't want to face the ordeal of the funeral in Niigata or the long train ride with his mother. If it was just a matter of making excuses to get out of it, he could have managed, but for once, his mother outmanoeuvred him. Not that she did it on purpose; she was just doing what was natural for her, calling everyone she knew with the news. Her first call was to her late husband's brother, Hideo's uncle and boss. That afternoon Hideo was told he had the next two days off to go to Niigata. His mistress, Fumiko, was not pleased.

Misako took Hideo's presence at the funeral as a positive turn in their marriage. The sadness she felt was softened by having her attractive husband at her side during the long ceremony on Thursday. Most of Shibata attended; the queue outside the temple extended a block. It was the second day of unseasonably warm weather. The bright sunshine mocked the mourners' black suits and kimonos.

Kensho couldn't control his jealousy at the sight of Misako sitting next to her handsome, impeccably groomed husband. Hideo's starched, startlingly white shirt particularly irritated him. The crisp white cuffs showed from the sleeve of his dark suit, boasting round gold cufflinks. Next to her husband, Misako looked like a sophisticated Tokyo woman, wearing pale pink lipstick. The priest had never seen Misako wearing makeup before. She's painted her face for him, he thought. Not even his quick sense of humour could help him today. Kensho sat through the ceremony looking grave. When it came time to go to the crematorium, the priest made profuse apologies to Keiko, saying that something important had come up and he had to rush back to Kamakura. No, he could make his way to the station. Would she please send his deep regrets to everyone, especially to Misako-*san*?

After the cremation, the old master's ashes were placed back on the main altar and a meal was served at the temple for selected mourners. Misako and her mother were now obligated to go to each person, pour sake and extend the family's thanks. Hideo watched Misako move around the room in her black kimono, with her hair swept off the graceful line of her neck. Her delicate beauty stirred old feelings.

Mother Imai sat by his side, enjoying the change from Tokyo life. She had never thought of Misako's grandfather as anything more than a humble country priest but now she was impressed with the numbers of mourners who held the old man in high esteem. This was certainly something to tell her sister about. If only Misako and Hideo would get on better. She wanted life back to normal as soon as possible.

"Ah," she purred into Hideo's ear, "look how graciously Misako is behaving. Aren't you lucky to have such a wife?"

Like a young bamboo, Hideo's guilt was growing in leaps and bounds. By the end of the dinner, his face was flushed with sake and his heart was full of tender feelings for his wife. He told himself he had to end the affair with Fumiko. Too many people would be hurt if it went on. He would have to tell his mistress they were through, as soon as he returned to Tokyo. He lit a cigarette and silently vowed to do it, once and for all. No more Fumiko. He was tired of sneaking around corners and going to sleazy love hotels. It wasn't worth it.

That night he took his wife in his arms and, without naming his crime, told her he was sorry. Misako wept softly with the joy of having her husband loving her again. Mother Imai was right; husbands tire of their mistresses. A wife has to forgive.

They were in bed together in Misako's room. They were holding each other and whispering together like young lovers. "A new beginning," he said, and was extra tender in his lovemaking. It was like it used to be until his hands clutched at Misako's breasts. The hard little nipples were not centred on the generous hills of pleasure he had recently grown accustomed to. He missed his mistress's sexy touching, her teasing, her movements and moans. He was having sex with Misako but he couldn't help wishing it was Fumiko.

Later, while Misako slept, Hideo sat cross-legged on the *tatami* floor savouring a cigarette. Smoking was bad for him but the cigarette tasted so good, like Fumiko. As much as he told himself he cared for his wife, this attempt at lovemaking had left him unsatisfied. It had all seemed so bland. He held the cigarette in front of him and admired its glow in the dark room.

Now that's beautiful, he thought, hot and dangerous. I'm addicted to the damn things. I need cigarettes and I need Fumiko.

TEN

*T*hey met twice a week. Sometimes they went to a love hotel and other times Fumiko borrowed a friend's apartment. She was always delightfully funny and deliciously sexy, but Fumiko was beginning to make demands that Hideo didn't like, pressing him to divorce his wife and marry her. Sometimes Hideo felt as if he was strapped into a slowly tightening vise. He couldn't afford a scandal. His powerful uncle would be livid. This affair with Fumiko was dangerous. It couldn't go on, but Hideo didn't seem to have the strength to stay away from his mistress for any length of time.

It wasn't that he didn't try. Several times he told Fumiko that they had to stop seeing each other. She always cried and they always ended up in bed. Hideo had to admit that they were good together in bed, if that was love. At times he wasn't sure what love was supposed to feel like. Fumiko was sure. She was always saying, "I love you." She made it clear that she wanted him for her husband and she was not happy about having to wait.

During the second week of November, Hideo's uncle had been short with him about some minor business matter. The incident brought home how easy it would be for his uncle to kick him out of the company if his affair with Fumiko caused a family scandal. The time had come to put an end to it.

Hideo arranged a short business trip and left a message at Fumiko's office that he had to cancel their Monday meeting. Wednesday afternoon, Fumiko got him on the phone and demanded they meet that evening. "We have to talk." Hideo sighed and made another excuse.

Fumiko wasn't buying it. "We have to talk," she said. "I'm sure you don't want me to come to your office, do you?" Reluctantly he agreed to meet her at the usual coffee shop at seven o'clock.

Hideo was held up at the office and arrived twenty minutes late. Fumiko was sitting in a booth putting lipstick on her full mouth. All her attention was on her hand mirror. Even though Hideo didn't want this meeting, he couldn't help feeling a thrill at the sight of her. She looked delicious in her red silk shirt with the top button undone.

"I'm sorry I'm late," he said, flopping down on the seat across from her.

Fumiko got up. "Let's go," she said smiling.

"Don't you want something to eat?" he asked.

"My friend's out of town and we have her apartment. There's plenty to drink there and I already ordered Chinese food. We can pick it up on the way."

Hideo followed obediently. He couldn't really talk in the coffeehouse and he was hungry. After he had something to eat, he thought, they could talk. It was better that they would be totally alone. He had to tell her this was the end, once and for all.

They picked up the Chinese food and went to the apartment. Halfway through the meal he noticed she hadn't eaten much and hardly touched her whiskey and water. Her whole body seemed to droop.

"What's the matter?" he asked and reached across the table for her hand. "Aren't you feeling well tonight?"

"I have a big problem, if you want to know the truth." She looked like she was about to cry. Hideo took his hand away and frowned.

"Is this going to be one of those leave-your-wife nights?" he sneered. "We have gone over it time and time again. I can't do it, Fumiko. I just can't do it. This whole thing is getting far too complicated. I think the time has come for us to forget about each other. I don't think we should meet any more."

There, he had said it! He was in control. Fumiko burst into tears. He had known she would, but he was ready. He stood up, turned away and lit a cigarette, blowing smoke angrily into the air. Fumiko dabbed her eyes with her handkerchief. She spoke in such a tiny voice that Hideo could hardly hear.

"It's too late," she whispered. "I'm pregnant."

"What did you say?" he shot at her.

"It's too late. I'm pregnant."

This time he heard. "Damn!" he said, angrily turning to her.

She glared up at him. "Oh you can be angry if you like but I'm the one who has your child in my belly and it wasn't all my doing." Her voice was good and loud now.

Although livid with anger, he managed to speak in a soft, slow, determined tone. "We talked about it a hundred times, Fumiko. You told me not to worry, you were taking precautions. Now you tell me you are pregnant. What the hell am I supposed to think? Is this some kind of trick to force me into getting a divorce?"

"Precautions!" Fumiko screamed. "Precautions don't always work, I found out. Is that my fault? Do you think I'm crazy? Do you think I want to be pregnant with no husband? What will my family say?"

Hideo took another drag on the cigarette, sat down at the low table again and put the cigarette out in the ashtray.

"What are you going to do about it?" he asked.

Fumiko glared at him and spoke through clinched teeth. "What am I going to do?"

"Yes," he said calmly, "I think that is a reasonable question."

"Is it reasonable to ask what you are going to do about it?" she screamed back. "It is not only my problem."

"Look," he said. "Let's be calm. Screaming won't solve anything. It is not the first time this has happened to a couple. I can give you the money for an abortion. You can say you are sick at work for a few days. Make an excuse to your family and stay in a hotel for a couple of days. You can't be too far along if you didn't know about it last week. Early abortions are common."

Fumiko started to cry again and spoke through her tears. "You seem to have it all worked out like some business deal. Is that what you want me to do, really?"

"Yes," he answered firmly. "I don't see any other way out of this mess."

"Does that mean that you never wanted to marry me?"

"Come on, Fumiko," he said, showing his annoyance again. "We have gone over that a hundred times. If I didn't have a wife, it would be different, but I am married and I can't change that reality. My uncle would forbid it. He's the head of the family and my boss. There would be hell to pay. Do you want to marry a man without a job?"

"I don't believe it," she cried. "If you loved me you would find a way. Now you want me to have an abortion. You are asking me to go to a doctor's office and murder your son. This may be the only son you will ever make."

"What do you mean, my son?" he demanded. "You can't know that yet."

"Whatever it is, it is your child and there is a good chance that it is a boy." She put her hands on her stomach. "I just know it's a boy. Women get feelings and they are often right. Your skinny, sexless wife will never give you any kind of child, that's for sure. Certainly, never a healthy son. When you are old and childless, with no one to burn incense and remember you after death, you can think about the son you had killed. Where will your mighty uncle be then?"

Hideo was stunned. He stood up, put his hands in his pockets and turned his back to her.

"I'm sorry. I'm really sorry," he said. His voice sounded shaken. "Give me some time to think, just a few minutes to think. I'm going for a walk. I'll be back in fifteen minutes, I promise."

Without turning to look at her, Hideo grabbed the pack of cigarettes from the table and went out the door. Lighting a cigarette, he sat on the metal staircase, his shoulders hunched against the chilly night air. The word "son" kept going around in his head. He had dreamed of having a son and it could be true that Misako might never be able to have a child. She claimed the doctor said there was nothing wrong, but she hadn't gotten pregnant and they had already been married for five years. Hideo shook his head. Their marriage really wasn't what he wanted. Misako was a sweet wife but they never had fun together; not the way he and Fumiko had. And what about their sex life? Didn't he deserve to enjoy his life? But divorce! That was drastic. His mother wouldn't accept it. She'd worry about what people would say. She wanted grandchildren badly. Maybe it would help if she knew about the baby. Why should it matter who the mother was? It would be a grandchild through him, not the mother. She and Misako had never really got along that well anyway. But it would be a pity to hurt Misako; she wasn't a fighter. If she knew, maybe she would just give up and leave. That would make it easier. Maybe she would agree to a divorce. She knew how much he wanted a son but Misako just hadn't been able to give him any children. Why should he be penalized for his wife's inadequacies?

Hideo's mind raced, trying to sort things out. When he finished the cigarette, he crushed it under his shoe and went back upstairs. Inside the apartment, the overhead light had been dimmed, giving the room a soft glow. The table had been put away and in its place, a futon bed had been laid out on the *tatami* floor. Fumiko stepped out of the bathroom and stood by the futon. She was naked except for a towel wrapped low on her full hips. Her breasts and shoulders shone as if they had been rubbed with oil and her hair flowed loose down her back. She looked like a healthy woman from an exotic tropical island. Cupping her breasts in her own hands she pushed them up, as if offering them to Hideo.

"Soon they will be filled with milk," she said softly.

She sank down on the futon. Hideo knelt in front of her, touching her face tenderly.

"I don't want you to have an abortion," he said. I want you to have my son. I want you to be my wife. We will find a way. I don't want to live with-out my darling, my little mother."

They kissed passionately before Fumiko gently moved his head to her breast and cradled him in her arms as he suckled like a baby.

❀ ❀ ❀

During the significant forty-nine days after her father's death, Keiko went to the temple every day, praying, freshening the rice offering on the altar, lighting incense and fussing over the flowers. The urn containing his ashes stood like a decoration; she always moved it a bit as she smoothed out the altar scarf or removed some fallen incense ash. Then she would stand back to assess the effect.

"There you are, Father," she would say like a mother to her child, "all tidy and ready for another day." The old face smiled down at her from his black-ribboned photograph. Then she would leave the altar room to seek out the priest, Teishin, for their daily chat.

In the belief that the soul would finally go on its way after the seven weeks, Keiko tried to clear up all her father's worldly affairs in that time frame. She wanted his spirit to be free. She felt her father would never be at peace unless the temple ran smoothly. He had left that responsibility to his assistant, but Keiko was not convinced of Teishin's abilities. She shivered to think of how disorganized the funeral would have been if the priest from Kamakura had not been visiting. No, she was going to have to observe Teishin-san very carefully these next weeks.

Another pressing situation that worried her was the white, silk-wrapped box of unknown ashes. "I found the box of remains that caused all the trouble in the old altar room," she had told her husband over afternoon tea. "I won't rest until it is out of the temple."

Keiko blamed the ashes for her father's death. From the day they arrived at the temple, her father had acted foolishly. The outcome was tragic. No, she no longer wanted that box in any room in the temple, but to remove it by herself would undermine Teishin's authority. That wouldn't do, especially now, when she was trying to help Teishin overcome his insecurities.

"I'll say nothing at the moment, but I intend to bring this matter up when things are back to normal. I don't like that box being in the temple at all, not even in the back altar room. It would bring back terrible memories if Misako were to see it. Teishin-*san* will agree with me, I'm sure." She slapped the table with the palm of her hand and continued, "I'll have no more of the spooky game that Misako and Grandfather were getting up to."

The good doctor raised his eyebrows in surprise. He had never seen his wife so firm on any subject. "*Hai!* I understand," he said in the same firm tone, and he too slapped the table. Then he laughed, but his wife only smiled.

Keiko had also issued some no-nonsense orders to Misako's husband and mother-in-law before they left Niigata. She served them tea in her home and spoke to them very candidly.

"Misako has had a serious shock seeing her grandfather die. My husband and I are worried about her and hope that you will take care that she will not be subjected to any undue stress. When she comes back to Niigata for her grandfather's forty-ninth-day ceremony, we hope that she will be recovered, with your help."

Although Hideo listened to this speech before he left Niigata and moved his head in agreement, he wasn't finding it easy to keep stress away from home. With Fumiko's pregnancy, he now really wanted a divorce, but his mother was being so nice to Misako that domestic matters were running as smooth as silk. To his chagrin, all of his efforts to cause discord were in vain. Misako just smiled and avoided anything that could cause an argument.

The timing was impossible. He didn't see how he could tell his wife, who was still mourning her grandfather's death, that he wanted to replace her with a wonderfully sexy, pregnant mistress, six years her junior. But Fumiko kept nagging. Considering her condition, she was not willing to wait forty-nine hours, never mind forty-nine days.

Breaking the news to his mother and uncle was going to be really difficult. It wasn't even reasonable to expect his mother to understand. How was his mother to take a brand new daughter-in-law into the house after living with Misako for more than five years? It was unthinkable for him to move out of the house. Besides his duty toward his mother, it would be financially impossible to move to another house as comfortable. Yet he wanted to marry Fumiko. She suited him better and it was unacceptable to him to not have a son. His thirty-fifth birthday was coming soon and it was time to have a family. Surely Misako would understand his needs.

The situation wasn't helped by the general good humour Misako and his mother were sharing. They were involved in the wedding plans of his cousin, his mother's niece. It was all the women ever talked about. Instead of asking him why he was out so late, breakfast was filled with talk of how many outfits his cousin would change into during the wedding.

"At the reception hall," his mother went on excitedly, "she will change from her white wedding gown to a formal kimono. My goodness, you should see the *obi* her fiancé's parents have given her. It cost a fortune! Handwoven in Kyoto! Then, at the reception, when everyone is just finishing the main course, the bride will leave the room again to change into a long Western evening gown."

"And," Misako added, "I heard she will wear real orchids in her hair with the evening gown."

"Stupid women talk!" Hideo complained, but his outburst just made them laugh. He banged down his chopsticks and left the room. The more he complained, the funnier Misako and his mother thought it was. It was not part of his plan that they should be getting on so well. He had counted on the usual tensions to lay the groundwork for his big move. With all the nonsense about the wedding, he couldn't start an argument in the house, no matter how he tried.

The new closeness between Mother Imai and Misako brought on franker conversations between the two women. "Don't be so serious," Mother Imai advised Misako. "Be more cheerful. You think too much. Take up a hobby. A man has his own world and a woman must have her own world too."

She was trying. Misako made an effort to stop nagging Hideo about his late hours. She controlled her emotions and avoided complaining, even when he stayed out all night. She made an effort to get more exercise as well. Every Wednesday she got on a train to attend a swimming class that was held in the official 1964 Tokyo Olympics pool. That gave her an entire afternoon out of the house.

She went back to playing tennis with her friend, Yuri, on Saturdays. Mother Imai didn't seem to object to her daughter-in-law being active. Misako was feeling better. Her sleeping habits were improving. She rarely took sleeping pills and she had experienced no visions or bad dreams since her return to Tokyo.

It was true that Hideo was irritable but that was easier to handle now that Mother Imai seemed to be on Misako's side. There had been no more lovemaking between them since that one night in Niigata, but Misako told herself that it was natural after five years of marriage for that to cool down. She had never been keen on sex in the Imai house with Hideo's mother within earshot. Still, she was determined now to see a new doctor and get a second opinion on her chances of having a baby. A doctor had assured her there was nothing wrong. He told her to take her temperature every day to find out when the best time was to conceive. He advised the couple to go to a love hotel for a night when the time was right. "You need to relax," he said. That made Misako laugh at the time, but now she was thinking of suggesting that they go away to a hot spring for a romantic weekend, someplace where no one would listen on the other side of the wall.

Sometimes she worried that Hideo might still be having an affair but she didn't let herself dwell on it. She confessed her suspicions to Yuri after a tennis game. Yuri smiled and said that men were like that, they never stuck with anything very long. "Haven't you noticed how they buy golf equipment and fishing gear and never use them after a few months?" The girl-talk convinced Misako that Hideo had probably tired of the woman with the broad feet by now. All they needed was a short, romantic vacation together.

Misako was in a state of mind that denied anything unpleasant. When Hideo frowned, she turned her head to look in another direction. When she found lipstick on one of his white shirts, she told herself that it must be from months ago; the laundry probably wasn't able to remove it.

Denial worked well until the November day when she had another vision. This vision was too disturbing and vivid to dismiss. It happened on an evening when Hideo called and said he would not be home until late. Misako and her mother-in-law had dinner and sat down in front of the television. Misako was working on a sweater she was knitting and only glanced at the set from time to time. The program wasn't very interesting for her, although Mother Imai was enjoying it. The story was about the hard times of an old woman living in northern Hokkaido.

At one point, Misako looked up from her knitting and saw a scene on the screen that had nothing to do with what they had been watching, nor did it match the dialogue. It was too erotic for this time of evening. A man was standing before a naked woman who was kneeling on a futon. The woman had large, well-formed breasts. The man looked exactly like Hideo. He was pulling off a blue shirt. Hideo had a shirt like that; he had worn it this morning. Now he was kneeling before the woman and they were kissing hungrily. Misako closed her eyes in horror and made a little sound. Her mother-in-law shook her hand at her for silence. When Misako looked at the television set again, the picture was of an old woman walking through the snow.

The more Misako thought about it later, the more she was sure that she had seen Hideo with the same woman in her other vision. This time she saw the face clearly. It wasn't anyone she had ever seen in Hideo's office. But how could it be possible? If only she could call Kensho. He was the only person she could talk to about visions. Visions, yes, but how could she discuss her husband's infidelities with such a man? Impossible! Then she decided that, if she chose her words carefully, she might be able to confide in her mother-in-law, at least partly.

"What would be the best thing for a woman to do if she was sure her husband had a mistress?" she asked the next day.

Mother Imai raised her eyebrows and understood. She knew that Misako had cause to worry and she wondered why her daughter-in-law hadn't mentioned it before.

"It can happen in the best of marriages," she said. "Men are childish creatures, you must know that. Papa was involved with a geisha years ago, when Hideo was a baby. Of course in those days it was not uncommon. I ignored it and it was over soon."

"But suppose the wife was having a hard time ignoring it? Things are different now than in the old days. I mean, suppose it had been a love marriage?"

"My generation isn't sure what you call a love marriage but the wife should still ignore it. Anyway, few men can afford to keep a geisha these days. It's too expensive." Mother Imai laughed, remembering the experience that the years had softened. "Your generation is luckier than mine."

"But Mother, suppose it is not a geisha but a common bar girl." The idea that the other woman was a common bar girl appealed to Misako. It seemed less threatening.

Mother Imai let out a hearty laugh. She had been enjoying this hiatus from the tension with her daughter-in-law. She wanted it to continue, each of them shining a light only on what they wanted each other to see. She didn't want their conversation to get really serious.

"You are not suspecting Hideo, are you? You are thinking too much again. Even if it were true, you would be secure. You are the wife. We Imais don't get divorced."

103

"Sometimes I worry because Hideo stays out so late," Misako said, looking into her tea cup.

Mother Imai laughed. "Don't be foolish! All men have to work late from time to time. He is out less than before, only about twice a week. Where would he find the time for a mistress?"

"I wish I could be sure," Misako said and bit her lip.

They were sitting at the dining-room table with a box of fancy cookies opened before them. Mother Imai held her tea cup in both hands and hesitated slightly before she spoke.

"Misako. I haven't mentioned it in a while, but the trouble with your marriage is that there are no children. What are you waiting for? If you had a baby, you would be too busy to worry."

The words pulled the bandage and exposed the wound. Misako's eyes filled with tears from the sting. The softness she had felt for her mother-in-law faded.

"Don't you think I'm even more disappointed than you are? Of course I want a baby."

"It doesn't seem to me that you and Hideo try very hard." Mother Imai knew she was treading in dangerous waters but couldn't help herself. She avoided Misako's eyes by taking her time choosing the next cookie.

Misako glared at the older woman. She wanted to shriek, "What wife could be comfortable with sex with her mother-in-law always listening behind the bedroom door?" Instead, she controlled herself and talked about her visit to the doctor. "The doctor can find nothing wrong with me," she said truthfully, "but I'm going to see a new doctor for another opinion."

A cloud came over Mother Imai's face. "You don't think there is something wrong with you, do you? I mean your periods are normal and all that sort of thing?"

There was something about the expression on the older woman's face that angered Misako. It was bad enough that she had to sleep in her shadow but going into the details of her periods was too much. She knew the subject would fade away by simply answering "yes." Then she realized that she was actually taking some pleasure from Mother Imai's obvious irritation.

"I don't know," she said, shrugging her shoulders. "That's why I'm going to see a different doctor. I suppose it is possible that I can't have children. After all, we have been married for five years. Most people have a least one baby by the time they are married five years."

Mother Imai sat up very straight in her chair. Until this moment, the possibility that Misako would never have a child hadn't seemed real. "You mean there is a chance that you can't have any children at all?" Her voice sounded indignant, as if Misako had no right to even suggest such a thing.

Misako shrugged her shoulders again and reached over to cover the cookie box. "There is always that chance. We'll see what the new doctor has to say." She got up and carried the box over to the china closet, hiding the smile she was enjoying.

"Well, you tell that doctor that you have to have a child," Mother Imai barked as she leaned over to turn on the television set. "See him as soon as possible and then do whatever is necessary. There has to be a grandchild in this house, and soon. I can't wait forever."

Misako slipped away, beyond the beaded curtains, and leaned on the kitchen counter, doubled over in silent laughter.

ELEVEN

*T*he ceremony commemorating the forty-ninth-day memorial was to take place on Monday the twenty-ninth of November. Mother Imai's niece's wedding was scheduled for the Saturday before, on the twenty-seventh. Misako planned to leave for Niigata the day after the wedding, so she could attend the memorial. She would go alone. Hideo had a business trip with his uncle. Mother Imai had to stay home and watch the house.

Hideo hadn't succeeded in introducing the subject of divorce at home. Fumiko was not taking the procrastination well. She was beginning to think that Hideo was backing down from his promise. He hadn't called her in over a week and she was getting panicky.

The Wednesday before the wedding was a national holiday. Most offices were closed and people were out enjoying Tokyo's sunny weather. Hideo, depressed about his personal problems, wanted to be alone. He said he had a cold and stayed in bed until noon. His mother and Misako, in their new-found comradeship, went to the Ginza to shop and have lunch. When they were safely out of the house, Hideo went downstairs to watch television. At about two o'clock, the telephone rang. To his annoyance, it was Fumiko.

"You must be crazy calling me at home. I told you never to call here. Do you want to make things worse?"

"Don't get excited," she said. "I wasn't going to say a word if a woman answered. I would have hung up or said it was a wrong number."

"What's so important that you have to take such a chance?"

"Our baby is important! I have to see you today."

"Damn it, Fumiko! I can't, not today."

"You have to, Hideo. I'm at Shibuya Station now. It's not far from your house. Meet me at the Russian Tea Room on the top floor of the Daiwa Department Store."

"I can't," he said. "I have a bad cold. I have been in bed all day. I feel terrible."

"You'll feel worse if I go to your house. I can be there in ten minutes."

"You must be joking."

"No joke, Hideo-*chan*, I'll be ringing your door bell in ten minutes. I promise."

"Damn it, Fumiko, I don't like threats and I don't like meeting so close to home. Someone might see us."

Fumiko laughed. "It is so crowded here, no one will notice. I'll be waiting." She hung up.

Hideo slammed down the phone. He couldn't have her ringing his doorbell; he had to go. He ran up the stairs to get dressed, cursing.

It took him thirty minutes to find a place to park. He entered the tea room with a stern face and his hands thrust deep into his trouser pockets. Fumiko was at a table drinking a tall glass of Russian tea. She looked up at him and smiled. There was no hint of the threatening tone she had used on the phone.

"Hello, darling," she said brightly.

Hideo slid into the seat. He knew when she started throwing English words around that she was trying to be cute to soften a bad situation.

"I won't put up with your threats, Fumiko. You understand?"

"I'm sorry," Fumiko said, still smiling. "I didn't mean to threaten you. It is just that I'm desperate, and please don't look so glum or you will attract attention."

Hideo put his hands on the table and tried to look normal. "Why do you have to be so difficult?" he asked. "Can't you understand that I am doing my best under the circumstances?"

A waitress came over and Fumiko ordered more tea and two cakes. Hideo waited until the girl left before he spoke again.

"This cold has me feeling rotten and your demands don't help. I told you I have to wait until the wedding and memorial service are over. The timing is wrong. How can I drop this bomb right now? I just need a little more time."

"Time!" Fumiko said and rolled her eyes. "Time happens to be particularly precious to me these days. This morning my sister noticed that I threw up in the toilet and she told my mother. I had to say I had eaten a bad clam and felt sick all night. What if it happens again tomorrow? My mother isn't stupid. I'm worried and upset. It's not easy being pregnant and upset."

The waitress served the tea and cakes. "Will there be anything else?" she asked. Fumiko shook her head and the girl left.

"I have a plan," Hideo said as he lit a cigarette, "but I do need time. Give me a few more days, please."

Fumiko narrowed her eyes. "Exactly how many days?"

"Not that many. Misako leaves for Niigata on Sunday. Sunday night I'll have a chance to talk to my mother alone."

"Your mother!" Fumiko's voice came out louder than she wanted. "Why should you tell your mother you want to divorce your wife before you tell your wife?" She was keeping her voice down now, leaning across the table toward him.

"You don't know the situation," he said and took a long drag on his cigarette. "My mother is very kind, really, but she can have spells of hysteria. Her generation is not used to divorce. If I tell her Sunday night when we are alone, she'll have until Wednesday to get over it. I'll be away on business Tuesday and Misako isn't due back until Wednesday."

"I don't understand why it has to be so complicated," Fumiko pouted.

"The complication is that the two of them are getting on really well these days. As soon as I break the news to my mother, she'll side with Misako. I can't have the two of them against me. Handled right, Mother will think about it and come over to my side before Misako comes back from Niigata."

Fumiko seemed to be digesting what he said as she chewed her cake. "But," she said after a moment, "suppose your mother doesn't side with you? Then the waiting will be for nothing. You say they are on good terms. In the past you gave me the impression that they didn't get along."

Hideo blew smoke up at the ceiling. "They don't, not really. The good feelings won't last. I can see what is happening. My mother felt sorry for Misako and is trying to take her mind off her grandfather's recent death by getting her excited about my cousin's wedding. If I tell Misako I want a divorce before the wedding, she will run to my mother. That will ruin everything. We have to wait. I need time to prepare my mother first. I can handle her." He was sounding more confident now, and leaned over to take Fumiko's hand. She toyed with a spoon and pouted.

Neither of them noticed that a woman, smoking a cigarette over a cup of tea, was watching them with great interest. She was sitting alone, but from the expression on her face, she seemed to be enjoying herself very much.

On the morning of the wedding, Misako went to the local beauty salon to have her hair done and to have her black *tomesode*, the formal kimono worn by married women, put on professionally. She stood in the tiny two-*tatami* mat room in the back of the shop while the middle-aged beautician tugged and tied the silk garments around her. Since the woman had owned the shop for many years, she knew everyone in the neighbourhood. Mother Imai was a good customer. She had her hair done every week and always exchanged local gossip with her. Talking to her customers was one of the owner's main pleasures in life. The best days were when she heard some new morsel to pass on, especially if it smacked at a possible scandal.

"Take a deep breath and let me know if I am pulling the *obi* too tight," she said as she wound and pulled the brocade sash around Misako's slender waist.

"*Maa*! This *obi* is a beauty! Very expensive. Did your husband give it to you?" the owner asked with a sly smile.

"No," Misako answered, slightly annoyed at the personal nature of the question.

"I suppose it was your mother-in-law's. She is such an outgoing woman and a good customer."

"This *obi* was part of my wedding trousseau. My parents gave it to me at the time of my marriage." Misako was forced to give her the information and resented it.

"*Maa*! How wonderful. You must be from a good family. Niigata isn't it? A real Niigata beauty." Her words dripped.

Misako pulled herself to her full height and made no answer. The woman couldn't stand the silence very long.

"Today is Mrs. Imai's niece's wedding, isn't it? "

Misako gave her a small "Yes" and that was all. The silence hung.

"Your mother-in-law told me about it. I'm sure you and your husband will be the best-looking couple at the wedding. The groom can't be as hand-some as your husband and you look beautiful in this fabulous kimono. I don't see this quality silk every day and not many girls can wear kimono as well as you do."

Misako loathed the kind of compliment that tradespeople were so good at, especially this one. Unfortunately she had to finish having her *obi* tied and this woman was very skilled at it. Misako could only smile and say "Thank you."

"Your husband doesn't seem to change," the woman went on. "I saw him just last Wednesday in that Russian Tea Room in Shibuya and he's as handsome as ever. He was with an interesting looking woman, one of those modern beauties. The two of them seemed to be having a serious conversation."

The bait was cast. Misako's spine went rigid. She knew immediately that the woman had seen Hideo with his mistress. In the mirror she watched the owner's self-satisfied expression as she worked on the *obi* behind her back.

"Oh yes," Misako lied. "That must have been my friend. We went shopping and my husband and my friend were waiting for me. I had to return an item and you know that can take so long these days. I asked them to wait for me at the tea room. You know how men hate standing around. Yes, it must have been them. A plumpish girl, wasn't she?"

"Yes, the girl was slightly plump," the owner said with disappointment. But she wasn't convinced. After all, she had seen Hideo reaching out for the girl's hand in a very familiar way.

"Now take that girl's figure, your friend. With those big breasts, she could never wear kimono well. Even if you bind them down and fill in the waist with a towel, it still never looks graceful. I dread it when a customer who is built like that comes in here and expects me to make her look good in kimono. Not that there are many around with figures like that, but kimono wasn't made for them. They should stick to Western dresses. To wear kimono well, you can't have much on top." With those words, she smoothed down the front of Misako's kimono. "There, you look beautiful."

Something had changed Misako. Hideo noticed it at the wedding. Most of the time she acted normally, but there was something different about the way she looked at him. Several times he saw a coldness in her eyes that he had never seen before. It made him feel miserable and guilty.

She knows! he told himself. She knows about Fumiko. As soon as the wedding speeches were over, he left their table to join a group of men at the other side of the banquet room. They were throwing down sake, beer and whisky. He got so drunk that two young men drove him home and put him to bed on a futon thrown down in the Imai living room. It was easier than trying to get him up the narrow stairs to their bedroom.

Early on Sunday, Hideo made his usual amazing morning-after recovery and came to the breakfast table feigning good spirits. He knew he was expected to drive Misako to the train station. If his mother had not been there, he would have tried to get out of it, but he couldn't risk annoying his mother, not today.

Misako said very little to him. Her demeanour seemed defiant. A couple of times he caught something like loathing in her eyes. He didn't like it. He wanted to tell her to go to hell.

They drove in icy silence until she reminded him that they should stop at a certain sweet shop on a street they were approaching. The unexpected request caused the tension to snap and he cursed.

"I'm sorry," she said, looking straight ahead, "but you know I always stop at that bakery before getting on a train for Niigata. I can't go empty-handed."

Hideo's temper erupted. "Why do you leave things for the last minute? How long have you known that you were leaving today?"

"You know that I always buy the cakes on the way to the station." Her voice was laced with sarcasm. She felt brazen. "You don't have to be so mean. It's bad enough that you make me the butt of neighbourhood gossip by being seen with your mistress so close to home. Tell me, how are the cakes at the Russian Tea Room in Shibuya?"

Hideo turned the car sharply into the side street where the bakery was and jammed on the brakes. Misako was thrown forward, forcing her to put out her hands to stop her head from hitting the windshield. She looked at him with burning eyes. He glared back with contempt.

"Never mind taking me to the station," she said, pulling her suitcase from the back seat. "I think you are going crazy. I can get to the station without you."

"I don't need you either!" he threw back at her.

Misako got out and slammed the car door. Hideo put his foot down on the accelerator and sped away, making the tires screech.

"Spoiled brat!" she called after the car. A man passing looked at her with surprise and continued on, smiling to himself. Misako composed herself and went into the bakery. She came out with a large box of cakes. There was no taxi in sight.

Tokyo's Ueno Station teemed with people, giving it the movement of an ant colony. Perspiration ran down the back of Misako's neck as she made her way through the crowds. It had taken almost fifteen minutes to find a taxi. Fortunately, she had bought her ticket weeks in advance. Even then, there had only been first-class tickets available. It would be impossible to find a seat on another train to Niigata today.

Through the ticket punch and into the main part of the station, she moved as fast as she could, dodging people as she went. Balancing her suitcase and cake box, she ran up the stairs. The conductor was walking down the platform waving his red flag. The train door began to close as she lunged at it and squeezed through. The door snapped and jerked back for a second, allowing her to pull her suitcase through. The train lurched and started to roll. Her heart was pounding as she leaned against the door. This was only the entrance to car number four; her ticket was for car number six. She closed her eyes and sighed. It meant she had to make her way through two cars on a crowded, moving train, carrying a suitcase and delicate cake box.

The door to the first compartment was stiff. It was awkward having to hold it open as she tried to drag the box and suitcase through. Everyone in car number four looked at her, but no one offered assistance. Misako's face was hot with embarrassment. Walking sideways, she bumped down the narrow aisle. The car was already heavy with cigarette smoke.

The door to the next compartment was even more difficult to open. She managed by struggling in backwards, clutching the box with one hand, while pulling the suitcase with the other. The pressure on her back suddenly decreased and she realized that someone was holding the door open. She turned to see the priest from Kamakura smiling down on her.

"Oh! Misako-*san*, let me help you," he said as he took her suitcase.

"What a surprise," she said, feeling even more embarrassed that someone she knew had seen her in this awkward situation.

"It looks like you almost missed the train," he grinned. "Here, sit in my seat a minute and catch your breath."

All eyes were on them. It was obvious that the young woman and the very tall priest knew each other. A woman started to whisper to her companion behind her hand. The man in the seat next to the priest's stood up and offered to change seats.

"Thank you. That's very kind," Misako said, taking her ticket from her coat pocket and handing it to the man.

The man looked at the ticket and hesitated. "But," he said slowly, "your ticket is for the first-class car. It wouldn't be fair."

"Please," Misako pleaded. "You would be doing me a great favour."

"But—" the man protested mildly.

"Please! This priest is my good friend and I would like to sit with him," Misako insisted. "I don't care about the first-class seat. Please, take it."

The man picked up his briefcase and book. "If you are sure, thank you." He bowed and moved up the aisle. The whispering woman put her hand up again to talk to her companion.

Misako sat down in the seat next to the window and smiled. The morning had gone so badly but here was this great stroke of luck meeting Kensho on the train to Niigata. There was so much she wanted to ask him about that terrible day her grandfather died, so much she still didn't understand. The thought of it made her sigh.

"Are you all right?" he asked. "You look so tired."

"It's because I was running. I'm fine now."

They both sat back in comfortable silence as the train picked up speed.

"How is the weather in Kamakura these days?" Misako asked. It wasn't what she wanted to say, but it was a start.

"Very good. It has been clear enough to enjoy the view of Mt. Fuji," he answered. He had worked hard to put Misako out of his mind when he returned to Kamakura, but now her calling him her "very good friend" made his heart race with joy.

"How is life in Tokyo?" he asked.

"As always," she said and turned her head to the window, allowing a spell of silence to fall between them. She was beginning to wonder if this meeting was a coincidence or if it was like the day they had met at the Shibata garden.

The truth was that the priest had not planned it. At one point, he had actually decided not to go to Niigata for the memorial ceremony. His emotions were already dangerously entangled with the matters of Misako and Shibata. It was all so magnetic that his instincts told him to back off. The Buddha had written: "Indulge in lust but a little and lust like a child will grow."

As a rule, Zen priests take no vows of celibacy, even though marriage is seen as a hindrance to gaining *satori*. Nevertheless, some Zen priests prefer to marry and run their temples with the help of their wives, living a normal family life. A wife leaves the priest free to expand his parish and do his priest's work. Kensho had chosen celibacy. The training temple in Kamakura was his home and the community of monks, his family. It was the prudent path for a man of his unusual appearance and circumstances to walk. His decision hadn't been made lightly; it came through endless hours of meditation, that eternity of silence in which he had grappled with the twin mysteries of self and the world. Peace in a simple life was his goal, but achieving it meant winning a struggle between the mundane senses and the Inner Light. Kensho knew that this fascination with the paranormal, now seemingly linked to the lovely Misako, could play havoc with his carefully balanced life. Yet he could not ignore his obligation to her. Not only was he present when her grandfather had his fatal stroke, but he still harboured guilty feelings. He should not have gone along with the naïve old priest's plans. He could have stopped it. If only!

The city streaked past the train window like smears of dull paint. The passengers settled into the various occupations of transit. Food was unpacked, books appeared and some people fell asleep. Misako and Kensho continued to exchange polite phrases. The two men sitting directly behind them exchanged business cards. The women across the aisle were talking and laughing.

The fight with Hideo and the rush to the train had left Misako feeling agitated and untidy. She went to the washroom to comb her hair. As she looked in the mirror to touch up her lipstick, she realized she was feeling better. There was something soothing about this man with the strange eyes. What did her mother call them? Foreigners' eyes? No, more like monkeys' eyes! Yes, that was it, speckled with gold and full of mischief. The thought made her smile at him when she returned to her seat.

"This meeting isn't one of your brainwaves to me, is it?" she teased as she got comfortable in her seat again. "You didn't call me to this train like you did in the garden in Shibata?"

The priest fell victim to one of his uncontrollable blushes. He ran his hand over his bald head. "No, no, I promise. I'm as surprised as you are."

"Well, I am glad to see you, coincidence or not," she said warmly. "I want you to know how much you helped me in Niigata. The things you told me made me understand myself better."

"Well, if there is anything you would like to ask or tell me, I'm all ears," he said, putting up his hands and pulling his big ears forward.

Misako put her hand over her mouth and giggled. When that passed, she folded her hands in her lap and posed her question timidly. "*Sensei*, do you mind me talking about the morning my grandfather died?"

"Are you sure you want to talk about it?"

"At least I want to ask if you are as confused as I am about what happened."

Kensho rubbed his head. One part of him wanted to ask her what she

114

remembered. Another part of him wanted to draw back, to tell her that they should put the entire thing behind them. But there she was sitting so close, smelling so fresh and clean, looking up at him with her big, trusting eyes. Kensho felt his heart squeeze as he leaned toward her and dropped his voice. "Well, yes. About the trance you went into during the ceremony. What do you remember about that?"

"Was I in a trance?" she asked slowly. "I thought I fainted."

"You were in a trance for some minutes before you fainted."

"How can you be sure?" Her eyes grew wide with amazement.

"Oh, I'm sure. It was frightening to see your body there with your mind and spirit off somewhere else."

"Strange you should say 'off somewhere else.' I remember looking down on the scene, as if I was hovering over the bridge."

"Can you tell me what you saw?"

"Yes," she said and hesitated. "I saw the three of us kneeling and praying on the mat. I could see the altar and the white, silk-wrapped box. And at the same time I saw the girl squatting on the bridge. She was piling rocks on a square of material. Then she pulled it up on her shoulders and tied a knot across her chest. I clearly saw her lean forward and fall off the bridge. No one pushed her. She simply held onto the material tied over her shoulders and fell forward into the water, like a pearl diver with a basket on her back. I saw and heard the splash. There were bubbles. The patch of blue from the girl's garment sank under the water."

Kensho remained silent because he was stunned at the details she remembered. Misako bowed her head and examined her hands for at least a minute before she spoke again.

"She must have been very miserable to die like that."

"*Hai*," he whispered, not knowing what else to say. He wanted to tell her that he believed in her vision but he was afraid of making another bad judgement; afraid of exposing her to more danger. When he spoke again, his words were measured and laced with circumspection.

"Misako-*san*, you must be aware that there is no proof that what you saw in your vision was what really happened."

How different his voice was now from the authority with which he had spoken within the big garden. Misako felt her mentor and friend backing off.

"You have taught me so much," she whispered.

"You do me too much honour. I am an amateur, not worthy to be a

115

teacher. I do believe you have a great gift. Then again, it can happen that when the body is stressed and weakened, the imagination can take terrible liberties."

His words stung. Her face went pale. She closed her eyes and turned to the window. If her friend and teacher didn't truly believe in her visions, maybe she did have some kind of mental illness.

Kensho's sudden shame stabbed him like a knife in his gut. His head and shoulders drooped. "Misako-*san*, I am a coward. I said that because I am afraid you look to me for answers that I don't have. In my heart, I believe that whatever you saw during your trance was something that took place in the past. But what if I am misleading you? Misako-*san*, please forgive me."

"I am the one who should ask forgiveness," she said.

He closed his eyes and took a deep breath. "No more apologies. The next step is the memorial service tomorrow. Then we will go over everything that has happened. It is possible that we will decide to let it go, rather then allowing it to cause more grief." He touched her hand and it was the touch of a butterfly pausing on a flower. His touch calmed her more than a thousand words. She understood. A true friend must be allowed to express his doubts and fears.

Adjusting the seat, Misako leaned back and began to talk with a familiarity matching her relaxed posture. A little playfulness entered her voice. "We don't have much choice. We have to let it go because there is no way of getting any more information about the girl in the pond. What is the point of trying to find out who she was? We don't even know how long ago she died."

"No way?" he repeated and couldn't resist wiggling two fingers discreetly behind his other hand so that only she could see it.

She knew he was signing "antenna," and it made her smile and sigh. "I wish I could retire my antenna for life," she said. "It is causing me trouble again and I hate it."

"Recent visions?" Kensho couldn't help asking.

Misako hesitated and then spoke looking down at her hands. "Yes, nasty visions about my husband, his mistress and our crumbling marriage."

The priest rubbed his bald head. "I didn't mean to pry into your personal life."

"The truth is I need to tell someone and who else would believe me? Do you mind if I talk to you about my personal problems?"

"You can tell me anything you want, if you think it will help," he said. Another butterfly touch on her arm gave her courage.

Misako closed her eyes and thought for a moment. Then she folded her hands in her lap and began to tell her story in a soft, sad voice.

"You see, *Sensei*, Hideo and I didn't have an arranged marriage. Ours was a real love story."

TWELVE

*A*t my stage in life there is nothing as sweet as being appreciated. It makes the eyes clear and refreshes the skin, Mother Imai told herself as she smiled at her own reflection in the mirror over the bathroom sink. She gave her cheeks a little pinch. Her excellent mood was the result of being a hit at her niece's wedding reception.

Most of the other ladies were too shy to stand up and speak, but not Mother Imai. She didn't hesitate. After the usual speeches, she stood up and sang a song in her fine, strong voice. It was the best performance by a guest at the wedding. Everyone in the room applauded loudly, even her son, who rarely gave her a word of praise at home.

And then there was the matter of the new Western toilet that Hideo had bought to ease the pain in her knee. How she enjoyed bragging about it to her sister. It had been installed on Friday. She just couldn't get over the positive change in her son's attitude toward her.

Hideo had taken Misako to the train station and didn't return until late that afternoon. He walked into the dining room where his mother was watching television and put a large paper bag down on the table. He had never gone grocery shopping in the past but this Sunday he came home with the makings of a festive *sukiyaki* dinner. He was all sweetness and smiles.

"Just the two of us," he said with a wink, "like the old days. Remember Papa used to do the cooking at the table. Tonight I'm the chef. How do you like that?"

She liked it very much. It was wonderful. They sat at the dining-room table with the *sukiyaki* pot between them. Hideo surprised his mother by cooking so well. He knew just how much sugar and soy sauce to add to the meat and vegetables. The meal was turning into a party with hot sake and laughter about incidents from years gone by.

"If only Papa could be with us now," Mother Imai said with misty eyes. She was feeling a little tipsy. She always got sentimental drinking sake and Hideo was being diligent about refilling her cup. "Papa would like to see us enjoying a meal like this together," she said. "It is like the

118

old days, when he was alive." Resting her chin on her hand, she looked at her son sadly. "But I don't think Papa would like the long faces you and Misako show so often in this house. He certainly would be disappointed that there are no grandchildren. Misako said she may not be able to have children. That's not true, is it, Hideo? Is it true that Misako will never be able to have a baby?"

Hideo had never expected such a question from his mother. To have her start on this subject all by herself was a tremendous stroke of luck. He had to take advantage of it. Immediately, his face fell into his funeral expression and he shook his head.

"Oh, poor you," his mother said, pushing back the lock of hair that fell over her forehead. "Why didn't you tell me sooner?"

Hideo put his elbows on the table and his head between his hands. "I didn't want to make you unhappy. I had to let you hope as I did. Now I've lost that hope and our marriage is breaking up because of it. Misako and I are no longer happy together."

His deeply sad answer almost broke his mother's heart. "Is that what you are fighting about?" she asked.

Hideo milked her sympathy more by simply moaning into his hands. A kabuki actor couldn't have given a better performance.

"Well," she sighed and took a deep audible breath, "if it can't be helped, it can't be helped. One day you will have to adopt a son to carry on the family name. You might consider the youngest of your cousin Yoshi's three boys. I can talk to him if you like."

"No!" Hideo said loudly. "Never." He banged on the table hard. Dishes rattled and a little sauce slopped on the tablecloth. "I want my own son and I will have my own son! There is nothing wrong with me. Why should our family suffer for Misako's weakness?"

Mother Imai's eyes opened wide. "What are you saying? How can you have your own son when your wife is not able to have a child?"

"By divorcing Misako and marrying a woman who can give me a son." His words were forceful and angry.

She put down her sake cup, narrowed her eyes and looked into her son's face. "What is this?" she asked. "Are you planning to divorce your wife?"

"Yes," he said. "I have been thinking about it for some time and now I am decided. We don't suit each other. We made a mistake getting married."

"Are you crazy?" Mother Imai said, raising her voice. She was sobering up quickly. She couldn't believe what she was hearing. "You're crazy! Your

119

marriage wasn't arranged. It was a love match, don't you remember? Now you tell me you made a mistake? What kind of talk is that? You can't change a wife like you would a car. Marriage is for life."

"Mother, please, don't go against me when I need your support so much." He reached over to touch her hand. "Why go on making all of us unhappy when I have found the girl who really should be my wife?"

"Ah! So that's it!" she shouted, pulling her hand away from his reach. "You want a divorce because you are having an affair with some hussy."

"She's not a hussy."

"No!" said Mother Imai speaking very fast. "No! There will be no divorce in this family. Misako knows you have a girlfriend, but she's not crying divorce. Go to bed with the slut but don't divorce your wife. What would your uncle say?"

Hideo pushed away the plates in front of him in disgust. "What would Uncle say? What would Uncle say?" he repeated. "That's all you worry about. What Uncle thinks is more important to you than my happiness."

Mother Imai never could stand her son's anger, especially when it was directed at her. She softened the tone of her voice. "Hideo, I do want you to be happy, but a new wife won't guarantee that. You don't know enough about this woman. You don't even know if she can have children. What kind of a woman has an affair with a married man? Is she a bar girl?"

Hideo was indignant. "Of course not! Give me more credit than that. She's a wonderful young woman."

Mother Imai started to cry. "No, I won't let you do this to Misako. Maybe she can't have children, but she has tried to be a good wife and a good daughter."

Hideo stood up. "I'm warning you, Mother. If you go against me, I'll get the divorce anyway and move out of this house completely. This isn't the only roof in Tokyo. I'll get an apartment and you'll see how lonely life can be."

On the edge of hysteria, Mother Imai stood up to face her son and knocked over her sake cup. "You talk like a complete fool."

He slammed the table again and shouted, "I'm not the fool! Can't you see your son is a man who needs a real wife, not a cold stick like Misako? The woman I want to marry is already pregnant with my baby and I don't want my son born a bastard. If you want your grandchild born that way, you just keep on fighting me."

Mother Imai fell back heavily on the chair. Her crying swelled to screams. Hideo grabbed a jacket from the hook near the kitchen door and ran out, banging the sliding door as he went. The bell jingled madly, accompanying his mother's loud crying. Hideo gave a loud laugh as he backed out of the garage and sped down the street to the tobacco shop where he used the public telephone. Luckily, Fumiko answered.

"Listen," he said excitedly, "make an excuse and get out of the house. I'll meet you where I usually leave you off."

"What happened?" Fumiko caught the intensity in his voice.

"You won't believe how well the dinner went. My mother will be in the palm of my hand by tomorrow. I'll let her stew tonight. She'll be on our side in the morning and I don't think Misako cares if she ever sees me again. We had a big quarrel on the way to the train station. She knows about us, I'm sure of that. She got out of the car and went to the station alone."

"That's good news. Give me thirty minutes. My mother is the only one home and she'll ask questions if I rush off after this call. Wait for me."

"I'll be waiting," he said happily. "We have a lot to talk about. Arrange to stay the night and we'll go to a hotel. I don't want to go home. I want to be with my sexy girl tonight. I'm really excited."

Fumiko laughed into the phone. "Okay!" she said in English. "OKAY!"

❀ ❀ ❀

Teishin's shadow reflected across the *shoji* doors, waving and flickering with the movement of the flames of the two big candles that stood on either side of the altar. As a Buddhist, he believed the spirit of his dead master lingered about the eaves of the temple for forty-nine days. Tomorrow was the last day. The thought of it plunged his heart into night. One more sunrise and the master's close friends and family would return to the temple for their last farewells. The chants and incense would be offered again and the old priest's ashes placed in his ancestral tomb. This night's vigil was Teishin's way of attending to his beloved master's spirit before the final flight to the beyond. At dinner he had announced to Konein and the visiting priest from Kamakura that he would spend the night in the altar room. They had both moved their heads in understanding.

Except for the yellow glow of the candle, the room was dark. Teishin sat cross-legged in front of the altar. The dead priest's small face in the photograph seemed to smile down at his faithful assistant. Characteristically, the unhappy priest wrung his hands and fidgeted. He tried to sit calmly,

121

with his thumbs together as his master did, but Teishin could only maintain that posture for twenty minutes.

"Oh, Master," he murmured, "How am I to carry on without you? If I am incompetent, your spirit will not be free to go on peacefully. Your daughter has helped me but after tomorrow I am afraid she won't come to the temple as often. How can this miserable country fellow take your place?"

When he stopped praying, the room fell utterly silent again. The mute picture smiled, offering no hint of advice or comfort. Teishin covered his face with his hands and rocked back and forth. Although he was determined to spend the night praying, his prayers were only whispered worries. It was still fairly early but already his eyes were closing. He mustered his fleeting energy to hold back sleepiness. When he no longer could stifle a yawn, he almost cried with shame.

❋ ❋ ❋

"I will never know why Grandfather left things like this," Keiko said to her husband and Misako, seated around the dining table. The meal was late because the doctor had been delivering a baby.

"I am not sure if Teishin-*san* is going to be able to carry on. Grandfather should have known that and trained someone more capable."

"I don't agree with you," Dr. Ichimura said as he chose a morsel of fish with his chopsticks. "Your father saw something special in Teishin-*san*. He trusted him. The real tragedy is that your brothers were killed in the war."

"I am not sure that either of them would have followed in his footsteps even if they had lived. They dreamed of being pilots, not priests. Teishin-*san* has been as devoted to my father as any son would have been, but he should have been better prepared to take over."

"Poor Grandfather," Misako said as she ladled hot rice into the bowls. "If only he had adopted a nephew. Wasn't there some blood relative in the family who wanted to carry on the Tanaka name?"

Keiko accepted the rice and shook her head. "That generation was wrapped up in the war. Two of my male cousins were killed as well and I don't remember any other talk about adopting a son. When I first married, my brothers were still alive. After I was widowed and the madness of the war was over, Grandfather suggested I marry a priest. It was a great disappointment to him when we married." She said this smiling at her husband.

A tall man with a dramatic shock of white hair combed back off his intelligent face, Dr. Ichimura made a little bow to his wife. "Thank you very much," he said with mock formality.

"You mean you went against your family's wishes to marry Papa?" Misako asked.

"I wouldn't say that, but Grandfather did suggest that I marry a priest. That way my husband could be put into the Tanaka family register and carry on at the temple after he died. It was the usual way to do things, but my mother took my side. She knew I wanted to marry Dr. Ichimura. My father gave in but never gave up his dream. Once he told me that he hoped that you, Misako, would marry a priest."

"Me?" Misako gulped with surprise.

"Oh yes," said Keiko." Don't you remember how he was against your going to university in Tokyo? It wasn't until you left home that he formally named Teishin-*san* as his successor."

"But he never said a word about it to me," Misako said.

Keiko laughed. "How could anyone talk to you? You and your girlfriends were only interested in American movies and giggling about love."

"How is it that I never heard any of this before?" Dr. Ichimura said between mouthfuls of rice.

"Because, my dear, there was no reason to tell you. Men tend to stick together. Do you know how hard the life of a temple wife can be? It means work from morning to night with very little money, especially in those days. That is why my mother encouraged me to accept the offer to marry you. My mother was right. I have been very happy. Could I consider less for my own daughter?"

"I'm learning a lot tonight," the doctor said with a broad smile, offering to fill his wife's sake cup. "However, it seems to me you are working hard at the temple even though you married me. Have you decided what you are going to do about Teishin-*san*? Is it not true that he is growing more and more dependent on you? You are there every day."

"*Umm,*" Keiko said with understanding. "Right now I go mainly to honour my father's ashes and make sure there are fresh flowers on the altar. Sometimes I look at the schedules and books and I ask Teishin-*san* questions. Even though he is keeping up with the schedule, he still hasn't got it into his head that he is in charge. I tried to get him to move into Grandfather's room but he won't do it. He says he's not worthy."

"Maybe he needs more time to gain confidence," Dr. Ichimura offered.

Keiko frowned. "You may be right but I'm afraid I was hard on him yesterday. I told him outright that he has to stop worrying about minor things like meals. It is not right that he is always fussing about food. We can get a woman to work in the kitchen."

Misako was appalled. "Mother, how could you say anything unkind to Teishin-*san*?"

"Someone has to make him understand that he has to show leadership."

"You said that to him?" Dr. Ichimura asked after exchanging glances with Misako.

"No, not exactly, but I did tell him that he had to become stronger and take charge. What he needs is a good wife. The elders in the congregation have been proposing that for some time. It is Teishin-*san* who keeps putting them off."

"Well," Misako said with a shrug, maybe he doesn't want a wife."

"Why not?" Keiko asked. "Teishin-*san* is a normal man. He's very shy but a good country woman would change all that."

Misako giggled. "Does he know about the 'wife' plot?"

"Oh, he knows what the congregation wants. There is too much work at the temple for only two priests. Sometimes they are both called out at the same time and they have to find someone to come to look after the temple. A wife would be a tremendous asset. She could take over the cooking and free Teishin-*san* for his priestly duties. Yes, if things progress well, after the New Year, I'll do as my dear husband's mother once did. I'll look around for a hard-working country girl. There are a couple of unmarried farmers' daughters around. No one too old. It would be good for the temple to have a child or two."

Both Dr. Ichimura and Misako burst out laughing. "There is nothing to laugh about," Keiko said indignantly. "I'm serious."

❀ ❀ ❀

Late that night, black clouds rolled over Shibata on a stream of icy air from Siberia. Trembling trees released their leaves to the force. Cold breezes took the leaves skipping along the dark streets. Some stuck to wet spots; others rushed onto the abandoned rice fields on the outskirts of the city.

Misako slept peacefully under her parents' roof, snuggled deep in the warm futon. Before dawn, she dreamed that her body lifted effortlessly off the bed and floated out through the wall into the night. It was as if she were a long silk scarf being carried on a rush of wind. Shadowy buildings and trees swept past as she flew. In a fleeting moment she was sailing past the familiar temple walk, up the pathway and through the heavy wooden doors, stopping in the main altar room. Her grandfather's picture smiled from the black-ribboned frame resting near the urn of his ashes. The priest Teishin was there as well, sprawled out like a sleeping child on the *tatami* floor. The flame of a single candle sputtered and drowned in a hot pool of its own melted wax.

As the flame died, a dark figure appeared on the altar's top step. It seemed to have come from the picture, from the urn of ashes. It moved toward the sleeping priest. Even in the dark, Misako knew it was her dead grandfather. As the face became clearer, she saw it had the same grey pallor she had seen when he lay in his coffin seven weeks before.

The old man's shadowy form came forward, hovered over Teishin, and evaporated into a mist that settled down into the sleeping body. It happened slowly, like the movement in a classical Noh dance. Equally slow-moving was the scream that gathered and struggled up in Misako's throat. Teishin lifted his head and turned to her. His round face suddenly had bushy white eyebrows, old watery eyes and a small, fixed smile on its pale lips. He extended his arms in an offered embrace.

Misako woke up in a sweat. At first she thought she was in the altar room. It was cold and she could smell burning incense. When she sat up she realized that she was in her bed, in the semi-darkness of early morning.

The room was icy, colder than it had ever had been before, even in the dead of winter. She shivered and reached down to the bottom of the futon for her flannel robe. The shoulder of her soft cotton sleeping kimono brushed against her face. It smelled of incense even though it had been fresh from the laundry that morning. Unbelieving, she grabbed the garment and buried her nose in it. The entire thing reeked with the sweet, deathly smell. Misako felt repulsed. Her hair and skin smelled of it too. Forgetting the dream for a moment, she got out of bed. She could only think of going to the bath, washing her hair and putting on a clean garment. She had to rid herself of the death perfume that permeated her body and night clothes.

At the temple, Teishin awoke in the dark and silent altar room. He was uncomfortable, bone-cold, and the left side of his face was red with the imprint of the *tatami* floor. He rubbed his shoulders and got to his knees before remembering where he was and why. The shame of failure made him bow his head to the floor. In spite of his intentions, he hadn't managed to keep the all-night vigil and he was still terribly tired. It was the worst fatigue he had ever known, but he had to recover by sunrise. He couldn't carry on the memorial service in this condition.

It took great effort to get to his feet. He crawled to the *shoji* door and pulled himself up on the support beam between the room and the hallway. Staggering, he made his way down the hall to the old master's bedroom. He removed the futon from the closet and spread it on the floor. Soon, he was fast asleep under the dark-plaid quilt.

THIRTEEN

*E*ver since the old master's wife had died, Teishin had taken charge of the temple kitchen. He was the first one up shuffling pots and pans, humming happily before the morning slowly shrugged off its dark shroud.

"Good morning, Konein-*san*," he would sing out to the young priest who faithfully made his sleepy way through the kitchen on his way to the bell tower. Konein usually managed to bob his head and grunt. Unlike Teishin, his energy built slowly and he spent it slipping into sandals and fumbling in his sleeve for a cigarette before stepping out into that tenebrous stretch between night's death and dawn's birth.

But this morning the long fluorescent ceiling light had not been turned on. Konein paused at the kitchen entrance, peering into the dark room. This was only the second morning in his memory that Teishin was not performing his morning magic feat of water and fire, chopping and stirring. The room was a lifeless scene of scrubbed wood and cluttered shelves. There was no rice cooking on the stove, no pungent smell of miso or onions, no cheerful "Good morning." Konein took a black slicker off a hook near the door and stepped out into the wet darkness. He lit his cigarette outside the kitchen door and took a couple of fast puffs, standing under the eaves.

"Teishin-*san* must be exhausted," he murmured, remembering that the grieving priest had planned an all-night vigil with the master's ashes. Pinching the end of the cigarette, he placed what was left into his sleeve and dashed across the courtyard. He had to hurry. If Teishin wasn't up yet, he would have to start the rice himself.

Today was the forty-ninth-day-after-death ceremony for their master. Later, women from the congregation would be swarming over the kitchen. No part of the schedule could fall behind. Konein took a deep breath and climbed the bell tower.

Just under the edge of sleep, Teishin slipped in and out of familiar and unfamiliar worlds. One minute he was a small boy, sitting on the floor, practicing calligraphy with a large brush. The paper was spread out before him, receiving the wet, black strokes as his father instructed him. He felt the larger hand on his, guiding the strokes. But this can't be my father, he thought. "No," he said. "You don't do that. You're a farmer."

The words faded in his head and he rolled from side to side, throwing off the quilt. Then he dreamed he was a baby, a fat dozing baby tied to the back of a little girl. The girl was rocking back and forth, singing a child's song. It was comfortable, very comfortable hearing his sister's voice. She was singing a song from his babyhood. "Toyoko-*chan*," he whispered and saw the back of her thick black hair, smelled the pomade scent, felt her hands behind her back holding him securely as she rocked and sang. Sweet memories, warm memories that were now being chased away by the voice of a woman who was sharing the futon. He lifted his head to see her face and was shocked to see the old master's wife. He went to shake her, to tell her it was time to make breakfast, when he heard his own mother's voice. She was kneeling by his bed, slapping his shoulder.

"Wake up you lazy boy," she was saying. "Wake up!" The Master's wife was gone. Seeing his own dear mother sent a wash of joy over him. Her death had been painful for Teishin. It happened when he was fifteen, but there she was now, round and pleasant, dressed in a familiar dark cotton kimono. He heard her laugh and he could see her plump red hands on his shoulder. "I've cooked all the things you like for breakfast and here you are sleeping the morning away. Wake up sleepy boy." She slapped him lightly again. Her laugh tinkled like wind chimes. Teishin sprang to a sitting position. "Mother!" he said to the empty room.

There was no mistaking the smell of freshly cooked rice. Teishin rubbed his eyes, thinking he was home in the old farmhouse. Confused, he stood up and made his way to the water closet, slowly understanding that he was at the temple. "Dreams?" he asked himself as he looked down at his own stream splashing against the urinal. It wasn't until he threw cold water on his face at the wooden sink that he remembered failing to sit up all night with the master's remains. Today they would go into the Tanaka family tomb. His stomach churned and everything was getting dark. As he tried to hold onto the edge of the sink, he let out a moan and slipped to the floor. The priest from Kamakura found him sprawled outside the water closet, his face pressed in a pool of vomit.

Teishin opened his eyes and saw the looming figure of Kensho kneeling by his futon. It all flooded into his brain at once—last night's failed attempt to sit up with the master's august ashes in the altar room, sleeping in the master's bedroom, the confused dreams, passing out and even a vague sense of being carried by Kensho and Konein. Now he pulled himself up to a sitting position and buried his head in his hands.

"It's all right," the tall priest said softly. "You have been under a great deal of stress."

"I am ashamed of my weakness," Teishin bawled.

"No, no," Kensho said softly. "During a long pilgrimage, many will faint. You will continue when you are able."

"The problem is I never have been able." He looked at the priest through eyes brimming with misery. "I have let everyone down. I am a weak man, depending on Keiko-*san* for everything. My spirit is so weak it couldn't keep this miserable body awake for one night's vigil."

Still kneeling by the futon, Kensho placed his hands on his own knees, striking a formal pose. His face fell into a stony expression as he spoke in a low, stern voice. "Teishin-*san*! Stop this self-pity and be a man. Your master chose you to take his place and prepared you well. He was not a foolish man. Why can't you see in yourself those qualities that your master saw in you? He trusted you to carry on. Trust yourself and do what must be done."

The priest bowed and left the room. Stunned, Teishin sat up straight. The words entered his body, bypassed his stomach, and travelled to his heart. For the first time in his life, pain didn't make him hungry. Slowly he stood and made his way to the altar room. He didn't notice the youngest priest cleaning the floor outside the water closet. He didn't hear him call his name. The food smells didn't invite him into the kitchen. Only the black-ribboned portrait of his master drew him. It smiled down on him as Teishin fell prostrate before the altar.

The room was filled with the mute harmonies of incense and flowers. In the silent language of the heart, Teishin asked forgiveness and made brave new vows. And then gradually, a deft and beautiful change took place in the room. Teishin became aware of the ascent of incense smoke, of a section of a large chrysanthemum that weakened and slowly fell to spread its white petals like floral snowflakes on the altar. The petals made the faintest sounds as they fell, like the tread of a spirit.

❀ ❀ ❀

Dr. Ichimura, Keiko and Misako arrived at the temple at eight o'clock. When they heard that Teishin had collapsed, the good doctor wanted to examine him. They were surprised to see Teishin dressed in his ceremonial robes, intending to take part in the ceremony.

"Go to bed and rest, Teishin-*san*," Keiko insisted. "Konein-*san* can perform the ceremony. People will understand that you are ill. It can't be helped."

Teishin allowed the doctor to take his blood pressure and listen to his heart but he made it clear that he had no intention of going to bed.

"Your blood pressure is on the high side. I think the stress you have been going through is affecting your body. Passing out is a serious warning. I am afraid I am going to have to insist that you rest."

"I can't do that, I'm sorry," Teishin said. "I am fine now."

Keiko was kneeling on the *tatami* in front of him. She leaned forward and peered into his face. "You don't look fine. You look pale. You should be in bed."

"Impossible." Teishin said in an uncharacteristically serious voice. "Thank you for your concern but you know that I must take part in my master's burial service. Not to do so is unthinkable."

Teishin's show of defiance was a side of the priest that no one had ever seen before. Keiko worried it was a result of the talk she had had with him two days before. She hadn't meant to be so hard on him. She never meant for him to leave a sickbed to carry on! Dr. Ichimura frowned at his wife and shook his head. She knew he disapproved of her interfering in Teishin's business.

"Very well, have it your way," Keiko sighed. She knew people were beginning to arrive and they couldn't discuss the situation in front of strangers. The ceremony was set for ten o'clock.

※　※　※

"No matter what you say, or how you try to excuse it, the entire situation sounds terrible to me. I know Hideo has always been the apple of your eye, but you have spoiled him with your overindulgence. Now you see the results. Selfishness! I'm sorry if it hurts your feelings, but even if you are my older sister, I can't pretend to approve of what your son is about to do to his wife. What is Misako-*san* to do? It's awful."

Mother Imai sat in her sister's Western-style living room, her face registering the pain of the words being flung at her over the English bone china. After their argument, Hideo had left the house and didn't return until early that morning. His mother tried to talk to him, but he only changed clothes and went right out again, refusing to say a word to her. He wouldn't even sit down for the breakfast she made. When he slammed the kitchen door, Mother Imai felt frustrated and confused.

As soon as she was dressed, she went to pay her sister an early morning visit. She wasn't sure she was doing the right thing but she had to talk to someone. For the entire twenty-minute ride, Mother Imai sat in the back of the taxi mumbling to herself, trying to justify her actions. "Men don't realize what a woman of my age goes through. Putting such a burden on me and then leaving me alone with no one to turn to was cruel. It would be difficult enough for a woman half my age."

The sisters sat on big, stuffed chairs with a French provincial coffee table between them. They were four years apart in age, but it looked more like ten. Mother Imai's sister was slim and dressed expensively. A two-carat emerald-cut diamond flashed on her hand, broadcasting her husband's success.

The only door to the room was closed to keep the maid from listening. Although the mistress of the house was accustomed to her older sister's excitable nature, she couldn't help but react to the extraordinary news with horror.

"How perfectly awful to treat a young wife that way," she snapped, thinking of her own recently married daughter. Mother Imai stiffened and realized that coming here had been a mistake. She had said more than she intended. She really only meant to tell her sister that Hideo was thinking of divorcing Misako because Misako couldn't have children, which she now believed to be true. Once she started talking, she got carried away and blurted out that there was a pregnant mistress he wanted to marry as soon as possible.

"Dreadful," the sister said. "Hideo is acting like a selfish child. I hope you told him how disgraceful his actions are."

Poor Mother Imai cried into her lace-trimmed handkerchief, muttering about her shame and helplessness. "If I don't cooperate with Hideo," she said between sobs, "he said he will divorce Misako anyway, marry the other woman and move out of the house. Then I would be alone and you know I couldn't stand that." Her lower lip quivered as she spoke. "I always hated to be alone, even as a child, you must remember that. With Papa dead, what am I to do?"

Her sister jumped from her seat and paced around the room. "What a dastardly threat!" she said angrily. "What is happening to the younger generation? They are losing their values, their sense of responsibility. A son would never say such a thing to his mother before."

Mother Imai looked up at her sister with the expression of an abandoned child. "What can I do? I know I have spoiled Hideo but after a miscarriage, and then losing my infant girl, I was so happy to have a son. He is all I have."

Her sister had heard the bid for sympathy and frowned. At least this complaining older sister had a son. She herself had only two daughters.

"And what does Misako-*san* think of all this?" the younger sister asked.

Mother Imai answered in a small, tearful voice, "I don't know. I don't think Hideo has told her yet. She left for Niigata yesterday and Hideo just gave me the news last night."

"Unbelievable!" her sister snapped, and continued to walk around the room.

"Today is the forty-ninth-day ceremony of her grandfather's death. She will be back in Tokyo in a couple of days." Mother Imai sobbed into her handkerchief again. "I don't know how I am going to face my daughter-in-law."

The younger sister took a box of tissues from a cupboard and placed them on the table next to the tea cups. "Here, blow your nose, it's getting red," she said in a softer tone of voice. Sitting back down in the chair, she leaned toward Mother Imai.

"Listen," she said, "you have to take Misako-*san*'s side in this. She is your daughter now. She left her home in Niigata to come into your home as a bride. It is not her fault she hasn't had a child. Probably she suffers from it more than you know. Stand by her and ignore Hideo's empty threats. It's nonsense. How could he afford such comfortable quarters to live in these days? Don't you let him twist you around his finger. Be strong."

Mother Imai blew her nose. "What about the child that the girl is carrying?" she asked in a small voice. "It is Hideo's child, my grandchild. He told me."

"Honestly, you can be so naive," her sister said, pouring fresh tea into their cups.

"Don't even think about it. You don't know if there really is a child. You believe whatever he tells you. Those kind of girls are always pulling that trick to get a man to marry them. Where is the proof? My guess is there is no baby."

"No baby?" Mother Imai repeated the words and then started to cry again, this time much louder.

❀ ❀ ❀

Neither mother nor daughter wore kimono for the forty-ninth-day memorial service. Keiko was business-like in her tailored black suit. Misako wore her long-sleeved, black dress. The flared skirt spread out around her gracefully as she knelt during the ceremony. The dress had a small white collar that gave her face that innocent schoolgirl look Kensho so admired. He couldn't help stealing discreet glances in her direction. He noticed something different about her lovely eyes this morning, a new intensity. Every time he looked her way, she seemed to be staring at Teishin.

No matter how she tried, Misako wasn't able to give today's ceremony the concentration the memory of her grandfather deserved. There were moments when she managed to think of the times they had spent together, but those thoughts were like small birds, never staying long enough on any one branch.

Stubbornly, the nightmare image of her grandfather's shadowy figure melting into Teishin's body dominated her mind's eye. It was so real! She kept looking at his back as he chanted the sutra, half expecting him to turn his head at any moment and reveal an old smiling face. The fright she had experienced the night before was still clutching at her heart. If she could talk to him alone, perhaps Kensho could help her understand.

A fine, cold rain was falling as the old priest's ashes were finally placed in his family's tomb. The temple's graveyard was a soggy space invaded by people, flowers and prayer boards. Clouds of blue incense smoke continued to rise toward the dreary sky even after the chants had faded. Everyone spoke in hushed tones and drifted away in small groups. Keiko was trapped in conversation by two elderly women. She excused herself and left to make sure that the arrangements for lunch were going well.

Kensho saw Misako and Teishin together under an umbrella, their heads bent in serious conversation. Misako took a white handkerchief from her sleeve and touched it to Teishin's forehead. There was something surprisingly tender and intimate about this interaction. "Of course," Kensho thought, "they have known each other for years. He is like her uncle." Under his breath, he once again called himself a fool for almost allowing another pang of jealousy.

133

With Misako away, Hideo went to see a lawyer. He sat at an office desk belonging to Yukio Fukusawa, attorney-at-law, and talked about his desire to divorce his wife and marry his younger, pregnant mistress. Both men wore starched white shirts and the same shade of grey wool suits. Only their ties differed. The lawyer's was a deeper shade of blue.

"Well, there it is," Hideo said. "I don't want to hurt my wife too much but because of the circumstances, I want the divorce as soon as possible."

The lawyer leaned back in his chair and played with a pencil as he spoke. "In this day and age, you don't have the best of cases. Are you sure your wife hasn't had a boyfriend, a lover during your marriage, anything that could justify your infidelity?"

Hideo dragged on his cigarette and laughed nervously. "No, never, I'm sure of that. Why talk about infidelity at all? Can't I get a divorce because the marriage isn't working? What about the fact that there are no children?"

"Not a case these days," the lawyer said, removing his thick glasses and polishing them with a handkerchief. "I am sure you have heard the cliché that since the end of the war, Japanese women and nylon stockings have gotten stronger. Women have more rights, these days. Ha, ha! Not having a son is no longer a reason to divorce a woman. I have known men who put off entering the name of their wife in their family register until she has produced a son. Maybe you should have thought about that."

"Are you telling me it is not possible to get a divorce under the circumstances?" Hideo was becoming annoyed with the lawyer.

"Imai-*san*, I didn't say that. I am making the point that it is not as easy as it once was. A mistress isn't a valid reason for divorce, unless your wife agrees to it. No problem with a mutual-agreement divorce. Just a matter of signing papers. If that's not possible, you will have to go to family court and that can take a very long time."

"How long?" Hideo asked.

"Usually you attend one session a month. It all depends on how stubborn your wife is."

"Damn!" Hideo cursed. "Time is important." He puffed on his cigarette and slumped in the chair, pouting like a child. He was used to getting his own way and had not foreseen such a complicated process. He looked at the small man with the heavy glasses and regretted his choice of lawyers. He wasn't telling Hideo what he wanted to hear.

"All right then, you're the lawyer. How would you advise me?"

"Ah," the lawyer grinned, showing his protruding teeth. "It is better to avoid any domestic fights. You want her to sign a paper saying she agrees to a divorce and she will give up any claims to the Imai family. That will be difficult if she is really angry. Then, you are going to have to offer her some sort of a settlement. Better a lump sum rather than a monthly allowance. In the long run, it is cheaper. Besides, new wives don't like their husbands shelling out money to an ex every month." He winked and lit a cigarette. "How much can you afford?" The cigarette smoke carried the words across the desk.

Hideo sucked air through his clenched teeth, the sound that Japanese men make when they are perplexed. "I'll have to discuss it with my uncle. He's in charge of our family business. I'm not sure what I am entitled to since my father's death."

"These things are never pleasant. Fortunately there are no children, but still it will be difficult for her to go back into the work force."

Both men sucked on their cigarettes for a few silent seconds and blew smoke in each other's direction.

"Can't send a wife off to a Buddhist nunnery anymore," the lawyer laughed, enjoying his own joke. Hideo didn't join in. The lawyer became serious and leaned across the desk. "Imai-*san*, the answer to your problem is to get your wife to agree to a mutual-agreement divorce. That is the fastest road. Otherwise, it will take time and trouble."

"I need to know how much time and how much trouble," Hideo said.

The lawyer shook his head. It was his turn to make the tooth-sucking expression of difficulty. "Family courts have gotten tough since women were allowed to become board members. If you run into a modern woman, she won't be sympathetic to a man wanting to divorce his wife for a pregnant mistress. It only takes one board member to put you up against a wall." He clenched his teeth and sucked in more air. "It is a matter of great delicacy."

"I understand," Hideo said and stood up. The men put their cigarettes out in different ashtrays. The lawyer came around the desk to see his client out. He was almost a head shorter than Hideo. They bowed to each other and Hideo left. He wasn't satisfied. He wanted a lawyer who would fix things, but this one had thrown the ball back into Hideo's court. This lawyer must be dreaming, he thought. How was he going to get Misako to sign a mutual-agreement divorce paper? He wasn't sure how much she knew about Fumiko, but she knew something. Hideo decided that he was the one who should talk to Misako. He knew he would be better at sweet-talking her into signing an agreement than his foolish lawyer.

"Shit!" he said and punched the elevator button several times. It seemed to be stuck two floors above. "Nothing works in this damned building! Shit!"

FOURTEEN

*T*he women from the congregation tied their kimono sleeves back with colourful cords and began to clear the luncheon remains. Laughter and clinking dish sounds came from the kitchen. Keiko and Misako worked to arrange the altar room as it had been before the death. The old master's mortuary tablet and picture joined those of his wife, sons and parents in their family shrine, a gorgeous upright chest in gold and black lacquer. It stood in the corner of an enclosed eight-*tatami* mat space off the big altar room.

By early evening, the pulse of the temple slowed to a sigh. After all these weeks of mourning, something was released. It floated from room to room, soundless and odourless. Misako felt its soothing touch as she sat alone before the family shrine. Was this the lingering whisper of the tranquility of the man who had lived within these walls for so very long? Misako studied the writing on her grandfather's mortuary tablet, slowly mouthing his Buddha name: *Shaku Chiken*, meaning wisdom, manifestation and revelation.

It is in Teishin's hands, she thought with a sigh. Grandfather had no living blood sons but he has Teishin-*san*, who is as devoted as any son could be. He also has a very strong daughter. The second part of that thought comforted Misako. "And a granddaughter," a voice said from somewhere in her head. Why had it never occurred to her before that she too carried a responsibility to the Tanaka family? Wasn't she the only blood link to her grandfather in her generation? She had been surprised to learn that he had wanted her to marry a priest and carry on the family line. That made her smile. Of course she would never have considered it. All that dedication to the family was old stuff from the Meiji era. Girls of her generation dreamed of a modern love marriage, wearing a white wedding dress, walking up the aisle of a foreign church, like Elizabeth Taylor in *Father of the Bride*. Now that seemed shallow and selfish. A love marriage to a handsome man had not brought her happiness. It hadn't brought her the security of a kind husband, children and a sweet home. As the approaching night sucked the light from the room, Misako bowed her head before the family shrine and shed silent tears.

Dr. Ichimura arrived at the temple to examine Teishin again. Misako waited for him, sitting with Kensho, warming their hands over a ceramic hibachi. Weakened by emotion, she started to tell the priest about her strange nightmare. Calmly and softly, Misako spoke of flying through the night, down the cold streets. She described the altar, the way it looked and smelled, and the way the candles burned out. She recounted how Teishin was sleeping and how she watched something leave the altar and melt down into his body. Kensho listened to this fantastic story in amazement. When she stopped talking, he could do nothing but shake his head.

"I don't know what it means," he said honestly. "A dream usually needs unravelling. You describe it so vividly, like something that really happened."

"It felt so real, especially with the incense smell on my sleeping kimono. I swear it reeked, as if I had been burning incense for hours. I smelled it when I was awake. It wasn't my imagination."

"Has the sleeping kimono been washed?" he asked.

Misako put her hand over her mouth. "I threw it in the laundry basket. Mother has a maid who does the laundry twice a week. I don't know if it has been washed or not."

Two rooms away, the priest, Teishin, looked at a folded piece of paper that contained a sedative. "I'll take it tonight," he told Dr. Ichimura.

"No, you will take it now. You put a futon down and I'll get you a glass of water. I'm serious, Teishin-*san*. I'm ordering you to go to bed and get some real rest. I'm not leaving this room until you are completely settled. I am going to make an appointment for you at the Shibata General Hospital for a complete examination."

"But I have important things to do," Teishin protested.

"Not as important as your health. I don't want to hear any more excuses. Do you want me to tell my wife to talk to you? "

The thought of Keiko's displeasure ended the discussion. "This day is almost over. I might as well get a good sleep," he said.

"That's a good fellow," the doctor said. "You can start tomorrow feeling better."

Kensho looked troubled as he rubbed his hands together over the hibachi. "There must be an explanation," he told Misako. "If the sleeping kimono is still there, check it again. Smelling the incense may have been part of the dream."

"Teishin-*san* had strange dreams last night as well. He told me about them after the ceremony. He said he felt very shaken and tired from the dreams. Did you notice how different he is today?"

"Teishin-*san* stayed up most of the night in the altar room. Anyone could have strange dreams after the stress that you both have been experiencing."

Misako's eyes darkened. "You think I am exaggerating, don't you?"

Kensho wanted to be able to comfort her, to tell her what it all meant, but this dream experience was beyond him. "I can only say again that there is so much I don't know. I have heard of long-distance out-of-body experiences but it is far, far beyond my understanding."

"Out-of-body experience? What exactly are you talking about?" Misako was puzzled.

"I meant a spirit leaving its body and travelling to another place. I thought that was what you were describing."

"But, I have never even heard of such a thing," Misako said with wonder. "Is it possible?"

"Some people believe it is indeed possible. Frankly, I'm not comfortable with the idea of spirits floating around while people sleep."

Beginning to sweat, Kensho removed a wad of tissues from his sleeve and began to wipe his brow. "Honestly, Misako-*san*, this is confusing. Could you have picked up the vibrations of Teishin-*san*'s struggle to keep his vigil last night? You were asleep but your antenna was also attuned to what was going on at the temple. Perhaps that may have resulted in your dream."

"But, what about the incense smell? It was real. I swear it."

Kensho rested his right elbow on his left wrist and covered his eyes with his hand as if this pose could help him think. "If it was possible for your energy or spirit to travel to the altar room last night, could it have brought the incense smell back with it? Certainly your body didn't travel there and your sleeping kimono was on your body."

Misako moved her head in agreement and stared into the glowing coals in the hibachi. "Can two different people's dreams be connected? In my dream I saw Grandfather enter what looked like Teishin-*san*'s body. Today, he told me that in his dream, he sometimes felt as if he was reliving parts of Grandfather's life. In other parts of Teishin-*san*'s dream, he was himself reliving his own past."

"Did he tell you his actual dream?" the priest asked.

"It was all a jumble, but he did say that he dreamed he was a young boy being taught calligraphy by his father. Teishin-*san*'s own father never studied calligraphy. It was my grandfather who was taught calligraphy by his father."

Kensho frowned and thought a moment. Did he use any of your grandfather's mannerisms?"

"I don't think so," Misako said with a little shiver. "He wasn't like Grandfather, but he wasn't entirely like himself either. He seemed depressed and the box of cakes I brought from Tokyo is still sitting on the shelf unopened. In the past, he would have eaten them all in one day."

"Poor Teishin-*san* has been through a great deal since your grandfather's death. I don't doubt that he is depressed and has lost his interest in food."

"That's true," she said with a sigh.

Kensho shook his head sadly. "We should try to forget all this and go back to our own lives. We both have problems to face. I have to leave tomorrow."

"I go back the day after," Misako said. "I certainly have problems to face at home, but I just can't forget how Grandfather died. I will always know that he wanted the unknown girl's ashes to be returned to her ancestors. I really feel I let him down."

The priest felt a wash of tenderness for her and wished they were standing at the kitchen entrance. He longed to hold her once again.

"Give it time," he said softly. You will feel better about it in a few months. The box of unknown ashes is in the altar room, out of the way. Perhaps it will all soon be forgotten."

They heard Dr. Ichimura's voice in the hallway. It was time for Misako to leave. She and the priest looked at each other in silence for a long two seconds before she got up to greet her stepfather. Volumes of thoughts and emotions silently passed between them.

They said goodbye at the temple gate. There were bows and promises to contact each other. Kensho watched the car drive away and then went into the temple through the kitchen entrance. He sat down on the step where Misako had once stood and put her head on his shoulder. Then he took a black slicker from a hook and set out for a walk in the rain.

❀ ❀ ❀

Barren Twisted Tree
The Nightingale stops to sing
Forgotten Life Stirs.

Writing poems was the tall priest's secret pleasure. No one suspected it of him, not even the other priests at his temple in Kamakura. Considering his poems poor and his reasons personal, he had never shared even one of them. The poems did not follow prescribed rules; they were simply words that came to him in quiet hours, bits of deeply felt emotion.

It was his habit to write these poems on small pieces of rice paper. After reading his poem several times, he would fold the paper and carry it on his person until he threw it away in some fashion that was meaningful to him. Once or twice, he even ate them.

Some of the poem papers were folded into small birds that were sent flying from high places. Other poems ended as up as boats or fish that would journey down a river or a stream. Most often, he would tie the bit of paper to a tree in a secluded place where only the breeze found it of interest.

That night, Kensho wrote his poem in the silence of the temple. Indeed, he thought of himself as a barren, twisted tree and Misako as the delicate nightingale that had brought a new dimension of love to his life. He had felt it when she confided in him during the train ride to Niigata and again when they warmed their hands together and talked.

After putting the writing brushes away, he turned off the small lamp and sat with his back against the wall. He was too emotionally exhausted to meditate or practice any form of discipline tonight. He could only stretch out his long legs on the *tatami* floor and give himself to the pleasure of thinking of Misako.

Misako, sweet Misako. As if to pray, he pressed his hands together with the poem paper flattened between his palms. There had been so much sadness since that first telephone call from the old master. He heard Misako's pain from her own lips on the train, not only for her grandfather but the sadness of her failing marriage. Was he the only one who experienced a portion of joy during this terrible time? The joy came from being with Misako and the way she had confided in him, trusted him.

Alone now, he was too tired to judge himself, to be brave or noble. He simply needed to let go. He was allowing himself to remember her eyes and rejoicing in the memory of holding her for just that short minute, of touching her hand for barely a second. Oh joy!

The other priests were deep in sleep. The only sound was the rain beating hard on the temple's roof. The tall, strange, misfit of a priest sat alone in the dark, unfamiliar room feeling utterly elated. The personal vow he had made not to desire a woman was now a lifeline lost in the flow of rushing waters. He could do nothing but swim with the flow and relish the sensation of life before drowning. He put his hand in his sleeping kimono and pressed the poem paper against his most tender self. "Misako-*san*," he murmured again and again, and gave himself up to being a man.

FIFTEEN

*A*s soon as Misako entered the house in Tokyo she felt a smothering sense of oppression. Something was different. She stood in the foyer and sniffed the air like an animal. "*Tadaima,*" she called into the stillness. There was no answer. She put her suitcase down and called again. "I'm home." Silence was a rare occupant in the home where the senior Mrs. Imai lived, and now silence hovered about like a sinister presence.

"Mother? Are you here?" Misako went through to the dining room and into the sitting room. Misako felt short of breath as she climbed the stairs and stood outside her mother-in-law's closed bedroom door.

"Mother? Are you in there?" She knocked and heard a small whimper.

"What's wrong?" Misako cried as she slid open the door and rushed to kneel beside the futon. Mrs. Imai was in her bed with the covers pulled over her head.

"What's the matter? Are you ill?" Misako asked the faceless mound of quilts.

"No! No!" came the muffled voice. "I'm tired. Just let me sleep."

"Mother, come out of there and let me see you or I will call the doctor."

"No, I want to sleep," Mrs. Imai answered, still covered.

"You never sleep in the daytime. Let me see your face or I'll call the doctor right now."

Slowly the covers came down and Mother Imai's head emerged, looking up at Misako with red, mournful eyes.

"What's the matter? What happened?" Misako was frightened.

"Nothing, nothing," she said, but the tears rolling down her cheeks told another story.

"Mother, look at you. I have never seen you in such a state. Tell me, please, what is wrong?"

Mother Imai managed to sit up and brushed at her tears with the sleeve of her cotton kimono. "It's too much! I am so ashamed of my son. What am I to do, caught in the middle like this? It's too much for me. I'm not young anymore. It's too much." Her whole body was shaking as she spoke.

"What is too much? Mother tell me. What?"

143

She looked at her daughter-in-law through pools of tears. "Misako. No matter what happens, I am on your side. I know we haven't always been on good terms but, I don't want you to leave this house. You have been a good daughter." She kept dabbing her eyes and sniffing as she spoke. Her words were coming out at a feverish pace. "Don't let him do it," she pleaded, catching Misako's sleeve and pulling her toward her. "Don't let him send you away. Fight back!"

"Who is going to send me away? Where? What are you talking about?"

"Hideo! He wants to divorce you. He wants to marry that young hussy because she tells him she is having his baby. He said he wants a son and you will never be able to have a child. I believe she's lying. She isn't pregnant at all. It's her trick to get Hideo to divorce you and marry her."

Misako was stunned. She felt as if cement was being poured over her head and she was slowly turning into a lifeless statue. It seemed an eternity before she could speak.

"Divorce? Wants me out of this house? And when is Hideo supposed to tell me all this?"

Mother Imai looked at her with the expression of a frightened animal. "As soon as you came home from Niigata. I think tonight."

Misako's gaze turned icy through half-closed eyes. "Why then are you telling me before he does? Did Hideo tell you to tell me?"

"No, No! I did it because I want to help you. I want you to be prepared. I can help you fight. With the two of us against him, he'll forget that hussy. My sister said so."

"Your sister knows about this?" Misako stood up and turned quickly, bolting out of the room and down the stairs. She picked up her blue suitcase and left the house. The bell on the kitchen door jingled violently. Upstairs Mother Imai heard the bell. She got up from her bed and staggered toward the stairs.

"Misako, Misako," she called. "Where are you going? Wait!" The bell faded into a tinkle and stopped. Mother Imai sat on the top step pushing the hair from her forehead. Then she put her head in her hand and sobbed. "Hideo will be furious with me. Furious."

A surge of blind fury sent Misako flying out of the house and up the street. Everything she saw had turned to a vivid shade of red. Red children passed on their way home from school as red housewives stood outside a store in red aprons with red baskets on their arms. They turned to watch the intense young woman running past them with a blue suitcase.

Misako wasn't thinking of where she was going or what she was going to do. She was so angry that she just had to get away from the Imai house. At a busy intersection, she stopped in time to see the traffic light change from one red to another. Her head was spinning. She couldn't decide whether to cross the street or stay standing on the curb. A taxi turned the corner and she hailed it.

"Ueno Station, please." The words were automatic, programmed. Whenever she left the house with a suitcase, she went to Ueno Station for a train to Niigata. The driver pulled the lever to close the door behind her. She slumped into the corner of the back seat, relieved that the taxi would take her further away from the house. She closed her eyes and the spinning in her head became slower and slower. When she opened them, the red glow had faded to a pale pink. The driver was looking at her through the rearview mirror.

"Are you ill, Miss?" he asked.

"No, I'm all right. I mean, I felt faint for a moment, but it has passed now. Thank you."

She took a handkerchief from her purse and wiped her face and neck. The taxi was making its way through the big, impersonal city. Normal city greys were washing away the pink. She could see people on the streets and in cars, on their way to various destinations, and she began to ask herself why she was going to Ueno Station. She had just come back from Niigata. Going back wouldn't solve anything. But if she went back to the Imai house there would be a terrible scene with her mother-in-law.

The taxi had stopped for a light. On the street ahead she saw the marquee of a movie theatre. It featured the famous face of the actor Toshio Mifune dressed as a samurai.

"I'd like to get out here, please," she said to the surprised taxi driver.

"Here? I thought you wanted to go to Ueno Station." The light changed to green.

"I've changed my mind. Please let me out here." The car behind them honked its horn. The driver flipped the meter and opened the door, cursing under his breath. Misako handed him a thousand-yen note for a five-hundred-yen fare and dashed out of the car.

The man who took her movie ticket eyed her suitcase with suspicion and informed her that the movie was halfway finished. She sat in the back of the theatre and soon became absorbed with a roving samurai of old Japan as he defended a helpless village of peasants against a band of nasty bandits. The sword-fighting scenes were particularly gratifying and justice prevailed. Somehow, it gave her a sense of hope. She sat through the entire film a second time.

After the movie, she ate a bowl of hot noodles at a corner shop and found herself thinking about bamboo. There was an earthquake in the film and the samurai had directed the village children to the bamboo grove. The bamboo survives the cataclysmic whims of nature because bamboo bends and moves with the earth. One can't run away from an earthquake. Misako knew from experience that her mother-in-law overreacted to everything. Now she wondered if everything that Mother Imai told her was true. It was better to go home, to calmly hear what Hideo had to say.

The television was on when she returned home. Mother Imai got out of her chair to greet her but the older woman looked exhausted. Misako apologized for dashing out of the house. "It was a shock but I know it is not your fault. I would prefer to speak to Hideo before discussing it again."

Mother Imai went back to her television drama and Misako took a bath and went to her room. Hideo had not returned home. It was after nine-thirty.

He arrived after eleven. She heard his steps on the stairs, rather soft, not the heavy, banging steps of his usual late return. At least he wasn't drunk. He slid open their bedroom door and found Misako kneeling before her dressing table, clad in her sleeping kimono. Their futon beds were made up, close together. Hideo raised his eyebrows when he saw them. She was calmly brushing her hair. All he could think to say was, "I'm home." It came out in a small guilty voice. Misako bowed her head in response. Be calm, she told herself with each stroke of her hair brush.

Not prepared for this scene, Hideo faced the wall closet and slowly began to undress, trying to think of his next move. He knew he couldn't stay silent. This was the time to talk about the divorce. He had promised Fumiko. With the beds laid out so close together, he guessed that there was still a chance to tell Misako he was sorry and all would be forgiven. He was tempted to grasp at this chance. He didn't want to hurt his wife. Somehow it could all be worked out, he thought as he loosened his tie. If only they could talk. He moved toward her as he took off his jacket. Something dropped from his pocket and hit the *tatami* floor. The

146

dull thump made her look around. Hideo recognized Fumiko's lipstick. Misako moved quickly and picked it up. His face flushed. Damn Fumiko! he thought. Damn her!

"You dropped something," Misako's voice was bitter.

"What?" he asked trying to sound as if he hadn't noticed.

"This lipstick. It fell from your pocket when you took your jacket off."

Hideo let out an angry grunt and moved back to the closet. "I don't feel like joking. I don't wear lipstick. It's yours. I didn't drop it. It must have been on the floor and I accidentally kicked it."

"Impossible! It's not mine," Misako said, tossing it at him. He kicked it aside and turned his back to her again, taking off his shirt.

"Does it belong to her? Your mistress?" she asked.

Hideo managed a brave laugh and simply said: "Crazy."

"I am not so crazy that I don't know my own lipstick. I don't buy that kind. It's a cheap brand. It fell out of your pocket."

"I've never seen it before," he insisted in a perfectly controlled, flat voice.

Misako's calm was melting away. The rejection hurt badly; her hands began to shake. The wall of tranquillity that she had worked to build up was crumbling. There was no bamboo grove here. Flames were igniting. This was a war zone. Her anger exploded.

"You are a liar!" she shouted. "Liar! Cheat! Coward! You couldn't even tell me to my face about wanting a divorce. You had your mother do it."

Hideo went on folding his trousers. The thought of apologizing vanished. He hated a screaming scene but he knew it would be easier now; Misako was losing control. He kept himself from lashing back. He ignored her angry words. His indifference infuriated her more. Without even trying he was going to turn things around to his advantage. She was shouting and she knew it was ugly, yet she couldn't stop.

"It's true, isn't it? Answer me. It's true!" Having no response, she threw the hairbrush across the room. It bounced off his shoulder. The action surprised her more than it did Hideo. Immediately she knew it was a mistake and now she was making it even worse by standing up and facing him as if in battle. "Aren't you going to say anything?" she screamed. "Or should we call your mother in here to talk for you?"

"Sit down and stop acting like a maniac. Control yourself," he commanded.

Misako fell back down on her knees. The tide had turned, as it always did when she argued with Hideo. No matter what he did, she was the one who ended up in the wrong.

"I do want a divorce, but I didn't want my mother to tell you first. That was an accident, it just happened. We are adults here, I think. No one is murdering you. There is no need to carry on like this. We can talk things out and decide the best course to take."

Misako stayed sitting on her knees trying to control herself. "Is it true that your mistress is pregnant?" Her voice was normal again.

"Yes," he answered without emotion.

"And you want to divorce me to marry her? Is that right?"

"That's right. I'm sure you can understand it." He made it sound so simple, as if he was saying: "I'm sure you will understand my being late for dinner."

"Because I haven't gotten pregnant? "

"I didn't expect that when we married. It is a disappointment to me. Now I have conceived a child and I want to marry the mother. It's natural."

"Natural," Misako repeated.

"Absolutely normal!" he said. "A man must be a man. A woman must be a woman." His tone was that of a teacher speaking to a student. "It is natural for a man to want a son."

"And is it natural to get a woman pregnant when you already have a wife?" Misako asked with more spirit. She knew now there was no turning back. She was hurt and she wanted to strike.

"Already have a wife?" he mocked by repeating her words. I have a wife who not only can't give me a son, but a wife who doesn't know how to please her husband. That's the kind of wife I have."

"*Ah so!*" was all she could think to say. The sting of his words was sharp. She was no match for Hideo in this kind of exchange. Tears rolled down her cheeks.

"Anyway, what's done is done," Hideo said. There is no use in fighting over what can't be helped. The only thing to do is to agree on an amicable divorce. The quicker the better."

"You make it sound so easy." Misako said in defeat.

"It will be difficult only if you insist on making it that way. My lawyer said that if we both agree, it could be done quickly and cleanly."

"But I'm your wife! What am I to do? Where am I to go?"

"Your family will take you back. Of course, I will give you money to start a new life."

Misako's eyes widened as she echoed his words. "A new life."

"Why not? You are not so old and you are still pretty. Maybe you can marry a nice widower with children like your mother did. If you could have children, this wouldn't have happened."

"So, you are saying it is all my fault," Misako said, dabbing her tears with the sleeve of her sleeping kimono.

"It certainly isn't my fault," Hideo said with a sneer. "I've proved I can father a child."

Trying to control the flood of tears, Misako turned away. Hideo sat down on the futon.

"You are a weak man," she said softly to his back, "not the man I married. You have changed. You hide behind the fact that we have no children to justify your lust for another woman. We could adopt a son like other childless couples. It is not unusual. You are just using it as an excuse to get rid of me." Her feelings had shaken loose and now they tumbled out.

"I've had enough," Hideo cut her off. "I'm tired. I worked all day and I have a busy day tomorrow. You can talk to my lawyer or get your own. I don't want to hear any more tonight." He fell back on the futon and pulled the quilt up over his shoulders.

"In other words, the subject is closed," Misako hissed at him, but he turned his back to her and put his head under the quilt.

Frustration made her want to stand up and shout but there was no use. The lord and master had spoken; the subject was closed. He outranked her and she had been cast aside. It was so unfair!

A sound from the other side of the bedroom wall told her that Mother Imai was at her listening post. She knew there was nothing more to do or say. If she went out into the hallway, her mother-in-law would be out of her room in a flash and she didn't want to face her. Misako hated sleeping in this room tonight, so close to Hideo. She was trapped.

She took a sleeping pill from the dressing table and swallowed it without water. The black and gold lipstick case caught her eye on the other side of the room where Hideo had kicked it. She moved softly and picked it up before she turned off the light.

There was something new in her mind now. Something the priest from Kamakura had said. It was about a clairvoyant who located a child by holding an object belonging to the missing child. The clairvoyant had a vision through the vibrations from the object. It was mildly interesting when she first heard it, but now it seemed important. Misako wanted to see this mistress of Hideo's. She wanted to face the woman who was stealing her husband, who was having the child she should be having. Who is this woman? If she's not a bar girl, then perhaps someone new at the office. Where else would he meet a woman?

Misako's eyes were growing heavy. She felt as if she was in an airplane, descending and descending and descending, until the little pill took her to a place of suspended consciousness which she entered with her hand tightly enclosed around the lipstick.

In the hours before dawn, Misako slowly ascended, corpse-like in her futon, free of her pain, keenly aware of every soft utterance, every dim sound of night and nature. Behind closed eyes, she saw the sliver of a bright new moon. It hung in the dark void of her mind, appealing with its beauty and crystal aspiration to the silent intellect that survives at the core of every human heart. When the temple bell droned in the distance, it formed a sound bridge to a deep and healing sleep.

SIXTEEN

Plunk, plunk, plunk. The sound of the three-stringed *samisen*, followed by Mother Imai's melodious wailing, flushed up through the floor and woke Misako. It was eight o'clock in the morning, the day of her mother-in-law's classical singing lesson. For a few minutes, Misako lay very still, lost in listening. And then the lipstick caught her eye. It was on the *tatami* floor, next to the futon. The sun coming in the bedroom window sparkled off the black and gold case. It flashed back all the details of her ruined marriage. Misako sprang from the bed, retrieved the lipstick and examined it carefully in the morning light. It wasn't true that it was a cheap brand; she had said that out of jealousy. It actually was an expensive American brand. She uncapped it, observed the bright red colour and smelled it.

The old teacher was singing with Mother Imai. They repeated two lines of a song over and over again until Mother Imai broke into a fit of giggles.

"Who do you belong to?" Misako asked the lipstick as she placed it down on her dressing table. "Some new female working in Hideo's office?"

Plunk, plunk, plunk. Downstairs the two women carried on with sheets of music spread out before them on the *tatami* floor. "One more time," the old one demanded, plunking away and singing the line slowly for her student to repeat. Mother Imai tried her best. The kimono-clad teacher moved her head in approval even though her student was not doing well today. The problem was that Mother Imai had completely forgotten it was the day for her music lesson until the teacher was standing in the Imai foyer, calling out, "*Ohayo gozaimasu*, good morning." Fortunately, Mother Imai was dressed and could cover her surprise and lack of preparation with a laugh. What she couldn't cover was the absence of her daughter-in-law, who was usually in attendance, preparing tea and serving fruit and cakes.

When the lesson was over, the ancient one lit a cigarette and waited until her student had served her tea before asking about the absent daughter-in-law.

Mother Imai was by nature a truthful person. "Poor Misako-*san* is not

151

well this morning," she managed to answer without giving the details. She certainly was not lying.

"Morning sickness?" the teacher asked with a puff of smoke and a knowing wink. "Am I right in thinking that you are at long last going to be a grandmother?"

Mother Imai flushed and stammered another evasive but truthful answer. "So it seems." Then she hesitated and added, "but not Misako. I mean, Misako is not well from something else this morning."

The old face fell into a sly smile as she lifted her tea cup in a mock toast. "Am I to understand congratulations are in order?"

Mother Imai was mortified by this exchange and petrified that her barren daughter-in-law would come down the stairs and be congratulated for the child that her husband's mistress was in fact carrying. She clasped her bosom and turned pale as a ghost. Sweat broke out on her forehead.

"I'm so sorry, *Sensei*, but I'm not well myself this morning. I've had a headache since last night and neither Misako nor I managed to get much sleep."

"*Ah so!*" The old woman became concerned. The last thing she needed was to get sick. Suppose it was flu! A lot of it has been going around and very early this year. That would be very bad at her age. She finished her cigarette and made an excuse to leave the house that seemed to be contaminated with infectious germs.

"Call me when you are well again. We'll make our next appointment then. Take care of your health." The *Sensei* had packed up her *samisen* in its brocade bag and was bowing herself out the door.

With the teacher gone, Mother Imai realized how exhausted she felt. The day had started in a terrible jumble. After all the unsettling anger she heard pass between her son and his wife last night, she didn't know what was going to happen next. Misako hadn't appeared in the kitchen to make breakfast and Hideo dashed out thirty minutes earlier than usual without uttering a word. Then there was the loss of face, forgetting about the singing lesson. She turned on the television set, sat in her usual chair and mindlessly watched a cooking lesson, mopping her brow with a handkerchief.

Misako finally descended the stairs, poked her head into the dining room and almost sang, "Good Morning," on the way to the kitchen entrance. Mother Imai abandoned the television and quickly moved her ample body to see that Misako was wearing her new red wool suit and putting on her best black leather pumps. She looked as if she was on her way to a fashion show.

"Where are you going so dressed up?"

"Out," was Misako's only reply.

"Out? Where?" the older woman barked.

Misako pulled on her soft black leather gloves and picked up her purse. "Just out!" She smiled, waved and stepped outside into the sunny November day.

Mother Imai stood blinking with surprise. "Where are you going?" she screamed. The kitchen door raced on its rollers and slammed shut. The bell jingled merrily. The senior Mrs. Imai burst into tears.

It was such a beautiful morning that Misako walked to Shibuya Station. She stopped for coffee and toast at one of the coffee bars that had been built around the city for the Tokyo Olympics the year before. The rush hour was over by the time she boarded a train to the Marunouchi area, where Hideo's office was located. All during the fifteen-minute train ride, she held the lipstick case in her hand and rubbed the top of it like a worry stone.

When she emerged from the three-flight walk-up of the Hibiya subway station, a poster in the window of the corner travel agency caught her eye. It drew her to the window like a magnet. It showed a snow-covered Swiss mountain and urged people to come and ski where the slopes were uncrowded. Skiing was not in her mind at that moment but there she was, impelled to stand there staring at the poster as she fingered the lipstick case. That was when it happened. Inside the office, behind the counter, was the young woman in her vision, the girl she had seen Hideo with in those two awful scenes. There was no mistake, it was the girl with the big breasts, the bright red mouth, now laughing as she talked to a customer. Misako dropped the lipstick into her handbag and went in.

It promised to be a hectic day at the Marunouchi Branch of the Japan Travel Centre. It was only ten-thirty in the morning and already all three clerks were busy with customers. With the New Year holiday just a little over a month away, people were making their travel arrangements.

Fumiko sat opposite a middle-aged man who was joining a group tour bound for California. Full of happy anticipation, the man joked about the experience he had gained in handling American money during a visit to Okinawa, "Now I am prepared to leave my heart in San Francisco."

Fumiko giggled at his tired joke and tried to wrap things up. His passport and other papers were spread out on the counter between them.

When an attractive young woman in a smart red suit entered the office, Fumiko looked up and watched her examine the brochure rack, take one and sit down. Probably wants to go to Europe, she thought, hurrying the middle-aged man along.

Fumiko was an aggressive salesperson and she wanted to talk to this new potential customer before the other clerks were free. The man finally put his tickets and papers into his briefcase. Fumiko observed that the young woman in the red suit was staring at her rather intensely. She assumed that this meant that the lady was pressed for time. When the man left, Fumiko stood up and called out an apology for the delay.

"I'm in no hurry," the young woman said coldly as she approached the counter.

"Well then, what can I do for you?" Fumiko said, flashing one of her winning smiles and presenting her card. "A shopping trip to Paris perhaps?" A flattering remark. She had considerable talent handling customers and much of it was in the way she could make them feel at ease right from the start. But this wasn't happening. Miss Red Suit wasn't warming to her at all. She had taken the card and rudely shoved it into her jacket pocket. The stern expression in her eyes made Fumiko uneasy.

"I'm not here to plan a trip. I'm here to give you something you lost."

"Lost?" Fumiko said in complete bewilderment. "I don't believe I have lost anything."

"Oh, but you have," Misako assured her, reaching into her handbag and producing a black and gold lipstick case. "You lost this last night."

The lipstick stood upright on the counter that separated them. Fumiko's eyes travelled from the lipstick up to the stranger's face. "Do I know you?" she asked.

"No, you don't know me, but I believe you know my husband, intimately." Before Fumiko could react, the back of the red suit was rushing out the door. The haste with which Misako left was so unusual that the other clerks and customers looked after her. Damn! Fumiko thought as she sat down trying to look composed. Hideo led me to believe his wife was nothing to look at, but that woman was pretty. It had to be his wife. In a state of great irritation, she reached for the phone and dialled Hideo's office number.

Misako escaped down the avenue toward Hibiya Park. She looked

154

like someone desperately trying to catch a bus. Her pulse raced. Her feet moved half a beat under a run. Thoughts roared through her brain like water in a raging mountain stream.

"I can't believe I did that," she told herself. "I can't believe I had the nerve. The expression on that woman's face! Hideo will be seething when he hears. What made me do it? It wasn't a nice thing to do. I should be ashamed."

But Misako wasn't ashamed. She was tasting a drop of revenge which was far sweeter than the utter humiliation she'd had to swallow recently. She crossed the street and slowed her pace. She tried to take a couple of deep breaths as she entered Hibiya Park. Several office workers were out strolling in their shirtsleeves, enjoying the late November sun. Misako sat down on an empty bench and read the name card. Fumiko, is it? So that's my replacement. She put her hand over her mouth. How could I have approached her on something as flimsy as an impulse? No, I am sure I saw her in the visions. But suppose I'm wrong? Suppose that wasn't Hideo's mistress at all?

Misako couldn't suppress a giggle, saying out loud, "If I'm wrong, that travel lady must have thought me a madwoman."

A young man was walking past the bench thrust his hands in his pockets and squinted up at the sky. His good manners demanded that he ignore her, but Misako realized he had heard her. She stood up and started toward the busy Ginza area. She would go to a movie. Everyone was talking about *Dr. Zhivago*, but that was just another sad love story that would make her cry. It was better to go shopping, to walk through the department stores and get lost in a crowd.

The Wako Department Store was one of the best in Tokyo. Misako took time to walk around and admire the expensive merchandise. Upstairs, there was a print exhibition by Toko Shinoda, one of Japan's celebrated women artists. The works were a series of bold black and blue strokes on white backgrounds. There was something calming about the prints. The minimal strokes seemed to be all about inner peace. Misako stood back to study a print when she sensed a very close, very strong presence. She straightened and looked around into the face of one of the most stunning women she had ever seen.

"Misako-*san*? Is that you?" the stranger asked.

Misako caught her breath. She thought the woman must be a movie actress. The beautiful face was highlighted by large pearl earrings and her pencil-thin figure was elegant in a cream-coloured Chanel suit. Her shiny black hair was pulled back and held in a bun at the back of her long neck. Her smile revealed amazingly perfect white teeth.

Misako cocked her head. "I'm sorry, have we met before?."

"Look again. It's me, Sachiko. We went to school together in Shibata."

Misako gasped, "Impossible."

"You can't have forgotten me. We were best friends. I used to call you Chibi-*chan*."

"Sachiko! Is it really you? You are so changed."

"Only the packaging," Sachiko laughed. "Only the packaging."

"But what have you done to yourself?"

"Everything," Sachiko said and let out the infectious giggle that Misako remembered so well. A guard standing in the corner gave them a stern look. Sachiko took Misako's arm and moved her out of the exhibition hall. She looked at her watch. "Let's go someplace quiet. I know a little French restaurant in Roppongi. We can have lunch and talk. How long has it been? Ten, twelve years?"

Their taxi sped across the city while they shared their memories. "Remember Mrs. Arai? We used to call her Old Pumpkin Face. Whatever happened to that boy in the tenth grade you thought you liked? What was his name?" Misako was so caught up in the joy of the moment that Hideo and all their troubles were totally flushed out of her mind.

In spite of the metamorphosis, this was indeed Sachiko Kimura, the kid from the kimono shop. Misako couldn't keep her eyes off her. How could this be the skinny childhood friend? And the teeth! The Sachiko she knew had a mouthful of crooked teeth. This woman's smile was good enough for a toothpaste commercial.

During and after the war, Sachiko and her mother had had to endure more than their share of misery, barely surviving from the earnings from their small kimono shop. Like the father Misako couldn't remember, Sachiko's father had also been a soldier. The difference was that Corporal Kimura had the misfortune of not being killed outright, only gravely wounded.

He returned home with a half-burned face and only one arm, which was merely the physical maiming of his body. Worse were the serious inner wounds, the trauma suffered to his spiritual self that bled every time he was made invisible by people's heads turning away from him. There was no compensation for Japanese war veterans, no cheering parades. Many disabled Japanese war veterans were reduced to donning their tattered uniforms and kneeling on the floors of train stations. Begging was the only occupation available to them. Mr. Kimura's scarred face and empty sleeve announced that he had not been brave enough to die. War heroes of a defeated army were honoured only when they were dead heroes.

On a hot summer day in 1949, Sachiko's father drowned in the waters of the Japan Sea. His mother and wife knew that he had been deeply depressed. They thought it was a positive sign when he set off that morning with a bucket to hunt small shellfish at the seashore. He had promised his thirteen-year-old daughter that they would enjoy a fine soup from his catch that evening. Sachiko, her mother and grandmother stayed up late waiting. He never returned. Days later, his body washed up on a distant beach.

Most small kimono businesses had all but died during the war years. There was no money for luxuries. Civilians no longer had occasions to dress up for. They went to work in factories or helped out in the rice fields.

By 1950, however, the women had survived the desperate years and their small kimono shop was beginning to limp back to life. Sachiko's mother and grandmother were capable of handling the business while Sachiko spent her spare hours learning the technique needed to create tiny, perfect stitches. Things were actually improving until the old woman began fretting about not having a man in the house. The day she invited her youngest son and his family to move back home was the day that Sachiko and her mother's life changed for the worse. Immediately, their living space shrank to one six-*tatami*-mat room in the rear of the shop. The fact that Sachiko's mother was the widow of the eldest son meant nothing. She was now the lowest ranking adult female in the house. The brother's wife treated her and her daughter like the poor rice relatives they had become.

The family's saving grace was Sachiko's mother's skill at sewing; it was the reason she had been chosen as the bride of a kimono shop. She had come from a family of kimono makers. Sewing was in their blood. Her younger sister had married a tailor in Yokohama and it was this "Auntie Yokohama" who was the topic of many conversations between Sachiko and her mother.

After the war, Auntie Yokohama and her husband's business greatly expanded with the influx of foreigners, especially American military personnel. It was a time when impoverished Japanese were selling their skills for almost nothing. American military families were living high on the hog in Japan. Women who had never had domestic help in their lives could now afford two maids. The maids cleaned their houses and took care of their children. That new leisure allowed the ladies to socialize, to play cards in the afternoon and attend parties with their husbands in the evenings. Looking good had never been easier for them. Why do your own hair and nails when the beauty parlours were so cheap? When they needed new clothes, all they had to do was find a picture in a fashion magazine, take it to a Japanese dressmaker, buy the fabric at the PX and in less than a week's time, look like a million bucks, for peanuts.

Auntie Yokohama jumped on that bandwagon early. By the time Sachiko graduated from high school in 1954, Auntie's business was well established. She could afford to do her poor Niigata sister a huge favour and take her daughter on as an apprentice. And because young people now studied English in high school, maybe Sachiko could help her communicate with the customers.

Bright and eager, Sachiko loved the city and she loved dressmaking. Auntie Yokohama was pleased. Her niece was a quick study and a hard worker.

"I am going to become a famous dress designer," Sachiko wrote to her mother that first year. "I can already make a dress pattern and Auntie says I have a real flair for design."

"Work hard and forget about boyfriends," her mother wrote back. "In a few years, your aunt will find you a good husband."

Sachiko laughed when she read the words. Her heart was too full of her own ambitions. There was no room for romantic love. She was already in love with the things that gave her pleasure. She loved the international flavour of Yokohama. She loved spending hours flipping through the shop's pile of foreign fashion magazines. On her days off, she took the train to Tokyo and walked through the best clothing shops. If she dressed nicely, no one was bothered if she sat in the lobby of the Imperial Hotel, notepad on her lap, dashing off quick sketches of a skirt or a jacket.

Within a year, the clothes Sachiko was making for herself had that expensive look and cut. It was amazing how different her long, skinny figure looked in a smart Western suit. She was beginning to look a little like the models in the fashion magazines, as long as she didn't smile. The change in Sachiko's appearance gave Auntie Yokohama mixed feelings. In one way, it was good for the business. The customers trusted Sachiko's taste and she had her own following. Her English had certainly made communication easier; she had even picked up a little French. No one could fault the young woman for not being diligent.

On the other hand, Auntie didn't like being usurped. Sachiko had matured. Many of the foreign customers now asked for Sachiko. They wanted her advice. They wanted her to do the fittings. Auntie worried that they might be confused about just who owned the business.

In 1957, Sachiko's mother died. Auntie Yokohama and Sachiko travelled back to Niigata for the funeral. Sachiko had never before realized how poor her mother had been until she went through her pitiful pile of personal belongings. Her mother hadn't owned one kimono that was made of a fabric worthy of the superb stitches that held it together. The thought of how her mother's talents had been taken advantage of infuriated and saddened Sachiko.

Auntie assumed that her niece's silence on the train ride back to Yokohama was the result of mourning. She never guessed at the volcano of emotions that were dangerously simmering in the young woman's heart. Two days later, Sachiko sat down to talk to her aunt and uncle. She let it be known that she felt she had learned all they had to teach her. She said she had no intentions of reliving her mother's life and that it was time for her to move onto the next level.

"How can you compare your life with your mother's?" Auntie was indignant. "We have given you opportunities your mother never had. We have brought you to a big city and taught you Western dressmaking. Kimono dressing is going to be a thing of the past. Western dresses are the wave of the future."

Being reminded of her debt made Sachiko bow, apologize and thank her aunt and uncle formally. Uncle sighed with relief. Auntie poured more tea, thinking it was the end of her niece's complaints. After all, the girl had just lost her mother.

A week later, Sachiko brought up the subject again. This time she requested a raise in salary. She said she knew that they had been good to her, taught her a trade and given her roof over her head and food in her stomach, but the little money she was given monthly hadn't been increased by a yen in the past three years. Sachiko told her aunt that she needed to save some money. Her plan was to move to Tokyo in the next year and find a job with one of the up-and-coming designers.

Auntie Yokohama's face nearly turned blue with anger. She accused Sachiko of being an ungrateful upstart. "I never heard of anything so crude," she yelled. "Who do you think you are to make such unreasonable demands? You, a penniless, country girl! Have you forgotten that we took you into our home and taught you a lucrative trade? Is that how you thank us?"

Even Sachiko was amazed at how ungrateful she really felt toward her Yokohama relatives. She had worked hard these past three years and she knew her talents had enhanced their business, which was something her aunt never acknowledged. Sachiko said she was tired and not feeling well. She needed some time off. "If I am not an asset to your business, then you can do without me for a week."

There was no doubt in Sachiko's mind that this next step would be a tough one. She was going to stay in a cheap hotel in Tokyo for a week and spend the days trying to find a job in the fashion world. If all else failed, she would become a nightclub hostess. She had heard it was a good way to save money. Once she had money, she could open up her own small shop.

She arrived in Tokyo on a Sunday, and by Friday knew that no one in any design house or high-quality clothing shop was going to give her a break. They looked at her portfolio and admired her drawings, but— "Sorry." Discouraged, Sachiko went for plan two, the temporary solution. She would find a job in a nightclub, and why not try the best ones first? The first two were an instant no-go. The third nightclub she tried was a fairly classy establishment. The woman owner saw potential in Sachiko. She was skinny, but not bad-looking. She already spoke some English and a smattering of French. The only flaw was those teeth. If she wanted to succeed as a hostess, she had to get her teeth fixed.

A curious combination of haughty confidence and rough edges, Mrs. Teguchi observed the young woman who had the nerve to walk in off the street and apply for a job. Carefully groomed and well-preserved, the sixty-something nightclub owner sat behind her desk, fingering her pearls with one hand while holding a cigarette with the other. She was no fool. She was a successful businesswoman who believed in her own gut feelings and she made quick decisions based on them. She had immediately felt that Sachiko was special.

"Miss Kimura, in spite of the fact that you have no experience, I'm willing to give you a chance," she said. "You will need some training but I can see that you are smart. However, I like my club to be a happy place, which means I like my ladies to have beautiful smiles. Forgive me for noticing your teeth."

Under her steady gaze, Sachiko did something she didn't do often; she blushed.

"I'm sorry. I know my teeth are crooked. I have always hated my teeth."

"Well," the older woman said with a shrug, "if you hate your teeth, get them fixed. It's easy. Anything can be fixed these days."

"Easy, but expensive," Sachiko said and smiled behind her hand. "I've been working as a dressmaker these past three years. I'm afraid I don't have extra money."

Mrs. Teguchi took a calling card from a small holder and wrote something on it. "Here, take my card to this dentist. He's a good customer here. If he knows I sent you, he'll do a good job and he'll give you a good price."

Sachiko shrugged. "A good price won't help me, Mrs. Teguchi. I simply can't afford it."

"Don't worry about the cost. You get those teeth fixed and I'll take care of the bill. You can pay me back a little every month. If you decide to take this job, that is. So, is it a deal?"

"This is very generous of you, Mrs. Teguchi. I don't know what to say."

"Say what you feel," the older woman smiled. "That may not be the Japanese way, but that is the way I operate."

Sachiko felt weak in the knees. She had been dealing with foreigners for three years and she knew what this woman meant, but did she dare just blurt out what she was thinking? Taking a deep breathe, she sat up straight and looked directly at Mrs. Teguchi. "Well," she began, "I do need a job and I need it fast. My instincts tell me you will be a fair employer, so, I guess we have a deal."

"Good," Mrs. Teguchi said and stood up. "I'll expect you tomorrow about this time. We can work out the details and I'll show you around." She crushed her cigarette in an ashtray and leaned across the desk. "Since this is a business deal," she grinned, "let's shake hands on it."

A little dazed, Sachiko walked out of the dark nightclub into the busy street. Suddenly, she had doubts. It struck her that it was odd to take a job and end up in debt to the employer before she had worked a day. She had agreed to take a job and she didn't even know what her salary was going to be.

The new job was in the world called *miszu shobai*, a place of illusion and entertainment. Sachiko was a little ashamed of her new profession.

She knew she would have to cut ties with her few Niigata friends. She didn't want them to know.

"Well, here goes Act Two," she told herself the day she moved into a small Tokyo apartment with another hostess. Mrs. Teguchi had arranged it. They would share the rent and Sachiko would absorb the finer points of their business. She had worked at the nightclub for a week and had started her sessions with the dentist. Soon she would be able to smile without putting her hand over her mouth. That reward would almost balance out the fact that she hated her job.

The joy was in the hours of preparing to go to work. She loved dressing up and walking down the street perfectly turned out. It was like getting ready for the stage. Her performance was brilliant but the script was stupid. Most of all, she hated lighting cigarettes and allowing half-drunken men to paw her. It won't be forever, she told herself. She was already plotting her next career move. In the daytime, Sachiko was seriously studying French. France was the home of great designers of women's clothing and Sachiko was not going to lose sight of her goal.

As a result of the horrors of Hiroshima and Nagasaki, when the cities were destroyed by nuclear bombs and hundreds of thousands killed and injured, plastic surgery came of age in Japan. By the end of the 1950s a number of American-trained Japanese doctors excelled in the field. Their dedication took them beyond repairing burns and putting disfigured faces back together. Japanese standards of beauty were changing. Higher noses and round eyes became the rage. Sachiko knew two hostesses who had had their faces changed. She decided to take a month away from work for her own transformation.

Just as it had been in Auntie Yokohama's shop, the doctor's office had magazines with styles to choose from. But in the doctor's office, the pictures were of faces rather than frocks. There were pictures of "dream" noses with text under them, naming the American movie star who had a similar nose.

"The Doris Day nose is very cute," the nurse told her while she waited for the doctor to come into the room. Sachiko smiled and said nothing. When she was alone with the doctor, she produced a picture of the famous statue of the Egyptian Queen Neferetiti.

"This is what I want," she said. "Can you make me look something like this?"

The doctor was fascinated with the challenge. It would be unlike every other operation he had ever performed. But he could see that there was a good chance it could work. Sachiko had darker skin than the average Japanese. She also had a long neck and the gaunt, high-cheekboned face one needed for such an exotic look. He would have to enlarge her eyes, try to make them almond-shaped. As for the nose, it was just a matter of building it up a little.

The operation was painful and it took almost the entire month for Sachiko's face to heal. When she went back to work, people commented on how much she reminded them of that famous Egyptian queen. If not exactly Neferetiti, she looked like no other woman in Tokyo. Sachiko was a sensation.

The real turning point came six months later. The man she would learn to call "Papa" walked into the nightclub on a chilly night in March of 1960. He was nothing much to look at—late fifties, portly—but he was rich. He was also intrigued by the hostess who reminded him of the statue that graced the bookcase in his office. He asked for Sachiko to sit at his table. From that evening on, he was a regular at the club.

One night Papa offered her a trip to Paris. He had to go there on business. He would give her a ticket to go ahead of him. They would meet there and travel back separately.

"I'll go," she said, "but let me go a week ahead. I want to study the way French women dress. I need a week by myself."

Papa laughed. "Sure, why not. If that would make you happy."

"That would make me very happy. Two weeks would make me happier," she answered, flashing a perfect smile. Papa wasn't the man of her dreams, but Paris was the city of her dreams. One dream out of two wasn't bad.

To make the most of the experience, Sachiko planned the trip with her French teacher. By the time Papa arrived in Paris, she was right at home. When his business was over, she took him through a world he had never seen, although this was his sixth trip to the City of Lights.

For three days she was his guide, his teacher and his lover. They had dinner at Maxim's and drank champagne. He didn't need a blonde on his arm. Men of all nationalities turned to look at him with envy in their eyes. Waiters and shopkeepers went out of their way to serve her. Even women smiled at the elegant Sachiko. She turned heads. Papa loved it. He was having the vacation of his life.

Back in Tokyo, he wanted her to be there for him. "Leave the club and I'll buy you a business," he told her. "Anything you like, within reason."

This was her golden opportunity and Sachiko wasn't about to waste it. The business had to be something that made money. With Mrs. Teguchi's reluctant blessings, she planned Act Three. It took five months of hard work to open her small boutique in the nightclub district. Her immediate plan was to cater to the hostess trade. Sachiko knew from experience that nightclub hostesses needed lots of clothes and she knew what they wanted. One of the two rooms in the rear of the shop was turned into a studio and a seamstress was hired.

Besides dresses, Sachiko carried a full line of beautiful expensive lingerie and she let it be known that she was open all night. A hostess had only to make a telephone call. The best business was done in the small hours of the morning, when the girls were on their way home with their gentlemen. The men were well-lubricated and could easily be talked into buying the teasing dolls something sexy and expensive. The business quickly turned a profit.

The only one who was not thrilled with the business success was Papa. He didn't care if the shop made money; he wanted Sachiko to be available for him at his convenience. He also didn't like going to the shop; he preferred to have her tucked away in an apartment. Sachiko hired a salesgirl to live in the back of her shop and keep her night business going. But Papa had to be careful; he didn't want a scandal. He was what is known in Japan as a *yoshi*, meaning that he had been adopted into his wife's family as a son. It was a way to keep the bloodline pure, but it gave the wife a strong position in the household. His wife wouldn't put up with her husband having a so-called second wife, not with her family's fortune.

Sachiko proposed a deal. If he lent her the money to buy a comfortable apartment, she would pay him back with interest with the profits from her business. The kicker was a promise that as long as she owed him money, she would not leave him for any reason. Papa agreed. In a short time, she was not only making money but she was beginning to design clothes for well-known entertainers. Within months, she had three seamstresses working in the back of her boutique.

One very exciting day, she bought her apartment with Papa's cash. How he got it out of the business without anyone knowing was something she didn't ask. He arrived with a big, fat briefcase filled with nicely wrapped ten-thousand-yen bills. Privately, they signed a note saying she owed him the money and promised to pay it back by giving him one-fourth of her business profits, in twice-a-year payments.

They toasted the deal with French champagne in bed. Although everything had been done in a party mood, Sachiko had every intention of keeping to the contract. The first payment was due at the beginning of the New Year. In the last week of December, however, Papa had a massive brain hemorrhage while at his office. He was dead by the time the ambulance got him to the hospital.

Other than the paper they had signed together, there was no record of the money he had given her. Forty-nine days after his death, Sachiko planned a night alone at home. In her bedroom, atop a dresser, were his picture, flowers, a candle and an incense burner. Standing before the picture, she touched the promissory note with the flame of her Cartier lighter and then lit incense sticks for him with the burning paper. She toasted her benefactor, friend and lover with a glass of champagne. It was 1963: several months later she opened Atelier Sachi. She now had five girls working for her.

Over stuffed quail with grapes, Sachiko gave Misako a thumbnail sketch of her life since working with her aunt in Yokohama.

"Think how much you have accomplished since we left high school," Misako said with admiration. "I was able to go on to university but I only managed an office job, which I left after a couple of years to get married."

"That's called normal life," Sachiko said. "Nothing wrong with that."

"What is wrong is that my husband has a mistress and he wants a divorce. She's pregnant and Hideo is serious about her. Last night he told me that he wants this child. He wants a son. I really don't know what to do about it," Misako said, twisting her plain gold wedding ring. "My mother-in-law said he is going to send me away from our home. My marriage is totally over and I haven't even told my mother. Instead, I got dressed and ran out of the house this morning. I don't know what to do."

Sachiko lit a cigarette and blew the smoke toward the ceiling. When she spoke, her eyes were half closed and her voice was low and serious. "What you are going to do, Chibi-*chan*, is stay with me for a while. I have room."

Misako's eyes widened. "I couldn't impose on you like that."

"When we were kids, I spent a lot of time at your house. I often stayed over night and ate many meals with your family. Your parents were very kind to me. Now I have a chance to pay back that debt."

Misako sighed. "You don't owe me anything."

"Listen to me. I think it was fate that made us meet today. We are going to my apartment and you are going to tell me all the details. After that, you will call your mother. She has a right to know. Tell her what is happening and tell her that you are staying with me. Surely she will remember me."

"My mother will worry," Misako said, brushing away a tear.

"Good! You need people who will worry about you. I'm worried about you. That's why I am going to make a telephone call as soon as we get home. The most important thing you are going to do is see my lawyer. Tomorrow. Understand?"

"Your lawyer? Hideo said I should see a lawyer."

"A lawyer maybe, but I am sure he didn't mean Isao Ogawa."

*T*wenty-two boxes of rice crackers! Teishin piled the boxes in three neat stacks against the wall in a small room off the kitchen. Never in his memory had the temple had such a supply of rice crackers, incense and tea. Absolute superfluity! They were all gift offerings given to the temple at the time of the master's funeral. Arranging the storeroom was on the top of a list of things that had to be done this week. Keiko had written it out for him and he didn't want to disappoint her.

When everything was neatly arranged, Teishin chose the best box of rice crackers and carefully wrapped it in an indigo cotton *furoshiki*. He wanted to take it to the caretakers of the big garden. The visit was long overdue and Keiko had put it on her list. He had to express his regrets for the trouble the unfortunate death of his master had caused them.

The caretaker was at home; the wife was out shopping. He welcomed the priest warmly, invited him into the cottage and clucked over the priest's weight loss. Teishin sat cross-legged on the *tatami* floor, smiling, blushing and waving his hand in front of his face.

"No, no, you must not concern yourself about me. The doctor said it is good for my health. I am sure when my appetite returns I'll be as fat as ever."

He patted his tummy and laughed. It was a flash of his former jolly self, but after a cup of tea Teishin became serious and timidly asked if he could see inside the tea house where his master's body had rested immediately after his death.

"Of course," the caretaker said with something in his voice that smacked of glee, even though he had been specifically instructed to stop talking about the priest's death in the garden. The director clearly wanted all that forgotten. He didn't want the tea house to be associated with death. He had been quite disturbed to hear that the caretaker and his wife were conducting mini tours, showing people where the tragedy had taken place. Mr. Saito had spoken very sternly and put a stop to it. Still, the caretaker couldn't refuse the priest's request.

"Come with me. I'll show you exactly where it happened," the caretaker said, looking around to make sure they were alone.

Half an hour later, Saito was on his way to the storage building when he saw the priest and the caretaker coming out of the teahouse. He guessed what the caretaker was up to and it made him frown. When Teishin saw the director, he stopped on the path and gave a little bow. Good manners made Saito return the bow and go up the path to greet the old master's assistant.

How he regretted giving the unknown girl's ashes to the temple. The results had been disastrous. How could he have known that the old man would become obsessed and end up dying in the very area where the bones had been found? It was not the kind of story he wanted associated with this garden. He wanted people to come here for the garden's historical significance and its beauty. But what was done was done. All he could do was keep the gossiping caretaker couple under control and hope the unusual circumstances of the priest's death would be forgotten in time.

As Saito made his way to the teahouse, his smile was warm but it held a certain degree of apprehension. He liked this priest, but the director couldn't help wonder if this visit would lead to some new misfortune.

"Saito-*sama*," Teishin said, making another deep bow. "Forgive me for intruding. I came to apologize in person for all the trouble this affair has caused you. Your caretaker has very kindly shown me the tea house where my master rested after his death. It has given me some peace to see it." He bowed low and added, "Thank you for the many kindnesses you have extended to my master, myself and our temple."

The caretaker squirmed but Saito was touched. It was such a sincere little speech, delivered with a smiling face and deeply sad eyes. He noticed that the priest's face was no longer as full or as rosy as he remembered.

"*Dozo*," the director said. "See anything you like. Have you been inside the storage house, where we house the museum exhibits?"

"No, never, I'm ashamed to say," Teishin stammered.

"Well then, it happens I am on my way there now. Come along and I'll give you a personal tour."

Teishin bowed. "I would be honoured but I am afraid it would inconvenience you. We have troubled you enough."

"Not at all," the director said with a friendly smile. "Come along, I insist. It is good for me to go over the present display from time to time."

Teishin followed and entered with his head bowed and shoulders bent, a humble posture, befitting, he thought, a country bumpkin visiting such a grand building. It didn't matter that this was a storage house; it was a wonderful building. The director was going to point out only a few highlights, but when the priest recognized the Mizoguchi family crest on a helmet, Saito was pleased. After all, he had personally arranged the museum and only he could conduct a tour that was rich with details, and he liked to be appreciated. How many other people had followed him around in a cloud of apathy?

The priest began to ask questions, so many questions. When the director gave his replies, Teishin listened carefully, his eyes wide.

"Is it so? How wonderful."

"*Hai*, this storehouse has been renovated to display cultural items of the Momoyama and Edo eras. Actually, anything relating to the history of Shimizuen. We have historical data, arts and many other items that were used in life as it was lived here."

"*Soooo desuka? Ah so!*"

History poured from the director. He pointed out works of art, samurai armour, saddles, swords, pottery, items of furniture and incredible images of the last century, even rare photographs of the Mizoguchi family with samurai and ordinary folk going about their business. Miraculously, someone had an early camera to record Shibata's original castle before it was burned to the ground in the Meiji uprising.

What Teishin found most fascinating was a great paper map of Shibata City. It was unique because it clearly showed the location of every house. Each had the name of the family that lived there written on it. Many had layer after layer of small papers attached to the house square showing the different family names as dwellings were bought and sold, rented and re-rented. It was all there, a detailed history of who lived where and when.

"What a marvellous record of Shibata's history," Teishin exclaimed.

Saito was impressed. Many a distinguished guest had followed him around this room and never commented on this highly important piece of Shibata's history. Yet here was a simple priest, peering over the glass case in wonder, asking questions. The director was delighted to explain.

"Castles were always in danger from rival clans. In those days they were afraid of spies. Strangers were watched and the records of local people were strictly kept."

"Then the family name of the girl whose bones were found in the pond is probably registered on one of these tiny papers."

The director was taken aback. He had not expected any mention of the subject he wanted to forget, but the priest had a point.

"That may very well be so," he said, and added the very information that he had intended to keep secret. "Unfortunately, there is no way to know her name. However, if these papers gave a physical description of the people in the homes we would know without a doubt."

"Oh, and why would that be?" the priest asked innocently.

"Because the girl had only one ear. There was no ear hole on the right side of her skull. That is most unusual, I am told."

The priest's eyes widened. "I never heard of such a thing. How pitiful," he said, shaking his head, and turned his attention to a glass display case holding the most exquisite lacquer boxes and small tables.

"Were these beautiful items actually used in the Mizoguchi household?"

Every time he was with one of these priests, Saito seemed to be saying or doing something that he regretted. He had never meant to give anyone these details. With some relief, he noted that the priest didn't dwell on the information. He could have asked Teishin not to mention the missing ear hole to others but thought it unwise to put importance on the matter. The director decided to leave it alone and hoped this fellow would forget the detail. They were onto another subject now, the wonderful collection of old lacquer.

The facts entered Teishin's mind and joined the other bits of information he had taken in that day. He didn't think about it until a few days later, when he was holding the monthly meeting of the temple's Old People's Society. Eight elderly ladies and three elderly men attended. They sat on the *tatami* floor in a circle, with their teacups and various plates of sweets. The group had been started by the master some ten years before, but it had recently taken on a very different air. They had become more active. Today they were planning a day-trip to Deyu, a nearby hot spring, to be taken in March. The members looked forward to soaking their old bones in the healing hot water and enjoying a boxed lunch together.

"There are other small outings we could go on as well," Teishin suggested. "Recently, the director of Shimizuen gave me a wonderful tour of the storage house museum. It was so interesting. Perhaps he would be willing to give the same tour to our group."

"Oh, I've been there several times," said grandmother Sugimoto. "Too close to home. I like to ride the minibus."

"But did the director give you a personal tour?" Teishin asked.

"Certainly not! We are not big shots," the woman answered, covering her mouth with her hand to laugh. Her eyes travelled around the group to encourage them to join in. Teishin's laugh was the loudest.

"I am not a big shot either," the priest said in the same spirit of jest. "But I was fortunate. It was really interesting. Mr. Saito explained everything so clearly. Did you know there is a map there that recorded all Shibata houses and who lived in them during the old castle days?"

A murmur went around the circle. None of the old people had remembered seeing such a thing before and the thought of looking up their own family homes delighted them. It was then that, totally innocent of any desire to enhance his image by sharing gossip, Teishin blabbed out the morsel about the bones found in the garden belonging to a girl who probably had only one ear.

A few whispered exclamations went around the room. *"Ah so! Ah soooo! Maa!"* And then there was an explosion of creaky voices that hit the walls with all the animation of a group of children. To Teishin's surprise, he realized that these people knew very little about the skeleton found in the pond. Only a few had heard that bones were found in the garden. It finally dawned on Teishin that the details he had heard from the master, from Misako, the caretaker, Keiko and especially from Saito were privileged information. It was too late. The questions and comments were circulating around the room like a dog chasing his tail.

"Just a minute, please!" Teishin said, holding up his arms in alarm. His face was pink and he began to sweat like his former fat self. "Maybe you had better forget what I said as you know I am a foolish fellow and probably heard the details wrong."

How animated the group became, tossing about this sensational bit of news. Poor Teishin couldn't calm them down. Finally, he chewed on two sweet cakes and let the old folks chatter. The meeting lasted fifteen minutes longer than usual.

One of the members of the Old People's Society had a particularly good appetite that noon. Grandmother Sugimoto's daughter-in-law asked her about the meeting as they ate their meal.

"Very good. Very interesting. I don't know why you don't want to attend," grandmother Sugimoto said, waving her chopsticks toward her eighty-two-year-old husband. He was sitting across the *kotatsu* table slurping soup.

"What could be so interesting? Old people nattering at each other," he grumped. "I have more important things to do tending the garden."

"Did you know," grandmother Sugimoto said, addressing her daughter-in-law, "that they found human bones in the pond at Shimizuen? Thrown up with the big storm."

"Yes, I heard that last year," the daughter-in-law said as she filled a bowl of rice.

The old man made a mocking sound. "Everyone in town has heard that old news. Is that all the old people have to talk about, old news?"

Ignoring her husband, grandmother Sugimoto kept talking to her daughter-in-law. "The bones, they say, belonged to a young girl and the girl had no ear hole on the right side of her skull."

"Never heard such a thing," the younger woman said as she ate her pickled cucumbers.

"Certainly you never heard of it," the old woman said, "no one at the meeting ever heard of it either and we all have lived a long time. This girl couldn't possibly have had hearing on that side and probably didn't even have an ear on that side."

"No ear?" the old man inquired putting his chopsticks down.

"That's what I heard today. The right side of the girl's head could have been as smooth as an egg."

The daughter-in-law's eyes widened. "*Maa!* That must have frightened people."

"Her hair hid it most of the time," old Mr. Sugimoto offered.

"What?" both women asked.

"There was a girl like that years ago. Lived near here when I was a boy. Must have been almost seventy years back. A nursemaid of some kind. Baby always tied to her back. The baby sometimes pulled the long hair away from her face. We kids saw it. We used to run away from her. We called her Ghostlady."

"*Maa!* How cruel. Poor thing," the women said, almost together.

"It was teasing," the old man said in his defence. "We were only kids."

The old woman put down her rice bowl. "What happened to this poor little nursemaid? Do you remember?"

"No. That was a long time ago. I think she was related to the people she lived with. Can't remember their name now. Too long ago."

Even the sweet-tempered Teishin could be out of sorts on occasions and today things weren't going well. He was annoyed at himself for giving out so much information at the Old People's meeting that morning. The next mishap was when he went to the kitchen to prepare lunch and found an elderly woman already at work. She bowed and said that Keiko had arranged for her to come and cook for the priests. As far as Teishin was concerned, the midday meal was terrible. Everything was so salty. He couldn't eat the fish. It was a piece of dried salmon and he was sure that the woman hadn't taken the time to soak the fish to get the salt out before cooking it. To make things worse, the miso soup tasted like water and the meal was late. He and his new assistant, the priest Konein, had to rush off without a post-lunch rest. People had to wait for them at a house where they were scheduled to chant sutras for a departed soul.

What does it look like when a priest is late? What would the master have said? Teishin was sitting in his room, grumbling to himself. This was the old master's room into which he had officially moved a week before, as a result of Keiko's nagging. He still was uncomfortable here. It would be easier if the master's parents' pictures on the wall didn't look so disapproving. Their faces seemed to get sterner every day. It was unnerving to look at them first thing every morning. When he had mentioned this to Keiko she laughed at him.

"Pictures don't change their expressions. I never heard such nonsense. If it makes you uncomfortable, move the pictures to another room."

Teishin was shocked. He couldn't take the images away from their own room. Instead, he hung his master's picture on the wall next to his parents. That was at least one smiling face to greet him every morning.

Konein called from outside the *shoji* door to tell him that he had a guest. Grandmother Sugimoto was asking to speak to him. No, she didn't say why. With a great sigh, Teishin got up and went to see what the old woman wanted.

❀ ❀ ❀

Keiko put down the telephone after a long conversation with Misako. She couldn't believe what her daughter told her was happening, and here she was alone. Doctor Ichimura was away at a medical convention and wouldn't return until the following day. With shaking hands, Keiko poured herself a cup of tea and sat at the *kotatsu* looking out on her tiny garden. It looked shabby, all brown and dark. Even the tiny star-like leaves of the small maple had fallen. "What am I to do?" she asked herself. Now that she knew her daughter's troubles, of course she wanted to go to Tokyo as soon as possible, but Misako had refused. She said she didn't need her mother complicating things by talking to Hideo or Mother Imai. Misako was insisting on handling things herself.

Keiko was eager to see where Misako was living. Sachiko Kimura? Yes, she did remember that skinny girl from the kimono shop. She and Misako had been very close friends. But there was something unpleasant that Keiko remembered, something she had heard a few years ago: that Sachiko was working in a nightclub in Tokyo. If that was true, she certainly didn't want Misako living with a nightclub hostess. If Hideo really wanted a divorce, leaving him to live with a nightclub hostess would be the worst mistake that her daughter could make.

Keiko stood up and paced around the room. She was very worried now and couldn't wait to talk this over with her husband. Why did he have to be away when she needed him so badly? She sat back down at the *kotatsu* to think. No matter what anyone said, Misako was her daughter and she was going to go to Tokyo to get a better idea of what was going on. Better pack tonight.

"Oh, what a fool! This is all Hideo's fault. He is behaving like an undisciplined child." Keiko—usually sensible and calm—was talking to herself, out loud. The telephone rang. Keiko jumped up and grabbed it, hoping that it was the doctor. Teishin's excited voice came over the wire.

"What bones?" Keiko asked. "Teishin-*san*, what are you talking about? The girl in the pond? Oh, no. I don't want to hear any more about that subject. What do you mean no ear? Teishin-*san*, the last thing I want to hear about is anything connected with those troublesome bones." Her voice sounded angry. "I can't talk now. I'm sorry. Goodbye."

Teishin looked into the earpiece of the telephone with horror. Never, never had he heard Keiko raise her voice to him like that. She had always wanted to know everything that was going on at the temple. Suddenly, it dawned on him that talking about the bones was reopening the wound of her father's death. "I shouldn't have called. Now what have I done?"

Teishin was standing by the telephone in the kitchen wringing his hands. Old habits kicked in and he wanted to eat something sweet. He was looking for the opened box of cookies when he saw two beautiful melons Saito had brought to the temple. Teishin picked them up, each in a different hand. He chose the heavier melon. It was resting in its own white net wrapping with a tag telling where it came from and how it was grown. Such melons were frightfully expensive, something Teishin would rarely have enjoyed. One was enough for two poor priests. Wrapping the melon in his indigo cotton *furoshiki*, he carried it outside and down the temple steps with great care. It nested cozily in his bicycle basket as he rode slowly to Keiko's house. He didn't want to bruise the precious cargo.

The outside lights were off at the Ichimura Clinic. Only one window glowed in the back living quarters. Teishin rolled the door open as quietly as he could and placed the gift melon on the bookcase-like box that held shoes in the entranceway. He almost tiptoed back to his bicycle. Before he reached it, he heard the door roll back. He stood still and saw Keiko standing with the light behind her. It was obvious that she couldn't make out his motionless figure in the darkness. He was about to say something when he heard her irritated voice say: "I can't believe what an undisciplined child that man is!" The remark stunned Teishin. He didn't know she was furious with her son-in-law's behaviour. He didn't dream that Keiko was talking to herself.

It was hard pedalling home with such a heavy heart. Keiko was the last person in the world he wished to upset; she had been like a good older sister. Now he had displeased her. The master would have wanted to know the information about the ear. He thought she would as well, but he'd made it worse with one of his impulsive acts. She had called him an undisciplined child!

Everything had gone wrong today. Now dinner would be late. Quickly, he found the biggest, strongest onion in the vegetable bin. As he cut it, the tears came. His eyes burned and tears rolled down his face. Konein, came into the kitchen.

"What's the matter?" he asked in a concerned voice. "What are you doing?"

"Cutting an onion for dinner," Teishin answered through the tears.

Konein came closer and frowned. "I've never seen anyone cry so much just from cutting an onion. Here, let me help you. Your eyes must be painful. You look like you are suffering."

Teishin pulled away and kept on chopping. "It can't be helped," he sobbed.

EIGHTEEN

*I*f life at the Imai household was a slow and predictable two-step, Sachiko's world was a quick and intricate tango. Sachiko's set seemed to communicate in some secret thought pattern that Misako didn't understand. Misako's session with her lawyer, Mr. Ogawa, was her first lesson.

The meeting was set for eleven o'clock. By eleven twenty-five, Misako was leaving through the revolving door of the high-rent office building, not sure of what exactly had transpired. She'd arrived five minutes early and was ushered into the office by a young, sweet-faced secretary. As a large wall clock finished striking eleven, the lawyer rushed in spouting apologies. He had an unusual barrel chest and a deep voice. Misako thought he looked like a bullfrog. When he sat down, he placed his hands far apart, palms down on his large desk, and leaned forward to scrutinize her with his swampy little eyes. His posture suggested an imminent spring to another rock. Misako braced herself at the edge of her chair and became the target of a series of rapid-fire questions.

Yes, it was her husband who wanted the divorce, and no, she wasn't happy about it. Yes, the Imai family owned their own home in Shibuya and no, there were no children but they lived with her husband's mother.

"Hideo is an only child. His father died some years ago. . . . The company's name is Imai Exports Ltd. . . . Yes, family-owned. . . . No, my husband isn't president. My husband's uncle, who is head of the main branch of the Imai family, is president. My late father-in-law was his younger brother. He was a vice-president. . . . No, I have no idea what he did or did not own. . . . No, I have never asked about stocks and bonds or any other holdings. I only know my husband is a salary man. . . . No, we have no country villa. His uncle has a summer home in Karuizawa. We usually spend a few days there every summer. . . . Yes, only one car."

The interrogation was over before she had a chance to finish the little cup of strong coffee his secretary served her. The lawyer asked more questions about the Imai family finances than why Misako's husband wanted a divorce.

"Well," the legal frog said, "I'll put a detective on this case right away.

We'll have all the information we need in a short time. I'll be in touch."
Misako was being walked out the door.

"And what information do you want the detective to find?" Misako asked. "Perhaps I can tell you."

The lawyer smiled painfully, like a polite dance partner who just had his toes stepped on. "I am afraid you don't understand, Mrs. Imai. We must have a full record of your husband's financial holdings before we can decide the strategy for our case. The only advice I have at this time is not to sign any papers pertaining to a divorce."

He checked his watch and pushed his chin down and in toward his chest, giving him a roll of fleshy neck he hadn't had a minute before. "Frankly, I squeezed this appointment into my schedule when Miss Kimura telephoned. So sorry, but I'm already late for my next meeting. Give my regards to Miss Kimura. So sorry. Good-day."

Not knowing what else to do, Misako took the subway back to Hiroo Station and walked the three blocks to Sachiko's apartment in the rain.

Keiko had arrived in Tokyo and found her way to the address Misako gave her on the phone. The man behind the reception desk at Sachiko's apartment building said Miss Kimura and her guest had gone out. Keiko settled herself on the sofa opposite his desk and waited. Outside, dark thunder clouds rumbled over the city. The drizzle suddenly became white sheets of rain. When Misako pushed through the doors of the apartment building, she looked as if she had been for a swim in her red suit.

"Mother, I asked you not to come," Misako said as she tried to brush some of the water from her shoulders.

"Of course I had to come. Oh, look at you, you are soaking wet. Where is your raincoat?"

"I haven't gotten my things from the Imai house yet."

Keiko was indignant. "You sound as if your name isn't Imai. It is your house too. You shouldn't be living here with Sachiko when you have your own home. The worst thing you can do in this situation is leave the family home."

Misako silently accepted the lecture on the elevator ride up to the eighth floor. There was so much to explain. Misako made tea and changed into the sweater and the jeans she'd borrowed from Sachiko. The jeans were too long and too tight. She looked like a child sitting on the big white sofa as she tried to explain the situation to her mother. Keiko gradually calmed down, especially when she heard that Sachiko was not a nightclub hostess but a fairly successful designer with her own studio. After two cups of tea, they discussed a course of action.

They would go to the Imai house together. Misako could pack some of her things and Keiko would talk to Hideo's mother. "Not too many clothes," Keiko warned.

"Remember, you are just visiting your friend for a few days. You must make that very clear."

Since Misako was insisting on staying at her friend's apartment, the Imai family had to know that it was with her mother's approval. As soon as that was over with, Keiko said she would go back to Niigata. Misako was firm about wanting to handle this her own way. The compromise was that Misako would visit her parents, as soon as possible, and stay until after the New Year holidays.

Now that they had both agreed on the plan, Misako picked up the telephone to inform Mother Imai that she and her mother were on their way over to the Imai house. Keiko almost grabbed the telephone out of her daughter's hand.

"What are you doing? It is still your home. Calling first gives the impression that you have moved out."

Misako claimed that she felt awkward. Keiko insisted that there was nothing to feel awkward about since she was still part of the Imai family.

Mother Imai was surprised and deeply embarrassed when she saw Misako's mother. Keiko was friendly, assuring her that she knew this terrible situation wasn't caused by anything Hideo's mother had done. She had only come to talk. Surely between the two mothers, something could be done. They sat on either side of the dining table, sipping tea and eating fancy cookies as they discussed the family disaster. Mother Imai constantly flourished her handkerchief to dab at her eyes. She told Keiko how her brother-in-law, Hideo's boss, strongly disapproved of Hideo's actions. He was calling a family meeting in a few days.

"Will Misako be invited to this family meeting?" Keiko asked.

"Oh, no, I don't think so," the weepy woman stammered.

"I see," said Keiko, stiffening in her seat.

"I'm afraid nothing much can be done at this point," Mother Imai said through her tears. "Hideo and Fumiko are determined to have this child and be married."

Fumiko, is it? How intimate, Keiko thought, and bit into a cookie. Not even a formal *san* attached to the pompom's name. This woman is already thinking of her son's mistress as her new daughter-in-law.

Mother Imai saw the look on Keiko's face and felt the drops of sweat form on her own forehead. Her handkerchief threw a light floral scent into the air as she waved it around her face and neck. She wasn't sure what she had said wrong. She could see Misako's mother turning to stone before her eyes.

"Well, then. I suppose there is nothing more to discuss." Keiko stood up as she spoke. "Misako! Please hurry!" Keiko called out. "I've decided I want to catch the next possible train to Niigata."

The crying came when Misako returned to the apartment alone. It had been one of the most difficult days of her life. It was now almost five-thirty and the rain had stopped. She hung up her coat and turned on the television set. Then she dragged her suitcase into Sachiko's spare bedroom. Music from the television was filling the apartment. Someone was playing a guitar and crooning the Beatles' song "Yesterday." The singer sang the word "yesterday" in English. The rest of the slow, sad lyrics were in Japanese. The words seemed to have been written to express her personal pain. Misako sat on the narrow bed listening to the music, tears rolling down her face.

When the song was over she broke down and really cried. Gone was the brave voice she had found when talking to her mother. Gone was the slightly arrogant air she had managed for Mother Imai. Here was a frightened, rejected, confused and miserable young woman crying as if her heart was broken.

When Sachiko came home, she found her friend asleep holding a framed picture of Hideo. Sachiko bent over the bed to take a good look at the handsome face. I could handle this one, she thought.

Misako opened her eyes, sat up and brushed the hair away from her face.

"Been crying?" Sachiko asked.

Misako nodded. "I'm all right. I need some sleep, that's all."

"Sleep is the last thing you need," Sachiko said. "I am not going to let you feel sorry for yourself. Now open up your suitcase and find something to wear. We are going to a party. Two parties! Maybe three!"

Misako rubbed her eyes. "I can't. I'm in no mood for a party. Besides, I don't know any of your friends."

"That doesn't matter. A party will change your mood. You can make new friends. Two good reasons to go. We leave in an hour."

"An hour? Why didn't you tell me this morning?"

"Because I didn't know I wanted to go to a party until I saw your sad face. A party is exactly what you need."

Parties were not part of Misako's lifestyle. On the rare occasions when there was a wedding or a school reunion, she thought about what she would wear for weeks in advance and prepared for the big occasion all day. There was excitement, clothes to be arranged and hours spent at the hairdressers.

"I don't understand," Misako moaned. "You mean you knew about the party invitation this morning?"

Sachiko laughed. "There are always party invitations in my world. The problem is deciding which to attend. You use the shower first and come into my room when you are ready. Now move!"

Years ago, when Sachiko had studied and helped her mother sew kimono late into the night, she learned the art of being refreshed by taking small naps during the day. Now she went to her room for that ten-minute rest. It had been such a hectic day, paying the price for being away from the studio the day before. Things were getting frantic. Her head pounded.

Really, she needed a secretary, someone smart, someone she could trust. With the New Year fast approaching, all her show-business clients needed new costumes and yesterday she had to take the time to go to the Ginza to shop for year-end presents. Ah, but that outing was well worth it. Not only did she connect with an old friend, she may have found exactly the right person to bring into her business. Misako might be suffering from a blow to her self-confidence now but Sachiko remembered how organized she had been in school. Sachiko stretched and made her way to the shower. Yes, they just might make a terrific team.

It took Misako forty-five minutes to get dressed. She looked very pretty in her black wool dress with the little white collar. Sachiko looked spectacular, poured into a silver-grey knit, draped in ropes of grey pearls.

"You need a little help, Chibi-*chan*," Sachiko said and sat her friend at her dressing table. With a tiny pin, she skilfully removed the white collar and replaced it with a necklace of intertwined pearls and coral beads. Then she added a touch of colour on Misako's cheeks and a stroke of liner on her lovely eyes.

"You have to have those eyebrows professionally shaped tomorrow. I'll tell you where to go and you tell them 'Audrey Hepburn.' You have no idea how beautiful those big, innocent eyes of yours can be."

She rearranged Misako's hair and snapped on a pair of dramatic earrings that matched the necklace. "*Bon!*" Sachiko said. "Niigata would never recognize you."

The first party was at a Middle Eastern embassy. The bright, white home of the ambassador was overflowing with beautifully dressed people, both Japanese and foreign.

"I don't know what to do," Misako whispered as they made their way up the marble steps.

"Put your head up and follow me," Sachiko said, and sailed into the crowded room with Misako in tow.

"Ah, Mademoiselle Kimura." The tall, handsome ambassador spoke a fast stream of French to Sachiko. She rattled a stream of words back at him. Then he turned to Misako.

"Your houseguest. Charmed," he said in English. He took her hand and kissed the air just above it. "So pleased you could join us this evening."

Misako smiled shyly and wished she were anywhere other than this party. Though she had studied English in school, could read it fairly well and could catch the meaning of the words of a song, she had never actually spoken it with a foreigner. All she could say haltingly was "How do you do?" and "Thank you."

Misako accepted a glass of champagne and found it was easier to bob her head slightly while sipping it. Then it looked as if she was agreeing with whatever was being said and that provided a wonderful excuse not to pour forth the obviously expected waterfall of English or French.

It was a trial by fire, until they moved onto a group of Japanese. At least she could understand their words, if not the body language. All the kissing! Everyone seemed to kiss everyone. Cheeks, hands, even the Japanese were doing it. Misako was petrified that someone was going to kiss her. She used her champagne glass like a shield whenever anyone came too close.

Sachiko pushed Misako toward a very long table blanketed with beautiful dishes of strange food. The centrepiece, a large carved-ice crab, had a hollow middle that was filled with at least two kilos of black and grey caviar. Sachiko heaped tablespoons of it onto Misako's plate.

"Feast on this and forget the other stuff," Sachiko whispered.

A middle-aged foreign man approached them. Sachiko introduced him as a diplomat from Latin America. He looked down at Misako as if she were one of the luscious dinner offerings. At least he spoke Japanese.

"I am glad you speak Japanese so well." Misako said with a measure of relief.

"Not well, of course, but I try. When one is assigned to an embassy, it is always worthwhile to make the effort to learn the language of the country. Don't you agree?"

Misako was impressed. He might have an air of arrogance, but at least she could eat without fear of being spoken to in a foreign language. Plate in hand, she followed him to a corner sofa.

"Imai, Misako-*san*. Why have I never seen you before? I would never forget those eyes."

Misako blushed and her eyes became larger. No man had ever said such a thing to her in her life. She didn't know what to say.

"I don't go to many parties. I'm staying with Sachiko-*san* for a few days."

"Have you known Sachiko-*san* long?"

How nice, Misako thought, to be asked a normal question. "Oh yes. We went to school together in Niigata."

"Ah, Niigata! So that is the source of the mysterious Sachiko-*san*. Some of us thought she was a gift of the Nile. The daughter of a Sphinx."

Misako had no idea what this man was talking about. She ate the caviar and grinned as the delicate flavours burst in her mouth.

The foreigner was gazing down, watching her lips move. After she swallowed, she had to say something. It was always safe to talk about food. "The caviar is delicious," she said, "really delicious."

"Yes," the man said, "probably the main reason the parties at this embassy are well attended. These Middle Eastern countries are so rich. They serve the very best caviar and champagne."

"Champagne," Misako giggled and held up her empty glass.

The man reached for the glass, pressing her fingers as he took it from her hand. "Niigata beauty," he purred. "I'll get you more champagne if you will promise to have lunch with me tomorrow."

His touch, and the surprise of what he was saying, stunned Misako. She had no idea how to handle such flirtation. This man had only known her for ten minutes. She had her wedding ring on. What was he thinking? She fluttered her long lashes and grinned stupidly in sheer terror. The Latin lover read her response as a coquettish "yes."

"What eyes! I'll be back," he said and blew a kiss over his shoulder. Misako sat on the sofa like a limp doll. The timing was perfect for Sachiko to appear and announce they were off to the next party.

"Why did that diplomat call you the daughter of a Sphinx?" Misako asked Sachiko as they rode in a taxi to the next party.

"Did he?" Sachiko laughed. "Good! I like that! The less they know about me, the better."

Misako moaned. "I'm afraid I told him we went to school in Niigata together."

Sachiko leaned her head back and closed her eyes as if to nap. "Don't worry about it. I never really lie about my background. I don't volunteer any information to that kind of man. He is one of those libidinous foreign peacocks who think every Japanese woman is eager to roll on her back for the honour of being the recipient of their momentary lust. Ha! He called me a Sphinx! Probably because I ignore his phone calls."

Misako simply whispered, "*Ah so.*" She didn't want to admit that she really had no idea what her friend was talking about.

"You'll like this next place better. It is the home of a French art dealer with a long Russian name. His American wife is very clever."

"That's nice," Misako said. "Is she a teacher?"

"Not that kind of clever," Sachiko laughed. "She's the rare American woman who doesn't make a public fuss about her husband misbehaving, which he does very often."

Misako flinched and Sachiko giggled. "Better say no if he wants to show you his collection of Japanese prints on the third floor."

Misako gave out a low mock scream. "Ahhh!"

"Don't worry," Sachiko said. "His new mistress is sure to be there. Anyway, you'll see a lot of familiar faces at the party. Mostly Japanese show-people, and many are my clients." She patted Misako's hand. "You see, Chibi-*chan*, I'm simply making my business rounds."

The minute she walked in the door, Misako saw a famous actor standing in the crowd. The house was packed with people holding drinks, talking and laughing. Sachiko pulled her through the crowd to introduce her to their host. Misako liked his dark, friendly eyes. More kissing and English, but the host managed to put her at ease.

"Good tennis player," Sachiko commented as she steered her little friend toward the bar. Misako asked for a soft drink and noticed that the crowd parted when an elegant young woman came into the room. Her long face and prominent jaw were very familiar.

"Is she an actress?" Misako whispered in Sachiko's ear.

Sachiko laughed. "We are all actors here, with the possible exception of Chibi-*chan*."

Misako made a face. "I can't place her. I know I've seen her picture."

Sachiko leaned close and spoke softly into Misako's ear. "Let's say, high born."

"Ohhhhhh yes," Misako hummed. She started to say a name, but a warning look from Sachiko cut it short.

Sachiko spoke slowly through her beautiful, expensive teeth. "I can't think what she sees in him. Easing her aristocratic ennui, I suppose."

"*Maa!*" was all Misako could manage to say. Sachiko lightly tapped under Misako's chin to close her gaping mouth.

❀ ❀ ❀

The Imai family meeting did not happen as Mother Imai imagined. Instead, late one night, Hideo alone was summoned to his uncle's office to receive the elder's shouting wrath.

"You are a disgrace! No fidelity to your family! No fidelity to your company!"

Head down, Hideo spoke softly and tried to explain, man to man. Uncle would have none of it. This young fool had talked him and his wife into acting as go-betweens for his so-called love marriage more than five years before. Now he wanted a divorce to marry a pregnant mistress! Everyone would lose face.

"Idiot!" he screamed at his nephew. Hideo started to talk. Uncle wasn't receptive. Hideo kept talking, pleading. He might lose his job, but he had to marry Fumiko. He couldn't give in. In the end, Uncle agreed to talk to Hideo's lawyer. He controlled the money. He would have the last say on any settlement. The meeting was set for the following week at the lawyer's office.

Mr. Fukusawa bowed deeply several times, adjusted his Coke-bottle glasses and handed the head of the Imai family the papers drawn up for a mutual-agreement divorce. Everything looked official. All that was needed was the amount of the settlement to be printed into the blank space. Uncle sat in a chair like the Buddha, with his thick legs wide apart, his arms folded across his chest and his face looking as if it was carved from dark stone.

"One million yen," he said. "That's final." He glared over at his nephew who was sitting up straight in a chair like an obedient schoolboy.

"*Hai*, Honourable Uncle." Hideo leaned forward in a bow. "I understand. Thank you."

Uncle grunted and lifted his chin to affirm his decision.

"Excuse me, Honourable President." The lawyer had to address this Buddha with the greatest expression of respect. "I have to point out that one million yen may not be enough. Divorced women are not usually entitled to much money, but times are changing. It is understandable that your nephew's wife and her family are very upset at this course of events. She may feel vindictive. There must be sufficient incentive for her to sign divorce papers."

Now the Buddha growled. Ignoring the lawyer, he pointed a fat finger at Hideo. "You should have thought of that before you got into this mess. One and a half million yen, and half a million yen from your personal finances. That's final." The lawyer and Hideo exchanged glances. They both knew there was no room for argument. Hideo jumped to his feet and stood like a soldier with his hands at his sides and bowed deeply.

"Honourable Uncle, thank you. Really, thank you, sir." If they had been in a *tatami* room, he would have fallen on his knees and touched his forehead to the floor. The lawyer lined up next to him and joined in the bows. "Shacho-*sama*, truly, thank you. Thank you, sir."

The Buddha grunted, stood up, bent his neck slightly and marched past them like a samurai disgusted with his foot soldiers after a lost battle.

Fukusawa instructed his secretary to print "two million yen" into the blank space on the divorce papers. But first she had to make fresh tea.

"I'm still concerned that this is not enough," said Fukusawa. "Your wife has to start a new life and even renting an apartment these days takes big key money."

"Two million yen is a fortune to Misako," Hideo assured the lawyer. "My wife won't give you any trouble. She'll go back to Niigata. It is not so expensive to live in the country. Her parents will help her. I'm sure she will realize this is for the best."

The lawyer sat at his desk, chain-smoking over his teacup. His secretary finally entered the room with the completed document. He examined it and grunted approval. Now he had to earn his fee. His smile made his teeth protrude and his eyes closed into slits behind the thick lenses.

"When it comes to presenting such difficult documents, I always need information from my client." He took off his glasses and looked up at the ceiling as if he was about to compose a poem.

"Imai-*san*, tell me, what would be the best time of day to present these papers? I mean, what time would she be sure to be home and perhaps, in the best frame of mind?"

Hideo's face fell. "Uh, I forgot to tell you she is not at home. She stayed away one night and then appeared the next day with her mother. She packed a suitcase and said she was staying with an old friend. She gave my mother the friend's name, address and telephone number." He opened his wallet and handed the paper to the lawyer.

"Good!" Fukusawa seemed excited. "If she moved out of the house, she's taking action. That is excellent news." He examined the paper and asked, "Who is this Sachiko Kimura?"

"I don't know. Never heard her name before. Misako told my mother they went to school together."

"And you never met this Kimura-*san*?"

"No," Hideo said.

The lawyer shook his head. "Strange. This sounds very strange. Something is funny here. And look at this address. It is in one of Tokyo's highest rent districts." He looked at his watch and picked up the phone. "All I can do is try to make an appointment. I know this kind of fancy apartment house. I would never get past the reception desk without an appointment."

It was nine-thirty in the morning and Sachiko answered the phone.

"May I speak to Mrs. Misako Imai, please? I understand she can be reached at this number."

"May I ask who is calling, please?" Sachiko was using her professional voice.

"My name is Fukusawa. I am the attorney for Mr. Hideo Imai. I have a document I would like to have Mrs. Imai look over and sign."

"Ahh, would you?" Sachiko purred. "All legal matters are handled by Mrs. Imai's attorney. You will have to contact him."

The bottle bottoms began to steam. "*Ah so.* May I ask to whom I am speaking, please?"

"My name is Kimura and this is my home you are calling."

"I beg your pardon, Kimura-*sama*. May I have the name and telephone number of Mrs. Imai's attorney please?"

"His name is Mr. Ogawa. Mr. Isao Ogawa." Sachiko heard his muffled gasp. "As for his telephone number, you can consult either the Tokyo directory or any first-year law student." Sachiko hung up.

Fukusawa cursed and a surprised Hideo asked, "What happened?"

The lawyer glared over the desk at his client. His voice was laced with irritation. "I am afraid this is going to be more complicated than we thought, Imai-*san*. Let's go over this again." The lawyer leaned back in his chair and crossed his arms and spoke slowly. "You said your wife took one suitcase with her. That means she will be back for more clothes." The thought made him put his head back and gaze at the ceiling. "This is going to take wits and imagination. We have to be ready. You will have to make sure you have the money in your home. Tell anyone at home to let me know the minute your wife telephones or comes to the door."

"Just a minute," Hideo said, showing his own annoyance. "That sounds like some kind of ploy. Surely that won't be necessary. I think you are overreacting."

"No, I am not overreacting," the lawyer said firmly. "I can tell that Kimura woman will never let me see your wife alone. We have to make a plan if you want a divorce, especially if you want to get away with only two million yen."

"What are you talking about? Two million yen is a great deal of money. My wife is not the mercenary type."

The lawyer stood behind his desk and smiled. "Imai-*san*, excuse me, but I must tell you that you are naive. Things have changed here. Your wife may be a sweet woman but she has that hotshot lawyer Ogawa representing her. You don't know his reputation. That guy will be out for every asset you have, every share you own in the company."

"I can't believe that. Misako wouldn't let that happen," Hideo said, shaking his head.

The exasperated lawyer leaned across the desk and glared at his client. "Imai-*san*! Can't you understand? Of all the lawyers in Tokyo your wife just happens to have Isao Ogawa to represent her. Something doesn't add up here."

"Don't worry. I know Misako. We don't have to play tricks on her."

"Oh, Imai-*san*, you don't know anything about her lawyer. We have to act fast and take him by surprise. There is no other way to beat a guy like Isao Ogawa." Fukusawa's voice had grown louder; now he was shouting. "You think two million yen will buy you a quick divorce from your innocent wife? Listen, Imai-*san*, two million yen won't even pay Ogawa's fee!"

NINETEEN

*I*t came silently in the middle of the night, causing an eerie glow behind the small, high window. Teishin heard it with his heart and smiled in his sleep. It was so familiar, so comfortable, exactly the atmosphere to coax a buried seed of memory into a dream flower.

He is a child, bundled and padded, waddling in the cold, white winter world of his native mountain village. He is wearing small straw boots. His big sister Toyoko shuffles close behind, hovering with her arms open, ready to steady his baby steps. As they shuffle toward their waiting mother, she is chanting a song about falling snow.

"Sho-*chan*! Sho-*chan*!" His mother is smiling and calling his childhood name. He reaches her with a scream of baby glee and is swept up into her arms. She wipes his running nose and pats his apple cheeks. His sister claps her hands and cheers. "What a good boy!"

"What a good job!" His mind rocketed through the years. "What a good job," Keiko said as she was going over the temple's schedules and accounts. Teishin's schoolboy characters were written neatly in the exercise book she had given him. He was awake now, trying to remember when it had happened, when she had paid him that compliment. Was it two days ago?

Teishin had worked hard at learning Keiko's system of bookkeeping. He became particular about recording all financial transactions, where and when the priests held ceremonies, as well as what monies were received, when and from whom. All the details of all expenditures were put down in the book. The old master had been casual about such things. In all his years, he had hardly ever had the word "money" in his mouth. It was totally unpalatable to him. Keiko closed the book and smiled. "What a good job, Teishin-*san*!"

Teishin blushed. "You must tell Konein-*san*. I couldn't do it without him. He is very good with his abacus. He often helps me."

Keiko couldn't help but smile at this man who sometimes infuriated her and at other times exhibited such sweetness.

"It takes more than an abacus," she said. "You are the one who is recording what comes in and what goes out. The accounts are complete and very nicely arranged. I would say you both did a good job."

Before she left the temple, Keiko paused at the entrance as if she had forgotten something. "Oh, by the way," she said as she fished the indigo square from her handbag, "This is yours, isn't it? I am sorry I haven't thanked you earlier for the beautiful melon. I didn't see it until I returned from Tokyo. I'm afraid it got buried under the year-end presents that are beginning to pile up on the entrance shoe box. Thank you, but you and Konein-*san* should have enjoyed it yourselves."

Teishin lay on his futon, thinking about Keiko, staring at the high window, watching the soft, tremulous snow shadows. If Keiko hadn't seen him in the shadows then it must have been someone else she had been angry with. Still, he realized the mistake he had made calling her about the bones. He was beginning to understand that Keiko blamed that strange business for her father's death. Hadn't she called the box of unknown ashes "bad luck"?

"Those mysterious ashes shouldn't be in this temple at all," she had said. "It was foolish of Grandfather to agree to keep them; they have brought nothing but bad luck. Every time I think about it, I want to remove that box from under the temple's roof."

"She wouldn't, would she?" Teishin asked himself. The mere thought made him spring from the futon with fear. Taking a few seconds to regain his composure, he quietly slid open the *shoji* door and listened. There was no sound. The only movement was the cascading snow shadows on the other side of the corridor's *shoji* windows, like a great lantern spreading soft, flickering light along the polished floors. Softly, very softly, the barefoot priest made his way to the back altar room.

The box containing the unknown ashes was still where Kensho had put it. Even in the dim light, he could see that the silk wrapping was no longer perfectly white. He could smell the dust as he removed the box from the shelf. In a few minutes, he was back in his room and the box was in the *tokonoma* alcove where it had rested during the last months of the master's life.

Until that was settled, Teishin hadn't been aware of the freezing temperature. All at once, he felt as if he was being massaged by hundreds of icy fingers. He wrapped himself in his quilt and sat cross-legged before the *tokonoma*. "Who are you?" His whisper blew puffs of mist into the freezing air. "Why was my master so keen on finding your identity?" Under the quilt, he folded his arms across his chest tightly and began to rock as he thought.

Master wanted these ashes to be returned to the girl's family. How can I discover her identity? It was only by chance that I gained information about her not having an ear. Or was it? Could it be my master's spirit guiding me? Is he allowing me to serve him still?

The thought made Teishin both shiver and smile. With this new information about the bones, perhaps it was possible to learn who this person was, and how she died. The problem, as Teishin saw it, was Keiko. She hadn't liked her father keeping the ashes in his room; he could guess what her reaction would be if she knew what he had just done. His face wrinkled into an expression of pain.

Surely, Misako-*san* and the priest from Kamakura would be interested in the new information that has come my way. But I can't contact Misako-*san* directly; Keiko-*san* would be upset. Surely she couldn't object to me mentioning it to the priest from Kamakura, could she?

Teishin blew out a great cloud of breath. The New Year holiday was approaching. He could send a letter with his New Year's greetings. That decided, he cast off the quilt and lifted the silk-wrapped box into the back of the futon closet, carefully covering it with a thin summer quilt. He was doing what he felt was right, even though he knew he was going against Keiko's wishes. The old feeling of insecurity started to roll in his gut. He was craving something sweet.

"No," he whispered. "I must not be an undisciplined child. It is a matter of self-respect."

Instead of making his way to the kitchen, Teishin slid open the small window and stood under the cold flow of air and snow. For the first time in his life, he felt he was acting boldly, taking charge, being brave. A great rush of adrenaline sent fear, uncertainty and a wonderful tingle of happiness popping in his chest as he snuggled back into the futon. Tomorrow, he would carefully compose a letter to the Zen priest.

I'll start by telling Kensho-*san* about our first snowfall, he thought as he closed his eyes and started to drift back to sleep. A lacy dusting of snow blew down from the open window and settled on his quilt.

❀ ❀ ❀

With the New Year less than two weeks away, Misako realized that she wasn't going to be able to keep her promise to return to Niigata before the holiday. It was simply far too busy at Sachiko's studio to leave. The telephone never stopped ringing. Every client wanted new clothes immediately. There were two extra seamstresses working. The sewing went on late into the evening and Sachiko was doing most of the fittings and delicate handiwork herself.

There was no time for parties now. Sometimes the designer and her new secretary didn't return to the apartment until after midnight. Often, they were back at the studio by nine o'clock the next morning.

"I'll come to Niigata when I can," Misako told her mother on the phone. "I've never been so busy in my life. The studio is like a madhouse. We sometimes work until ten or eleven at night."

"Sachiko is killing Misako," Keiko told her husband that evening. She would have been on a train back to Tokyo to see what was going on, but her youngest stepson was coming home from university and there was so much to do to prepare for the coming holidays.

"Leave her alone," the doctor said over his newspaper. "Misako is not a child. It is a good thing that she is working hard. Not being busy and thinking only about her troubles would hurt her more."

Keiko sighed. Her husband was right and she knew she should be concentrating on all that had to be done for the holidays. The year-end gifts had been sent, but Keiko felt she had to supervise the cleaning, decorations and activities at the hospital as well as in her own home. She was especially concerned about the temple. She noticed that a rip in the shoji in the altar room hadn't been repaired, and she was sure the window shutters were not always put in place in the evenings.

Would the temple be cleaned properly? Would there be enough tea and cakes? Would the charcoal braziers be kept going so that visitors could keep their hands warm? Could the two priests keep up conversations with the New Year callers? Her father had been talented at holding court. He would sit in his Buddha position smiling and keeping people happy with little stories about old happenings, mostly about the people who were present. It was true that Teishin could be a chatterbox, but the younger priest, Konein, hardly said a word to anyone.

Who would see that the guests' shoes were properly arranged at the temple's entrance? Old as he had been, her father had been very good at arranging these details. After all, this was the season when much of the temple's revenue came in from New Year gifts. It was important that people enjoyed their visit. Some women from the congregation would help, but they couldn't be depended on too much during the holidays. They had plenty to do in their own homes, as Keiko did. She had to honour her dead mother-in-law's strict tradition of a splendid New Year's morning feast.

Dr. Ichimura frowned when he looked up from his newspaper again. The worry lines on his wife's brow had deepened. "Still thinking about Misako?" he asked and turned a page.

"No," Keiko sighed, "I was thinking about what has to be done to prepare for the New Year holiday."

"You worry too much. I suppose you are fretting about the temple. Let Teishin-*san* handle his own affairs. He is capable. Why can't you believe it? Your father did."

Keiko raised her chin and smiled. "People will understand if things are not perfect. After all, this is the first New Year without Father. Hopefully, by a year this time, Teishin will be settled into family life. I'm determined to find him a nice country girl before next summer is over. The elders in the congregation agree. Teishin should be married. The temple has been too long without a priest's wife. What do you think of that plan?"

Dr. Ichimura smiled. "Excellent. Then I'll see more of my wife."

❀ ❀ ❀

Teishin's letter came as a surprise to the Zen priest. He sat in his temple in Kamakura and read it carefully. What did Teishin mean? Kensho read the letter again and understood that the skull had no external auditory canal on the right side. Because that was such a rare condition, someone might remember a story of a girl with that defect who had once lived in Shibata. The news was so stunning that the tall priest had to take a deep breath. Teishin wrote how he had learned about this from Shimizuen's director. He explained that a member of the temple's Old People's Society might have information concerning who the girl might have been, as well as where and when she had actually lived.

When Kensho absorbed the information, he got so excited that he rushed to the temple's office to call Misako, wondering why she had not let him know this important news. Quickly, he looked her telephone number up in his black notebook, dialled and found himself in a strange conversation with Misako's mother-in-law.

"I beg your pardon," he said, not believing his ears. "Did you say that Misako-*san* is no longer living at this residence?" Mother Imai was flustered, evasive and slightly hysterical. Yes, she remembered meeting the Zen priest at Misako's grandfather's funeral in Niigata. As if anyone could forget such an incredible appearance. No, she couldn't explain at this time why Misako was not living at home. Well, maybe it would be all right to give him her new telephone number. Misako was staying with a friend somewhere in Tokyo.

Kensho was confused and concerned. He promptly called the number that the senior Mrs. Imai had reluctantly given him. It was ten o'clock in the morning. No one answered. He tried telephoning again in the afternoon, in early evening and as late as nine-thirty at night. Again and again, there was no answer.

The next morning, after meditation, meals and morning chores, he sat at the low desk in the temple's office and dialled the number. It was a little after seven o'clock. Misako's sleepy voice answered after five or six rings.

"Good morning. Is this Misako-*san*?"

"Yes," she said.

"Ah, this is the priest, Kensho from Kamakura. I beg your pardon for calling early. I have obviously disturbed your sleep."

"Oh, Kensho-*san*. It's all right. I'm surprised to hear from you. How did you get this number?"

"From your mother-in-law. She told me you are staying with a friend."

"Yes, that's true."

"*Ah so*," was all he could say. Misako's tone clearly discouraged questions.

"Look, Kensho-*san*, I'd like to tell you all the details but not on the phone."

"Then may we meet some time soon to talk?" he asked.

"I am working and will be busy until the New Year. Kamakura is only a little over an hour by train. Perhaps I could come and visit your temple during the New Year holiday."

Kensho hesitated, trying to remember his schedule.

"I'm sorry, but the third of January is the first day I will have free time. I can see you that afternoon."

He knew the train schedules from Tokyo. He would be waiting at the Kamakura Station at 1:25 PM on the appointed day. Misako agreed.

"Will you take lunch at the temple?" Kensho asked.

"Yes, thank you."

"Very good. I will arrange it."

"Thank you," Misako said, and that was that. A short telephone conversation. She didn't seem eager to talk to him. Perhaps it was the early hour. He hadn't had the chance to tell her about Teishin's letter and the amazing new development, which was the main reason he had called her.

Keeping his hand on the phone after he'd hung up, he stayed seated on the *tatami*-mat floor, leaning over the low desk, deep in thought.

Something must have happened. Why was she not living with her husband? An image of Hideo came into Kensho's mind, his handsome face, his perfect white starched shirt and gold cufflinks. Kensho remembered the pangs of jealousy he experienced in Niigata on that last day of the funeral. Shamefully, he had left Shibata without saying goodbye to Misako. His thin face sagged with unhappiness. He put his head in his hands and moaned, "Oh, Misako!" He was so engrossed in reliving that pain that he wasn't aware of a grinning, young priest leaning against the door with his arms folded. He had obviously heard Kensho saying Misako's name with a measure of passion.

"Oh, Misako!" the young priest repeated. "Who's 'Oh, M-i-s-a-k-o?' Is she pretty?"

The tall priest felt his ears begin to glow. Ordinarily, he would have rubbed his bald head, smiled and left the room. This time he was more than painfully embarrassed; he was mortified. But his tormentor was a friend and colleague who was familiar with Kensho's antics.

He smiled and stood up, gathering the skirt of his kimono up in front, assuming the exaggerated demeanour of a geisha. Slapping the other priest playfully on the arm as he passed, he spoke in a practiced sing-song falsetto voice.

"Very pretty, don't you think?" Kensho put his hand over his mouth, imitating a giggling woman, and left the room in a mincing, pigeon-toed gait. The grotesque geisha stepped into the hallway and broke into a run, while his friend slid down the doorframe and collapsed in laughter.

❀ ❀ ❀

Misako and Sachiko had come home close to midnight the night before. Today's plan was to return to the studio at ten o'clock. Misako was glad

Kensho's call had woken her early. It gave her time to walk to the French bakery in Roppongi and surprise Sachiko with fresh croissants and coffee for breakfast. Sachiko loved anything French and Misako liked to do small things to please her. Right now, it was all Misako could do to express her appreciation.

Between her growing popularity and the coming holidays, Sachiko's business was being swamped with orders. Together they had decided to focus on the business until the New Year rush was over. It didn't seem likely that Hideo was going to move on the divorce within that time frame. The end of the year was hectic for everyone. Misako thought it was safe to put her own personal life on hold, even though there were telephone messages from Hideo's lawyer almost every day.

Sachiko put him off. "Mrs. Imai is not available to talk to you. Please contact her lawyer, Mr. Ogawa." After every such call, Sachiko would warn Misako again. "Under no conditions should you talk to Hideo or his lawyer."

Misako had never been busier in her life and hardly wanted to think about her failed marriage, much less talk to Hideo or his lawyer. She was running errands, handling clients and taking charge of the accounts. She was Sachiko's secretary, even though they had never discussed working hours or money. The unspoken understanding was that it all would be settled after the New Year. Right now, they would do whatever it took.

In one way, Misako found living with her childhood friend in a modern, Tokyo apartment a great experience. The negative was that she was not entirely comfortable about being dragged into Sachiko's social life. She didn't enjoy nightclubs or late night parties. It was all too fast for her liking.

She also wasn't used to Sachiko's two sleek, pampered Burmese cats. Coco and Cleo were not like any other cats Misako had ever seen. They were very beautiful and seemingly useless. In Misako's world, cats went out at night and caught rats. Sachiko's cats never ventured outside the apartment. Even though a maid came in to clean every day, there was always that slight unpleasant cat smell. Misako found her sensitive nose twitching every time she put turned the key to open the apartment door. Sachiko never noticed it.

The cats were not totally accepting of Misako either. When she entered her bedroom, Cleo was often on the bed. Misako would sit down and try to pet her, but Cleo would slink away. It was obvious that Misako had taken over Cleo's room.

The sister Coco had laid claim to the white sofa. Sometimes when Misako entered the room, Coco would lift her beautiful brown head and follow Misako with her jewel eyes. The cat's aloofness was not inviting. It discouraged Misako from sitting down.

And then there was Sachiko's dear friend, Auntie Kaz Teguchi. It was a new experience for Misako to meet a woman well into her seventies who had long red fingernails and always wore high-heeled shoes. Auntie Kaz was the only guest who came into the apartment who wasn't expected to remove her shoes. She was also the only person Misako had ever heard boss Sachiko around.

Dressed elegantly and wearing pearls the size of dove eggs, Auntie Kaz would arrive at the apartment about seven in the evening, totter over to the white sofa, light a cigarette and wait for Sachiko to fix her a scotch and soda. Misako noticed that the only time Sachiko drank hard liquor or smoked cigarettes was when she was with Auntie Kaz, which was a couple of times a week. After what they called their cocktail hour, they went out to their favourite sushi shop where they were treated like visiting royalty. That ritual finished, they always caught a cab to a piano bar or nightclub, even though it was almost midnight and the next day was not a holiday.

It wasn't that Misako was left out of the partying; quite to the contrary, Auntie Kaz was always very insistent that Misako join them. The trouble was that Misako didn't enjoy drinking or coming home so late that it was almost impossible to keep her eyes open the next day. Still, it was difficult to beg off such a jolly, expansive invitation.

And then there was the creepy feeling she experienced when she sensed the presence of a strange man in the apartment. Just before dawn that very morning, she woke up and heard whisperings in the hallway. Misako decided to ask about it over breakfast.

"Is it my imagination, or did you have a man in your room last night? I'm sure I heard someone leaving the apartment this morning."

The question came as Sachiko bit into the last morsel of her croissant. Sachiko chewed and smiled. She was sitting on the sofa with their breakfast on the coffee table. Cleo was rubbing against her shoulder and Coco was curled up in her lap. Misako sat on the thick, white rug, pouring another cup of coffee.

"Ummm," Sachiko finally said, still savouring the buttery flakiness. "Delicious!"

Misako gave her shoulders the same exaggerated shrug that Sachiko often performed. "If it is something you don't want to talk about, I won't ask again."

Sachiko let out one of her infectious, rich giggles. "Actually, I've been meaning to mention him to you. It's a private matter, so you must promise never to tell anyone. Understand?"

"Of course, I promise. Is he a secret lover?"

"I think of him more as a playmate than a lover."

"Now, that I don't understand!"

Sachiko laughed again. "No, I don't suppose you would. Let me put it this way. If I were a man and had a woman spend the night from time to time, you would understand?"

"Ah, I suppose so," Misako said, beginning to wish she had never brought up the subject.

"Then why should it be so different because I'm a woman? I'm human and there are times that I like to play." She let out another peal of laughter and poked Misako's knee with her bare foot under the coffee table. Cleo jumped off the sofa and examined the crumbs on the rug. Misako's face went blank.

Sachiko rolled her eyes. "Playmate, as in S-E-X, Chibi-*chan*. You know what you and Hideo used to do. It can be very relaxing." Sachiko shooed the other animal off her lap and stretched like one of her elegant pets. "It's not complicated. I have a special friend who is happy to come and play when I call him. We have fun together, and from time to time, I buy him something pretty."

Misako shook her head slowly. "But why, Sachiko? You are such a beautiful and talented woman. You could marry almost any man you want."

Sachiko folded her arms and looked down at her little friend. "If I am to keep building a successful career, I can't afford the time or the energy that goes into a serious relationship. This is a game where I call the shots. He does the work and I never have to fake it."

"Fake what?" Misako blurted out before she fully understood Sachiko's words.

Sachiko narrowed her eyes. "How can you have lived thirty years and still be so naive? I bet Hideo's mistress fakes orgasms. What's her name? Fumiko? I bet she does things for that spoiled brat that you couldn't imagine."

Misako bit her lip and avoided Sachiko's cat-like eyes. Sachiko stretched and arched her back. Her silicone breasts pressed against her soft sleeping kimono.

"Well, anyway," Sachiko said, flashing her perfect white teeth, "now you know my wicked little secret. It's a luxury I can afford."

"My goodness," Misako said, blushing crimson.

"My goodness indeed," Sachiko laughed. "I might have to deduct tutoring fees from your salary if I have to keep educating you like this."

❀ ❀ ❀

It didn't take Fukusawa long to get information on Miss Sachiko Kimura. After making a few phone calls, he learned that the lady was a rising star in the design world, working mostly with the show-business crowd. He also learned that Misako was working as her secretary and living in her apartment. As for Sachiko's past life, he found out that she came from the same town in Niigata as Misako, and since they were about the same age, they could have indeed been classmates and friends. There was also some gossip that Sachiko had once worked as a hostess in a Tokyo nightclub, but no one seemed to know the details. Nevertheless, the lawyer had enough information to drop off a thin report at Hideo's office.

Hideo read it through and wrote down Miss Kimura's home and business addresses. Labouring under the illusion that he was still capable of sweet-talking Misako into signing the divorce papers, he wanted to talk to her in person. There wasn't much chance of getting past the security at the apartment house. He decided to try the Atelier and hoped that the Kimura woman was out of town.

As fortune would have it, it was Misako who was out of town. She had gone to Kyoto to carry back some very special fabric for a major television star's costume. Sachiko happened to come out of her office when Hideo was approaching the receptionist. The sight of him stopped her in her tracks: he was even more handsome than his photograph. As she sailed forward to greet him, she took in his well-cut clothes and impeccable grooming.

"Ah, you must be Mr. Imai. If you are here to see Misako, I am afraid she is out of town. Perhaps there is something I can do for you."

It was Hideo's turn to be dazzled. Suddenly he was the male peacock looking at a female whose polished feathers were more glorious than his own. She smiled coolly as she performed the minimum polite bow. His bow was deeper. It was the first time in his life that he was conscious of blushing. Sachiko read it, knew she had stunned this mouse and decided to play with it a while. He just could be a good candidate for new playmate down the road. He and Misako were practically divorced. Always calculating for her future, Sachiko could see the day when the new wife would be too wrapped up in domestic bliss and motherhood to care about his conjugal needs. Hideo said something about the important matter he had to discuss with his wife.

"Your wife has been put through a terrible ordeal, and as her friend, I am one hundred per cent on her side. She cannot talk to you, Mr. Imai. Her lawyer has forbidden it." Then she tilted her lovely head sideways and blinked. "However," she said slowly, "since I am not directly involved, I suppose there would be no harm in my listening to what you have to say. Of course, I don't promise to be your messenger. If fact, I think it would be better if you and I keep this conversation to ourselves. Can you do that, Mr. Imai?"

Hideo stood there nonplussed as Sachiko looked at her watch. "I was about to go to lunch. Why don't you join me? There is a good little restaurant a short walk from here. We can talk privately there."

She threw her cashmere shawl over her Chanel suit and they were on their way to lunch. Suddenly, all thoughts of wife and mistress were gone from Hideo's head. At that moment, he was just another guy being led down the street by an exotically beautiful woman and his libido.

TWENTY

The Fire Horse returns
Other than the moon
Few had witnessed her departure.

*A*waning moon made a bright crescent-shaped scratch in the dark sky over the ancient city of Kamakura as Kensho folded his poem paper into the shape of a horse. Just before midnight, he went for a walk in the temple grounds. He wanted to experience the first second of the New Year alone, with no one trespassing on his inner reflections. He stood at the edge of the bamboo grove waiting, his arms folded across his chest and his big head thrown back looking up at the sky.

Past the wall on the far side of the garden, throngs of people passed, talking and laughing, on their way to the great Shinto shrines. Dressed in their best clothing, they had come out, on this mild last night of December, to court the gods of good fortune.

The bells started to toll. It was the start of 1966, the forty-first year of the reign of the Emperor Hirohito, known as *Showa yonju-ichi*. It was also the rare year of the fire horse, a year when the national birthrate would drop dramatically, a year in which abortions would increase. It would be a most unlucky year for baby girls.

In the twelve-year, twelve-animal Oriental zodiac, the fire horse came only once in a sixty-year cycle. The last year of the fire horse had fallen in 1906, when the present Emperor's grandfather, Emperor Meiji, was on the throne. That had been a lifetime away. Few people would ever experience more than one Fire Horse Year in their lifetime.

An undercurrent of holiday excitement infected the mood of the shrine visitors passing the temple's garden wall. The sound of their voices stopped at the priest's ears. None of it reached his consciousness for he was wrapped in his own self-spun cloud of absorption. He was alone with his thoughts and the mellow voices of the bells.

As he stood there, so close to hundreds of people, yet so solitary, his thoughts flipped over and rippled like the pages of an open book exposed to a breeze. With both the finger of pleasure and the finger of pain, Kensho mentally began to hold down a page here, another there. Misako's face and moments of the old year came and faded, each leaving a different flash of emotion. When the bells sang their last note, he slowly started to live within the New Year.

"The bridge has been crossed," he whispered to the night. "I now walk a virgin path." With an exaggerated gesture, he put his right foot out to take the first step of the New Year. He strolled around the garden, talking to himself as he went. "Each waking a birth, each sleep a death. Life is born and dies each day. Living is to drink from the cup we ourselves brew—bitter, sweet, nourishing, poisonous or merely sustaining."

He passed the temple's entrance and strode through the gates, walking against the crowds. He passed the wide and narrow streets on his way to the road that wound up the steep hills away from the city. The shadows of houses became the shadows of trees and bushes. Pavement gave way under his feet to earth and rocks. His walk turned into a climb. His destination was a large flat rock that sat among the crooked pines on the highest point, overlooking Sagami Bay. When he arrived there, he stood with his feet spread apart, breathing in the night, marvelling at its tranquillity. Overhead, the moon seemed to hang lower here, bright and placid among a myriad of distant stars. Below, the dark ocean moaned and heaved, its waves crashing against the foot of the cliff, tossing up great sprays of water, salt and mysterious smells.

Kensho removed the little paper horse poem from the sleeve of his woolen kimono coat and sent it sailing down into the darkness. The white paper glided, growing tinier and tinier, until it was a mere white speck caught by a leaping wave of watery tongues. Pleased with his humble offering, Kensho sat on the rocky cliff and folded his body in the zazen position. His eyes closed out the beauty of the night as his spirit began to suck in its essence. Slowly, the meditation cleared his mind of everything, save the budding anticipation of experiencing the first sunrise of the New Year.

❀ ❀ ❀

At fifteen minutes before the New Year, Teishin left his temple's kitchen door and shuffled across the courtyard under an oiled paper umbrella. Smudged prints from his rubber boots followed him across the newly fallen snow. The Niigata night air was crisp and cold, leaving a pleasant sting in his lungs. Mercifully, there was no wind.

At the bottom of the wooden bell tower, he shook the umbrella and set it against the post before climbing the narrow ladder. Under the protection of the tower's tiled roof, the bell looked dark and luminous against the frosty scene. Teishin stood for a moment to survey the night. The snow was coming down very quickly, as if in a hurry to add to the already white roofs and trees. The night was utterly silent. He squinted, hoping for a better view of his surroundings. Not even the outline of the temple was visible through the dancing white curtain.

A mass of beams and planks, the tower creaked as Teishin moved about. A box holding irregular, small stones rested on a piece of wood that served as a shelf. There were one hundred and eight stones in the box. From the folds of his kimono Teishin took out an old-fashioned pocket watch that had belonged to his master. Lovingly, he placed it on the shelf next to the box of stones. There were only two minutes left in the old year, the year that had taken his master, the year that had changed his life and position so drastically. Teishin folded his hands and bowed his head in prayer as he prepared for his holy task.

As Teishin waited for the stroke of midnight, so too were other Buddhist priests all over Japan, standing by their temple bells, ready to announce the New Year by tolling one hundred and eight times. The year before, Teishin and the younger priest, Konein, jointly performed the ringing of the bells. It was a bitterly cold night. To fortify themselves, they drank small cups of hot sake before going outside to face the Siberian blast. They actually had fun, joking as they took turns swinging the heavy log. Later, when they slurped their bowls of hot noodles, to assure good fortune in the New Year, the Master looked at the young men with stern eyes.

'"Tell me, how many times does a temple bell ring to announce the New Year?"

Teishin put down his bowl of noodles and looked sheepishly over at the younger priest.

"One hundred and eight, Master," he said in a small voice.

"And, how many times did you and Konein-*san* strike the bell to announce this New Year?"

Both priests flushed to the top of their bald heads. As the older of the two priests, it was again Teishin's responsibility to speak. "About one hundred and eight times, I think. We used the small stones to keep count."

"And I used a pencil and paper to count the rings. Are there now only ninety-nine known evils in the world instead of one hundred and eight? "

Both priests abandoned their bowls of noodles and bowed in apology, their heads touching the *tatami* mat.

The shame of that memory had made Teishin insist on ringing the bell by himself this year. He had taken care to count out all the small stones in the old box that morning. The stones had a way of disappearing over the year and now there were only eighty-nine. It was difficult to find nineteen small stones under the snow, but he managed, carrying them to the box with red, freezing hands.

"Pay attention to details," he repeated his master's remembered words. "You would be an excellent priest, if you would pay more attention to the little things. It is all very well to be a jolly fellow, but not at the expense of your duty." This is what the master had said.

Trying to live up to his dead master's expectations was becoming an obsession. As he went about his duties, it was as if he was being followed by an overseer who carried a large stick. It made him try harder. In the hope of becoming a disciplined person, he even gave up the pleasure of eating sweets between meals.

With great care, he removed the stones from the box and piled them in little mounds on the plank. The large hand of his watch moved toward the small hand over the Roman numeral XII. Teishin bowed to the bell with his hands folded in reverence. Slowly, he pulled the log back and then pushed it forwards against the waiting bell. The bronze voice sang out in all directions, cutting through the white night. Undaunted by the explosion of sound, the snow continued its race to the ground. Teishin removed one stone from the plank and dropped it back into the empty box, then prepared to hit the bell again. The second smash of the log, the second bell-song, the second stone dropped into the box. He imagined his master smiling at him. "Well done," the voice in his head whispered. His heart pounded. His face flushed with excitement.

By the tenth ring, the cold air began to feel warm. He tugged at the collar of his kimono to expose some of his sweating chest. Ringing the bell was hard, physical work. He peeled off his outer kimono jacket. There were more than ninety strikes to go. He knew that Konein would appear under the tower soon, wanting to help. Teishin was determined to decline the offer.

The night resonated with the solemn, mighty voice of the bell, each boom spreading on the air to chase the last echo. It was taking all his concentration to lift his aching arms. Fifty-two stones still waited to be counted.

Konein called from the bottom of the tower. "Teishin-*san*, please let me take over ringing the bell."

"I don't need help," Teishin yelled into the night.

"You must be very tired," the younger priest called.

"Thank you, but I can do it. I am strong. I can do it." The umbrella under the bell tower turned and moved slowly toward the temple. Teishin stepped out of his rubber boots and threw them tumbling down onto the snowy ground. The ice on the platform stung his bare feet. The repenting priest welcomed the pain as a wash of pleasure.

❀ ❀ ❀

As worldly as Fumiko considered herself to be, speaking English and having had experience with foreign men, she still wasn't truly comfortable turning her back on Japanese superstition. A girl child born in the year of the fire horse was thought to grow up with a vicious temper. It was said that they have been known to kill their husbands. Understandably, fire horse females often ended up old maids. The realization that her child was to be born during this unlucky year distressed Fumiko more than she was willing to admit. Still, she knew that the only chance she had to marry Hideo was by hanging onto this pregnancy.

Even though Hideo's lawyer informed him that he was confident that he could bypass Misako's fancy attorney and get her to sign the divorce papers after the holidays, Fumiko was nervous. If they had been already married, she could have had an abortion, as many women do in a Fire Horse Year. Under the present circumstances, she couldn't risk it. There were too many times that she saw something in Hideo's eyes that looked like doubt or rejection. When it happened, she pressed his hand pressed against her stomach, reminding him that his son was alive and growing inside her. A fire horse baby is better than no baby, she thought, and went on to convince herself that the child was certainly a boy. Boys born in the Fire Horse Year didn't suffer the stigma that girls did.

The lovers spent a lot of time together during the month of December. Fumiko's girlfriend, who often lent them her apartment, left Tokyo for several months. They spent time there together almost every day. Hideo insisted that Fumiko go to her own home to sleep, although he often stayed the night. He knew his mother's opposition to his marriage to Fumiko would lessen when she became lonely. As soon as the divorce went through, Misako's name could be taken off the Imai family register and his mother would have little choice but to welcome the new bride to the house.

The next step toward this goal was taken when Mother Imai reluctantly agreed to meet Fumiko on New Year's Day. Hideo was to bring her to the house, but not before he planned the visit like a master strategist at war.

"Be sure to wear kimono," he told Fumiko. "One with purple in it, if possible. My mother loves the colour purple."

"Kimono makes me look fat!" Fumiko protested.

"Good," Hideo said laughing. "My mother is fat. She will like it and think you are strong and healthy."

Fumiko was distressed. "The kimono I wore for graduation from junior college has purple flowers in the design, but it has the unmarried girl's long sleeves. What shall I do?"

"What difference does it make? You aren't married yet, are you?" Hideo wasn't helping. He seemed amused at her dilemma.

"Not married but pregnant! Your mother knows. What will she think of me in virginal flowing sleeves with a baby under my *obi*? It will give her a chance to ridicule me." She said this on the verge of tears.

"It doesn't matter," he said. "This is going to be an important meeting. Our future happiness depends on it. If the sleeves bother you, find a kimono that's right . . . borrow one."

Fumiko wore her aunt's pre-war kimono. It was purple with a classic arrow design and enough pink in the pattern to make it suitable for a young woman. To complete the picture, she sat in the beauty parlour for hours having her thick tresses dressed in a spectacular, old-fashioned style, complete with purple, pink and yellow silk ropes wound in and out of the sculpture. Mother Imai almost lost her breath at the sight of the gorgeous creature standing next to her son in the entrance of her home on New Year's Day. This woman was so different from the conservative, petite Misako. The unexpected first impression completely deflated the puff of authority Mother Imai wanted to display.

Under Hideo's tutoring, Fumiko played the part very well, stunning the older woman even further when she unwrapped her gift: within a deep purple square of silk lay a lacquered box filled with delectable New Year delicacies.

"*Maa*! Did you make all of this beautiful food?"

"I love to cook," Fumiko said demurely.

Hideo had in fact bought and arranged the goodies. He had also gone over all the things he thought could happen on such a visit. He told Fumiko how she was to handle herself. When more hot water was needed for the tea, Fumiko quickly got up from the table and pleaded to be allowed to fetch the hot water. She rushed into the kitchen and effortlessly found everything without having to call out one question about where things were kept.

Hideo made sure that his mother noticed this. Mrs. Imai was impressed. She hadn't dreamt that her son would go so far as to draw a sketch of the kitchen for Fumiko and even drill her on how to turn on the gas stove.

The evening went perfectly except for one incident. It happened after the meal, as they were sitting around the table talking. Mother Imai suddenly blurted out, in her slightly hysterical way, the dreaded question. "Fumiko-*san*, is it true you are pregnant with my son's child?"

"Yes," Fumiko answered with her eyes cast down on the table. Then she reached for Hideo's hand and added, "Our baby is due in June."

"June?" Mother Imai frowned. "That's only six months away. Aren't you nervous about having a baby during the year of the fire horse? Suppose it's a girl? The child will have a strike against her for the rest of her life. She'll never get a husband or live a normal life."

"Oh, don't worry. It's a boy. I know I'm carrying a boy," Fumiko said, sounding confident.

"Know?" Mother Imai repeated. "How can you know?"

Fumiko broke into a radiant smile and looked boldly into the older woman's eyes.

"Didn't you know that Hideo was a boy when you were carrying him? Think back."

Mother Imai blinked in surprise. "Come to think about it," she said slowly, "yes, I didn't even consider my baby being a girl." She moved her head indicating that she felt foolish. "Well, you know, it probably was because I wanted the child to be a boy. Maybe that's what is happening to you."

"I don't think that is the case," Fumiko said. "It is more than wishful thinking. I believe that we motherly type women have a way of knowing about our children, even before they are born." As she spoke, Fumiko put her hand across her breasts that were swelling against the bindings under her kimono.

"Do you really think so?" asked Mother Imai sitting up tall in her seat, reminded of her own large bosom.

"Oh yes," Fumiko said, leaning across the table to pour Mother Imai more tea. "Which reminds me of a drama I saw on television a few months back. The story took place in a remote mountain area during the Edo period. A woman with large breasts had a baby a few weeks before her neighbour had a baby boy. Shortly after the boy was born, the neighbour died leaving her infant without milk. In desperation, the husband of the dead woman took his tiny son to the other new mother and pleaded for her to suckle his child as well. The mother with the large breasts had plenty of milk and willingly agreed. When that little motherless boy grew up, he was healthy, brave and strong. He became a leader and saved the village from being destroyed by bandits."

"Oh yes!" Mother Imai almost screamed with glee. "I saw that drama too. That plump young actress played the nursing mother. Oh, what is her name? If the mother hadn't had so much milk, that baby wouldn't have grown up to be the hero who saved the village. Oh yes! I saw that too," she said, smiling over her own fond memory. "You know, I had so much milk when I was nursing Hideo, I could have nursed another child. *Maa*, he was a greedy little boy. It took me a very long time to wean him away from my breast."

"Really?" Fumiko said and shot Hideo a knowing glance.

Hideo missed the look because he was busy pouring himself another whiskey. Mentally he was patting himself on the back. Fumiko was as good as tucked into the upstairs futon.

❀ ❀ ❀

"Here's to you, Chibi-*chan*. I couldn't have managed this rush of business without you."

"Here's to you, Sachi-*chan*. I couldn't have gotten through these last weeks without you." The friends clinked champagne glasses and drank to their recent success. The holiday rush was over, the bookkeeping done, the employees paid, the stack of invoices folded into addressed envelopes ready to mail on the first working day of the New Year. The clothes were delivered and all the customers were satisfied.

Sachiko knew that it could not have been accomplished without Misako. Having a smart, trusted friend to take charge of the office allowed

Sachiko to concentrate on designing, working with the seamstresses and keeping the temperamental clients happy. Without such a devoted assistant, the amount of sudden new business could have been her undoing. Word would have gotten around if there was even one unsatisfied customer.

It was seven-thirty on New Year's Eve. They sat in one of Sachiko's favourite French restaurants in the hip Roppongi area. It was all part of Sachiko's efforts to show her appreciation to her new secretary. Before they left the office that day, she presented Misako with a fat pay envelope and an invitation to "celebrate . . . my way."

The waiter served their first course of individual mushroom soufflés. Sachiko sent her compliments to the chef. Misako had never eaten a soufflé before. "This is so delicious," she said after the first mouthful of the luscious stuff.

"I'm glad you like it. This is a special dinner to thank you for working so hard."

Misako looked fondly across the table at her friend. "Really, Sachiko, I wish you didn't thank me so much. I am the one who is thankful. I'm not sure how I could have gotten through these last weeks without this job. It kept me from thinking of . . . you know."

"You'll get through this, Chibi. Don't worry," Sachiko said as she put her fork down to pat Misako's hand.

"I know. I'm fine," Misako said, but she wasn't feeling fine. She was feeling some unpleasant vibrations going on behind her back.

Two heavily made-up dark eyes were staring at Misako and Sachiko from a table on the other side of the room. The dramatic-looking woman spoke to her slightly built male partner behind a large, black lace fan. "Look, Cheri, there's my costume designer being very cozy with that petite femme in the red suit. Very interesting. I always wondered about Sachiko's love life. Never saw her with a man. Never saw her being that familiar with anyone. They call her a sphinx."

The waiter removed the soufflé dishes and set down the main course of fillets of sole with lemon, potato, leek purée and French beans in butter.

Sachiko fairly purred over the dish. Misako felt the heat on the back of her head again, sensing that she was being stared at. Suddenly, a striking woman in a black Spanish-style lace gown and mantilla stopped at their table. Her black hair was piled up and held by an enormous silver comb. As soon as she began to speak, Misako realized that it wasn't a woman at all, but a famous transvestite entertainer who specialized in French *chanson*. Misako had seen him on television hundreds of times. Mother Imai never missed his shows.

Sachiko exchanged pecks on the cheek with the singer and asked him to join them.

"Well, for just for a moment," he said, flourishing the black lace fan. "I simply had to say hello and tell you how much I adore my new dress." The fan fluttered, but his eyes stayed rivetted on Misako.

There was a quick introduction. A few polite murmured words and head bows, and then the singer broke into French. It was awkward for a few minutes, but Misako sat quietly fascinated. The singer was moving his fan and batting his luxuriant false eyelashes, seemingly to make points in his arcane conversation. A great peal of throaty laughter, more pecks exchanged and the Spanish beauty was up and rustling his skirts across the room to his own table, but not before he snapped the fan shut and looked at Misako with a very knowing smile.

"Very pleased to meet you, Misako-*san*. I'm sure I'll see you again."

There was something about the way he threw the words over his shoulder. Misako almost shuddered.

"One of my best customers," Sachiko said, going back to her meal. "I always have a problem with that horrid Adam's apple. I have to add a choker or a scarf. I think the black lace dogcollar worked well this time. Poor thing. He does so want to be a beautiful woman, but his voice is so deep and his feet are so big."

Misako didn't laugh. "Why did he look at me that way? What did he say about me in French?"

"He wanted to know if we were lovers."

Misako gasped. "I told him you were my secretary . . . that's all." She let out her famous giggle. "I don't think he believed me."

Misako was completely taken aback. The expression on her face only made Sachiko laugh more.

"Don't be so serious, Chibi. It's really very funny."

Misako turned to shoot daggers across the room into the broad lacy back.

"He makes a striking woman, don't you think?" Sachiko was still laughing.

"He's a regular clothes horse. Very good for business."

Sachiko called over the waiter and had a bottle of champagne sent over to the singer's table. It was just being poured as Sachiko and Misako were leaving.

"*Merci*, Sachiko-*san*, *Merci*. Have a good time tonight." The last remark was punctuated with a peal of laughter. Misako felt her face burn again. Sachiko put her arm around Misako and steered her toward the door, while waving good night.

"I suppose," Misako finally giggled when they were outside the restaurant, "my tutoring bill for education has just increased." The joke and the champagne sent them laughing as they walked the three blocks to a place that Sachiko promised would be another educational experience.

The next destination was The Gas Light, a piano bar owned by an American couple. It was a home away from home for Americans in Tokyo and popular with Japanese who thought it was like a mini-trip to the States. To Misako, the atmosphere seemed outlandish. The place was crowded with people wearing funny paper hats. Everyone, standing or sitting, had a drink in their hands.

Grasping the edge of the cream-coloured cashmere shawl that Sachiko wore over her Chanel suit, Misako was led to the piano bar, seated and handed yet another glass of bubbly. Inwardly, she groaned. Outwardly she smiled until Sachiko felt that it would be all right to leave her little friend for a few minutes. Sitting on the other side of the room was an actress whom Sachiko had long wanted as a client. She had to say hello, buy a bottle of champagne, and make a subtle sales pitch. As Sachiko walked away, Misako had a silent panic attack. She smiled at the piano player and tried to mouth some of the English words of the song "Bye, Bye, Blackbird." She turned with admiration to the Japanese girl sitting next to her. This girl knew every English word and was obviously having a very good time . . . all by herself.

"It's really amazing how you know the American songs. Have you lived in America?" Misako asked.

"No," the girl smiled. "But I've been studying English for some time. Do you come here to meet Americans too?"

Misako was almost getting used to these rude verbal slaps. "Certainly not!" The two words had hardly passed her lips when a big American man with a drink in his hand loomed over her. He swayed slightly as he breathed his drunken dragon breath.

"Oh, oh, oh! Lookee here at this little Japanese doll," he slurred. "I know who I'll be looking for when the clock strikes twelve."

Misako drew back in horror. His wet, pink mouth widened into a knowing smile as his friend dragged him away. "It's a date, sweetheart."

"What did that man mean?" Misako nervously asked the American-loving Japanese girl sitting beside her. "What happens at twelve o'clock?"

"Don't you know how foreigners celebrate the New Year?"

"No," Misako said. "I've always been home on New Year's Eve, except to go to the shrine."

Her neighbour's laugh made the young piano player look up and wink at them. A cigarette dangled from his smiling lips as his hands skilfully ran up and down the keyboard.

"I'll tell you what will happen," the girl said. "Just before midnight, everyone in the room starts counting down from ten. Exactly at twelve o'clock, the whole room goes wild with everyone yelling 'Happy New Year!' People kiss each other. The piano player plays 'Auld Lang Syne.' Everybody sings and blows paper horns. Then the real kissing starts."

"Kissing?" Misako asked. "Who does the real kissing?"

"Everyone kisses everyone. It's fun, but stay away from the fool that just talked to you. He kisses with his tongue."

"What do you mean, with his tongue?" Misako asked in horror.

"You know, he tries to shove his tongue in your mouth. And don't stand up when he kisses you. He's an ass-grabber." Misako went pale and felt dizzy but the girl didn't notice. "I know exactly who I intend to be standing next to at midnight," the girl went on. "Do you see that guy with the crewcut at the end of the bar? I'm about to start making my way down there now."

Misako couldn't see anyone. The room was filling up with dark spots. She was on the verge of hyperventilating. She grabbed up her black shawl and purse and slid off the barstool. "Please," she said weakly, "do me a favour and tell my friend that Misako got sick from the champagne and had to go home. Her name is Sachiko and she'll be back looking for me soon. Thanks."

"Okay," the girl said. "You do look pale." Misako didn't hear her. She was already pushing through a hazy fog of celebrants standing near the door.

There wasn't a taxi that would stop for her. It was a busy night and Misako didn't know the hand signals to indicate that she would pay double the fare. After five minutes standing on the corner, she gave up.

Breathe deeply and walk quickly. That was the advice Misako gave herself as she headed home. It was going to be a dozen blocks or more. At least, she consoled herself, she could walk through the Ju-Bon area, which was several busy streets of neighbourhood stores. There would be people there doing their last-minute shopping for the three-day holiday.

All the stores were open and the streets were crowded with ordinary people going about their business. The familiar sounds and smells calmed her. Misako began to feel safe. She thought about how she used to shop for the holidays and wondered how Mother Imai was managing alone. She pictured the Imai kitchen and her mother-in-law trying to work and still peek past the bamboo curtain to see the seasonal extravaganza on the television set. She passed a red public phone and actually fished a ten-yen coin from her purse before she thought better of the impulse.

Suppose Hideo was home? She was feeling sorry for Mother Imai, but she couldn't face Hideo, not even his voice. Even Mother Imai's voice would make her cry. Misako put the coin away and walked on, feeling totally dejected. It would have been nice if she could have shopped for tomorrow's New Year's breakfast, but Sachiko had told her it wasn't necessary. Everything was arranged.

The stalls jutting out from the stores were loaded with lavish food for the feasts. Misako bought two large apples, just for the pleasure of carrying a paper bag, and crossed the street. That's when she saw the *sento*, or public bath. It was down the street, perhaps a half a block away. She could see the sign with the large red character that means "hot water." Misako hadn't been in a public bath since her university days. It seemed exactly the right healing treatment after the awful experience in the foreign bar. She wanted to be among Japanese who were comfortable in their ordinary Japanese skins. She wanted to wash away the horror of those scotch-stinking, pink, wet lips telling her they would force themselves on her at midnight. Oh yes, she wanted a body scrub and a long soak in a deep, hot bath.

Stopping at a small shop that specialized in sleepwear, she bought a soft cotton sleeping kimono and a flannel kimono robe. Next stop was a drugstore where she bought a plastic basin and a packet of two small towels. As she headed toward the bath, she made one more stop for a pair of common wooden clogs.

Misako could imagine herself scrubbed and clean, wearing her shawl over her sleeping kimono and robe, carrying the plastic basin and making that unmistakably Japanese music of wooden clogs on the pavement as she walked home. She looked at her watch. It was a quarter past eleven. If she hurried with the bath, she could make her way home through the back streets and hope to hear the last drones of some temple bell.

The bathhouse had two sliding doors of frosted glass. Misako entered the one marked "female" and bought a ticket from a man sitting up on a high stool, behind a high, narrow desk. The man took her 200 yen, bobbed his balding head and went back to rubber-necking over the glass wall that separated him from the baths.

Misako removed her shoes and entered the dressing room, where she undressed, neatly folding her clothes into a rattan basket. With only the skimpy bath towel held modestly in front of her, she slid open another glass door and entered the steamy bathing room. Ignoring the other nude women, she knelt on the tile floor before a set of hot and cold faucets and filled her plastic basin to wash. At the next set of faucets, a woman was washing her daughter's back as the child sat on a small stool. Men's voices could be heard over the tile wall that separated the two baths.

Twice, Misako rubbed herself with soap and rinsed it off by filling the basin several times and throwing it over her body. When she finally felt clean, she eased her body into the far end of the large rectangular tub where there was only one elderly woman soaking. The almost scalding water covered Misako's shoulders and turned her skin the colour of cooked shrimp. The few seconds of pain had its rewards. Slowly, Misako could feel the stiffness in her muscles loosen. It had been such a long, difficult day. Her neck and shoulders felt as if they had been bound up with large, coarse rope. Now, the tension was softening, unknotting and floating away to be dissolved in the healing heat.

She took a deep breath and smelled the men's hair tonic drifting with the steam over the wall that separated the sexes. Hideo had used the same hair tonic. It was called *Kami no moto*; the bathroom in the Imai house always smelled of it. She still loved that smell. Closing her eyes, Misako could picture the handsome Hideo as he had looked, standing nude before the mirror combing his thick, black hair. She pressed her back against the side of the bath, wishing the hot water could ease the ache in her heart. Softly, very softly, she began to hum to herself as the words of the song "Yesterday" ran through her head.

Misako leisurely strolled home through the back streets, feeling relaxed and loving the *clip-clop* sound of the wooden sandals. The night watchman at the apartment house smiled at the sight of a tenant of his fancy apartment house obviously returning home from a public bath. Sachiko was far less amused. She was standing in the living room with her hands on the back of her hips, a pose she had copied years ago from photographs of her ideal, Coco Chanel.

"Where have you been?" Her voice sounded cross. "I've been very, very worried about you. When I heard you left feeling ill, I rushed home. That was over an hour ago."

"I'm sorry," Misako said softly. "I went to the public bath."

"I can see that. You look like you're staying at a hot spring resort. We have a bath and a shower in this apartment. Why would you go walking around looking like that?"

Misako left her clogs at the entrance, and put down the plastic basin and the shopping bag holding her red suit and shoes. Removing her shawl, she stepped into the living room before answering. "I am Japanese," she said firmly. "I am not ashamed to go to a public bath."

"That's not what I mean," Sachiko protested.

"Once more," Misako continued, "I am not comfortable in foreign bars. I don't know how to sing 'Bye, Bye Bird.' I don't want to yell 'Happy New Year.' And, I especially don't want to kiss drunken foreigners."

"What are you talking about?" Sachiko was beginning to get a hint of the problem. She was also amazed at her friend's tone. It put Sachiko on the defensive.

"I don't want to do those things either," she said. "I only planned for us to stay there for a short time. It was a business call and I wanted you to experience something different. I intended us to go to Meiji Shrine at eleven o'clock."

"Then why didn't you tell me?" Misako was standing with her head bowed, looking at the white living room rug. Tears began to roll down her cheeks. Sachiko sank down on the white rug to sit Japanese style. The posture spoke volumes about her feelings. She put her hand over her mouth and thought for a moment before she spoke.

"I'm sorry, Chibi-*chan*. I've been a one-woman act for so long, I'm not used to talking over my plans with anyone. I just wanted to show you a memorable New Year's Eve."

Misako came and sat across from her. "I'm sorry too."

"Well, it can't be helped now," Sachiko said with that little French shrug of the shoulders that accepted whatever fate had dished out.

"It can't be helped," Misako repeated.

That was the end of their first adult disagreement. Before they said goodnight, each woman bowed formally to the other on the white rug. "*Akemashite o-medeto gozaimasu,*" they said to one another. "The New Year has begun—Congratulations!"

They left each other smiling, looking forward to their New Year's breakfast. Sachiko was had taken care of everything. The food would be delivered about ten in the morning.

Misako's smile faded when she closed the door to her own room. She opened the desk drawer, took out Hideo's picture and started to cry. This was the worst New Year of her life. The thought of him spending it with Fumiko was almost too painful to bear. Misako threw the picture back into the desk drawer and slammed it shut. At least it gave her some small satisfaction to lock up his likeness in a small dark space.

Sachiko was in her room, still feeling annoyed at Misako for running off to a common public bathing house. Well, maybe she was expecting too much. Misako was still a country girl at heart. However, she certainly had a talent for organization and her Japanese script was beautiful. It gave an enormous touch of class to the handwritten invitations and notes that were sent to customers. All in all, it was working out nicely. Their meeting in Wako Department Store had been a stroke of serendipity for both of them.

Sachiko knew that for a woman who had no family, it was a gift to have someone she could totally trust. Every successful samurai needed a faithful retainer. Having Misako live in the same apartment wasn't the best arrangement but it wouldn't be forever. It was almost time to talk to Misako about finding her own place; something small but nice. Sachiko was prepared to pay the expensive key money for her. It was something like Auntie Kaz paying for Sachiko's teeth.

And then there was that very handsome, soon-to-be ex-husband of Misako's. Their meeting had been another bit of serendipity. He was a black-haired rat for sure, but he was a very sleek, cocky black-haired rat, exactly the type that excited her hunting instincts.

TWENTY-ONE
January 1966

With Keiko in charge, the Ichimura hospital and household were greeting the New Year in perfect order. Everything had been cleaned, all the bills had been paid and the *juzume* traditional New Year delicacies were ready. There were plum blossom eggs, sweet soya beans, rising sun fish cakes, glazed sardines, gingko nuts on pine needles, brush-shaped ginger, lotus root pickles, spinach dressed with sesame and many more of the traditional delicacies which have been offered and eaten at New Year since time immemorial. The many-tiered nests of lacquer boxes were put together in a presentation that amounted to nothing short of an artistic triumph. Each tier of the gastronomical treasure chest contained three, five or seven types of food. There was a box for grilled food, mostly fish; another for boiled food, mostly vegetables; another for appetite teasers, pretty hors d'oeuvres and sweetmeats. Keiko arranged it all, carefully conforming to what her mother-in-law had taught her, aware that few modern house-wives managed to carry on the old traditions to the letter.

Keiko's talent for organization was connected with her passion for order and numbers. As a child, the abacus had been her favourite toy. Anyone who knew her understood that even now she could take that implement of taut wire in a frame, slide the counters on the wires and solve mathematical problems with lightning speed.

Early in their marriage, Dr. Ichimura's mother observed this talent and asked her new daughter-in-law to help with the hospital's books. Keiko obliged by spending a few hours perusing the big old-fashioned ledgers. The books turned out to be testimonials to several amateur interpretations of account keeping. She could make out three different hands, and three different lines of rationale, juxtaposed in rows of jumbled notations and even mistakes in simple arithmetic. Keiko shook her abacus and ordered a brand new ledger. She started with the payroll, sitting in the office for hours on end, content to swim in a sea of figures. The ledgers and desk became Keiko's domain.

Dr. Ichimura padded in his favourite slippers from the hospital to his living quarters in anticipation of the New Year's breakfast. His youngest son, Taro, was home from university. His eldest son was still doing his internship at a hospital in far off Buffalo, New York. The doctor smiled when he saw his wife wearing a large white apron over her kimono. It reminded him of his mother. It was her generation that had always worn kimono. When she was alive, she had insisted that Keiko wear kimono on New Year's Day.

"If Japanese holiday traditions are completely put aside, then all our old values will soon be lost," the older woman often said. Keiko kept the New Year kimono custom to please her husband and honour her mother-in-law's memory, even though she would have been far more comfortable in her brown wool slacks and turtleneck sweater.

By nine-thirty, Keiko had removed her apron and joined her family at the table. Dr. Ichimura poured the warm *otoso*, a sweet sake, from the decorated pot and they congratulated each other on the New Year. Keiko smiled even though she was thinking of her daughter in Tokyo. Since Misako was not celebrating in the Imai home, why couldn't she have come home to Niigata for the holiday? Would there be a New Year's breakfast in Sachiko's Tokyo apartment?

Worrying about Misako in Tokyo weighed heavier on her heart than concern for Teishin at the temple. By noon, she would find that New Year's morning at the temple was more of a disaster than she could have imagined. The news came from a nurse at the hospital.

"I thought you would like to know that I heard Teishin-*san* is not well enough to receive New Year's callers today."

"What? Not well? What's wrong with him?" Keiko asked. The nurse didn't know the details. Keiko got on the phone. It rang for a long time before the priest Konein answered.

"Yes, Teishin-*san* has a very bad cold. Most of the guests didn't stay more than a few minutes. Some of the women from the congregation tried to get him to go to bed, but he insisted he had to stay up to greet callers."

Keiko drove to the temple immediately.

Obviously sick, but still stubborn, Teishin sat in the receiving room, looking miserable, huddled over a small charcoal hibachi, trying to warm his hands. His face was partly covered by a surgical mask to prevent others from being infected with his horrendous cold. He coughed and his eyes were red and watery.

"You look terrible," Keiko told him. "Why aren't you in bed?"

"I have to be here to greet the New Year's callers." His voice filtered weakly through the mask.

"Nonsense! Anyone can see you are sick. Have you eaten breakfast?"

Teishin shook his head. His eyes had the expression of a helpless animal. Keiko tied back her kimono sleeves, put on the apron she kept at the temple, and began issuing orders. First, she told Konein to heat some soup, and then she went directly to her father's old room, which was now Teishin's, to prepare his futon. The moment she slid the *shoji* door open, she felt the dampness. She stepped on the *tatami* floor and could feel the wet cold through her white *tabi* socks. The window wasn't entirely closed and the place felt like the inside of a refrigerator. When she opened the closet, she smelled mildew.

Keiko tried to control a mounting anger. This had been her parents' room. Her grandparents had spent much of their lives here. Her father was born in this room. How dare anyone contaminate it like this?

"What has happened here?" she shouted as she started to pull the futons out of the closet onto the floor. Everything was damp. "How did these quilts get so wet?" she spoke in a loud, agitated voice. Konein appeared at the door, looking nervous. "How did these quilts get in this condition?" Keiko demanded. "No wonder Teishin-*san* is sick. Has he been sleeping on these?"

Konein hunched his shoulders and answered in a small voice. "I'm not sure," he said. "Teishin-*san* keeps the window open at night. The snow sometimes comes into the room."

"Is he going mad?" she almost screamed. With this rush of rage, Keiko began to pull all the quilts out of the closet. "All damp," she said. "Everything is damp!" She reached into the very back of the closet and pulled hard on the summer quilt. It flew out onto the pile that already lay on the floor. The white silk-covered box of the unknown ashes flew with it and bounced against the wall. The silk knot held fast, but there was a cracking sound when the wooden box broke inside the wrapping. Keiko stared at it in horror. She slammed the *shoji* shut and rushed down the hallway to the room where Teishin was sitting shivering as he sipped his soup.

Two hours later, Teishin was fast asleep in a dry, windowless room, located behind the big altar. With the help of two male members of the congregation who were still lingering, Keiko lit kerosene stoves to heat the temple. The damp futons were hung on bamboo poles set up in the long corridor and the *shoji* doors were removed from her father's former room. Keiko had Konein take the silk cloth that held the broken box and the unknown ashes to the back altar room. It was all she could do for the moment.

"Teishin-*san* needs a doctor's attention. You should have called me," she scolded as she left through the kitchen door. "I'll be back in an hour with my husband."

Konein sat on the broken chair near the telephone, chain-smoking, until several women arrived, asking if there was anything they could do to help. News travels fast, Konein thought. He was sure the entire neighbourhood had heard Keiko barking orders like a general on the battlefield.

⁂

Sachiko looked over the top of the newspaper at Misako and noticed she was chewing on her bottom lip. She remembered that it was a sign that all was not well with her friend.

"All right, out with it. What is on your mind this on beautiful second day of a brand new year?"

Misako hesitated before answering. "I know you told me not to contact the Imai house, but I have to pick up a kimono to wear to Kamakura tomorrow."

"Stay away from that house until Ogawa-*san* returns from abroad. Lawyers don't like their clients disregarding their advice."

"I can't stop living because Ogawa-*san* is out of the country. Tomorrow is the only outing I'm taking during this holiday and I want to wear kimono. It's the New Year!"

"Fine," Sachiko said, turning the pages of the newspaper. "I have all kinds of kimono stored in my closet. Take your choice."

Misako managed a small smile. "Thanks, but I really want to wear my own."

"Suit yourself," Sachiko said with a shrug, "but I think it's dangerous to go anywhere near that family. You could accidentally undo whatever your lawyer has done so far on your case."

Misako raised her hands in exasperation. "What has Ogawa-*san* done to undo? I've seen him once and never heard from him since."

"Have a little patience, Chibi-*chan*. You don't want to spend the rest of your life regretting a mistake made in haste."

Misako folded her arms over her chest. "What mistake can I make by simply fetching something that belongs to me?"

"Don't tell me I didn't warn you," Sachiko said. "I think you are just a little rabbit hopping into a den of wolves."

Misako was still hurt and angry about Hideo's betrayal, but she hardly thought of the Imai household as a den of wolves. She called, wished Mother Imai a Happy New Year and told her she would be around to get some of her things at four o'clock that afternoon.

Mother Imai hung up the phone and ran upstairs to wake Hideo with the news. He lit a cigarette and sat up in his bed thinking. Just before noon, he called his lawyer.

Mr. Fukusawa wasn't happy about being disturbed on the second day of the New Year holiday. He had been looking forward to the rest. He wanted to lie around the house and watch television all day long. But this Imai case was giving him trouble and he had bragged that he would get Mrs. Imai to sign the divorce papers soon. He had regretted his words because he had not been successful in even talking to her on the telephone. That woman she was living with was like a watchdog and the hotshot lawyer was sure to have something up his sleeve. However, he had a little something up his sleeve as well and it was time to put his plan in action.

"Listen," the lawyer said, "my wife and I will visit your home about three-thirty this afternoon. Have a friend—someone you can trust— there, someone your wife doesn't know. It will look as if we are New Year's callers when she arrives. I'll find a way to talk to your wife alone and see if we can't get these papers signed once and for all."

Hideo went along with the plan. When Misako arrived, Hideo would be in the living room entertaining their guests. When Misako went upstairs, Fukusawa would go into the dining room and make sure the papers were ready. When she came down the stairs, he would call her into the dining room and try to reason with her. If she agreed to sign, Fukusawa's wife and the other visitor could act as the two witnesses that were required. To cover any possible slip-up with the plan, Hideo put his mother in a taxi and sent her to visit her sister. He didn't want his mother saying anything that would make Misako suspicious.

Misako hesitated outside the house. She wasn't sure if she should ring the bell. At exactly four o'clock she merely slid open the kitchen door as if she was returning from the daily grocery shopping. No one was in sight, but she heard soft voices coming from the living room. She slipped out of her shoes and stood in the entrance, aware that something wasn't right.

"Excuse me," she called out as if she was a tradesperson at the kitchen door.

Hideo appeared and merely grunted a cold greeting. Again, his expression made her feel as if all this unhappiness was her fault. He told her he had guests in the living room.

"I am sorry to disturb your guests," she said.

"You don't know them so there is no need to be introduced." It was as if she was the maid coming to pick up a forgotten umbrella. "*Dozo*," he said. "Your things are still upstairs. Go and get what you need."

As soon as she ascended the stairs, Hideo went back to the living room and Fukusawa took his briefcase into the dining room. Upstairs, Misako knelt before the open dresser in the hallway. Each kimono was separately wrapped in handmade rice paper. She opened several to find the one she wanted. It had white plum blossoms intertwined with an octagon design against a deep-blue background. The fragrance from the delicate wooden drawer was sweet, but it merely sharpened the sense of desolation that she had been feeling from the moment she'd entered the house. She touched the silk's softness and thought how wrong it was that her trousseau should be more enduring than her husband's love.

Her *zori* slippers and kimono handbag were kept in boxes in the bedroom. Nervously, she slid open the door to the place where she and Hideo had once slept happily in each other's arms. The room was different now: it felt cold, unlived-in. It reminded her of her step-grandmother's room after her death. The brocade cloth was pulled down over the mirror of her dressing table and her hairbrush, perfume bottles and hand-mirror were gone. She noticed her name written on a cardboard box in the corner. It was obvious that she was being moved out. As far as the Imai family was concerned, she was dead.

Misako found the boxes containing her *zori* slippers and kimono handbag and wrapped them in a silk *furoshiki*. The kimono, *obi*, socks, and underwear she wrapped in a large square of brightly coloured cotton. The two bundles were awkward to carry. Halfway through her struggle to get down the narrow stairs, Misako realized that a strange man was on a lower step, taking her bundles from her arms.

"Mrs. Imai, please, let me help you. Surely you can't see the steps. You

221

will fall." Confused, Misako allowed him to take her bundles and followed him down the stairs, into the dining room.

"Thank you," she said.

The man bowed. "You must be wondering who I am. My name is Fukusawa, and to be truthful, I am your husband's attorney. But," he added, lowering his head and lifting his hand in a sign of peace, "I am one man who knows that you have been treated very badly. If you would please sit down for just one minute, Mrs. Imai, I will explain."

There were a number of papers spread out neatly on the table, along with cups and the teapot she had made tea in for years. It occurred to Misako that this was exactly the kind of situation that Sachiko had tried to warn her about. Still, Misako knew she was dead to this family and she wanted to know what their spokesperson had to say. It would be like sitting in on the reading of one's own will. Misako imagined she was a ghost sitting down at her worldly dining-room table.

"Mrs. Imai," the lawyer started, as he eased himself into the chair next to her. "I can only imagine what you have suffered. This must be a terrible time for you. Would you allow me to ask you one question?"

"All right," Misako said. Her voice was barely audible.

The lawyer poured tea and handed Misako a cup. "Mrs. Imai, do you have any hope that this divorce will not take place?"

Misako took a sip of tea. When she placed the cup back on the table, she shook her head slowly.

"Let me assure you," the lawyer's voice was placating, "that I realize that you deserve every consideration possible. If there is unfortunately no hope for this marriage—and it is my understanding from your husband, as well as from yourself, that there is not—then, well, you should have the most generous amount of compensation possible."

Misako looked up and stared at the man in the thick glasses. She hadn't even considered "compensation." What did he mean by compensation?

Fukusawa was beginning to get slightly rattled by this woman's silence and her large sad eyes. He had to make his pitch quickly, get to the point. He cleared his throat and sat up straight in his chair. "We are Japanese, Mrs. Imai. Proud of our country and our traditions. However, the truth is that in this country, women do not usually receive much monetary settlement in divorce cases. Here, look at this chart I have prepared." He dragged his chair slightly closer to Misako and placed a large graph on the table in front of her. "Here is a general graph of the amount of money that Tokyo women, in your husband's economic range, have received in divorces in the last ten years. Look here, the usual amount is about five hundred thousand yen. There are only ten cases in which it has been one million yen or over, only two cases in which it has been two million."

Misako blinked at the paper and felt a lump growing in her throat.

"You see," he went on speaking very kindly, "I have been working on your behalf. Sign this paper and you will go down on this chart as one of only three women who have received the generous sum of two million yen. That's a great deal of money, Mrs. Imai. Think about it. Your husband is determined to divorce you. No court will give you more and think of the long, drawn-out pain of going into family court, month after month, after month. A new year, Mrs. Imai. A time to start a new life."

Misako pressed her hands on her ears and stood up. "Please, I don't want to hear any more. I have to call a taxi. I just want to leave."

"Of course, Mrs. Imai. I understand. I don't want to distress you more. I'll call you a taxi immediately."

He leaned over to the telephone and dialled. "There you are, Mrs. Imai. The taxi will be here in ten minutes." Then he pushed the papers in front of her and spoke in a whining tone.

"Oh, Mrs. Imai. Why don't you simply sign this paper so you can go on with your life? Why would you want to drag this pain out? I can see how you are suffering." He handed Misako the pen. "Your signature, Mrs. Imai. Right here. It's for the best."

"Please, leave me alone," Misako said almost in tears. Can't you leave me alone and let me have some peace?"

The lawyer's answer was well oiled. "The truth is there will be no peace until this the divorce is over with. You have the power to make it happen now. All you have to do is sign your name and it is finished."

"All right!" Misako said in defeat. "I hate this whole situation. I just want it to be over."

"That's right, Mrs. Imai. That's right. Of course you understand, we need two witnesses. Do you mind if my wife and friend come in to witness the signing of this document?"

Without waiting for an answer, Fukusawa made a noise in his throat and Misako sensed people entering the room. She accepted the pen. The strangers were standing behind her chair.

"You understand you will be divorced, and no longer have any claim on the Imai family?"

Misako shivered at the cold words. "Yes," she said in a small voice.

"Good," the lawyer said. "Then please sign here, Mrs. Imai. Good, now, here and here. I need three copies. Yes, that's fine. Thank you."

Misako took a deep breath. "Now, Mr. Imai," she heard the lawyer say, "if you will kindly do the same." His voice was very formal. Misako hadn't realized that Hideo was in the room.

The bell tinkled as the kitchen door slid open. The taxi driver stood in the entrance and called. Misako stood up and made a quick bow to the group that was bent over the dining table, signing papers. She kept her head down because her eyes were brimming with tears. All she wanted to do was gather up her bundles and escape. Fukusawa already was carrying her things. She put her shoes on and started out the door. Fukusawa followed and handed the bundles to the driver. Before Misako climbed into the car, Fukusawa bowed to her and handed her an ordinary paper shopping bag that she had never seen before.

"I'm afraid this isn't mine," she said.

"You are mistaken, Mrs. Imai. This most certainly is yours. You agreed to it in the document." With that he bowed again. The taxi backed out the driveway.

Hideo hadn't come out of the house to say goodbye. Five years of marriage and he couldn't even say goodbye. The thought was so painful that she began to cry. The driver kept his eyes on the road, pretending not to notice. After a few minutes, she pulled herself together and wiped her eyes. Along with the pain, there was a strange feeling of relief. Well, she thought, being dead to the Imai family doesn't make me dead to the world. I'll survive.

She sat trying to calm herself for a minute and then, purely out of curiosity, looked into the shopping bag that was on the seat next to her. There were two layers of white tissue paper, which she removed. The taxi driver glanced back when he heard a gasp. The shopping bag was full of new ten-thousand yen notes. Two million yen in cash, all stacked neatly in an ordinary paper shopping bag.

Misako stared down at the money and bit her lip as the world took on the pinkish hue she saw when she was angry. Damn them! Damn the whole Imai family, she thought and pushed the shopping bag away. She folded her arms across her chest trying to swallow down the fury. "How insulting," she said under her breath. "An ordinary paper shopping bag. How did I ever marry into such a vulgar family? They didn't even have the manners to wrap the money in a silk *furoshiki*."

TWENTY-TWO

$\mathcal{T}$okyo's weather was glorious for the first two days of the New Year. The winter sun polished the streets while gusts of playful wind pushed white clouds across a China-blue sky. Sometimes, the wind swept down to catch the long silk sleeves of the young girls' holiday kimonos, making them flap and wave like colourful sails in a festive regatta. On both mornings, Sachiko and Misako enjoyed a rare view of Mount Fuji from their living-room window.

On the third morning, the sacred mountain disappeared behind a veil of cold rain and Misako woke up steeped in melancholy. Her pounding head reminded her of yesterday's calamity at the Imai house. "I can't go to Kamakura today," she told the bathroom mirror. "I'll call and say I'm sick. It wouldn't be a lie." The face that looked back at her was puffy and the eyes looked empty; it was shocking. It reminded her of a homeless, drunken man she once saw emptying his bowels on a piece of newspaper in a deserted alley. Misako had been horrified and had run from the scene. But she had never forgotten the dull expression of irremediable defeat in that man's eyes as he looked up at her. The loss of dignity was almost more shocking than what the man was doing. Misako was appalled that she should think of that scene now as she looked at her own face.

"Will I allow Hideo to destroy me?" she asked the mirror. There was only one answer to that question: an unequivocal "No." The determination in her voice seemed to switch the light back on behind her eyes. "I will not!"

Misako washed her face, applied some beauty cream, got into her jeans and braved the wet walk to Roppongi. She knew the French bakery was open this morning, making the first croissants of the New Year. The thought of Sachiko's pleasure hurried Misako along the dreary streets. Giving her friend this small gift was a way of saying she was sorry. Misako didn't blame Sachiko for being upset with her. The lawyer Ogawa wouldn't have considered taking her on as a client if it weren't for Sachiko. Now, her stupid action was going to make Sachiko lose face.

The rain weakened into a drizzle on the walk back home. Misako carried the bag carefully against her chest to keep it well under the umbrella. The

225

warmth felt good through her jacket. For the first time, Coco ran to meet her when she entered the apartment.

"What's attracting you, Coco? Is it me or the croissants?" she asked as she bent down to pet the cat. "I hope it's me because I need a friend today." After that confession, Misako decided that she wouldn't cancel the trip to Kamakura. Kensho was her friend, her very good friend, even though Sachiko did not approve.

"What could you possibly have in common with a Zen monk?" Sachiko asked during breakfast.

"He's just my friend," Misako said in a serious voice.

"Ummmm," Sachiko said, still savouring the croissant. "I'm always suspicious when a woman says that about a man. Men and woman can't be just friends, unless they are both at least seventy years old."

"Not true," Misako said, feeding Coco bits of the buttery treat. "Kensho-*san* is not like other men. I told you he is very tall and strange looking. Not attractive. Besides, he's a priest, very spiritual."

The room rang with Sachiko's wonderful laugh. "Not like other men?" she said. "Tell me, Chibi-*chan*, what makes him different? Does he squat when he pees?"

Misako sat up so quickly with surprise that the cat jumped off her lap. "Really, Sachiko, you say such shocking things."

"Well, come on, answer me," Sachiko said, still laughing. "Do you think he squats or stands?"

Misako was beginning to understand how much Sachiko enjoyed shocking her. She decided not to wilt under the candid inquiry. "I suppose like all men, he stands to relieve himself."

"Then he has to have something to hold in his hands and you had better be careful." Sachiko warned.

Misako felt her cheeks burning with shame. I wish you wouldn't talk like that, it seems so crude. Kensho-*san* is a wonderful man, intelligent and spiritual."

"Excuse me for laughing," Sachiko said. "There is one part of a man that is not capable of spirituality. That part has only two practical functions; most men think peeing is the less important of the two."

"How did you become so cynical about men?"

Sachiko grinned. "Let's say that working as a nightclub hostess was educational. Aren't you even a little bitter about the way Hideo treated you?"

"Kensho-*san* is nothing like Hideo."

"*Umm*," Sachiko purred. "If you say so, but if you find yourself alone with him in some isolated temple room, you might be in for a surprise."

Misako moaned and put her head in her hands as a gesture of protest.

Sachiko performed one of her great French shrugs and put the breakfast remains on a tray. "I don't know why I bother to give you advice. You never take it and you have no sense of humour." She stood up and started for the kitchen.

Misako sat petting the cat and chewing her lip. She didn't want to argue, especially since they wouldn't be seeing each other for a while. They had made their separate plans for this week when clients were recovering from the holidays. Sachiko was going off to Hawaii for a sunny rest with Auntie Kaz. Maybe with a mystery man as well, for all she knew. Misako was too busy thinking about how she would get through the next few days.

Going to Kamakura would probably be agreeable; going to Niigata tomorrow was cause for trepidation. Misako had to tell her parents the details of her divorce and her plans to find an apartment in Tokyo. She would have preferred to be going to Hawaii.

Sachiko came back into the room clapping her hands like a school teacher organizing a class. "If you are going to Kamakura, you had better get going. I'll do your hair and help you put your kimono on. You'll look so beautiful, the poor priest won't be able to control himself. Then you'll know Sachiko was right." It was so like Sachiko to still be expansive, even when they had disagreements.

The results of Sachiko's creative talent turned Misako into the most elegant lady boarding the train for Kamakura. Two older women riding in the same car judged her to be a high-class geisha. Not only was her hair and makeup perfect, but her impeccably arranged blue kimono was accented by a silk *haori* jacket that was the colour of ripe persimmons. Little touches of Sachiko's own expensive accessories were used as enchanters: the coral hairpin, the flower-embossed leather handbag and even the Kyoto hand-tie-dyed, purple *furoshiki* that wrapped the gift box of cookies. The colours blended together as skilfully as in a fine kabuki costume.

Kensho made his way to the Kamakura Station, asking himself why his heart was racing. He could hear it pounding in his chest as he walked, and was afraid that others on the street could hear it as well. It made him blush. He looked up at the sky, trying to control the urge to rub his bald head. The sun had come out to pull a pale rainbow ribbon across the sky.

No one else on the street seemed to notice it. Kensho managed to tell himself that everything was planned to the last detail. Misako's visit to the temple would go well.

Misako stepped from the train and stood on the platform. Kensho saw her and quickly stepped back into the station building. He needed a moment to recover. She looked so beautiful! It was as if the rainbow had come down from the sky and touched her. In his eyes she was sparkling. His big, bony knees were threatening to collapse. He swallowed hard and walked back out on the platform—terrified.

The two ladies from the train found an excuse to linger on the platform. They had to see who this geisha was meeting. Some rich businessman they speculated, perhaps a politician, off for a secret rendezvous. Who else could afford such an exquisite creature?

Their mouths fell open when they saw a gangling giant in priest's clothing, galumphing up the platform toward them. He was rubbing his bald head, his ears glowed like neon and he was grinning like an idiot. The lovely little creature was smiling. She looked perfectly delighted to see the walking skeleton.

"*Maa!*" one of the ladies said.

"He must be a go-between," the other whispered. "Perhaps the man she's really meeting is too famous to be seen in a public place."

"Never happened!" her travel partner said. "No discreet person would send such a go-between. Look at the attention he is attracting. Everyone is staring at them."

"Maybe her lover is a rich comedian. Only someone with a sense of humour would send that priest." Both women giggled, shrugged and went off on their outing in the ancient city of Kamakura.

Kensho's temple was a compound of several splendid buildings, nothing like the humble country temple where Misako spent her formative years. The altar room was large and elegant. Misako noticed the lack of clutter. The family temples that Misako knew usually had a great deal of decorative clutter. Here, the *tatami* mats were fresh and there were no patches in the *shoji* doors.

There were many monks walking about, including a couple of bald-headed foreigners. Kensho took Misako to view the meditation room. It was a big space with rows of *tatami* mats laid out separately on a plain, wooden platform. He explained that each priest had his own mat to sit and meditate on, as an assigned priest walked around with a stick, in the event

228

anyone was tempted to doze. He stepped up on one of the *tatami* mats and acted out the scenario of a novice monk trying to meditate, trying to stay awake, falling asleep and finally having a great whack come down on his shoulder. His mime was so funny that Misako clutched her tight *obi* and laughed until her body shook. As she laughed, one gossamer layer of the pain she had been living with loosened and fluttered away from her heart.

"Please, don't make me laugh anymore," she said, feeling grateful that there was no one else in the room.

"Why not?" he asked, "Laughter is nature's medicine."

"That may be so," she said, but something very sad happened yesterday. It doesn't seem right to laugh so soon."

"Did someone besides your grandfather die? Your grandfather wouldn't have wanted you to stop laughing on his account."

"No, it's not because of Grandfather. It is not *someone*, but *something* that died. Something precious. And I should be in mourning. Laughing seems disrespectful."

Kensho moved his head in understanding. He didn't want to pull on something not freely given. She'll tell me if she wants to, he thought.

They joined other guests in the eating hall for a simple lunch of miso soup, grilled ricecakes and sauce-simmered vegetables. Misako spoke politely to the people around her, but the tall priest said very little. He shifted uncomfortably and his ears had not gone back to their normal colour. The monks who served the individual trays of food kept their eyes lowered, but Kensho could tell they were dazzled by Misako. He caught the subtle looks they exchanged and he inwardly moaned at the thought of the teasing he would have to endure.

After lunch they heard chanting coming from the scriptures' hall. The *bok-bok* of the fish drum, punctuated by the delicate *ping* made by tapping a bronze bowl with a stick, were soothing sounds to Misako. She wanted to stay and listen. Kensho seemed impatient to leave.

"If you don't mind, I'd like to take you to another place," he said.

"I haven't seen everything here, have I?"

"No," he said and hesitated. "We should talk and we can't talk privately here."

Misako responded with a smile. She noticed his discomfort.

"I have arranged for us to have tea at a friend's villa," Kensho said. "My friend and his wife are in Tokyo, but their maid lives at the villa. It is only a short taxi ride away and we are expected."

The short taxi ride turned out to be almost fifteen minutes toward the hills that slope down to the ocean. An elderly maid met them at the door of an antiquated, sprawling, one-storey house. She was smiling and bowing. It was apparent that she knew Kensho very well. She said "Welcome" to Misako, but she said "Welcome back" to the priest as she helped them remove their *zori* slippers and *haori* jackets. She led them to a lovely eight-mat room where the maid moved about, plugging in a small electric heater, offering them cushions to sit on and serving steaming cups of hot tea. After a moment of comments about the weather, she excused herself, leaving the priest and Misako alone behind the closed *shoji* door.

Everything was suddenly very quiet. It was the silence that can settle down over an isolated house on a grey afternoon. No footsteps, no voices. Even the crows seemed to be resting.

They sat on their knees facing each other with only the tea cups and cakes between them. Kensho smiled and looked at her with adoring eyes. It was then that Sachiko's warning popped into Misako's mind. For the first time she felt uncomfortable being alone with this man. She sipped her tea to avoid his admiring gaze.

"Misako-*san*," he said with unaccustomed emotion. "Forgive me, but I have to say you look so beautiful in kimono."

"Thank you," she said softly and looked down into her tea cup. The air in the room was growing heavy with sentimental tension. Misako was beginning to feel edgy. Suppose Sachiko was right? she thought. Suppose this priest had more on his mind than friendship?

Not knowing what to do, Misako took a deep breath and nervously began to talk quickly about anything that came into her head, hoping to break the spell. "Actually, Kensho-*san*, I'm embarrassed. You see, Sachiko-*san*, the friend I am staying with in Tokyo, was responsible for dressing me up like this today. She was brought up in a kimono shop in Shibata and she knows all about wearing kimono. Sachiko-*san* and I went to school together and she can pull the collar tighter and tie an *obi* better than anyone I've ever known, better than the professionals in the beauty parlours."

"*Ah so*," the priest said. His eyes took on a slight glazed look.

"Some of these things belong to her," Misako chatted on as she touched the hairpin and the little decorations hanging from the front of her *obi*. "The jacket I wore belongs to her."

"Very beautiful," Kensho said quietly, referring to the accessories that she was jabbering on about. In her nervousness, Misako thought he was saying she was beautiful again and she panicked.

"Oh no," she stammered, "I'm only a fancy-wrapped package today, really," she went on. "I'm afraid you would be very disappointed if you unwrapped the package." Then she stopped, realizing she had said something perfectly silly and possibly suggestive. Her face flushed scarlet. "I didn't mean that the way it sounded."

The priest was looking at her with his head tilted sideways, wearing an expression of bemusement. "Misako-*san*, there is something very important that I have been wanting to tell you. It is the reason I called you in Tokyo and invited you to Kamakura."

"And the reason you have taken me to this place?" Misako asked, backing up slightly on her cushion.

"Well, yes," he said. "I'm sorry we didn't spend more time at the temple but we couldn't talk privately there."

"Is it important that we talk privately?" she asked, sitting up rigidly on the cushion.

Kensho's broke into a big smile. "Yes. I mean, really. Every time I think about it, I get so excited."

"Every time you think about what?" Misako asked with a gulp.

"Teishin-*san* wrote me saying that the skull showed a rare defect."

"Skull?"

"The skull of the bones found in the pond in Shibata," he said.

"Oh . . . *hai* . . . Shibata. Teishin-*san* wrote you? What kind of a defect?"

"The doctor who examined the skull told Mr. Saito that the girl had been born with no external auditory canal on the right side of her head." Kensho leaned forward. "Which means that she couldn't have had any hearing on her right side and probably had no ear."

"Which means," Misako began to slowly talk out her thoughts, "that a girl with that kind of defect would be remembered; someone easy to identify."

"Exactly. Teishin-*san* thinks there may be someone in Shibata who might remember hearing a story about a girl with only one ear. He is going to continue his investigation."

Misako couldn't help smiling. "Teishin-*san* has been investigating on his own?"

Kensho rubbed his head. "I'm not sure of the details."

"Grandfather would have been pleased." Misako said, finally letting her face relax into a smile. "What very good news. Maybe one day we will be able to bury the ashes in the girl's own family grave."

Kensho smiled and rubbed his hands. "I want to be there when that happens."

"So do I," Misako said. "Now I can't wait to talk to Teishin-*san*."

Misako's misunderstanding had been settled. They began talking as they had in the past. Just two friends sharing thoughts and experiences, comfortable as an old shoe before Sachiko had planted the pebble in it.

When she told him about signing her divorce papers, she managed to evoke yet another kind of emotion in Kensho's heart. She seemed so vulnerable, like a delicate bird, out of its cage, not knowing exactly how to fly in a large space. He wanted to reach out his hands to enfold the bird, to protect her, but knew he couldn't. It was best to change the subject. There was still one thing that he really wanted to ask.

"And how is your antenna these days?"

"Weak," she answered. "Very weak. I hardly get an advance signal that the telephone is going to ring. My mind has been so full of things that concern the office that I have no time to brood over my own problems."

"If you really wanted to snap off your antenna, you are in the right lifestyle."

"I don't know what I want anymore," Misako said, and changed the subject, her voice taking on a teasing tone. "By the way, why did the maid say 'welcome back' to you when we arrived? Do you live here as well as in the temple?"

"I was here this morning, before I met you at the station," he said. The owner of this house has a teahouse in the garden. Tea ceremony is his hobby and sometimes we practice together. Would you be willing to take tea made by such an amateur?"

Misako bowed and said, "I would be honoured."

He returned the bow. "Then I had better go ahead and light the charcoal burner in the tea house. I'll wait for you there."

Misako sat for a moment to prepare for the ceremony. First she removed her watch, as there should be no reminder of time in a teahouse, then she removed her rings to eliminate the chance of scratching a precious tea bowl. Fortunately, she had a clean pair of *tabi*-socks in her purse. When she was ready, she followed Kensho's directions to the sliding glass doors at the end of the hallway. There was a pair of straw sandals waiting on the rocky step into the garden. Carefully, she stepped down into them and followed the stone path to a small, thatch-roofed hut, stopping to wash her hands at a small stone fountain. Mentally cleansing her mind as well, she paused a moment to stand on the carpet of strewn pine needles, smelling the cool, wet air, before removing her sandals, sliding open the small door and crawling through the *nijiri-guchi*, the low entrance. The four-and-a-half *tatami* mat room had one window covered with crosspieces of bamboo. The hearth was sunken into the floor in a corner space and a kettle stood on a trivet over the charcoal fire. Misako kneeled before the *tokonoma* alcove and examined the scroll and flower arrangement. The flower arrangement was a single thin, barely flowering branch from a plum tree in an unglazed vase. The scroll was blank.

The puzzle demanded concentration. She stared at the blank scroll and felt a strong urge to write on it. "Love is pain," her mind wrote in flowing invisible characters down the white space. As she thought about it, the words slowly dissolved. She became aware of the soft bubbling of the kettle boiling on the brazier.

Kensho entered the room smiling. He knelt by the sunken hearth and bowed, but there was nothing stiff or formal about his greeting. Misako returned his bow.

"I'm not sure I understand," she said, indicating the blank scroll and plum branch with her eyes.

"Ah," he said and placed his big hands on his knees, "the plum branch promises spring."

"And the blank scroll?"

Kensho chuckled. "Since you are so skilled in the art of calligraphy, I had hoped you would honour the occasion by writing something."

Misako pulled herself, still kneeling, closer to the brazier. "Not so skilled," she said. "But if I was, what would you have me write?"

He tilted his head sideways for a moment, thinking. "Perhaps" he said slowly, " 'happiness is reached through the comprehension of sorrow.' Would that be appropriate, considering?"

"Too many words," Misako said teasingly.

Kensho rubbed his head. "And how would you say it?"

Misako folded her hands on her lap in silent thought. "Maybe," she said, "maybe, I would write: 'Love is pain.' "

The priest smiled. "Too few words."

"Then please add to my few words."

He hesitated and spoke slowly. "Love is pain. Pain is life. Life is love."

"Excellent," Misako whispered and bowed deeply.

Kensho returned the bow, stood up and went silently to the tiny adjoining room where the tea utensils were kept. Misako sat, allowing a new sense of peace to wash over her. The priest re-entered the room, walking in slow measured steps, hardly raising his feet from the floor, carefully carrying the tea vessel. When he was settled again by the sunken hearth, he paused for a few reflective seconds to mentally go over the prescribed ritual that was designed to reduce necessary motions to a minimum. The kettle's murmur bubbled a healing song. The tea ceremony had commenced.

TWENTY-THREE

*A*t a quarter after two in the morning of January fourth, an old rat in the Shibata temple heard a noise and stopped nibbling on a potato. He stretched his grey head and waddled across the kitchen before dropping down into a hole between the floorboards.

The noise the rat heard was Teishin's painful fit of coughing. The priest felt as if he was burning up, his throat was parched and his head ached. When he tried to raise himself on one elbow, pain stabbed his chest.

The coughing disturbed Konein, who was sleeping across the hall. The young priest left his warm futon to investigate. He found Teishin complaining of a terrible thirst and trying to throw off his quilts. Konein went to the kitchen to get a glass of water.

Exhausted from coughing, Teishin only took a few sips of the water before he fell back on his pillow. Konein felt Teishin's hot, dry forehead and ran to the bathroom for a wet towel. Wiping down the sick man's face and arms seemed to help. Teishin managed a nod of the head and a faint smile. Relieved, Konein went back to wet the towel again. When he returned, Teishin appeared to have fallen asleep; his breathing was laboured. Konein wiped the burning brow once more and sat cross-legged on the *tatami* next to Teishin's futon.

After a while, Konein himself fell asleep. When he woke up, Teishin's teeth were chattering; he said that his feet were freezing. Konein put the quilts back on him and ran to the kitchen again, this time for the hot water bottle. As he waited for the water to heat on the stove, he sat on the dilapidated chair and worried. His gaze went from the telephone on the wall, to the round clock that was ticking away steadily. It was almost three-thirty in the morning. It was no time to call Keiko, but his concern was blooming into fright. He knelt on the chair, dialled the number and waited. It seemed like an eternity of ringing in his ear. By now the kettle was steaming on the stove and he thought he could hear Teishin's voice calling faintly within the temple. The ringing continued.

Still, no answer and the kettle's steam was turning into a threatening billow. He tried to turn off the stove by reaching over the back of the chair.

The uneven pressure collapsed the already cracked leg. Konein fell over, hit his forehead and lay, face down on the floor while the telephone dangled in the air. The crashing sounds flowed up into the speaker. Konein could hear an anxious voice repeating "Hello, hello." He was trying to get up when the confused old rat chose that moment to leave his hole and scamper across the kitchen. Trying to escape out into the hallway, the rat passed close to the priest's feet. Konein sent a mulekick out at it, missed and fell flat again. When he finally was able to speak on the telephone, he was crying.

Dr. Ichimura and Keiko arrived at the temple in less than twenty minutes. The doctor listened to Teishin's chest and took the priest's temperature; it was 103 degrees. "Double pneumonia," he announced. "He has to be hospitalized."

Keiko felt overwhelmed. How would they care for such a sick man? Japanese country hospitals had very little nursing staff. The custom was for a family member to pack up a futon and tea kettle and move into the hospital with the patient. Keiko was like an older sister, but she couldn't possibly move into a ward in the Shibata General Hospital. The solution was to admit the priest as the first male patient at the Ichimura Women's Hospital.

Misako learned of Teishin's condition when she arrived at her mother's home that evening.

"He's very sick," Keiko told her. "It will be at least a day before the antibiotics take effect. He has trouble breathing. Papa is with him now. His temperature is 104. We have to get that down. Tonight could be critical."

The small private hospital was a one-and-a-half storey wooden building. Almost everything happened on the main floor where the operating-cum-delivery room was located. Along with the office and other needed spaces, there were two large rooms with six beds each and one room with two beds. Since most women were there for normal childbearing, there was no special recovery room. If one was needed, a space near the delivery room was sectioned off with a white screen. This happened when there was a birth by caesarean section, or a hysterectomy.

The hospital had two full-time doctors, Dr. Ichimura and Dr. Goto. Dr. Goto was sixty-three years old. He was thinking of retirement but agreed to stay until Dr. Ichimura's eldest son returned from his training in the United States. When needed, an anesthesiologist was called in from either the Shibata General Hospital, or from a hospital in Niigata City.

The upstairs of the building held three small single-bed rooms that were rarely used. They were reserved for a visiting doctor who had to stay the night, a patient who was very sick, or a place to hold the body of an unfortunate patient who had died. There was no elevator. Patients had to be carried up the stairs on a stretcher and the nurses and doctors had to climb up and down the stairs to care for them. It was an ideal out-of-the-way place to house the one and only male patient.

Teishin was lying on the narrow hospital bed in the small room at the end of the upstairs corridor. He was attached to intravenous tubes and an oxygen tank. Misako entered the room while a nurse was sponging him down. He wasn't aware of either of the women being there.

The priest was adrift on his own strange sea of illusion. As if reliving some shadowy prenatal memory, he floated over swells of warmth and wet, until a wave pulled him down, down into a stifling, esoteric breadth. Then, a painful struggle to swim up . . . up . . . until a deep kiss of air slowly returned him to floating in the endless dark sea. Sometimes he could hear the wind murmuring over his head, a muffled female voice. It sounded like the cooing of his mother.

Misako made it clear that she was there to help. The nurse taught her the basics of the sponge bath, and left the room. Sometimes the nurse would come back to check on the priest's temperature and breathing. She noted everything on the patient's chart.

Once the nurse pulled down the bed sheet and placed Teishin's limp penis into a urinal and encouraged the half-conscious priest to urinate, like a doting mother with her two-year-old, sitting on the potty. Misako blushed and looked away. "That's a good boy," the nurse said as she wiped him and returned the bed clothes. Teishin fluttered his eyes and went back to his own mysterious journey. "That goes with the job," the nurse grinned as she recorded the information on his chart.

Since Misako insisted on staying with the patient, she was told to wipe his face and arms with the cool cloth when needed and call a nurse if he had trouble breathing. This she did earnestly. Sometimes he stirred and mumbled ambiguous words; he would even open his eyes, but he never seemed to know her.

Dr. Ichimura came into the room about one in the morning. He had just delivered a healthy baby and wanted to check on the priest before finally going home to bed. He looked at the chart and took the patient's temperature.

"It's down a fraction," he told Misako. "Why don't you go to your own bed? Mother doesn't want you sitting up here all night."

Misako shook her head. "I want to help."

"Well, it is good that he is not alone. The staff is busy tonight."

"Papa, is he going to be all right?" Misako asked.

Dr. Ichimura took another look at the chart and frowned. "He's almost forty years old and usually in good health, which is very good. However, I'm told that he has been neglecting himself lately and that may be why his resistance to infection was low. Teishin-*san* is a very sick man right now. The antibiotics should be doing their work soon. We'll know more by tomorrow afternoon."

"That doesn't sound very promising," Misako said, a worried tone in her voice.

The doctor gave her an encouraging pat on the shoulder. "I think he will come through this, but it will take time and effort to clear those lungs and build up his strength."

Misako stood up and shook out the large, white apron she was wearing over her jeans and sweater. She stretched her arms and went to the window. A bright slice of moon hung over the snow-covered roof. "I never realized how much I cared about Teishin-*san*. He has always been so kind to us all. I want to help get him well, Papa."

"You are helping. He needs someone to keep an eye on him tonight," the doctor said and yawned. "Sorry, but it has been a long day. Call the nurse if there is a problem."

Misako sat by the bed again and looked into the sleeping face. Teishin didn't look like the jolly, chubby priest who had come to her grandfather's temple when she was still a schoolgirl. It seemed that he had always been part of their family. It felt right that she was here with him now. Misako put her head down on the bed and closed her eyes.

About four in the morning, Teishin became restless; she could tell he was not comfortable. His eyes fluttered and she thought he might be trying to say something. Misako removed the oxygen mask and put her ear down close to his lips, but couldn't understand what he was mumbling. Then she knew, the same way she sometimes knew the telephone was going to ring. He had to urinate, that had to be it. He must be feeling pressure on his bladder. After a moment of panic, she left the room to find a nurse. There was no one around. She stood on the top of the stairway and listened. Everything was silent. The lights downstairs were dim.

When Misako got back to the room, Teishin seemed to be trying to raise his shoulders. There was nothing she could do but a take a deep breath and do what she had seen the nurse do, remove the clean urinal from the cabinet next to the bed, quickly whip off the bed clothing and fold over his sleeping kimono so that his private parts were exposed. She hesitated, and then with one hand on each of his upper legs, pulled them apart. He looked like a big baby waiting for a diaper change. Misako made a face and lifted his soft penis gingerly, dropped it once in horror and then picked it up again. Her hand had to surround the thing before it could be shoved into the neck of the urinal. A minute passed and nothing happened. Misako tried to imitate the nurse, tapping him lightly on the shoulder, urging him on. Finally it came, flowing into the receptacle, making a sound like the rain running off the eaves of a house. Just as the nurse had done, Misako found herself saying "Good boy, good boy." When he was finished, his eyes fluttered.

Not knowing exactly how to write on the chart, Misako made a note on a pad. She wrote down the time and the amount of urine. After emptying the urine and washing her hands, she went back to the room and took the patient's temperature. It was hovering around the 103 mark. Misako added this information to her note. The patient looked pink and sweaty. She started wiping his face and arms again. A nurse came into the room carrying a replacement bottle for the intravenous and a large cup of tea for Misako.

"How is he doing?" the nurse asked.

"I thought he needed to urinate and I couldn't find anyone to help, so I managed myself. I wrote down the amount and time on that note pad. I took his temperature a few minutes ago. The information is on the note as well. He's been sweating a lot."

The nurse raised her eyebrows and read the note. "It's the high fever," she said, and went about her work changing the intravenous bottle. "Hopefully, he will be more alert and able to swallow tomorrow. Then we can get some real food into him."

Misako was standing by the bed with her rolled-up sleeves and white apron, wringing out the washcloth. The nurse smiled at her.

"You make a good nurse."

"Thank you," Misako said and took a sip of tea.

"You are lucky you can visit your parents around the holidays," the nurse commented. "I was married two years ago, but my husband is not keen on my being away from home for even a couple of days. How long do you plan to stay?"

"I'm not sure. I planned to stay five or six days. Now I want to wait until Teishin-*san* is well."

"That could be a while. I suppose your husband will complain."

"No," Misako said. "He doesn't care."

"You are the lucky one," the nurse said, raising her eyebrows again before she left the room.

Misako bit her lip and wondered what the nurse would say if she knew the truth; that she didn't have a husband anymore. She pulled the chair close to the bed, rested her elbows on her knees and clasped her hands, one over the other, under her chin.

"Neither you nor I are lucky," she said as she looked into the sick priest's face. His sagging cheeks were covered with dark stubble and his bald head was shadowy with the beginnings of hair growth. Poor Teishin-*san*," she whispered. "It has been so hard for you since Grandfather died, hasn't it? I understand. Sometimes it is difficult to find the strength to carry on."

In the silent, dim room, Misako began to cry. "Grandfather wouldn't want to see you like this. You have to get well again."

Under her clasped fingers, she was becoming aware of an unfamiliar heat radiating in the palms of her hands. It made her remember what the priest from Kamakura had told her about people's inner energy leaving their bodies through the palms of their hands. The realization that she was feeling her own energy pouring from one hand to another filled Misako with a kind of awe. Clasping her hands tighter and closing her eyes, she sat still and concentrated on feeling the surge of heat travelling from her navel, up to her shoulders, down her arms, out of the palm of one hand and into the other, to return back up her arms. Her energy was flowing up and around and down again, like an endless stream in her body. Gradually, the tiredness she had felt was being replaced with a glow of strength. Even the sadness she had been filled with minutes before was being washed away in the flow of her own recycled energy.

Very gently, Misako took Teishin's limp right hand and pressed it between her warm palms, thinking that it might be possible to pass some of this new-found strength to the sick priest.

"You are going to get well, Teishin-*san*," she whispered. "We are both going to grow strong and well."

⊕ ⊕ ⊕

The day was everything the travel agent had promised. The flower island of Kuai had blue skies, sparkling water, white sandy beaches and waving palm trees.

"Good morning," Auntie Kaz called, between coughs. She was leaning over the rail that separated the two hotel room balconies, wearing red silk pajamas, and smoking.

"Good morning," Sachiko said and waved a hand.

"Really, Sachi, if you lay out in that sun much longer you will look like an African."

Sachiko lowered her big sunglasses and grinned. "That's the idea! What are you doing up so early?"

Auntie Kaz blew a puff of smoke out toward the ocean. "Can't sleep in this place. It's too damn quiet. Anyway, I'm hungry."

"Okay, go brush your teeth and I'll be over to help you get dressed."

"Oh, good, good," Auntie Kaz giggled. "How about a neck massage?"

"Don't push your luck, dear. I'll be over in ten minutes."

The exchange between them was as usual, playful and loving. Long ago, they had unofficially adopted each other as family. Sachiko had never forgotten the day when she was desperate enough to ask the formidable Mrs. Teguchi for a job in the murky world of *misu shobai*. A different kind of nightclub owner could have taken advantage of the naive young woman from Niigata. It was tremendous luck that she walked into a nightclub that was owned by a lady who was already wealthy, who was contemplating retirement and had never wanted to run anything but a first-rate establishment. It was also fortunate that Sachiko brought out the maternal instinct in the hard-nosed businesswoman.

"How is this little protégé of yours turning out?" Auntie Kaz asked over broiled *mahi-mahi* and a large glass of wine. "Do you think she'll stay in Tokyo?"

"I don't know," Sachiko said. "Misako's work is wonderful but her personal life is complicated. In spite of all my warnings, she still allowed herself to be tricked by that bastard of a husband."

"Are you going to tell me the story?" Auntie asked, putting her wine glass down in anticipation.

"The story is still in progress, although she has already signed the divorce papers."

"*Maa*, that was fast! So, if the divorce is done, why is her life still complicated?"

Sachiko sighed. "Her mother doesn't like her working in Tokyo and Misako seems to keep getting involved in the lives of Buddhist priests."

Auntie Kaz's eyebrows shot half way up her forehead. "Priests? This sounds too rich. You have to tell me more."

Sachiko laughed. "I will, but right now I want to pick your brains about this coming interview on NHK. The interviewer wants to talk about the costumes I designed for the New Year Special. Rather than describing my designs, I am thinking of asking them to show a few film clips from the show. What do you think? How can I get the most out of a five-minute interview?"

Auntie Kaz reached for a cigarette. "Are you sure you want to have this interview? Most of your work is designing costumes for show-people. Your name is already well known in their circle. If you want national exposure, you are going to have gossips poking around in your private life. Are you ready for that?"

Sachiko did the exaggerated Gallic shrug. "Let them poke! People want me to design for them because they admire my work. I have never lied about my past."

Auntie Kaz's little face wrinkled into a frown before she took a long, slow drag on her cigarette. Her one strict rule in her long climb to success was to keep within her own business circle. She never wanted people to know too much about her. She didn't want anyone to be able to capitalize on her life by writing her story. A spotlight on someone as close as Sachiko could be dangerous. With poking, the muck-rakers could find out that Sachiko's dear friend and former employer had started out in a small bar in Osaka. They could find out that she had been quietly buying real estate in downtown Tokyo for the last ten years. She put her little chin in the air and exhaled.

"I think this TV interview would be a mistake, Sachie. Why do you want to be known to every little shopkeeper and farmer's wife in Japan?"

"I don't see the harm in it and I can't understand why you wouldn't want me to enjoy this kind of exposure."

Auntie Kaz leaned into the young woman who was as dear to her as a daughter. "Sachi, dear, I want you to enjoy everything life has to offer. I just don't want you to have to pay too dearly for it."

"I'll take that chance," Sachiko shrugged.

"Fine," Auntie Kaz said as she blotted her red lipstick on the hotel's white linen napkin. "Just don't say I didn't warn you."

TWENTY-FOUR

*T*here had been no particular urgency in Keiko's mind about pressing her daughter for news of her personal life as they talked on the telephone for almost an hour on New Year's morning. That was the day before Misako went to the Imai house to pick up her kimono. Now that she was home, Misako knew she had to tell her parents that she had signed the divorce papers and received the money. Teishin's unfortunate illness made procrastination easy.

The antibiotics were at work marshalling the priest's white corpuscles against the attacking bacteria. The battle within his body was on. Besides Dr. Ichimura, three women looked after the priest. There was a nurse to administer the care that took special training, Keiko looked in on him many times during the day, and Misako sat by his bed in the evenings and stayed near him during the night.

All three rooms on the second floor of the hospital were identical in size and furnishings. There was a narrow bed facing the door, a wooden chair next to the bed, a window opposite the door and a small white cabinet under the window. The walls were painted off-white and the floors were plain wood. The windows looked out on the roof of the hospital's first floor, beyond that was a graveyard with two large twisted pine trees where a family of owls made their home. At night the owls became active, hunting and calling. Their occasional melancholy hooting outside the window added an eerie air to the already isolated second floor. It made Misako uneasy about leaving the priest alone during the night.

Misako took it upon herself to move the bed in the next room so that there was only a wall between that bed and the patient's bed. She stayed with him until after the nurse's last visit at one in the morning. When she was satisfied that Teishin was sleeping comfortably, she went into the next room to sleep in her sweater and jeans. If she heard him cough or stir during the night, she went in to check on him. Early in the morning, Keiko would awaken her and Misako would go back to the house, bathe and sleep for a few hours more.

By Saturday morning, Teishin's fever was lower and he no longer needed the support of an assortment of tubes. He could sit up in bed and was capable of eating bowls of rice gruel. In the late afternoon, Misako brought in cups of tea and sat by his bed peeling tangerines and apples. He obediently ate and drank what she offered, but it was clear that his old gusto for food was gone.

By Monday, he could shuffle to the water closet and take care of his personal needs himself. He was still weak and had to endure the dreaded postural breathing exercises several times a day. Those humbling moments came when the nurse entered his room wearing a large apron and with a determined glint in her eye. He knew he had to lie across his bed, let his shoulders and head hang over a stainless steel receptacle, and submit to a series of back clappings and poundings, until his lungs revolted and violently coughed up a repulsive concoction of rust-coloured sputum. His worst moments came when either Keiko or Misako was in the room and actually assisted in this effrontery. The fact that he even cared was testimony to his improving condition.

The schedule altered a little on Monday evening. It was Keiko's birthday and they planned a sukiyaki dinner for the family of three as Taro had already gone back to school. It was near the end of that dinner, after several cups of hot sake, that Misako told her parents about the day she had gone to the Imai house for her kimono and met Hideo's lawyer. Misako's voice reflected her humiliation and pain.

Dr. Ichimura listened intensely, shaking his head. "Unbelievable," he said. "Such behaviour is not to be believed."

Keiko listened with a face that seemed to slowly turn to stone. The final insult was the money in the paper shopping bag. Dr. Ichimura and his wife exchanged horrified glances when they heard this detail.

"Does Hideo's uncle know about this?" Keiko asked.

"He hasn't communicated with me at all," Misako answered.

Keiko straightened and assumed a haughty expression, raising her slightly hooked nose. "He will know," she said in a slow and determined voice. "I will write to him."

"Please Mother! There is no use writing to anyone. It won't do any good. The marriage is over and there is no changing the situation," Misako started to cry as she spoke. "Hideo's mistress is having his child. Let that be the end of it."

Keiko handed her daughter a tissue. "Here, dry your eyes. You won't have to deal with the Imai family ever again. From now on, it is the Imai family that has to deal with me." Her voice had the ring of steel.

Just after midnight, the grimy streets of Shibata got a new coat of fresh white snow. Misako saw the first flakes slowly float down, dancing to the ground. She clutched a shawl around her shoulders and looked out the window of Teishin's second-floor room. The priest was asleep. He didn't need her help, he was recovering well and settled for the night. Still, Misako lingered. She realized that she was staying not particularly for Teishin's sake, but for herself. When she was a small child, she sometimes went off and hid in the big futon closet in her grandmother's room. It was like that now; she felt safe here. There was something about this space where the priest was sleeping that reminded her of that big closet. It was a quiet place where she could be alone, yet not alone. It was a safe place to think, or not to think, just to be.

Soft as a whisper, Misako began to sing a child's song about the falling snow. The white stuff fell faster and finer past the window. Its fluttering light played on the wall of the small, darkened room. The light and the whispered song were soothing to the priest, even as he slept. It led him back in time to a snow hut that looked like a big, hollowed-out snowball. He and his sister were laughing and eating round cakes of sweet pounded rice as they crouched over the glow of a single candle. The children's shadows reflected on the low ceiling of the hut and danced when the breath of their laughter made the flame flicker.

The shadows in the priest's dream resembled the moving lights in the hospital room where Misako stood mesmerized by the snowfall. Beyond the window she too saw the hut and caught glimpses of the children's faces in the candlelight. The sound of their laughter was unlocking some long-forgotten moment of joy in her heart. She knew she would be happy if she could join the children in the snow hut.

Full of longing, Misako pressed her face and hands against the cold glass while the vision slowly faded. She closed her eyes, resting her forehead against the window, and left the vision with a new sense of peace. As always, the vision left her tired, so very tired. She wanted to go into the next room and sleep. As she passed the priest's bed, she heard him softly laugh in his sleep. It sounded like the child's laugh in her vision.

On the Tuesday morning, Keiko sent a fat envelope to Hideo's uncle. It contained a letter, beautifully written on elegant, handmade rice paper. The letter had a tone of noble acceptance of the unfortunate events, with a hint of personal outrage and a careful recounting of how Misako had been tricked by Hideo's lawyer into signing the divorce papers when she went to the Imai house. She also made mention of the two million yen given to Misako in a paper shopping bag and all the expensive items that Misako had brought into the Imai household as a bride. The envelope was sent by personal carrier service with instructions that it should be put into the addressee's hands no later than the next afternoon.

Misako had forgotten about her mother's intention to write to Hideo's uncle. Her mind was focussed on her vision of the children in the snow hut. It was a new experience to have a vision that was pleasant. Being in a snow hut was not one of her own childhood experiences, but she guessed that it had something to do with the priest who was sleeping in the room when the vision came to her. Misako could not remember a vision that had brought her anything but confusion and sorrow. This one was different.

That afternoon at three o'clock, Misako carried a tray of hot tea and cakes to Teishin's room, hoping that he would be well enough to talk. She found him sitting up in bed, looking drawn and wrinkled, a paper-doll version of his formerly plump self. His drawn face was cleanly shaven. When he saw her come into the room, he managed a bright smile of welcome.

"My! Look at you," she said. "You are well enough to shave."

Teishin rubbed his chin and grinned. "Konein-*san* was here this morning. I felt strong enough to sit on the chair while he shaved my face. It feels good but I was too tired for him to do my head."

"Are you strong enough to try the cakes I brought you?"

"I'll do my best," the priest said with a hint of his old jolly self, "but only because you brought them." He straightened the front of his sleeping kimono self-consciously as if suddenly aware that he was in bed and Misako was nursing him.

"I don't remember much about these past days," he said, blushing. "Have I thanked you for your kind care?"

"At least ten times," Misako said as she put the tray down on the cabinet under the window. She handed him a cup of tea and a cake before settling into the chair next to his bed.

"I have said that you are welcome ten times before and I say it again." She tilted her head and looked at him closely. "Is there some reason, other than the shave, that you feel better today?" she asked.

Teishin swallowed his tea and smiled. "I suppose the medicine is working and I have to say I felt well-rested this morning. I had a good sleep and a nice dream last night, the first good sleep since I became ill."

"And your dream, Teishin-*san*? Do you remember it?"

The priest grinned and blushed. "Oh, it was nothing special. More like a childhood memory. I grew up in a Niigata mountain village and as children we used to make snow huts about this time of year. I dreamed that I was sitting in one with my sister. It was a nice dream."

"Tell me," Misako asked earnestly, "could you taste the little rice dumplings you were eating in your dream?"

The priest's mouth opened in surprise. "How would you know I dreamed I was eating dumplings?" Then he laughed and answered his own question. "Ah! Of course, what else would country kids eat in their snow hut?"

Misako stood up and put her empty cup on the tray. "Have you ever heard of two people sharing a dream?"

Teishin blinked and handed his cup to Misako. "No, never. I don't think it is possible. Do you?"

Misako sat back down in the chair and leaned in closer to the priest. "I am learning that all sorts of strange things are possible. Now, about the bones found in the pond. Kensho-*san* told me what you learned about the girl's skull. Why didn't you let me know as well?"

"Oh," he moaned, "I wanted to call you, but I was afraid."

"Afraid? What were you afraid of?"

Teishin lowered his head and spoke softly. "I was afraid that telling you would displease your mother. Your mother gets very upset when the subject of the unknown ashes is brought up. She blames your grandfather's death on his interest in those ashes."

"Oh, she couldn't. Surely you are misunderstanding her."

"No, she does," the priest said firmly. "Just this morning, Konein-*san* reminded me how angry your mother was when she found the box of ashes in my closet."

"In your closet?" Now it was Misako who was confused.

The priest's face flushed and he slid down in the bed. "Oh, please, Misako-*san*, don't ask me about it now. I'm too tired and the memory is too terrible."

"I'm sorry. You are still sick and I'm upsetting you. We'll talk when you are feeling better." She arranged the quilt around his neck. "You sleep now. I'll be back later." Misako's voice was sweet and soothing.

"I'm taking too much of your time. You don't have to come back tonight."

"I want to come back and spend time with you," she said. "I'll be here after dinner."

Misako left the room quietly and dashed down the stairs and back to her parents' living quarters to get her coat. She was not going to wait to visit the temple. It was important to speak to the priest, Konein, and find out what had happened on New Year's Day.

The streets were too snowy to ride her bicycle. Misako bundled up and set off on the thirty-minute walk. She arrived at the temple chilled to the bone; her boots were wet and feet were cold and damp. The young priest showed her into the sitting room, where a space heater gave out a welcoming dry heat. He fussed about bringing her hot tea and cakes. Misako warmed herself and put on the extra pair of dry socks she'd brought with her.

"How are you, Konein-*san*?" she asked, touched by the sad expression on the young priest's face.

"Thank you, I am well," he said in an unconvincing voice.

"It must be lonely being the only one at the temple," Misako said.

"I don't mind," Konein answered, and let a silence fall between them.

"I suppose you must be very busy," Misako commented after an awkward few seconds. "With Teishin-*san* in hospital, you would have to do the work of two priests. How are you managing with the memorial ceremonies?"

Konein lit a cigarette, screwed up his eyes and blew a perfect circle into the air. For just a second, it hovered above his head like a halo. Misako marvelled at his skill as the smoke circle got wider and wider until it dissolved into the air.

"There hasn't been much call for ceremonies," the priest said.

"*Ah so,*" Misako said and waited for him to elaborate, but he said nothing more.

"I understand you visited Teishin-*san* today, and shaved him," she offered, trying to keep a conversation going.

"*Hai,* I did," the priest said.

"Don't you think Teishin-*san* looks and feels very much better?" Misako went on, trying to make conversation. "He is making good progress, isn't he?"

"*Hai,* I think so," Konein said, examining his cigarette.

Misako drank her tea; the silence hung heavily. The priest frowned and made an effort to speak. "Excuse me, Misako-*san*, but is there anything special I can do for you? It seems very bad weather to come out in for no reason."

"Yes, there is," she said with obvious relief. "Teishin-*san* told me a little about the problem my mother is having with the unknown ashes. He said he is afraid to mention the subject in her presence."

"*Hai*, I understand," Konein said.

"Then please tell me. What has my mother said or done to make you both so nervous?"

The priest blew two small smoke circles and watched them with squinted eyes. "Because," he said after a pause, "of what happened here on New Year's Day."

Misako couldn't help but raise her eyebrows. She had never paid much attention to this priest in the past. She couldn't recall actually hearing him speak and she was now struck at how high his voice was, almost like a girl's. Then there was his annoying habit of letting what seemed like minutes elapse before he answered her questions. It was as if he had to wait for everything she said to be translated before he could answer. It was making her very impatient.

"I don't know anything about what happened here on New Year's Day," she said. "Teishin-*san* was too tired to talk about it. Please, Konein-*san*, I must know."

The priest stretched out his delicate hands to pour hot tea into their cups and offered her a sweet, which she declined with a shake of her head. His economy of words was affecting Misako. She decided that if she said little, he would have to talk. Finally, the priest broke the silence in his soft, high voice.

"I suppose it is all right to tell you, Misako-*san*."

"Yes. Certainly it is." She was trying to keep the annoyance out of her voice.

"*Hai*, I understand," he said and hesitated.

"What happened?" Misako was irked beyond words, but the young priest seemed completely oblivious to the urgency in her voice. He blew another slow, smoke circle and watched it waft toward the dark ceiling before beginning his calm narrative.

"Your mother came to the temple on New Year's Day. Teishin-*san* was ill. She also found that the dead master's room, where Teishin-*san* had been sleeping, was in poor condition. For some reason, he had been leaving his window open at night. Everything was damp and cold from the snow entering the room. I'm afraid your mother became very angry."

"What has that to do with the unknown ashes?" she asked.

"Because your mother was angry, the box of ashes was damaged."

"Damaged?"

"That is so," the priest said calmly and let another strip of silence fall between them. "It was an accident. Teishin-*san* had been keeping the box in his closet. When your mother pulled out a damp quilt, the box flew out and crashed against the wall."

"Oh, no!" Misako cried, clapping her hand over her mouth in horror. "Were the ashes spread all over the floor?"

"No," Konein said, "the box broke, but the ashes stayed inside the silk wrapping."

"And now? Where is it now?"

Konein crushed the tiny bit left of his cigarette into the ashtray. "In the old altar room," he answered.

"I see," Misako said and started to rise. "This is my fault. I had meant to arrange for the ashes to be put into a proper urn."

The priest waved his hand, indicating that she should stay seated. "I already took care of that. All is in order."

"You did all that? How did you transfer the ashes to a new box?"

"I called the funeral director for help. He came to the temple and together we opened the silk *furoshiki*, removed the broken box and put the ashes into an empty metal urn we found in the back altar room. The funeral director said it was all done properly and he didn't charge for his service."

Misako sat back down on her heels and sighed with relief. "That was very kind of him," she said and then narrowed her eyes to study this strange young man. "Thank you, Konein-*san*. I see you are very efficient."

The praise did not bring a smile to the priest's lips. He looked at her with his expressionless gaze and said, "There is no need for thanks. My job is to do what needs to be done."

That night, Misako returned to Teishin's hospital room. Knowing the ashes were safe made her happy and she brought that happiness with her to Teishin. At first they talked about her grandfather, but within a few minutes, they were laughing together. After a while, they were talking with such familiarity that their words were almost delicious in their spontaneity and ease. With such closeness, it was even possible for Misako to touch on the subject of her separation from her husband, without going into the details. She mentioned that she was now working with a former classmate from Niigata high school. "We were best friends in high school and now she is a successful designer in Tokyo."

"*Ah so,*" the priest said and sat up in bed, pulling a blanket around his shoulders. At first, he was terribly distressed to hear of her personal unhappiness. Then slowly, he became rivetted and charmed at the wonder of this intimate exchange with his dear master's granddaughter, even though she was talking about things he could not fully grasp. The small room was lit only by the bright pinkish glow of the snowy world outside the window. The dreamy ambiance made them speak softly, like children sharing secrets.

Misako told him about her visit to the temple and what the younger priest Konein had said. Teishin moved his head and listened, pleased to hear that all was in order at the temple.

"Why," Misako asked, "did you allow the snow to enter your room?"

The priest suffered a violent blush. "Because I was ashamed of myself. I've have always heard that children in samurai families endure such training to teach them discipline. I thought it would make me strong."

"Is that why you kept the box of ashes in your closet?

Teishin shook his head. "No, that's not why. I did it to keep the box hidden. I know now it was a mistake. I guess I am always making mistakes."

"That is not true. You do so many things right. My mother said you are doing a good job keeping the books, and think of the information you were able to find about the girl's bones! One day we will know enough to bury the ashes in that girl's own ancestral grave."

"Do you think it possible?" This was a new thought and it thrilled the priest.

"Finding that information was a very big step. You must continue to investigate when you are well."

"I don't know what to do next," the priest said.

"What you can do tonight is get some rest and get well," Misako said gently. "If you are nervous about my mother finding out that the unknown ashes are now in an urn and still at the temple, I will take the urn back with me to Tokyo. When you are ready, we will work together to find the answer. Then I will bring the ashes back and we will bury them properly."

"*Hai,*" Teishin said as he obediently slid down under the quilt. There was no need for Misako to stay in the next room tonight. Teishin was well on the road to recovery.

TWENTY-FIVE

*T*he blow came harder and faster than even Auntie Kaz could have imagined. Sachiko's interview was pre-taped and she was pleased with the result. What she didn't know was that the details of her interview was leaked in a conversation between one of the cameramen and a cute girl reporter who was working for a gossip magazine. She knew that Sachiko was a rising star on the Tokyo fashion scene and she saw an opportunity to scoop the television interview. To cause the sensation she wanted, she would have to dig into Sachiko's past and hope to find some dirt.

Looking and acting as harmless as a little brown wren, the reporter traced Sachiko from the humble kimono shop in Niigata to the dress-maker in Yokohama. Ever since Sachiko left, Auntie Yokohama's business had gone downhill so she was more than willing to complain about her uppity niece. Auntie Yokohama repeated the story she had been telling for years. It was all about how she had taken her niece, a poor, ignorant country girl into her business and trained to design and make western clothes. Then the ungrateful girl ran off to Tokyo to become a common bar girl."

"But, Miss Kimura is an accomplished and talented designer," Miss Brown Wren commented. "She even speaks French."

"I was the one who taught her how to design clothes and she learned French when she was living in Paris as a kept woman of some wealthy Japanese businessman."

The trashy magazine was on the newsstand the day before the interview was even broadcast. That evening the television show's producers had a long meeting in the back room of a tempura shop. After consuming a lot of sake, they decided that they would play the tape as planned, adding a telephone interview with Sachiko about the magazine article. It was already out; they couldn't ignore it. They called Sachiko and she agreed that it was the best way to handle the situation.

Sachiko was articulate. Her voice came over the television set loud and confident.

"The writer of that slanderous magazine article should be ashamed. I have nothing in my past to be ashamed of. I have always done my best, under what could be considered difficult circumstances.

"My father died when I was a child. He had never fully recovered from the wounds he received in the war. My mother died some years later. She had been overworked and underfed by her husband's relatives, especially his brother's wife. My mother had to fight to allow me to finish high school. The aunt that my mother and I lived with wanted me to quit school and go to work at age fourteen. After high school, my mother's sister, who had a dressmaking shop in Yokohama, did take me in and teach me the basics of her trade. However, I was not allowed time off. I had to work and sleep in a tiny space in the shop. I worked very hard and soon developed my own customers. Still, there was no chance for my life to improve. I saw myself going down the same road that took my mother to an early death. That is why I left and went to Tokyo with only enough money to last me a week. On the sixth day I gave up looking for a job as a dressmaker. The only job I could get was as a hostess in a nightclub."

At this point in the telling, there was a catch in Sachiko's voice. It wasn't put on. Older emotions were welling up. She took a deep breath and continued. "The owner of the nightclub was a woman who treated me fairly. She protected me as a mother protects her child. She never made me do anything bad and she encouraged me to continue my dressmaking studies in the daytime. As soon as I could, I stopped being a hostess and opened my own business.

"As for Paris, I did go there for two weeks to observe and study fashion. The magazine article was a lie. I never lived in a Paris apartment as a kept woman. If I speak any French, it is because I studied it in Tokyo, on my own. I paid for those lessons myself."

In countless homes, all over Japan, people listened to Sachiko's voice. Men blinked and women dabbed their eyes with tissues. Sympathetic hearts were touched by the saga of a poor girl who worked hard and succeeded, in spite of her terrible relatives. Mother Imai was not touched because she had mentally tuned out when the telephone interview started. She was still thinking about the feature in the gossip magazine that told a story that she wanted to believe. The last thing she wanted to hear was Sachiko defending herself. Mother Imai flipped off the television set.

"Sachiko Kimura, Kimura-*san*," she repeated to herself, until she made the connection. "*So da*! That was the woman Misako went to live with, the designer from Niigata, Misako's childhood friend. *Maa!*"

She rushed to the corner supermarket and bought a copy of the magazine. "*Maa!*" she said with a great deal of smug satisfaction as she read it at her dining-room table. "What a scandal! Hideo should know about this." Mother Imai was so excited that she had trouble dialling his office number. To add to her frustration, he wasn't at his desk. A woman answered his phone.

"Where is he?" she asked with a great deal of irritation. "In the president's office? Please tell him to call his mother the moment he returns to his desk." She dialled her sister because she had to tell someone. The maid answered and said that "madam" had already left the house and wasn't expected back until late afternoon. Mother Imai went back to reread the magazine. To soothe the frustration, she drank tea, talked to her dead husband's picture and kept looking at the telephone.

A little past noon, when she was eating lunch, the kitchen bell on the side door rang out. It was Hideo. He removed his coat, walked into the dining room and threw his briefcase on a chair. Mother Imai looked up from the magazine and started to bubble out the news. After about three sen-tences, she stopped. Hideo's face looked as if he had just returned from his own grave. He wasn't listening. He was clearly livid about something else.

"What's wrong?" his mother asked in a trembling voice.

"What's wrong?" he repeated. "Everything!"

"You were in Uncle's office when I called. Is there some problem?"

"Yes, there is a problem," he almost screamed. "Misako's mother sent him a letter accusing this family of being dishonourable. Dishonourable! She accused me of tricking Misako into signing the divorce papers."

"What?" Mother Imai said and stood up facing her son. "What did Uncle say?"

"There is nothing he didn't say. I thought he was going to have a heart attack. He ordered me to go to Niigata with him tomorrow. We have to go to Misako's parents' home and apologize."

The fury in her son's eyes made Mother Imai shake. She sat back down at the table. "Are you going?" she asked in a small voice.

"Going? What choice do I have? If I don't, he will kick me out of the company. Imagine, my own father's brother kicking me out of the family company!"

Mother Imai was about to say something when Hideo grabbed a

254

wooden chair and flung it down hard. There was a loud cracking sound as part of the chair back flew off. It hit the table and narrowly missed Mother Imai. Hideo rushed up the stairs as his mother sat stunned, breathing hard until she slowly worked herself into a major fit of hysterical sobs.

*A*s it turned out, Uncle Buddha had no intention of having Hideo go to Niigata with him. He knew that making Hideo apologize in person would mean more loss of face for the Imai family, not to mention the upset his presence would cause the Ichimura household. He was also too angry with his nephew to take a journey with him; he simply wanted to make the worm squirm, and it worked. Hideo was so unhinged after the great fracas that took place in his uncle's office that he refused to even talk to Fumiko. He went home, took a bottle of whiskey up to his room, ordered his mother not to disturb him and got drunk.

The next morning Hideo turned up at the Ueno Station platform as ordered, looking as if he was facing a death sentence. Uncle did not return his bow. Instead he glared at his nephew and announced that he had changed his mind, he was taking another employee to Niigata since everyone at the company now knew about the scandal. A young man, carrying his boss's briefcase and packages, stood with his eyes respectfully downcast.

"I couldn't stand to look at you for such a long train ride," Uncle Buddha told his nephew. Hideo stood at attention, apologizing and bowing until after the train had pulled out of the station.

Settled in a first-class seat, Uncle sent his employee to the dining car for a large whiskey. It was only seven-thirty in the morning. After drinking it, he fell asleep and snored loudly for over an hour. The train raced toward snow country while his employee read soft-porn comic books and cleaned out his ears with a long slender earbrush.

When the train pulled into Niigata Station, the two men were met by a hired car and driver. They were taken to the Toei Hotel for lunch because Uncle remembered liking their Chinese food. At two o'clock they left for Shibata. It was almost an hour's ride.

The appointment with the Ichimura family was for three o'clock. The hired car drove up to the Women's Hospital five minutes early. Uncle's lackey jumped out of the car, opened the back door and followed the portly, immaculately dressed gentleman up to the house carrying a gift box wrapped in blue silk. At the door, the employee rang the doorbell, handed his boss the box, bowed and returned to the car to wait.

At the entrance of the house, Keiko and Misako greeted the head of the Imai family with deep bows. It was here that the dialogue and dance of Japanese etiquette commenced. For the occasion, Keiko had made a sacrifice: she wore a kimono in a muted colour. Misako wore her black dress with the little round white collar. Both women bowed. Keiko said the words of welcome and ushered Uncle into the Ichimura's best *tatami* room where she placed a silk cushion at the position of honour in front of the *tokonoma*. When Uncle was seated, he removed the silk *furoshiki*, bowed and presented the gift of a large box of expensive Belgian chocolates to his hostess, apologizing for the poor quality of his gift. Both Keiko and Misako made a formal bow, kneeling on the *tatami* floor and thanked him. Keiko reached out and gently pulled the box toward herself, bowing again, and assuring Uncle that his gift was of the highest quality and a rare treat for the household.

Misako excused herself to see about the refreshments. While she was gone, Keiko expressed thanks for his visit, saying she was surprised and honoured that the busy president of such an important company would take the time to come all the way to Shibata. Uncle waved the compliment away with his pudgy hand and said a few words comparing Niigata's harsh weather to Tokyo's mild winter days.

To be polite, Dr. Ichimura came into the room to greet the guest and apologize for not being able to stay. He knelt on the *tatami* floor next to his wife and bowed a friendly welcome.

"Unfortunately, I have an operation to perform in five minutes."

Uncle let out an understanding grunt and gave another wave of his hand. In turn, he apologized for interrupting the doctor's important work and for the fact that this his nephew's disgraceful behaviour had made this visit necessary.

Dr. Ichimura replied that he remembered happier occasions when they had met and would keep those memories in his heart. There were more bows, the doctor left and it was time to get down to business.

Misako returned with a tray of tea and cakes, serving Uncle first. It was obvious that his bulk made sitting in the formal Japanese style uncomfortable. Keiko urged him to relax, but he declined. In spite of the discomfort, Uncle sat erect with his hands on his knees, looking down at the *tatami* mat in front of him.

He started his formal apology by acknowledging Keiko's letter in a dry, expressionless tone. He further expressed his deep regrets at the breakdown of Misako and Hideo's marriage, which he blamed entirely on Hideo. "I want you to know," Uncle Buddha said, "that I have made arrangements that the furniture and other items that Misako-*san* brought into the Imai house as a bride will be carefully packed and removed to my personal storage house, and remain there until I have instructions from your honourable selves."

The two women sat nobly erect listening, looking down at their hands that were folded in their laps.

"Once more," he said, "I realize that Misako-*san* has many personal items that she would like to pack herself. Therefore, I have arranged for both Hideo and his mother to be away from their home next Saturday and Sunday."

Keiko bent her head and cast her eyes down in a posture of regret. "We have no intention of inconveniencing Hideo's mother," Keiko said.

"Don't worry about that," Uncle assured her. "To avoid an awkward situation, I have arranged for my dead brother's wife to go to a hot spring with her sister next weekend. The poor lady has suffered greatly from her son's rash behaviour. The short rest will do her good and she welcomes the opportunity to get away. Have no fear, she will not be in Tokyo and therefore there will be no inconvenience."

Misako and her mother sat in respectful silence. They dared not even exchange a quick glance.

"As far as Hideo is concerned," and here Uncle Buddha's voice rang with his displeasure, I have ordered him not to be at home on either Saturday or Sunday. A trusted company employee will be at the house to render whatever assistance Misako-*san* may need."

Keiko bowed deeply and indicated that such arrangements were very satisfactory. Then she apologized for the harsh tone of her letter and said that she had been distraught for the sake of her daughter.

Uncle Buddha wiped his sweating brow with a linen handkerchief and said that he was glad that she had called the injustice to his attention and that he wanted to make amends on behalf of the Imai family. At that point, he removed an envelope of folded handmade rice paper from the breast pocket of his expensive suit. Misako's name was written on it in beautiful brush strokes. Uncle bowed and slid the envelope toward the two women. Startled, Misako hesitated.

"Misako-*san*, I know that nothing can replace your happiness, but please accept this small token of restitution from the Imai family."

Misako blushed, bowed and whispered her thanks. Keiko bowed deeply and simply said, "Thank you, sir. Your concern is most appreciated." Without having to take an extra breath, Keiko offered him more tea. Uncle Buddha politely declined, saying that he had to return to Tokyo on the six-thirty train.

The two women accompanied Uncle to his car, bowed several times and sighed when the car was out of sight. The performance was over. Misako was scowling. Keiko's face wore a subtle smile.

Some minutes later, mother and daughter sat down at the *kotatsu* to warm themselves. Both the box of chocolates and the envelope were on the table.

"I hope you will enjoy your chocolates," Misako said, "since your letter caused everyone so much discomfort."

"Don't you dare complain," Keiko said sternly. "You should be pleased to have such an apology from Hideo's uncle. He is a busy and important man. His coming here is far more than I expected. I am impressed."

Misako made a face. "I was very uncomfortable through the whole thing. I felt sorry for the man."

"He is a gentleman and took responsibility. He made a great effort to bring some kind of balance to this unfortunate situation. You should feel some satisfaction yourself and stop being ungrateful. Now open the envelope."

Misako frowned again and carefully unfolded the rice paper, lifting out a company cheque signed by Hideo's uncle, the president and very busy man. Misako gasped when she read the figure of two million yen.

"It is humiliating that your letter shamed them into parting with so much money!"

Keiko took the cheque and examined it. "My letter had nothing to do with shame. I merely gave them the opportunity to do the honourable thing."

Still, Misako remained upset and that night, phantom warriors of mind and emotions clashed in her dreams. As much as she loved her mother, she simply couldn't help resenting the intervention into her personal life. The cheque for two million yen was particularly distasteful.

Misako lay in bed talking to the darkened room: "No one asked her to write such a letter. If I came back to live and work here, she would be controlling my life. How mortifying to be treated like a child, to be pitied and patronized."

"How mortifying to have your husband discard you for another woman," another voice spoke from deeper in her head.

"What's done is done," she said to the phantoms, but they were not finished with her. "She deserves what happened. If she had been a better wife, been sweeter, sexier, her husband wouldn't have turned to another woman. What about all the unkind thoughts she harboured toward Mother Imai? How did that make her husband feel? It caused hard feelings in the household. Now she is resenting her own mother. How will she make a new life for herself without her mother's help?"

Misako tossed and turned and cried into her pillow. It wasn't until the healing call of the temple bell floated on the dark morning air that she fell asleep.

❀　❀　❀

The train to Tokyo was at three in the afternoon, but there were several things Misako had to do before she left Shibata. First she wanted to go to the temple to offer incense as a farewell to her grandfather's spirit. Her second reason was to take the urn holding the unknown ashes. Taking action on her own also helped to diminish the sense of helplessness her mother made her feel.

Konein was away performing a ceremony. The temple was being looked after by an elderly male member of the congregation. He sat cross-legged on the *tatami* floor, next to a hibachi, smoking a cigarette that was stuck upright in a tiny old-fashioned pipe. Misako entered the room to greet him, leaving her large leather handbag just outside the door. She chatted with him for a few minutes and then excused herself, explaining that she wished to burn incense at the family altar before she left Shibata. The old gentleman smiled and bowed, pleased that some young people still remembered to honour their ancestors.

Carrying her large handbag, she went first to the old altar room. She immediately spotted the urn because it was wrapped in the white silk *furoshiki*, which now looked wrinkled and dull. With great care, she took it off the shelf and placed it in her handbag. Then she bowed her head and said a hasty prayer. The room made her shiver. It was cold and musty. Once again, Misako noticed how worn everything in the room was. Even the bindings on the *tatami* mats were threadbare. Filled with a kind of protective energy toward the unknown ashes, she was glad that she was removing them from this broken-down room.

The Tanaka family altar was in an inner room where her grandfather used to receive guests. This space too now looked shabby. Small offerings of rice, fruit and flowers had been laid before the open black lacquer cabinet; at least something looked cared for. Misako wondered who was attending the altar now that Teishin was not here. Was it Konein, members of the congregation, or was it her mother?

Her grandfather's picture had now joined the likenesses of his wife and sons on the family altar. A Buddha sat on the altar's centre shelf and watched as Misako set her handbag down, knelt and lit sticks of incense. Bowing her head over her folded hands, Misako whispered an account of her plan to take the ashes to Tokyo and why. She couldn't help but let the anger she felt toward her mother seep into her words.

Grandfather had many disagreements with Mother over the years. He will understand how I feel, she reasoned.

She stayed kneeling on the *tatami* floor, looking up at her grandfather's smiling picture, wondering what he would have said to her if he was alive. The incense wavered up, perfuming the mortuary tablets, each inscribed with the consecrated post-funeral name of a family member. She reached out and tenderly pressed her fingertips against her grandfather's tablet, just as she had touched his face after his death. At that instant Misako felt compelled to turn her head and clearly saw her grandfather's body stretched out on a futon. Her mother was there as well, kneeling, bending, and arranging the old man's death kimono across his chest with all the reverence of giving a blessing. In that flash, Misako saw her mother's eyes wet with tears and brimming with love.

And then it was gone, vanished as if it never happened, but Misako knew that scene had taken place. This had to be the room where her mother had lovingly prepared her grandfather's body for his coffin. Kensho would tell her that the vibrations, the energy of the actions, still lingered. Misako was suddenly thankful for this strange gift. She could feel the anger slowly seeping out of her, and as it went she understood that her mother's actions had been reasonable and right.

The muted striking of the kitchen clock reminded her that there was little time left to say goodbye to Teishin and tell him that she had taken the urn of ashes from the altar room. Finding a chance to talk to him alone was

261

another problem. Now that the priest was well enough to soon leave the hospital, Dr. Ichimura had given his permission for a few members of the temple congregation to help care for the patient. It meant that there were always at least two women in his room fussing and clucking like mother hens. They never thought about leaving the room when the priest had a visitor. Misako couldn't say anything that hinted at how sorry she was to leave him, or how happy she was that they had been able to share their innocent words and dreams.

Teishin was sitting up in bed. He smiled as Misako entered the room. His head had still not been shaven and his hair was beginning to grow in. It made him look younger.

"I've come to say goodbye. We have to leave for Tokyo this afternoon." She knew he would grasp her use of the word "we."

"I understand," he said. "Thank you for all your kind help."

"I did nothing at all. Please take care of yourself and regain all your strength soon."

"Thank you, Misako-*san*. I hope you both have a safe trip."

The women from the congregation smiled at the farewell scene and urged Misako to stay a while and drink some tea. One of them produced a plate of round sweet dumplings that she had made. To be polite, Misako accepted two, wrapped them in a white napkin and promised to enjoy the dumplings on the train ride. Both ladies would go home later and tell people what a nice young woman the old master's granddaughter was. Only one of the ladies wondered out loud to her family about just who Misako was travelling back to Tokyo with.

TWENTY-SEVEN
February 1966

*T*he official divorce decree was to be placed in Misako's hands at Sachiko's office on the afternoon of Thursday, January twentieth. Fukusawa's secretary called the office first to make sure Misako would be there when the decree was delivered. Misako's hand shook when she hung up the phone. She felt weak and sat at her desk biting her lip until Sachiko noticed and asked what was wrong.

"Hideo's lawyer is on his way here with my divorce papers."

"Good!" Sachiko said. "It means that you are totally free."

"Is that supposed to make me feel better? Misako's voice dripped with misery. "I feel like something is being amputated, a whole section of my life cut off forever. Since that lawyer tricked me, I'm not sure I can even look at his face again."

"The divorce has been signed and sealed. Now, let it be delivered and forget about what he and Hideo did to you. Put your energy into your future, not your past."

Misako tried to embrace Sachiko's advice. She went back to working on invoices until a smiling Fukusawa came through the door at two o'clock. Misako's heart started to race when she looked up from her desk and saw his Coke-bottle glasses and prominent teeth.

"Good afternoon, Imai-*san*, or have you gone back to the name Ichimura now?"

Seeing the lawyer again and hearing his arrogant tone so rattled Misako that her knees felt wobbly and her voice refused to work. She stood up and said nothing as he put his briefcase on her desk and started to remove the official papers. Sachiko saw him through the glass partition that separated her office and immediately came to stand by Misako's side. She introduced herself coldly.

"Oh, Kimura-*san*. I know who you are," he said with an even wider grin. "I've seen your picture in a recent magazine."

"If you are here to give Mrs. Imai the final divorce papers, then do your job," Sachiko snapped.

The lawyer lost his smile, removed the brown envelope and handed it to Misako. "There is another paper that you must sign to confirm that you personally received the divorce document."

Misako removed the three pieces of paper from the envelope and handed them to Sachiko, who took her time examining them. Fukusawa shifted his weight from one foot to another. At least three minutes passed and no one had asked him to sit down.

Sachiko finally put the papers on the desk and told Misako where to sign. The lawyer had to swallow a growl. He liked being in control and now he was being challenged by a woman. Who did this ex-nightclub hostess think she was?

"I didn't know you were a lawyer, as well as your other occupations," he sneered.

Sachiko slowly focussed her unblinking cat eyes on his face. She looked like a panther about to pounce on her smaller prey. It made the lawyer so uncomfortable that he flushed and looked down at his shoes.

As soon as Misako put her name on the paper, Sachiko handed it to the little man. He was about to say something, but thought better of it. Misako and Sachiko were still standing like statues when the lawyer bowed, thanked them and left.

Misako looked at the papers in her hand and couldn't control her tears. "I can't believe it is over. I'm really divorced!"

"It's for the best," Sachiko said, looking at her watch. "We'll wrap up as early as possible and go for sushi. That will cheer you up."

Misako tried to get back to work but her mind fluttered off on its own, conjuring up images of Hideo having her name removed from the Imai family register and entering Fumiko's. All at once, Misako felt like a small plane flying around and around in the air, with no place to land. She remembered when she and Mother Imai used to sweep and water the Imai family tomb and how comforting it was to know that this lovely grave was where her own ashes would one day rest. Now Fumiko's urn would sit in her place. Misako had to admit that she mourned the loss of her place on that shelf more than she mourned the loss of her faithless husband.

❀ ❀ ❀

Through Uncle Buddha's arrangements, the removal of Misako's belongings from the Imai house went smoothly, even though Misako and Sachiko were too busy on Saturday to leave the office. They arrived at the Imai house at noon on Sunday the twenty-third. Uncle's two employees were there, as promised, explaining how they had worked the day before, packing and arranging all the items on the list. The large downstairs room now held Misako's dresser, dressing table, futons and boxes of clothing and other belongings, all covered with thick wrapping paper. By four in the afternoon, everything was ready. Misako and Sachiko carried the few things Misako wanted to keep at Sachiko's apartment; the rest was placed on a truck to be taken to Uncle's warehouse. For the moment, everything was in order.

Hideo and Fumiko were married the following week on a calendar day of good luck, called *tai-an*, or great peace. It was a scaled-down wedding attended by family and a few friends, thirty people in all. This was not the wedding that Fumiko's mother had dreamed of for her eldest daughter. Neither she nor her husband was happy that Fumiko was marrying out of her class and in a cloud of scandal. As she watched Fumiko and Hideo sipping the ceremonial sake during the Shinto ceremony, she couldn't help feeling bitter over the loss of face this daughter had caused the family. "Fumiko was never content," she thought. "She was never proud that her parents were hardworking shopkeepers. I suppose she got pregnant on purpose to steal that idiot away from his wife. She could fool him but she could never fool me. Speaking English and trying to be something she wasn't. I knew she was running around with that foreign journalist, going to love hotels, as soon as she was out of junior college. I saw the black and blue mark on her inner thighs when we were in the bath together. I know a disgusting love mark when I see it. Well, I suppose I should be grateful that she's at least marrying a Japanese. It would be far worse if she was marrying some big gaijin. That girl has always been foreigner-crazy."

The bride wore a rented traditional wedding kimono with an elaborate *obi* of red and gold. Because of her generous bust, and the long, padded bride's coat, no one really noticed that Fumiko was five months pregnant. She just looked a little fat. People commented that the bride had a body type similar to that of her new mother-in-law. But most overlooked her figure and praised her abundant black hair that had been arranged in a graceful, upswept Japanese style.

The reception was held at an upscale Chinese restaurant. The menu featured festive dishes made with fresh red snapper and lobster. Mother Imai made sure every thing was first class, including the generous gifts that waited in thirty shopping bags for the guests to take home.

Everyone displayed delight in the union by giving the newly married couple a round of applause as they made their way to the head table. Only Mother Imai's sister couldn't mask her disapproval. Expressionless, she pretended to clap, but made no sound. When the toast was given, she touched the glass to her lips and didn't drink. She looked Fumiko over carefully later, when her coat was off, and had to admit to her sister that at least Fumiko was not lying about being pregnant.

Uncle Buddha did not attend the ceremony or the reception, using an urgent business trip as an excuse. His wife disapproved of his absence. She alone could get away with calling her husband mean-spirited. She supported her dead brother-in-law's family by attending the wedding and by giving a generous cash gift of Uncle Buddha's money.

To Mother Imai's chagrin, she did not have a chance to show off either her storytelling or her singing ability, as it didn't turn out to be that kind of wedding. There were several lacklustre speeches wishing them happiness. In two hours, it was all over. Fumiko and Hideo were off for a onenight honeymoon in Hakone, a resort area not too far from Tokyo. The bride had wanted to take advantage of her travel agency connections and go to Europe for a week but Uncle Buddha said an unequivocal "No!" He wouldn't give Hideo time off from work and he reminded his nephew that he was in debt to the company for an extra two million yen.

The couple returned home on Sunday evening. Mother Imai exhausted herself by working for hours preparing a festive dinner to welcome Fumiko. The couple seemed pleased. The three of them laughed and drank a lot during the dinner. In fact, Mother Imai had never seen a woman throw down so many cups of sake as Fumiko did. By the time the dinner was over, Hideo had to help his giggling bride up the stairs. Mother Imai was left alone in the kitchen to do the washing up. Totally exhausted, she pulled herself up the stairs to go to bed at midnight. A chorus of snoring came from her son's bedroom.

At two in the morning, Mother Imai woke up to an unfamiliar noise. At first frightened, she sat up in her futon and quickly realized that the noises were coming from the next room. These were not the discreet little moans she had sometimes heard in the night when Misako was Hideo's wife; these were bellows of outright pleasure. As she had done in the past, the older woman quietly got up and went to her listening place at the wall, unfortunately stumbling in the dark. Fumiko heard the thump and smiled. The thought of her husband's mother listening to their lovemaking really turned her on. It was just what she wanted. If there was going to be a power struggle in this house, the old lady might as well understand right from the start just who came first with Hideo.

Mother Imai stood in the dark, pressing her ear against the thin wall, listening to sounds and words that she had never heard before. Her eyes were wide and she clapped her hand over her mouth until the couple finished with Fumiko's wild orgasmic screams. Mother Imai went back to her futon so upset that she couldn't get back to sleep.

The next morning Fumiko came down to help with the breakfast and sweetly apologized to Mother Imai for not being able to wash the dishes the night before. "I hope we didn't wake you up in the night with our lovemaking." She said this so frankly that her mother-in-law had to sit down to recover.

"You two make a lot of noise," Mother Imai finally managed to say, amazed that she was talking about sex with her new daughter-in-law. The word was hardly ever mentioned when Misako lived in the house.

Fumiko yawned and stretched. She was still in her sleeping kimono with her abundant cleavage showing. "I'm not like that sexless stick that used to be his wife. Hope you can get used to it."

Mother Imai blinked and thought for a minute. "Oh well, maybe it would be better for me to move downstairs," she said, fully expecting her new daughter-in-law to vigorously object to the suggestion, or at least to promise to be more considerate with their noise. "I suppose I could sleep on a futon in the living room at night."

"That's a good idea," Fumiko came back quickly. "Before long we are going to need your room for the baby. I mean, you wouldn't be comfortable trying to sleep with a baby crying in the next room. I think you know all babies cry at night and Hideo and I intend to have lots of babies."

※ ※ ※

On the evening of February twentieth, Tokyo had a rare snowfall. In her flannel pajamas, Misako watched from the eighth-storey window of Sachiko's apartment. The white streaks moving through the dark sky looked desolate and cold. Her head felt heavy. She was so very tired. Auntie Kaz and Sachiko must have seen that because they didn't object when she said she wasn't up to going out with them. The two women even put down their drinks and went to the kitchen to heat up some soup for her.

Wrapped in fur coats, Sachiko and Auntie Kaz left the building and hailed a taxi. Most of the snow was melting the second it touched the ground. The taxi drove through the white curtain on a black, shiny, wet road.

Auntie Kaz whipped off her scarf and shook it out. "I hope you are not over-working that girl," she scolded. "I've never seen her with such dark shadows under her eyes."

"We are all tired at the atelier, Auntie Kaz. Misako is getting a cold, that's all."

Up in the apartment, Misako turned from the window and climbed into bed. One of the cats crouched on the top shelf of the bookcase built above her desk. Cleo looked down at Misako as if she was a big mouse. Misako sat up and clapped her hands.

"Out, Cleo! I know you think this is your room, but I have to sleep. Go! Leave! Out!"

Cleo let out a loud meow and jumped down first onto the desk, and then the floor before dashing out of the room. Misako closed the door behind the cat. It wasn't a good idea to have a cat up on that particular shelf. It was where she had placed the urn of ashes. It was cleverly hidden behind a tacked up calendar picture of the big Kamakura Buddha. It was only one sheet of paper and certainly not cat-proof.

Alone in the quiet apartment, Misako settled back down, hoping to fall asleep, but the minute she put her head on the pillow, her mind started to run like a movie reel. Tonight the feature was all about guilt. Sachiko had told her everything about her trip to Hawaii. Misako told Sachiko only half of what had gone on in Niigata. She had explained how she nursed the priest, Teishin, and she described Uncle Buddha's visit with great animation. All that conversation came easily, but Misako had never been able to discuss the drama of the unknown ashes with her. Which was ironic, since Sachiko had been present when little Misako, as a young girl, first claimed to have seen a girl fall into the pond. It was likely that Sachiko didn't remember it. Certainly, she had never mentioned it in all their years of friendship. Then again, Sachiko never talked about her early childhood. Now that Misako thought about it, it didn't seem right to bring the dust of her grandfather's temple into Sachiko's fresh, white, modern apartment where the past was not welcome.

Bringing the urn here without Sachiko's permission had been a mistake. Why hadn't she thought it through? Now her guilt was keeping her awake at night. Another reason she couldn't sleep was because she kept thinking about her chance meeting with Hideo and Fumiko that very morning in Shibuya.

Sachiko had asked Misako to pick up a book of samples at a fabric showroom in Shibuya. As usual, the city traffic was jammed. To save time, Misako took the subway. She got off the train at Shibuya, a mere four or five blocks from the Imai home. A safe enough distance, she thought, and set out feeling confident that she wouldn't see anyone she knew.

An hour later, with the fabric book under her arm, Misako walked back toward the Shibuya train station. The entire area was crowded with shoppers, travellers and office people out for a quick lunch. Up ahead, Misako spotted the back of a familiar head. It was the way the thick black hair was cut that reminded her of Hideo. Misako elbowed her way through the crowd for a closer look. It was Hideo, with Fumiko walking a few paces behind him. Misako slowed down and gave in to the temptation to follow them.

The couple stepped into a cafe and sat down in a booth. Misako saw a seat opening up, a seat where she could look right into Hideo's face. Immediately, she sat down and hid behind a large menu. Even after she ordered sandwiches and tea, she held on to her menu shield.

She studied them all through her lunch, noticing that the couple hardly spoke to each other. When Misako and Hideo had been newly married, she remembered that they had talked and laughed together all the time. The man and woman who she was spying on were not happy in each other's company. The revelation released something inside of Misako. It reminded her of a day from her childhood, when she let go of a kite of on a blustery autumn day. She had watched the wind take it far away. She had loved that kite yet it flew away. Her grandfather wiped said there was no use even trying to find it. It had probably come down in a rice field and was now ruined with mud.

"I'll clean it off," she whimpered.

Her grandfather shook his head. "No, it's too late for that. Once the mud penetrates the kite, it will never fly again."

There in her Tokyo bedroom, she finally accepted that her marriage was totally over. That kite was never going to fly again.

Misako closed her eyes and tried to sleep but the thoughts kept rolling. Surprisingly, Sachiko's business was not suffering from the smutty magazine exposure. Hostesses from the best nightclubs were clamouring for appointments. Fortunately, Sachiko had returned from Hawaii with a sketchbook full of new design ideas. This year she was definitely leaning toward Gauguin's bright pallette and draping her dresses like sarongs. Business was so good that Sachiko was planning to hire another cutter and two more seamstresses.

It was no use. She couldn't stop her racing thoughts. For the first time since she had come to live with Sachiko, she had to get up and look for her sleeping pills.

TWENTY-EIGHT

*K*ensho-sama,
      The weather was very fine today and I had the
opportunity to leave the office to walk in the sunshine
during my lunch break. Passing a garden wall, I saw
a plum tree beginning to flower. Only a few branches
had white blossoms but it reminded me of the flowering
plum branch you had arranged for your tea ceremony.
Once more, I wish to express my thanks for the lovely
time in Kamakura.

   As you know, I returned to Shibata the day after our
meeting. What you probably don't know is that Teishin-san
was very ill with double pneumonia and was hospitalized
while I was there. Although he had a difficult time, my
mother tells me that he has now recovered and is back
living at the temple, enjoying the meticulous care of many
kind members of his congregation.

   It is rather difficult to explain in a letter all that has
happened in Shibata. On New Year's Day, my mother found
the box of unknown ashes in Teishin-san's room. Konein-
san tells me she was very angry. When I saw Teishin-san
in the hospital, he seemed very nervous about keeping the
unknown ashes at the temple as he doesn't want to upset
my mother again. To ease his mind, I have taken the urn of
ashes with me to Tokyo.

   You will be surprised to hear that the unknown girl's
ashes are now in an urn on a shelf in my bedroom in Tokyo.
I confess I have not yet let my friend know that I have
brought such a strange item into her home. I have brazenly
hidden it behind a calendar. It makes me uncomfortable and
guilty. Yet I must try to keep the urn safe until the day that
we will be able to place the ashes in the girl's family tomb. As
promised when I saw you last, I will keep you informed.

*In the meantime, we are very busy at the office and I
know there will be little free time until the new orders are
filled. The office is closed on Sundays, and perhaps, if we
both find a free Sunday, we could meet. I look forward to
seeing you again.*

Until then, I remain your devoted friend,
Misako Imai
February 23rd, 1966, Tokyo

Misako sat at her desk considering her signature. Was her name still
Imai? Maybe that hateful lawyer was right and she should no longer use
the Imai name. She had signed a paper saying she would have nothing
more to do with the Imai family. This problem was just another irritant
making her feel insecure.

Let it be, she thought. If I sign my name Ichimura, no one will know
who I am. Certainly Kensho-*san* would be confused. Let it be for now.

But it didn't feel comfortable. If she had lost her place in the Imai
ohaka, and was no longer in the Imai family register, then she had no right
to use the name Imai, or did she? Misako shivered. She had a terrible
feeling of being disconnected.

The long day's work at the office and these heavy thoughts made her
tired. One letter was all she could write tonight, the letter to Teishin would
have to wait for another day. It was late and somewhere in the city a temple
bell was tolling. The surrounding jungle of highrises ate Buddha's voice
before it could reach Misako's troubled heart.

Dear Misako-san,
*Thank you for your kind letter. I too have seen a plum tree
struggling to bloom here in Kamakura. I too have enjoyed
the memory of the tea ceremony in Kamakura. We must do
that again before long.*

*I wish very much to see you, especially now that you are
distressed with the matter of the urn. I will be in Yokohama
next Sunday attending a pottery exhibition for the work
of a friend and fellow monk. If you could manage to meet
me there and bring the urn with you, we will have time to
talk and I will be able to take the urn back to my temple.
Keeping it here in Kamakura will lighten your burden.*

> When the time is right, I will carry it back to the temple
> in Shibata.
>
> Enclosed you will find an invitation to attend
> the exhibition.
>
> Please come and bring the urn. I will be waiting
> for you most eagerly.
>
> Your friend,
> Kensho

Sachiko was away on business. This allowed Misako to prepare for her Sunday trip to Yokohama without having to explain her plans. She wrapped the urn in a purple silk square and placed the package in a white shopping bag bearing the logo of Atelier Sachi. It wasn't perfect but it was a discreet way to carry it on the train.

The day was clear and cold. Misako wore some of the new clothes that she had purchased for work, at Sachiko's suggestion. The outfit consisted of beautifully cut grey slacks, a matching turtleneck sweater and a classic camel hair coat. She looked smart enough to turn heads as she walked up Yokohama's Muromachi Street, looking for the address on the invitation. It turned out to be a large store for high-priced pottery, mostly items for ceremonial tea. Kensho's face broke into a joyous grin when he saw her.

The meeting was happy and productive. She met several interesting people, looked at beautiful pottery and ate a delicious boxed lunch. They sat on the *tatami* in a room within the store drinking tea. They had a limited amount of time, which allowed them to ignore protocol and talk about what really mattered.

Kensho's happiness at seeing Misako was doubled by the knowledge that he could take the worry of the urn off her hands.

"I have spoken to our Abbot. The place is prepared. When the time comes for it to be returned to Niigata, it will be my responsibility."

Misako handed over the urn with some hesitation. "It is possible that we will never find the correct resting place. I sometimes agree with my mother and feel my grandfather had no business starting this whole drama."

"He didn't start it, Misako. The girl started it when she tumbled into the pond. Your grandfather was caught up in her karma."

"Suppose we never find more information? Where will her ashes end up?"

Kensho tried to imitate Misako's little shrug, not knowing that Misako had adopted it from the mysterious Sachiko. "I believe that should be Teishin-*san*'s decision. When he is completely well, and the temple is running in a normal way, he will probably want to keep it in an appropriate place near him."

Misako sighed. "What about my mother?"

"Trust me," Kensho grinned. "The day will come when Teishin-*san* won't need your mother's advice."

"Trust me," Misako laughed, "you don't have to need my mother's advice to get it."

"The advice I need is how to contact her daughter. I am afraid of disturbing you if I call early in the morning, or at the office or late at night."

"*Hai*, I feel the same way about you," she said. "Let's agree that if it is important, we will call each other any reasonable time. If we can't talk, we can call back."

"Or how about these?" Kensho wiggled his fingers on the top of his head, a gesture that always made her laugh. "Are they sharp or dull these days?"

"Working, but not dependable. Sometimes I have strong intuitive feelings about everything around me. Then there are other times when I go through the day like a robot."

Kensho tapped the side of his head with a long finger. "All life experiences are locked up in there. No one can write a manual for the human brain. It is all too individual and complex."

"Lately I have thought a lot about our conversations and I want to talk a little more about this 'antenna' thing. I think I have changed my mind. Instead of snapping it off, I want you to tell me how would I go about making it stronger."

Kensho winced. "Misako-*san*, please. I keep telling you I am not a master of these matters. I can only tell you the bits of information I have heard or read."

"Then at least teach me how to meditate without playing silly games."

"I'll try," he sighed and tucked his kimono around his knees as he sat up very straight. "To keep it simple start by sitting up straight. Fold your hands in your lap, thumbs lightly touching. Put your head down and close your eyes, or keep them slightly open if you like. Be very quiet and think about your breathing. Count one, two, three. If you lose count go back and start again. That should make you feel calm and slowly clear your mind."

"Is that the technique you used when you called me to the big garden?"

"I don't recall," he said, looking down at his folded hands. "You have a way of taking things to another level so quickly that I am not even sure I should be trying to teach you."

"Well, I'm going to try it. I'm going to practice every day, starting tonight. It can't do any harm."

"Just think," Kensho said with a grin, "if we perfect this, we can solve our communication problems and save money on telephone calls as well."

Before Kensho went home, he found a shop on Muromachi Street and bought a black nylon sack. He just could not travel back to Kamakura carrying an Atelier Sachi shopping bag.

❀ ❀ ❀

New orders for Sachiko's designs kept coming into the office. They were so busy that March that most evening dinners were ordered into the office. When she got home, Misako usually was too tired to do anything but ar-range what she would wear the next day, take a hot bath and fall into bed.

"I'm trying to ride the wave while it is here," Sachiko told Misako in a taxi as they returned home one night too exhausted to stop and eat. "If things don't slow down by early May, I will have to consider expanding, maybe have a small factory outside Tokyo. I'm looking for another girl to help you in the office. She can be your assistant. I think we can squeeze another desk up against the glass partition."

Although it was gruelling, the job was never boring. Famous people came in and out of the atelier almost every day. One incredible commission came from a member of the Tokyo Ladies' Benevolent Society. The members, both Japanese and foreign, were the female crème de la crème of Tokyo. Their yearly charity ball was the highlight of Tokyo's social season.

Many of the ladies had their gowns made in Paris or New York. This year, however, would be different. It was to be a fancy-dress costume ball. The guests of honour included not only a Japanese prince and princess but a visiting British princess. That really caused a frenzy! Every member was busy planning their costume, hoping to make an impression.

The wife of the head honcho of a famous pearl company had her own idea of how she wanted to appear at that glittering event. She saw it as a chance to promote the Japanese pearl industry. Madame wanted to be

275

carried into the ballroom in a very large closed oyster shell. When the top was lifted, she would slowly stand up in a sensational dress and headpiece made from thousands of real pearls. She made it clear that she wanted her body to literally drip with the pearls that she, of course, would supply. Nothing had ever lit Sachiko's imagination like this challenge. She worked in her studio alone for two nights making attitude sketches. The purpose of this was to pinpoint the essence of her client's fantasy. When the design was approved, the pattern was cut and the dress shape was made up in paper. The dress was then made in muslin for more adjustments. Then the hunt started for the perfect fabric.

Madame Pearl was an attractive, middle-aged woman with a neat Japanese figure. Sachiko designed a long narrow dress of very pale turquoise silk, with a kimono-style coat made of a gauzy stuff that was so delicate it resembled the exquisite floss that covers silk cocoons. The front of the dress was to be hand-embroidered with crystal beaded swirls, suggesting waves that tossed off sprays of pearls. The fabric of the coat would be adorned with the same designs and include more than three thousand small pearls and about three thousand crystal beads. The design allowed for Madame to sit down to dinner as the back of the dress would not be embroidered and the pearl-covered coat could be lifted up to rest and flow over the back of the chair like jewelled butterfly wings. For the headpiece, Sachiko fashioned a sparkling helmet of crystals and pearls; drop pearls fell from the crown like luminous bangs. Naturally, the first lady of pearls owned many sensational ropes of the beautiful nacreous growths to adorn her neck and bosom.

In just two weeks the labourious hand-embroidering began, but not in Japan. Sachiko's usual source for this kind of work could not have it done in time, so she had to fly to Hong Kong where she had test samples made. Satisfied with the results, she entrusted the small factory with the precious dress panels and pearls. The beaded panels had to be back in Tokyo in thirty days. The dress had to be finished at least one week before the ball. The intricateness of this most important commission created a tension that filled the atelier. Everyone was fully occupied with other assignments, but still all eyes were on Sachiko when she entered a room, eager, nervous faces, never asking but always waiting for news of the progress.

Finally, Sachiko announced that the dress and coat panels had arrived from Hong Kong, beautifully done and three days before the deadline.

A cheer went up in the sewing room. When it was completed, Madame Pearl almost swooned from delight. Her husband almost swooned when he saw the bill.

All of Sachiko's employees were fiercely loyal to her. They never complained when they had to put in extra hours. In return, Sachiko made sure that all of her team felt appreciated. When a design was finished, it was placed on a mannequin and everyone who worked on it attended the viewing. Tea was served as Sachiko explained what the fabric was and how it was constructed, pointing out any fine stitching, beading or handwork. Everyone would applaud as the garment was carefully folded into layers of tissue and boxed. After a deep bow, everyone went back to work full of pride. The only exception to this rule was the pearl masterpiece. At that viewing, every woman who worked on the garment was presented with a small pearl on a gold chain. The incredible creation was hand delivered to Madame Pearl by Sachiko herself.

Misako was as devoted to Sachiko as anyone else, the difference being that beautiful clothes had never been her passion. Looking at a bolt of exquisite fabric did not make her pulse beat faster, but no one at the atelier would have guessed that. Sachiko had begun choosing Misako's clothes, slowly polishing her Tokyo image. It was as if, at least at work, Misako was another of Sachiko's creations. She was in fact living a double life.

The other Misako could only be herself when she entered her bedroom. That space was the small extension of her private self; its white-painted door the border between her two worlds. Slowly, Coco and Cleo had become comforting friends. Sachiko was rarely home and the cats were content to join Misako on her bed as she slept.

And now there were new, vivid dreams about the unknown girl. On three different occasions Misako dreamed she was once again in the big garden in Shibata, reliving the vision she had seen just before her grandfather died. Instead of wanting to rush toward the falling girl, now she was aware that she was dreaming and could calmly take in more details. This was something new to tell Kensho. When she woke up, she would stay in bed a few extra minutes, trying to remember. By the time she had dressed and walked through the white bedroom door, her mind had left that personal sphere and all thoughts of the dream had vanished. She was a working woman again, who worked long hours with little time for herself. It wasn't until after midnight that Misako finally sat at the desk in her small Tokyo bedroom and wrote to Teishin.

Teishin was so overjoyed to receive Misako's letter that he immediately took it, unopened, to the Tanaka family shrine box and placed it near his dead master's picture. After burning incense, he bowed and savoured the coming pleasure of reading it that evening.

Receiving a personal letter was a rare occurrence for Teishin. Every year the mail brought New Year and midsummer greeting cards and there were letters concerning temple business, but the year was still new and this was already the second personal letter he had received. The first one was a short note from Kensho. In it, Kensho had written that he had heard of Teishin's illness and wished him a speedy recovery. Teishin had treas-ured that note but this letter was even more precious. He couldn't recall receiving such a fine rice-paper envelope addressed personally to him in lovely flowing characters.

That afternoon Teishin and Konein, now working as his assistant, were to officiate at the seven-year death-anniversary memorial service for a wealthy farmer. Teishin had looked forward to the affair, as the two priests would be invited to stay for the wonderful meal that followed. Although his former passion for food had been tempered by his illness, his appetite was coming back and he was beginning to enjoy social functions again.

The priests were invited to sit in the honoured place, in front of the *tokonoma* alcove. Everyone in the room was seated on cushions behind footed lacquered trays laden with delicious dishes. After the speeches the hostess went from guest to guest, moving on her knees, bowing and refilling drinks.

"It is good to see you looking well, Teishin-*sama*," the daughter of the deceased farmer remarked as she knelt in front of his tray and offered sake. Teishin bowed and blushed as he held his little cup toward her to be refilled.

"Thank you, thank you," he said. "It is kind of you to notice. *Hai*, I do believe that I have not felt this well for a long time."

What he couldn't say was that he was filled with delicious anticipation because he had a beautifully written personal letter waiting for him at the temple. To Teishin, it was an amazing gift and he had decided to keep the pleasure of opening the letter until after the evening meal.

Which is what he did, sitting formal Japanese style on the worn *tatami* floor with the bare light bulb overhead. First he touched the letter to his forehead and then slit the envelope open reverently with a letter opener.

Removing the letter, he bowed to it before his eyes consumed the skillful pen strokes.

> Teishin-san,
> It feels like spring has come to Tokyo. The sun seems warmer and the plum blossoms are showing themselves. Yesterday I saw a tree near the office that was heavy with flowers.
> Mother tells me that you have fully recovered from your illness, that you are back to work and that you are even gaining a little weight. I look forward to seeing you healthy again.
> As for me, everyone at work here is busy, but I hope to return to Shibata over the holidays from the end of April into the first week of May.
> You will be glad to know that the honourable urn is safe. My room was not the proper place for it. Kensho-san was kind enough to take it to his temple in Kamakura. He tells me it is among other urns in a fine room where incense is burned daily. He has promised to return it to Niigata when you wish to receive it. For the present, I believe it is the best arrangement and respectfully hope you agree.
> I trust that your health will continue to improve and that winter will finally leave Niigata. Please take good care of yourself. Keep warm, get rest and eat lots of good food.
> Best regards,
> Misako
> March 9, 1966, Tokyo

After the first reading, Teishin smiled with his entire face. The second reading touched his heart and made him feel as if a lamp was burning in his chest. By the third reading his cheeks had some of their former pink bloom and his fingers tingled. Misako had written an almost hasty, ordinary, friendly letter. To Teishin, this was the sweetest epistle he had ever seen and tears began to flow down his face.

Whatever is the matter with me? he thought. These past weeks, I have hardly given a thought to that which was so important to my master. I have done nothing to gain more information about the unknown girl.

279

What would he think of such a lazy procrastinator? How can I disappoint Misako-*san*?

"*Yush!*" Teishin made the noise he had often heard movie samurai make before dashing off to battle. The gruffly spoken word sounded strong; an expression of his new determination. He folded the letter back into the envelope, placed it on the *tatami* mat and bowed. "*Yush!*" he said again. "It will be done."

The next afternoon, fuelled by this new determination, Teishin put on his padded jacket and slipped into his rubber boots to venture out on his quest for information. He couldn't wait, even though it was one of those dark, bone-chilling Niigata days where the wind raced snow-spitting clouds over the city. The logical place to start was the Sugimoto home, he thought, as it was old Mrs. Sugimoto who had told him that her husband had known of a girl with one ear when he was a boy.

The elderly Sugimoto couple welcomed his surprise visit. Their daughter-in-law ushered him in to join the old couple who were sitting at the warm *kotatsu*. Teishin accepted hot tea and rubbed his hands under a quilt warmed by a charcoal burner.

"We are always glad to welcome you to our humble home, but what could be so important to bring you out in this cold, so soon after your illness?" the old woman inquired.

As pumped up as Teishin was to do this job, he couldn't help but blush when the time came for him to ask questions. This urgency suddenly seemed foolish, and he wondered if he had been a bit rude to come into their home for such a purpose. For that reason, he bowed deeply before he spoke.

"Forgive me for disturbing your household, but I seek some information that perhaps only you can supply."

The formal tone of the priest's words and the seriousness of his facial expression made the old couple exchange anxious glances.

Teishin placed his hands on the *kotatsu* table and, like a movie detective, addressed his host. "Sugimoto-*san*, some time ago your honourable wife told me that when you were a boy, you knew a young girl who had no ear on the right side of her head. Can you tell me about that girl?"

The old man pulled his chin into his chest, which was his personal gesture of surprise. "Huh! Is that what you want to talk about? Is that what is so important?"

"*Hai*," the priest said.

"You are talking about seventy years ago!"

"I understand that, but can you tell me what you remember about the unfortunate girl with one ear? Do you remember where she lived or her name?"

The old man made a great sucking noise through his teeth. "Difficult! My memory isn't what it used to be," he said. He actually couldn't remember where he left his glasses ten minutes ago, but he did sometimes remember things about his childhood. "I think she was a kind of nursemaid for a family that lived two streets west of here."

"Ah, that is very good." Teishin was pleased. "And do you remember her name?"

The old man frowned and made another sucking sound. "How can I recall such a thing? I didn't know her well. She was five or six years older than I was—my friends and I teased her about having only one ear. We always wanted her to push her hair aside so we could see it. We called her 'Ghost.' I don't remember her real name, just Ghost."

"Oh, I see," Teishin said, feeling a great surge of pity for the ill-fated girl. "Well, at least you remember where she lived. Do you know if the house is still there?"

"No," the old man said. "That house has been gone for years. There is a modern house there now. I never noticed when it was built."

"*Ah so,*" Teishin said and his face reflected his disappointment. "Does it still belong to the same family?"

"How can I know such a thing?" The old man began to sound a little put out by the priest's questions. "Why do you want to know all this old stuff?"

Teishin flushed, not knowing what to say. If he told the truth, Keiko would surely hear about it. He hesitated.

"You should cooperate with the priest," the old woman said, scolding her husband. "Surely you can see that the priest wants to have more information about the remains found in Shimizuen garden."

"That is so," Teishin said with a new blush.

"Well," the old man said, rubbing his chin, "I don't remember the name of the people that nursemaid worked for, but it could be Nomura. The Nomura that lives there now must be about seventy years old. I met him through the Bonsai Society. He could have been the baby the nursemaid always had tied on her back."

"Good, that is very good," the priest said, regaining a bit of his excitement. "Perhaps, if you would be kind enough to draw me a map, I

281

can visit the Nomura home after I leave here."

"What?" the old woman said with surprise. "In this filthy weather? Teishin-*san*, you will be back in the hospital again tomorrow."

Her words embarrassed the priest. He smiled and bowed his head. "Perhaps you are right, Grandmother. I can inquire another day."

As they spoke, the old man had left the warmth of the *kotatsu*, and shuffled to a chest of drawers. "Here it is," he said and returned carrying a worn notebook. "These are my notes from the Bonsai Society. I'm sure I have his telephone number here."

"Good, very good," Teishin smiled. "Thank you."

Sugimoto looked at the book with his chin up, in order to see well from the bottom part of his loose-fitting bifocals. "Here, it is. I'll call him," he said as he reached out and pulled the telephone from the shelf behind him.

Teishin's heart almost stopped from the suspense of listening to the number being dialled. He realized that the old man was talking to Nomura, but Teishin was so nervous that he couldn't follow what was being said. Sugimoto hung up the phone and frowned.

"He doesn't remember anything, that guy. The family lived in the same place all right, but the house was rebuilt. This Nomura-*san* had to be the baby that was carried on that one-eared girl's back, but he doesn't remember anything."

"Too bad," Mrs. Sugimoto said, shaking her head.

"Well, I suppose it is to be expected, it was so long ago," the old man said.

Teishin bowed his head and thanked them for their trouble. He smiled to hide his disappointment. Only the old woman sensed it.

"Too bad," she said sympathetically.

"*Hai*, too bad," Teishin said and prepared to leave.

He walked home on wet streets, surrounded by piles of dirty snow. Funny he hadn't noticed them on the way to the Sugimoto house. The return walk seemed so much longer, and the wind was colder. When he got back to the temple, Teishin felt so tired that he went right to bed. The doctor had warned him not to do too much as it was going to take him a long while to get his strength back. What a fool, he told himself. All that effort for nothing.

Five days later, when the wet and cold had subsided, Mrs. Sugimoto visited the temple with another elderly lady. Her name was Mrs. Wada. She was the older sister of the Mr. Nomura who lived in the house where the one-eared girl had once lived.

"*Hai*, I remember that girl," she told the priest as they drank tea in the temple's small sitting room. Teishin had brought out his best cakes when he heard who his guests were.

"We children called her Kiku-*chan*. Yes, that was my brother she carried on her back. I was about six or seven when she lived with us."

Her words were so thrilling that Teishin could hardly sit still as she spoke. "Who was she? Where did she come from? What happened to her?" He had so many questions.

Old Mrs. Wada smiled; her false teeth were blocks of dull perfection. Her hand shook for a second as she was very old and it had been a long time since anyone asked her a real question.

"Kiku-*chan* was my cousin. She came to live with us before my brother was born. He was the fourth child in our family, the first boy. Kiku-*chan* was the daughter of my mother's older sister. They lived in a fishing village up north, on the Yamagata boarder. The poor girl was born with only one ear. Her hair covered the deformity, but we children knew about it. Our mother made us promise not to tell anyone. Still, some boys found out and teased her all the time."

"My husband!" Mrs. Sugimoto said, shaking her head. "He was one of those bad boys!"

Mrs. Wada shook her head with remorse. "It wasn't just the boys. We girls teased her at home as well."

"What happened to her?" Teishin asked.

"As I remember, she missed her mother very much. Actually, I don't remember that she said very much. She liked to go off by herself. When she ran away, my mother blamed us children for making fun of her. I'm sorry that it may have been true. She couldn't hear on her right side and we used to whisper to her on that side and laugh at her confusion. Children can be cruel!"

"Do you remember the name of the fishing village that she came from?" Teishin asked, almost holding his breath.

"Yes," the old woman said. "The village is called Neya. After my mother died, we lost track of those relatives. I suppose that family is still there. I'm not sure what happened to them."

Teishin shook his head in pity as he offered his best cakes to the ladies again and filled their tea cups. The question he was about to ask was so important that his hand shook. He sipped some tea, cleared his throat and asked: "What was the girl's family name?"

"The family name was Homma. That was her name, Kiku Homma of Neya. She must have been about fifteen or sixteen years old when she ran away from our home in Shibata."

Teishin leaned back on his heels and let out a great sigh.

"I hope this is a help," Mrs. Sugimoto said. "I felt so badly about not being able to give you information when you visited us last that I went over to talk to Mr. Nomura's wife. She told me that her husband had three older sisters and that one sister was still alive, living outside of town. This sister, Chiyeko-*san*, married Mr. Wada who had a general store close to Deyu. Their son runs the business now."

"And your husband, is he well?" Teishin asked out of politeness.

"Oh no," she said with an embarrassed laugh. "He died years ago."

"*Ah so*," Teishin said with the appropriate note of sympathy.

Old Mrs. Wada took another sip of tea. She had been living with her son's family for a very long time and she had been lonely since her grandchildren had grown up and left the house. But today was different. The trip to Shibata had been enjoyable. The priest's cakes were especially delicious and she hadn't felt so useful in a very long time.

When the ladies were about to leave, Teishin bowed to them with his head touching the *tatami* floor. "*Arigato gozaimasu*! I can't tell you how grateful I am," he said.

He walked with them down the temple path and through the big wooden gate where they exchanged a few more happy words. The priest bowed his goodbye and stood smiling.

Mrs. Wada was going home to tell her family about the long-lost cousin she had almost forgotten. Mrs. Sugimoto went home intending to scold her husband for having been so cruel to that poor girl seventy years ago.

Teishin watched them walk down the street, hardly able to contain his joy. His first impulse was to rush to the telephone. By the time he entered the kitchen, he had changed his mind. No, he wasn't going to send this news by telephone. This news was too important to throw across a wire to be absorbed without a trace. No, he had decided to take the time to send each of his friends the gift of a carefully composed letter.

❀ ❀ ❀

284

Ever since Misako had nursed the priest at the hospital, the nurses were always asking Keiko about her daughter.

"How is Misako-*san*? Was she glad to return to Tokyo? Misako-*san* must be happy to be back in the big city after her stay here in the country. . . . Give Misako-*san* my best. Tell her we miss her around the hospital."

Divorce always affects more people than just the couple. Keiko continued to feel a stab to her heart when well-intentioned people inquired about her daughter. What was she to say? That Misako was well and happy? That Misako and her husband were enjoying the spring weather in Tokyo? It hypocritical to keep saying that Misako was fine when she knew that her daughter had recently suffered a terrible rejection and a painful divorce. The fact that Hideo was already remarried and expecting a child only made it worse. She couldn't avoid the issue any longer, especially since Misako might decide to come back home.

Finally, after a morning hospital staff meeting, she asked the nurses and receptionist to stay and spoke to the small group of women.

"On a personal note," she began, "some of you got to know my daughter, Misako, when she helped me care for the priest during his illness. Many of you have been kind enough to inquire about her. It is very difficult for me to discuss such matters, but I thought it only fair to inform you that Misako's personal situation has recently changed. Unfortunately, she and her husband Hideo have been divorced. The cause was another woman. Hideo has remarried. Misako is staying in Tokyo for a while. Her father and I want her to return home."

The room was perfectly silent for a moment. The nurse who knew Misako best spoke up, expressing her regrets, and called Misako "a poor thing." She ended her little speech with what she felt was a great compliment: "Misako-*san* would make a wonderful nurse." A buzz of agreement went around the room.

"Perhaps that is so," Keiko said, accepting the well-meaning words. "We are hoping that she will come home and take over some of my work in the office. At the moment she is working as a secretary for her friend, Kimura-*san*, who is enjoying some success as a designer in Tokyo."

"Isn't that the designer from Shibata?" one of the nurses asked.

"Why, yes. My goodness," Keiko said, "she must be more famous than I thought. How do you know about her?"

"I read about her in a magazine," the nurse said uncomfortably, and one of the younger women giggled.

Later that day, the nurse came back to the office and placed the worn magazine on Keiko's desk. "A patient left this behind some time ago and I read it before I put it in the magazine rack in the waiting room. Maybe you ought to read it."

Keiko immediately read it and felt the blood drain from her head. What Sachiko's aunt had told her was true. She had been a nightclub hostess.

The nurse spoke up, trying to soften the shock. "You probably don't know about these muckraking magazines that have become popular recently. Really, they are often full of lies. Sachiko-*san* is a designer. She worked in a nightclub when she was down on her luck. It was a way to make a living. Those magazines try to make a scandal out of nothing."

Keiko stood up, closed the magazine and thanked the nurse. Maybe she was overreacting. Certainly she remembered that Misako's school friend had come from very unfortunate circumstances. That evening, she gave the article to Dr. Ichimura to read.

"What are we going to do?" a distressed Keiko asked.

"Nothing," the doctor said. "I keep telling you Misako is a grown woman."

"Grown woman or not, she is my daughter and I can't help worrying about her."

"Give Misako some credit. Your fretting won't help. Now please stop it."

Keiko smiled weakly. "I'll try," she said. But Keiko was a mother and the worry tendrils grew and grew and wound themselves ever more tightly around her heart.

TWENTY-NINE
Spring 1966

*T*eishin's letters reached their destinations on the same day. Kensho read his soon after it arrived, about ten o'clock in the morning. He had never expected Teishin to learn the identity of the unknown girl. The news caused him to become so excited that he rushed to the telephone. Only his well-honed discipline kept him from dialling.

At three o'clock the tall priest found a corner of the garden to meditate. He tried very hard to think of Misako and send the positive energy he was filled with by the good news. Misako also had time to be quiet at three o'clock. She had not yet received her letter but she came away from her meditation with a picture of a large, white chrysanthemum in her head. What did the vision mean?

The letter was in the mailbox when she returned from the office at about seven o'clock. Sachiko had a dinner meeting that evening. The maid had gone home at five o'clock and only the cats were in the apartment to witness Misako on the white rug, slitting the envelope with an ivory letter opener.

As Misako read her letter, both of the cats became restless and Cleo ran off to the bedroom. There was too much energy in the air for her feline liking. The entire room was bursting with whatever this human was feeling. Even Coco jumped off the sofa when Misako laughed out loud and rubbed her hands together saying, "Teishin-*san, arigato gozaimasu,* thank you!"

Misako reached for Sachiko's white telephone to call Kensho. They both marvelled at the information that the gentle Teishin was able to find on his own. They talked for almost an hour, making future plans that Misako promised to tell Teishin about by phone that same evening.

Late, when Misako was enjoying a bowl of rice and tea, she thought that it was ironic that the conclusion of this strange business, set in motion by a country priest's obsession, was being wound up in a Western-style, high-rise apartment in Tokyo. That night, she was comfortable enough to leave the white door to her bedroom ajar; the border no longer needed to be guarded. The cats purred. Cleo slept at her feet and Coco purred next to her shoulder. If Sachiko had been home, Misako would have told her friend the whole story.

❀ ❀ ❀

Golden Week is a series of holidays that all Japanese enjoy as a national vacation time. In 1966, it started with the Emperor Hirohito's birthday on April twenty-ninth, included Constitution Commemoration Day on May third and ended after Boy's Day, or Children's Day, on May fifth. That year, the twenty-ninth of April fell on a Friday and the fifth of May was on the following Thursday. It was a perfect time for Misako and the two priests to meet in Shibata.

Misako reserved her train ticket for the evening of April twenty-eighth. Kensho was involved in the training of a group of foreigners in the way of Zen and couldn't get away until May third. By the time Kensho arrived with the urn, Misako would have arranged to borrow Keiko's car and, with the priest Teishin, mapped out the trip. On the Wednesday morning, Misako and the two priests planned to drive north to the fishing village of Neya. There they would try to find the Homma family and return the ashes of the long lost Kiku.

Each of the three conspirators was excited by the impending adventure. Kensho, however, had to first deal with a group of American university students who were about to invade his temple. The sixteen men and seven women were coming as part of a study program created by a Zen temple in San Francisco.

In the past, the number of visiting foreigners at Kensho's temple had been a reasonable two or three at a time. The American visitors, usually men, would arrive with appropriately shaven heads and a serious desire to further their religious studies. Many of the novices had a basic knowledge of the Japanese language, dress and customs.

This new, larger experiment, however, brought an amazing array of energetic American youth, male and female. It had a most unsettling effect on the peaceful existence of the resident monks. Not only were their modest and restrained surroundings about to be filled with brightly coloured shirts and flowered skirts, but the level of sound would increase a thousand-fold. The hallowed halls of the Zen compound were about to ring with not only a foreign language, but one that was spoken so loudly that the quietude of the peaceful rock garden would never be the same again.

And the hair! Most of the foreign students of both sexes had an abundance of it. By the end of the first week, every one of the bald resident monks would face the distasteful experience of having to remove several long hairs from linens, sinks and bath. The task of taming these budding American flower children would fall heavily on the shoulders of the professor who was leading them and Kensho. He was after all, as tall as, if not taller than, most of these foreigners. He did seem, with his limited English vocabulary and a very un-Japanese talent for making faces and waving his long limbs, to be able to communicate with them. It was really impressive to watch him lecture. He even managed to make the foreigners laugh. Kensho was becoming a great asset to his temple.

As for Misako, enough time had passed that she could meet with people and even talk about the divorce without teetering on the verge of tears. Maybe it was possible to live in Tokyo, after all, she thought. Perhaps it was a good idea to try to get on with a Tokyo social life, at least until Golden Week. She telephoned her old friend Yuri who was delighted to return with her to the tennis court. That was a good step, Misako told herself. She might even try to go on a date with a man Yuri had told her about.

The promise of having Misako and Kensho visit Shibata inspired Teishin to burn a stick of *senko* on the temple's main altar and chant prayers of thanks.

It seemed that everyone was looking forward to Golden Week. Sachiko announced that the business would be closed from April twenty-eighth until Monday, May ninth. The rush was over and things were almost back to normal. Sachiko sighed with relief, not knowing that her name would once again be the talk of the town, after the Charity Costume Ball.

Madame Pearl's entrance caused a sensation at the Okura Hotel's ballroom.

Protocal demanded that the guests arrive after the Royals. This year, however, just after all were seated, there was a drum roll and a great oyster shell was carried onto the dance floor on the shoulders of four strong, young men dressed like fishermen. People stood transfixed as the giant oyster shell was gently lowered to the floor. The men disappeared, the top of the shell slowly opened and out stepped Madame Pearl in all her luminous glory. She looked sensational! The room erupted with applause. Madame was now a delicate, glittering dream of Japanese cultured pearls. Everyone loved it. Before the evening was over, every woman in the room wanted to know who the designer of the fabulous costume was.

The next day the wife of the French Ambassador called Sachiko to personally congratulate her.

"The ball was wonderful! Really, the pearl dress was superb. I heard that even the princess asked who designed it. Everyone is talking about it. You can't imagine how many people are raving about your work. You must come to our dinner party next Saturday. I know it is short notice, but please, you cannot disappoint us."

THIRTY

*K*eiko stood frowning down on two patches of red tulips that were just beginning to bloom in front of the hospital. The displeasure was still written on her face when she entered the office. Dr. Ichimura, who was going through a file cabinet, looked up and asked his wife what was wrong.

"Have you seen those red tulips? I distinctly remember buying two dozen pink tulip bulbs last fall and planting them myself. They must have sold me red tulip bulbs when I asked for pink."

"Mistakes happen. You can't control everything," the doctor said with a grin.

Keiko took no offence. Her husband often teased her about the way she managed the office, jokingly referring to his wife as "The General." The title made her laugh. After years of marriage and working together, the fondness and respect they felt for each other floated between them as naturally as air. Keiko had often tried to explain to her daughter that real love grew slowly and quietly. It wasn't a wave that knocked people down and swept them away. Love marriages indeed! She opened the ledger on her desk. Why hadn't Misako listened to her? Now what was she going to do?

Among other things, Keiko worried about the kind of woman Misako was living with, no matter how Misako had defended her friend. The magazine article made it sound as if there was some past scandal attached to Sachiko's name. Afraid that it could rub off on her daughter, Keiko wanted Misako to move back home, even if they no longer needed help in the hospital office. The superstitions about the Fire Horse Year had dramatically reduced patient numbers at the hospital. Keiko sighed.

And then there was Teishin. Finding him a wife was another problem. Everyone she spoke to in the congregation agreed that the temple would be better off if their senior priest was married, yet no one was able to suggest a suitable bride. There were several older unmarried ladies living around the area, but none of them was the least bit interested in becoming the wife of a country priest. But Keiko was not going to give up. There was one unmarried lady whose father had recently died. Keiko had seen her several times, at the temple. She would have to ask about her. Left alone, there was no telling what mischief Teishin would get into.

She had to admit he seemed to be pulling things together at the temple. Teshin was energetic and in excellent spirits. But Keiko still didn't have a lot of confidence in his common sense. He was being just as silly about those unknown ashes as her father had been. She was thinking about the bombshell her daughter had dropped on them the evening. Keiko still couldn't get over it, and again, she was powerless to do anything.

With so much happening since the New Year, Keiko wanted to forget the box of human ashes that had crashed to the floor when she pulled apart Teishin's closet. Just thinking about the mess made her shudder. She had no idea that Misako was involved in a conspiracy with the two priests. That's what made it so shocking when Misako broke the news at the dinner table that night with almost girlish delight. It was as if she was about to tell her parents she had won some sort of prize.

"I know you will have trouble believing this, but I have fantastic news."

Both parents put down their chopsticks and gave Misako their full atten-tion, Keiko thinking that a little good news would be nice for a change.

"It's about the bones that were found in the big garden," Misako said.

Keiko groaned. "Oh no. Will we ever be free of that trouble?"

"Yes, we will. That's the good news. We know who the mystery girl was, when she lived and where she came from."

The doctor was interested. "How did you ever find that kind of information?"

"It was Teishin-*san*. He did the detective work and found someone who knew the girl before she fell into the pond."

"Teishin-*san*? I can't believe it," Keiko said with authority. "He couldn't find anything out on his own."

"Well, you are wrong, Mother," Misako shot back, letting the im-patience she felt ring in her voice. "It annoys me that you don't give Teishin-*san* the credit he deserves. All on his own he found out the girl's name, when she lived and where she lived. He knows the very house in Shibata where she stayed. And he knows she came from a tiny fishing hamlet, north of Murakami."

"I'm impressed," the doctor said. "Now I suppose you will have to go the fishing village to investigate."

"That is exactly the plan. We hope to find someone there who will remember the girl with only one ear. We want to take her ashes to her family. Grandfather would have wanted that."

"We, meaning you and Teishin-*san*?" the doctor asked."

"And the priest from Kamakura. He has been in on this from the start."

"*Ah so*," Keiko said. "And of course, you will want to borrow our car to travel to this far away fishing village."

"Please, Mother," Misako said, her palms pressed together as in prayer.

The conversation had left Keiko frustrated. The only thing she had wanted to hear from her daughter's lips was what her personal plans were. Had she decided to stay in Tokyo or was she coming back to Shibata?

When Keiko went home for her mid-morning tea break, Misako finally opened up to her. She wanted her mother to know that she needed more time before she could decide her future. These months of trying to adapt to her new situation in Tokyo had not been easy and she confessed to her mother that she had often been often frightened and confused.

Keiko listened in silence, with a growing feeling of empathy and relief. She looked down into her teacup, nodding her head. She understood, and yes, she would be more patient. The only part of Misako's outpouring that Keiko was tempted to argue with was her claim that sharing the mystery of the unknown ashes with the two priests had given her a sense of balance. Keiko's mouth narrowed disdainfully, but she listened and said nothing.

"Otherwise, I would have felt like a robot going back and forth from the office to the apartment. At least it gave me a purpose other than my job, a connection to the temple. No matter how strange you think this whole affair is, I know Grandfather would have approved of what we are doing. It is what he wanted to do himself."

Keiko made a face. There was nothing more irritating than Misako going on about how all this was Grandfather's will. What made Misako so sure? There was no use arguing. She knew that there were intricacies to her daughter's character that she could never appreciate.

"I can't say I understand all this, Misako. I'm glad you told me how you feel. I only want your happiness."

Although the apprehensions still fluttered in Keiko's heart, at least she had a glimpse of what Misako was struggling with. She went back to the office, hoping for a chance to talk to her husband. Passing the tulips once again she thought that the red wasn't so bad. Something bright and optimistic was appropriate for the entrance of a hospital.

Misako rode her bicycle to the temple that afternoon, even though she knew Teishin would be away with his Old People's Club. They had gone to view what was left of the flowering cherry trees on the banks of the Black River. Last year's storm had caused many of the trees to be cut down.

Konein was alone in the temple when she arrived, examining the worn address book that hung next to the telephone.

"Ah, Misako-*san*. Forgive me but I have something important to attend to so I can't stay. I was trying to find someone to watch the temple for a couple of hours. Usually one of the elders is eager to help but Teishin-*san* has them on an outing."

Misako smiled at the priest's rare flow of words. "I'll be glad to stay. I intended to wait for Teishin-*san* anyway."

"He won't be back until almost four o'clock," Konein said, his face creased with concern.

"That's fine. For once, I am in no hurry." Misako said with a smile.

Konein bowed. "I'm sorry I have to leave you alone without offering you a cup of tea."

Misako waved her hand at him to go. "I'm not a guest. I used to live here, you know."

And that was how it happened that Misako was left alone in the temple. She felt like a child again, and set off to explore. Her first stop was the main altar room. She looked up at the ceiling's dark wooden beams and breathed in the *senko*-perfumed air. It gave her a sense of remembering something that had long lingered in the back of her mind, some fragment of a dream. As Kensho had suggested, this was the place where so much of her childhood imagination had been nurtured.

The revelation made her smile, a smile that resembled that of her late grandfather's. She wore it as she roamed around the building, opening sliding doors and peering into spaces that she had long forgotten about. There was the old storage room full of the temple's clutter that had been gathered over many years, a box or two of old scrolls, vases, a damaged tray, candlesticks and many personal boxes belonging to her ancestors.

Ah, there was a box Misako remembered. She and her mother had looked in that box many times during her childhood. It was full of pretty pictures painted by Grandfather's mother. Misako's great-grandmother had been a talented artist. Keiko sometimes displayed one of her scrolls at home. Misako took the box from the shelf and carefully removed the cover, unrolling the paintings one at a time.

They were all done with a brush, using the black ink made from rubbing a particular stone with water. Four of them were of flowers, two of birds, five of free flowing landscapes and one painting of the temple in winter. The temple's roof was high with snow and a small figure of a priest seemed to be walking up the path under an umbrella. Now she remembered that her mother thought that this one had not been done by her grandmother. There just was not the same loose touch, the same level of skill that her grandmother's paintings had. Perhaps her grandfather had done this when he was a schoolboy, or perhaps it was the work of one of his siblings.

Misako examined it closely, looking for the small stamp signature that her great-grandmother put on all her works. This one didn't have a signature, unless it was the small flower in the right-hand corner. It was a charming little work. Misako rolled it up and put it back in the box, intending to ask her mother if she could have it.

An hour had passed and Teishin still hadn't returned. Misako walked further into the private part of the temple, dismayed at the state of the *tatami* floors and *shoji* doors. Even the sliding wooden door to the bathroom was cracked, and a number of tiny tiles were missing from the bathroom floor. The old-fashioned wooden tub was in particularly poor condition. Although it was clean and empty, with the wooden-top, dippers and wash-bucket set neatly against the wall, she winced at the look of the decrepit tub. She went back to the room where the family altar was kept, to sit under the smiling gaze of her grandfather and ponder this troubling situation. It was all the more upsetting when she remembered the Zen temple in Kamakura with everything in pristine condition.

When Teishin returned, however, smiling and looking healthier than when she'd last seen him, Misako couldn't comment on the concerns she had for the temple. He was looking so well, and it would have been a shame to mar his happiness with anything unpleasant. He was most eager to talk about their coming trip. Teishin even produced a map and spread it on the floor, tracing the road they would take to Neya.

It was almost dark when Konein returned. Misako looked at her watch and said she had to dash home. Teishin snapped the light on in the kitchen and the resident rat scampered off into a corner. A feeling of horror welled up inside Misako and she let out a little scream.

"A rat," Teishin announced as if Misako hadn't known what it was. "The building is very old and stands too near the rice fields. It can't be helped."

"Why don't you have a cat?" she asked.

"A cat?" Teishin repeated. "The master never allowed a cat in the temple," he said, rubbing his bald head, obviously trying to remember why.

"Well, I think it is definitely time for this temple to have a cat to deal with the rats," Misako announced. Her voice sounded very much like her mother's.

THIRTY-ONE

*T*he plan to leave for the fishing village of Neya ran into its first major complication when Kensho was forced to miss his train to Niigata. The delay was caused by a general meeting called on the morning of May third to review and evaluate the study program for the foreign students.

Most of the members of the Zen community were present, sitting in rows on the *tatami* floor in the temple's large lecture room. The meeting started with a strong negative statement given by the most senior monk. He said that having foreigners at the temple was too disruptive and the program should not be repeated. Another monk said he respectfully agreed, but pointed out that it was only a test run. He suggested that, with more guidelines, and by limiting the program to only one or two groups a year, perhaps it could be successful. There were those who wanted to try again, seeing the advantages of cooperating with the temple in San Francisco and educating young foreigners in the way of Zen. The fact that every temple had to support itself was also brought up and, although some complained that such considerations were not in the Zen spirit, one brazen monk noted that having foreign student programs was lucrative. He even proposed that Kensho be sent to America to learn English.

Kensho had to stay for the entire discussion because everyone agreed that he was particularly suited for playing a major role in these programs. To reach a consensus, the meeting went on so long that he missed his train by three hours, arriving at Ueno Station at six o'clock. Since so many people were travelling during the holiday, there was no room on the next two trains, only a cancellation for a second-class sleeper on the very slow overnight train leaving at nine that evening. Kensho telephoned Teishin to tell him that he would not be arriving until seven o'clock the next morning. Teishin sounded flustered and said he would inform Misako of the change of plans.

"Don't worry," Teishin said nervously. "If Misako-*san* can't meet you at the station, I will try to make other arrangements." Both priests ended the conversation by stating that it couldn't be helped. "*Shikata ga nai.*"

Sick at heart about causing the snarl in their plans, Kensho checked his black bags and walked around the Ueno Station area. He needed to kill some time and find a bowl of noodles for his dinner. City life had never appealed to the tall priest, especially the busy, seedy streets around the station. Nevertheless, he kept searching for a place to eat, towering over everyone on the crowded street.

At the noodle shop, the heads of all six customers sitting at the counter jerked around when the hungry Kensho parted the curtain and had to bend in order to enter the tiny, steamy space.

"Is it a priest?" the owner-cook said with exaggerated surprise.

"*Hai, hai,*" Kensho said good-naturedly, "and I am sure you don't have a noodle in this shop as long as this hungry priest."

The owner was in the midst of draining a pot of hot noodles and burst into a hearty laugh. When he put the pot down, he removed the sweat towel that was tied on his semibald head and bobbed a little respectful bow.

"*Obosan,* look at these noodles here. If I press them from end to end, I think I can make it. How did you get so tall, anyway?"

"From eating noodles, of course," Kensho said as he sat on the only empty stool next to a man who was obviously a day-labourer.

"*Obosan,* here, let me pour you a beer," his slightly drunken neighbour offered through a smile that showed he was missing two front teeth.

"Thank you, but only one glass," Kensho said, still grinning. "If I drink too much alcohol, it might stunt my growth."

The noodle shop rocked with laughter. Two men passing on the street stopped to put their heads through the curtain to see what the merriment was about. None of the present customers were willing to give up their places at the counter, even though two of them had finished their noodles. This promised to be entertaining and they ordered more beer.

After two bowls of noodles and three glasses of beer, for which no one would allow him to pay, the priest made his way back to the station with a hot, glowing face and a growing feeling of depression. He was tired from working with the foreigners at the temple all week. He was tired from the anxiety he felt felt from missing his train. He was tired from worrying about the safety of the urn and he was especially tired of trying to entertain the men at the noodle shop. In spite of all the work he had done with meditation, exploring his own inner being, he didn't understand why he acted like a clown whenever he thought he was being mocked or teased.

"*Shikata ga nai,*" he told himself with a great sigh. No matter how much he wished it, it would be foolish to think of living a normal life. "It is my fate."

The only consolation was that he knew it would be easier to forget Misako now that he was being sent to America for a year to learn English. By the end of the summer he would be living at the Zen temple in far off California. It wasn't something he wanted to do, but it was unthinkable to refuse the wishes of his superiors. A year would go quickly and he would be back the following spring to run the next Zen seminar for foreign students; that is, if he could master English. And if they deemed him spiritually mature enough to teach on his own.

It didn't promise to be an easy night. The sink in the train was so low that the tall priest had to kneel on the floor in order to wash before he climbed up to the one available bunk of the three-tiered sleepers. The sleeping compartments were no more than stacked shelves with a black curtain for privacy. The bunk bed was so narrow and short that Kensho only just managed to close the curtains. In a short while, the lights went out in the train's corridor and a chorus of snores filled the air.

At first Kensho tried a fetal position, but his feet slowly edged out between the curtains. Next he tried lying on his back, bending his knees and pressing his feet against the compartment's edge. He managed to doze off until the train reduced speed and jolted into the next station. He finally sat up in the lotus position with his shoulders bent and the back of his head touching the top of the compartment. He tried not to think, not to imagine, not to feel, but the pain that stabbed the back of his neck couldn't be ignored; it really hurt. With his legs still locked, he tried to ease over on his side. Soon his legs cramped and his feet slowly edged back out into the aisle. At about three in the morning a conductor passed by and pushed at the two very large feet that were blocking the narrow aisle.

The rain started in Shibata during the night, just minutes before old Mr. Sugimoto died in his sleep. The news reached the temple about six in the morning, as Teishin was setting a fire under the old wooden bathtub. He had scrubbed it and filled it with clean water, hoping to have it ready for the priest from Kamakura. It certainly was in poor condition. Keiko had brought it to his attention and talked about the *shoji* and *tatami* as well. Teishin hadn't noticed that a new bath was needed. No one seemed to notice it. The old master didn't like change, but now Keiko was calling a meeting with the elders of the congregation to discuss the much-needed

299

repairs to the temple, even though nothing could be done until after the first anniversary of the old master's death. Teishin's thoughts were interrupted by Konein hurrying down the hallway with a message that had just come from the Sugimoto house.

The sky looked as dull as a tarnished pot as Misako drove from Shibata to the Niitsu Station. All of spring's wonderful colours were blurred and muted in a persistent rain, as if the new green and flowering trees were painted with wet, running watercolours. It was after seven by the time she reached the station. Kensho was already waiting outside, looking like the most dishevelled of passengers. She saw him before he saw her. He was carrying a black bag in each hand; his shoulders were sagging and his head was hanging down. It was a shock for Misako to see her friend and mentor looking so vulnerable. When he saw her drive up, he smiled, but his eyes looked as if they had retreated into their deep sockets.

Misako tried to be cheerful. "You must be very tired, but don't worry," she told him. "Teishin-*san* is preparing a hot bath and a good breakfast for you at the temple. Perhaps even the rain will let up. All will be well. We are going to enjoy the day."

But all was not well at the temple. Teishin met them with the news that he would not be able to go on their planned trip. Old Mr. Sugimoto was dead. A death in the congregation meant several busy days for the parish priest. There was no question of going with them now, duty called.

"Then we will put the trip to Neya off," Misako said.

"Yes, it can wait until another time," Kensho agreed.

"No," Teishin said, shaking his head. "There must be a reason for this. Perhaps I have done all that was meant for me to do. It is better that you two go and try to find the girl's family. This step in our plan must be taken before anything else can be decided." Teishin was once again showing his stubborn streak. "Now, Kensho-*san*, the bath is ready," he said. "Misako-*san*, come help me finish making Kensho-*san*'s breakfast. It will be ready in twenty minutes."

Misako raised her eyebrows, as she had never seen Teishin issue orders before. It seemed to her that the old Teishin would have sat still, wrung his hands and waited. She followed him to the kitchen, marvelling at his new-found health and strength.

As for Kensho, he had to once again fold himself into a fetal position, this time sitting in the temple's barrel-like bathtub, his knees drawn up and his head pushed down against his chest. The hot water was turning his skin a deep pink, slowly warming and dissolving the aches in his bones. He had washed before climbing into the hot water, folding his small towel and placing it on his bald head. The hot water caused both pleasure and pain. After ten minutes of sitting perfectly still, he sighed heavily. He closed his eyes and composed a small poem in his head. He imagined throwing it out to float on the bathroom's warm, steamy air.

> Spring blossoms and dreams
> By the mercy of the wind
> Stay or blow away.

It was eleven-thirty before Misako and Kensho left the temple. The urn of Kiku's ashes was back in the back altar room. They had decided that it was best to find the Homma family before taking the urn.

In the event that they would be received by anyone, Misako brought along a boxed bottle of good sake and a tin of rice crackers for gifts. Teishin wrapped all three lunch boxes that he had prepared that morning, even though he couldn't go along. The long ride and the sea air would make them hungry, he reasoned. Teishin placed the pretty indigo cotton package in Misako's hands. He bowed to his departing friends as their car passed through the temple gate. He went directly to the Tanaka family altar to light *senko* before his dead master's photograph and to pray. The telephone was ringing in the kitchen and no one was answering it—three, four, five rings. "Please excuse me," he told his master's photographed smile, "I must attend to the affairs of the temple." Brushing a tear from his face with his kimono sleeve, Teishin rushed down the hallway that led to the kitchen.

※　※　※

In the beating rain, Niigata's Highway No. 7 was like a shiny black streak laid down across miles of paddy land. There were few cars on the road and only an odd farmer out in the fields. Here and there large fish banners, limp with rain, hung over houses in honour of the next day's holiday, Boy's Day. The rain dissolved the colourful carp and the countryside into fluid, red-grey streaks. Kensho breathed in the cool, damp air, and wiped the haze from the windshield, straining to see a road sign. Neither of them felt much like talking. They drove in silence for over an hour, until they reached the town of Murakami. Kensho, with the map spread out on his lap, directed Misako to turn left into the town. Umbrellas bobbed on the wide shoplined street. Suddenly the asphalt ended and they were at the edge of a beach.

"I am afraid the highway going through the mountain hasn't been completed yet. We will have to turn right here and go along the old beach road. When we get around the mountain, there will be a sign to turn right and get back up on Highway No. 7."

They bumped along on the primitive road that strung a series of small fishing villages together. Misako drove slowly through the thin curtain of rain as they strained to see the dramatic rock formations, jutting from the grey sea, like small, narrow mountains. Waves played in and out of rocky caves, carved from an eternity of watery licks. Even in the rain, brown hawks glided and alighted on the pines that had been bent and twisted by Siberian-born winds.

"It's like a painting on a scroll, isn't it?" The priest's voice was almost a whisper.

"*Hai*," Misako answered, quietly trying to absorb the scene. She knew that they were sharing a moment that she would want to remember.

The road went through tight black tunnels, their interiors shiny rock running with water. At one point, their car almost collided head-on with a small truck. The driver stuck his smiling face out into the rain and waved his hand for Misako to back up. The car ended up on a sandy ledge so close to the water that the beach devouring waves spit white foamy spray at the car.

Kensho touched her shoulder lightly. "We must come again when the weather is better," he said smiling, knowing well that he would soon be going far away. His smile faded, his eyes darkened and he slumped in the seat as the car moved back onto the narrow road.

"I feel you have some sad news to tell me, Kensho-*san*. Why do you hesitate?"

"Not so sad," he said, trying to be cheerful.

"Then tell me. I can listen and drive at the same time."

"Please," he begged, "let me speak when we are on our way home."

"Are you ill?" she asked.

"No, nothing like that. Please, on the way home."

"*Hai*, I understand," Misako said and fell silent.

It was almost one o'clock before they found the road that led them back up on the highway. The rain slowly let up and patches of blue sky appeared over the new green of the mountain dotted with clusters of wild cherry trees. They came upon a gang of construction workers shovelling stones on the side of the road, men and women dressed in the uniform of peasants, dark-blue baggy pants and jackets. The women wore hoods and their faces were half-covered with blue cotton masks.

"Why do the women wear those masks? Do you know?" Kensho asked.

The question made Misako laugh. "I have heard that this area was once ruled by a cruel lord who kidnapped any pretty peasant girl he fancied. It's a nice story but the truth is that they probably wear the masks to keep from breathing in the dust on the roads."

"*Ah so*," Kensho said. Misako was surprised that he had nothing more to add; it seemed a perfect opportunity for the priest to make a joke. They drove on without talking.

When they turned off the highway, just before the city of Iwafune, exactly as Teishin had mapped out for them, they had to go back in the direction they had come from on another poor sandy road. They passed a great rock that jutted out of the sea. It stood like a petrified giant guarding the fishing hamlet. Misako stopped the car and gazed down on the monochromic scene. The only touch of colour was the blue of a young girl's kimono. The girl was lifting garlands of seaweed onto a bamboo pole.

The village of Neya consisted of two ribbons of wind-and-sea-beaten houses separated by a long narrow road cut into the sandy earth. It was a charcoal sketch of tremulous wooden structures, their roofs weighted down with rocks.

"It is like another world," Misako said.

"More like another time," Kensho offered.

Misako stopped the car. "This place is so unwelcoming. I'm beginning to feel that we shouldn't be here. How do we go about this?"

Kensho folded the map. "Let's see if we can find a store to ask questions. A temple is always a good place for me to take advantage of my bald head."

Misako agreed. "You keep an eye on the left side of the road and I'll watch the right." She started the car and drove at a snail's crawl. All the houses reminded her of driftwood. Near the end of the narrow street, Kensho pointed out what looked like a small grocery store. Misako parked beside the last house. No one was around and once again they were on a soft earth that sparkled with dark and silvery sand.

"It's chilly!" Misako said as she pulled the collar of her rain coat up around her neck. "Whoever thought it would be this cold in May?"

Kensho hunched his shoulders and folded his hands into his armpits as they made their way up the street. The store was built into the front of a house. They peered through the large glass door, surveying the clutter inside. Everything imaginable was piled on shelves, countertops and the floor. Even the ceiling was hung with all sorts of items. There was food, drinks, candy, toys, writing supplies, bolts of fabric, jackets, rubber boots, pots, pans and brooms.

"You go in and ask about the Homma family," Misako said. "I want to walk back up the road and ask the girl I saw on the beach."

Kensho straightened up to his full height. "What girl on the beach?"

"Down on the beach, on the side of the first house we came to on the right. Didn't you see her?"

"I've seen no one since we entered this place. Are you sure you saw a girl?"

Misako shoved her hands in her pockets and laughed. "Yes, I'm sure and I want to talk to her."

"I'll go with you," he said.

"No. I'm afraid the sight of a strange priest will frighten her. Let me go, please. We can meet after. There isn't much chance of getting lost in this tiny place."

"Maybe only ghosts live in Neya," Kensho joked as he slid open the glass door. "Excuse me, is anyone here?" Kensho called into the store.

"*Hai!*" a woman's voice rang from behind a patched *shoji* door. It separated the living quarters, which were built about two feet higher than the store. When the *shoji* slid open, Kensho saw a young woman holding a fat baby in her arms. She had a half-eaten cake in her hand.

"Is it a priest?" the woman asked in surprise and almost choked on her mouthful of cake.

"*Hai*, a priest passing through," Kensho said, greeting her with his palms pressed together in the Buddhist fashion. "A priest who is looking for a family named Homma. Do they live near here?"

"Oh yes," the woman said, passing the baby down to an old woman who was sitting at the *kotatsu* table. The old one had round pink cheeks and she smiled sweetly, bowing her head respectfully to the stranger as she put down the tangerine she was eating and received the child. The young woman stepped down from the raised living quarters into a waiting pair of plastic slippers. She wore dark slacks and a colourful quilted kimono jacket over a sweater. She went to the glass door at the shop's entrance and pointed to the right.

"There are two Homma families. Which one do you want?"

"I'm not sure," he said, unable to control a blush.

"One family lives just three houses to the right. The other is on the end of the street, the last house on the left."

"*Arigato gozaimasu,*" Kensho said, smiling and bowing again. "I'm sure I will find the family I want, if there is anyone around. I drove through the village and there was no one except a girl on the beach."

"It's unseasonably cold today. Everyone is home having their three o'clock tea," the woman said, hiding an embarrassed giggle with her hand. "Oh, I'm sorry, please come in and have a cup of tea to warm yourself."

"That's very kind, thank you. Perhaps, if I can't find the right house, I'll come back."

"Just take a minute. I was pouring fresh tea when you entered," the woman said. "It is not every day we see a priest here. My grandmother wants to see you closer. We have never seen anyone so tall."

The priest followed the woman in and sat down on the step-edge of their *tatami* room. The old woman smiled and bobbed her head at him.

"Good afternoon, Grandmother," he said.

"*Hai,*" the old woman said, still smiling at him and rocking the baby.

"How old are you, Grandmother?" he asked.

"You are very tall," she said and cackled.

"Grandmother! The priest asked you how old you are," the younger woman said in a loud voice.

"Eighty-three," she answered and let out another cackle. The baby screwed up his face and started to cry. His mother handed the priest a cup of tea and took the child away from the grandmother.

Kensho sipped the hot tea and tried to think what questions he should ask this old woman. If she was eighty-three, she was just three years younger than Kiku-*san* would have been if she had lived.

"Have you lived in Neya all your life, Grandmother?" the priest began.

The young woman answered for her. "My grandmother came when my father started this business in 1950. Their native village is up on the mountain."

"*Ah so,*" Kensho smiled and knew it was time to move on and ask his questions at the Homma house, three doors down to the right.

305

Instead of using the road, Misako wanted to walk on the beach. She slung her black handbag high on her shoulder, put her head into the wind and slipped through a space between two of the houses. The sand was grey and packed down from the rain; the soles of her rain shoes left little arrow designs where she walked. The wind was clearing patches of blue sky, and beams of sun, like heavenly searchlights, had lit sections of the dark, rolling sea. The waves looked angry as they crashed against the fishing boats lying upside-down on the beach. When Misako reached the last house, there was no sign of the girl, no sign of the bamboo poles. She walked around looking for a footprint, for any sign of what she had seen. There was nothing.

The last house was shuttered and looked like a closed-up, grey wooden box. At first Misako didn't notice an older man standing by the house watching her. He seemed to blend into the grey structure. His quilted jacket and trousers were faded brown and his skin had an ashen tint to it. His steel-grey hair was cropped close to his head and old-fashioned wire-framed glasses slipped down on his small nose. For some reason she couldn't understand, her heart began to pound when she saw him coming toward her. His bandy legs made him rock from side to side as he walked and his lips were moving, but his words were being carried off by the wind. He was very close before she could hear what he was saying.

"Young lady! What are you doing here? Are you lost?" His voice was gruff and his index finger kept going to the bridge of his nose to keep his glasses in place.

"Excuse me," Misako bowed while trying to keep her hair off her face, "I saw a girl hanging seaweed here a little while ago. I was wondering where she went."

The man looked at her suspiciously. "Seaweed? That's impossible! You must be mistaken; there was no girl here. Certainly no one would be hanging seaweed on such a cold day."

"Oh, I must have been mistaken," Misako said as the understanding of what she had seen began to swim in her brain. A vision, the girl must have been a vision, a vision of a girl who had in the past dried seaweed on this beach. She had seen Kiku-*san* as she had been long ago. The thought made her catch her breath. She swayed slightly and fought back a wave of nausea.

"Then this must be your house, sir. Is your name Homma?" But she couldn't go on because she felt the blood drain from her head and all the energy pour from her hands. Her life's energy was pouring like salt onto the beach.

"Hey! What's wrong with you?" the man said in a raised voice. Misako's eyes rolled in her head as she collapsed on the beach. The man stared down at her for a second, his glasses slipping off his face onto the sand. He bent to retrieve them and turned to the house, calling and waving his hand. "*Oi,* Jiro! Jirokun—*yo*—come here!" he yelled until a young man came running toward them. "I came to see what this girl wanted out here and she collapsed."

"I think she fainted," the young man said as he leaned over Misako, touching her forehead. "Better get her in the house," he said as he swept Misako up in his arms and carried her into the house. Jiro's grandfather came hobbling behind him, mumbling and shaking his head.

When Misako came out of her faint, she was lying on a *tatami* floor with a buckwheat-filled pillow under her head. A woman was arranging a quilt around her shoulders. Misako tried to sit up but the woman put her hand on her shoulder and eased her back down on the pillow.

"It's all right. Just rest a while. I'll get you some tea." The woman's face was slightly blurred and the room seemed to be moving. Misako closed her eyes again. The sound of the waves was washing over the house.

This is the house where Kiku must have lived, she thought, and made another effort to sit up. She pushed her dishevelled, thick hair away from her eyes and looked at the woman whose smooth tawny skin was pulled taut over her high cheekbones. She reminded Misako of a mummy she had seen in the museum near Ueno Station in Tokyo. The fans of wrinkles around this woman's eyes attested to smiles and life. A well-built young man knelt behind his mother with his mouth slightly open. The old man was sitting cross-legged by the shuttered window, scowling and smoking a cigarette. A light bulb swung from the ceiling.

"Young lady," the woman said in a sweet voice, "you fainted on the beach when you were talking to my father. My son carried you into the house. Are you feeling better?"

"Yes, yes. I'm sorry I have caused you such trouble."

The woman told her son to fetch a cup of tea, but he didn't move. His eyes were fixed on Misako.

"Maybe you are hungry," the woman said. "When have you eaten last? Perhaps that's why you fainted."

"That's what it must have been," Misako said with embarrassment.

307

"Who are you?" the old man asked, venting his irritation. "We don't know you. How did you know my name?"

"Oji-*san*! Please wait a minute until the lady has recovered. Jiro! Didn't I tell you to get some tea?"

Misako tried to fold the quilt and sat up on her knees. "No, no, your father is right. I must explain why I am here."

"Not before you have tea and something to eat," the woman insisted.

"Please don't bother," Misako said. "Our lunch is in my car parked at the end of the road. I came with a friend who is a priest. I was taking a walk on the beach while he went to the little store. He must be looking for me as we speak."

"*Ah so*," the woman said and turned to her son. "Jiro, go up the street and find the priest. Tell him this young woman is here."

"Oh yes, please," Misako said. "And ask him to bring our lunch boxes. Would you mind very much if my friend and I ate our lunch here in your home? I'm sure I will feel better."

"*Dozo*, please do," the woman said. "Jiro, you heard the young lady, go and find the priest. Ask him to bring the lunch boxes. I'll make the tea."

Jiro finally managed to close his mouth and left the room. Misako bowed to the woman and her father. "I am ashamed to have caused you so much trouble."

The old man waved his cigarette in the air. "No trouble. You gave me a start falling down like that. Don't mind me. My daughter here calls me a grumpy old man. I'm still wondering how you know my name."

Misako bowed her head. "I apologize again. I only know your family through a relative of yours."

"A relative?" the woman said as she came into the room carrying a large cup of tea on a plastic tray.

"It is a long story," Misako said, blushing, "and now I feel somewhat foolish telling it to you." She directed her words toward the suspicious Mr. Homma. "It has to do with a woman who is long dead, but I believe she must have been the sister of your father. If she was alive, she would be about eighty-five or eight-six years old."

Mr. Homma pulled a long breath of air through his false teeth. "My father's sister? My father had four sisters. Three of them are dead. One is still alive and lives a few houses from here, a ninety-year-old great-grandmother."

"The sister I am talking about was named Kiku. She went to Shibata

308

when she was very young, perhaps twelve years old. She lived with a cousin's family named Noguchi."

"*Horr*," the old man said. "I think I heard about her when I was a child. You are right, one sister went away. *Hai*! She disappeared, never came back. Ran away, my father thought."

"No," Misako said. "She didn't run away, she drowned in a pond about seventy years ago. Her remains were found last year after the big storm."

"How do you know they are her remains after so many years?" the woman asked.

"Because the skull was unusual. It was the skull of a girl with only one ear."

"*So ka*!" the grey man said. "Now I remember hearing about that too. So, she drowned, so long ago. How do you know this, young lady?"

"My grandfather was the priest at the temple in Shibata. He's dead now, but his wish was that this poor girl's ashes should be returned to her home. That is the reason the priest and I are here."

The woman moved her head in understanding as her top front teeth fell over her lower lip. "*Ah so ka*! Father's aunt, born in this house? It is hard to believe."

Jiro entered the room with the tall priest behind him. Kensho was carrying Teishin's lunches and the packages; his face was white with concern.

"*Obosan*, come in, come in," the grey man said. The sight of the priest changed his mood. "This young lady here has been telling us the strange story of my lost relative. I am so surprised."

The woman put her hands to her hair and looked around the room. "*Maa*! Oji-*san*, here, get a cushion for the priest. Jiro! Put the table down so the guests can have their meal."

"Please don't go to any bother," Kensho said, but the cushions were found. The guests sat and Misako shyly presented the gifts to their hostess.

"*Maa*! Such wonderful gifts," the woman said. "*Arigato gozaimasu*. Your gifts are too good for our humble home."

"The gifts are very poor, I'm afraid," Misako answered with a bow. "We are still ashamed about disturbing you."

"*Horr*!" The man said once more. "My father's sister?"

"Oji-*san*! You haven't said thank you for these wonderful gifts."

The old man rubbed the side of his head and bowed. "*Hai*, thank you," and went on shaking his head at the surprising news.

The woman took the box of rice crackers and placed it on a shelf that held mortuary tablets, old snapshots and the other trappings of an ancestor altar in a very poor home. She lit an incense stick, rang a tiny bell and rubbed her hands together. When she had finished the very short prayer, she turned back to her guests.

"My husband was drowned six years ago," she explained. The fishing boat he was working on sank in a storm near Korea. His body was never found. I suppose drowning is a fishing family karma."

Both Misako and Kensho bowed and expressed their regrets.

"Thank you," the woman said and fell silent for a few seconds.

Misako became aware of the constant sound of the waves crashing on the beach. It occurred to her that these were the very sounds that the long-dead girl had known as a child.

"*Horr!*" The old man said yet again. "It is something that is not to be believed."

Misako wondered how different the sound of the waves would be to someone with hearing in only one ear. She discreetly covered her right ear with her hand and was aware that Kensho was looking at her. When she caught his eye, she saw his ears grow pink and she knew that he understood what she was thinking.

"*Maa!*" the woman said, breaking into a warm smile. "Papa's spirit will be happy to have such fine sake in the house. Won't he, Jiro?"

"*Hai!* And Grandfather will be happy to drink it!" Jiro added with a great toothy grin.

THIRTY-TWO

On the morning of Boy's Day, Fumiko presented Hideo with a large silk carp banner. She said it was "to fly from this house next year in honour of our son."

Hideo smiled and slapped her lightly on the bottom. It had become a very big bottom; in fact, she had become big all over.

"Does every pregnant woman get so big?" Hideo asked his mother.

"Not all women carry a baby in the same way. The baby is due in six weeks, a big boy I suspect." He did wish that the two women would stop insisting that the baby was going to be a boy.

"You keep calling the baby a boy. You should be more careful, Mother. People are going to laugh if this baby is a girl."

"The baby is a boy!" Mother Imai said with conviction. Hideo shrugged and went out for a walk in the bright May sunshine.

But Hideo's words stayed with his mother. It made her mope all afternoon. The baby is a boy! She had to believe it would be a boy. How could she face her critical sister if her first grandchild was a girl, born in the year of the fire horse? Mother Imai couldn't block out the terrible thought. It was bad enough that her sister was mocking her for giving up her bedroom and moving downstairs. Her sister didn't understand. "I really don't mind," she told her sister. "In fact, I prefer having my room downstairs."

The *samisen* teacher had lifted her black-pencilled eyebrows when she had found out. "It saves me from going up and down the stairs to the toilet at night," Mother Imai told her. "I don't know why I didn't move downstairs years ago. Sleeping downstairs is very convenient."

"And how are you getting on with your new daughter-in-law?" the elderly teacher asked.

"Much better than with Misako, I have to say. The house isn't dreary anymore. *Maa!* Fumiko is cheerful and likes a joke! Hideo is happier, that's for sure. I only worry that he might be neglecting his job these days. He doesn't work late nearly as much any more."

"That's good," the *samisen* teacher smirked, and squashed her cigarette out in the ashtray. "Shall we start our lesson?"

The two ladies shifted onto their knees and started to discuss what they would work on that morning. The teacher played a tune on her instrument while Mother Imai placed sheet music on the low stand.

"Let's go over this," she said, pointing to a passage that she had found difficult at the last lesson.

"*Hai,*" the teacher said, and began. She played and sang the first verse before nodding to her student to sing it alone. Mother Imai stumbled, stopped and apologized.

"One more time," the teacher said, playing the introduction again and counting "*Ichi, ni, no!*"

Mother Imai, kneeling formally, with her reading glasses on the end of her nose, bent into the sheet music and picked up the cue. She was still having difficulty with it and on the third line of the song the teacher joined in to quicken the pace. Neither one of the singers heard Fumiko coming down the stairs, but they both stopped when they saw her standing by the sliding door. She was in her nightgown, loosely covered by a cotton kimono with a red sash tied high over her big belly. Her hair was cascading over her shoulders, with one long, black lock falling over her sleepy eyes.

"Good morning," the teacher said with a smile, thinking what a magnificent courtesan this one would have made.

"Good morning. Please forgive me for standing but, as you can see, it is difficult to kneel in this condition," Fumiko said demurely, placing her hand over her great protuberance.

"I hope we haven't disturbed you," Mother Imai said.

"I did have a bad night," Fumiko whined. "This boy does nothing but kick. He really wants to get out."

"When is the child due?" the teacher asked.

"About the middle of June," Fumiko sighed.

"*Maa!* That long! You are very big. Are you sure you are not carrying twins?"

"Twins!" Both Fumiko and Mother Imai said the word and exchanged shocked glances.

The old one shook her head and spoke with authority. "It is happening more and more these days. I knew one woman who had twins last year. She was very big like that a month before she delivered."

"Twins are not possible!" Mother Imai said. "No one in our family has ever given birth to twins."

"Oh, it happens," the old lady said with a little shrug.

Fumiko burst out laughing. "Maybe I'll have two boys. Wouldn't that be interesting. Maybe I'll have three."

"Don't talk crazy, Fumiko," Mother Imai scolded and blushed. She had read somewhere that twins and triplets were born to couples who had lots of sex. That certainly could be her son and daughter-in-law. As pregnant as Fumiko was, they still did something at night. She could hear them moving and laughing on the floor above. Fumiko couldn't be having sexual intercourse in her condition. Mother Imai picked up a sheet of music and started to fan herself; the room was suddenly very hot.

"Listen, *Sensei*, would you mind if we didn't have a lesson today? Come in the dining room and I'll make fresh tea. Fumiko had a difficult time last night with the baby kicking, and it would be better if she could go back to bed and get some sleep."

"*Hai*, I understand," the teacher said, and started to gather up the music. "We can have a lesson later in the day from now on. I have an afternoon free on Wednesdays."

Fumiko's face fell into a pout. "But what about after the baby comes? The baby will sleep during the day. If you don't mind, I think the lessons should be stopped for a while. I hate to ask you, Mother, but it could be very inconvenient with a baby in the house."

The teacher put her hand up in a gesture of agreement. "I understand perfectly. Fumiko-*san* is right. We can put it off for a while."

Mother Imai wrung her hands. "Well, yes, I guess so. We could start again in a few months, I suppose. Fumi-*chan*, you go back to bed and we won't make any more noise. *Sensei* and I will have our tea inside. I'll bring you up a fresh cup. Is there anything else you would like?"

"Maybe a piece of bread, lightly toasted with some honey. Thank you, Mother," Fumiko smiled, and took her leave. As the ladies went into the dining room, they saw Fumiko's broad back heavily climbing the stairs.

"Poor thing. The last month or so is always the hardest," the teacher said, lighting a new cigarette. Mother Imai put an ashtray down on the dining table and poured hot water into the tea pot.

"*Sensei*, if Fumiko were carrying twins, wouldn't the doctor have told her?"

The old woman lifted her face toward the ceiling and blew out smoke. "Maybe he doesn't know. The doctor has to hear two heart beats, or something like that. Have her ask him to check more carefully."

Twins—that was a complication that she hadn't considered. What would people say? She worried so much that she tossed and turned all night. The next morning she took a taxi to her sister's house. She knew it wasn't wise, but she had to talk to someone about this new possibility. Who can a woman talk to, if not her only sister?

"Twins!" her sister said, flashing her ring as she dropped sugar cubes into the English tea. "*Maa*! Like a cat or a dog!"

Mother Imai squirmed in the big stuffed chair and stirred her tea. "Don't say such a thing. Probably, Fumiko is just having a healthy child. If it did happen to be twins, well, that wouldn't be so bad. I mean one boy or two boys, I could help."

"Two boys!" her sister, who was, to her chagrin, the mother of only girls, laughed. "Listen to yourself! Do you realize how foolish that sounds? Has your new daughter-in-law managed to brainwash you completely? Just because you had a son doesn't mean your first grandchild will automatically be a boy. No one knows if she will have a boy or a girl. And who said she was having twins?"

Mother Imai held her ground. "Fumiko is carrying big, and my *samisen* teacher thinks it could be twins."

"I suppose that old second-class geisha is an expert on such things! Even if Fumiko had twins, they would not necessarily be boys. They could be two girls."

The thought delighted her. She just could not resist the chance to taunt her sister for the remark about her not having a son. "Can you imagine?" she said laughing, "not one but two fire-horse girls under the same roof!"

Mother Imai's face darkened as she put her teacup down on the coffee table. "What a terrible thing to say!"

Her sister saw her anger but wasn't about to let go. "It could happen, you know, and it would serve that couple right. I still think it was rotten what Hideo did to that sweet little wife he had. *Ha*! Misako would have the last laugh, wouldn't she? Imagine! Two fire-horse daughters could wreak havoc on any family."

By now, Mother Imai's face was scarlet with rage and she was sitting at the edge of the chair. "How mean you are! Why do I keep forgetting that? I was foolish to think I could come to my sister for comfort. I should remember that you have always been jealous because I had a son and you had only girls. That's why you are always finding fault with my Hideo."

"What? Jealous of you? I would rather have no child at all than have such an egotistical brat for a son." She leaned closer to the table and tried to lower her excited voice. Can't you understand that I am trying to keep you from making a fool of yourself? *Maa!* I'm embarrassed to think my own sister is babbling such nonsense. Do you know how silly it is for you to be talking about the sex of a child that hasn't been born yet?"

Mother Imai stood up and grabbed her purse. "I will never come here again. If I have to talk to someone, I'll talk to Fumiko. She's my family now. Hideo, Fumiko and my grandson and all the other children those two are going to make."

She was crying by the time she reached the entrance. The maid came running and tried to help her with her shoes, but Mother Imai pushed her away. Her sister always hated seeing her emotional older sibling cry. "Wait, *One-san*, maybe I was too harsh," she said, but Mother Imai was already rushing out the door.

⊕ ⊕ ⊕

Every sound, every smell, every sensation Misako experienced in the hamlet of Neya was still with her. She wore them like so many layers of kimono, close to her skin, waiting for the right moment to peel them off, one by one, to air and examine before folding everything away carefully in her cherished memories. She had hoped to do that during the trip back to Tokyo but it was impossible because the train was so overcrowded that people were standing in the aisles. The lineup for the dining car snaked into the next car. Some passengers without tickets had commandeered the tables and kept ordering more food and drink, anything to keep their seats. The air was thick with frustration and cigarette smoke.

Misako's head was pounding by the time she got off the train and entered the crush of Ueno Station. She almost burst into tears when she saw the long line of people waiting for a taxi. By the time she got home, she was ready to fall apart.

"Oh no," she moaned when she turned the key into the apartment door and heard laughter. Sachiko was entertaining. She had invited the French ambassador, his wife and another couple to drink champagne before she hosted a meal at a restaurant. A beautiful display of fruit and French cheese covered the coffee table. The gentlemen jumped to their feet when Misako appeared at the door looking as if she was about to face a firing squad. What was fired at her was the French language. All through the introductions, all the guests spoke French. Even the pencil-thin, elegant

315

Japanese wife of the French businessman appeared to speak only French.

Although longing to go to her room, Misako tried to be polite and sat next to the bony beauty on the white sofa. She hoped the Japanese woman would speak to her in their native language. Misako turned to her and spoke in Japanese. The woman stared at her, flashed a beautiful smile and said that she had been living in France for so many years that she was really more comfortable in French.

"*Ah so,*" Misako said shyly.

Sachiko tried to translate some of the conversation but it was awkward. Misako fell silent, sipped the champagne and to Sachiko's annoyance, made a face. The champagne was tickling her throat and bubbles went up her nose.

Why did Sachiko think champagne was so wonderful? Misako wondered and fumed. Why was Sachiko crazy about cheese? Misako had never been able to enjoy cheese; she didn't like the smell. How did Sachiko develop a taste for this smelly stuff? They never ate cheese in Niigata when they were growing up. Country people always said foreigners smelled of cheese and butter. It was never meant as a compliment.

Misako would have preferred to be snacking on the radish pickles she brought back from Niigata. She would have preferred little cups of hot sake to champagne. Of course she couldn't say that to Sachiko, but she preferred *daikon* pickles and sake instead of French cheese and champagne. Sachiko would be scandalized.

The torture didn't last long. Sachiko and the guests were out the door in twenty minutes. Misako put away the food to keep it safe from the cats. She washed the glasses, wiped away the crumbs and straightened the pillows on the sofa, even though she was very tired. It was ten o'clock before she finally ran the water for her bath, rejecting Sachiko's array of bath oils and bubble stuff.

Why do foreigners want everything to bubble and fizz? she thought, knowing that she was being cranky. This bouncing back and forth between her two worlds was becoming intolerable.

Which world do I belong in? she asked herself, sliding down in the tub. She was living and working in Sachiko's world but a big part of her was still hovering in the shadows of Niigata. There was a lot to be said for this world of white living rooms and central heating and views of Mt. Fuji from your bedroom window. Even though it was impossible to have a good bath in this semi-Western tub, she did have four million yen in a post office savings account and a salary that equalled that of many a salary man who was supporting a wife and a couple of children. No one could fault Sachiko for a lack of generosity. On the contrary, sometimes she was too generous. As a welcome-back gift, Sachiko had left a beautifully wrapped, expensive bottle of French perfume in Misako's room. Every gift she accepted made her obligation to Sachiko bigger.

The bath was not a place to worry about obligations. She wanted to finally be able to go over in her mind what had happened in Niigata. Going to Neya had been the right thing to do. Misako finally smiled and felt the steam from the hot water undoing that first layer of memories that she so wanted to keep alive. The locked bathroom afforded a secure space in which her thoughts could flow freely.

The Homma family had been receptive and kind to the two strangers who had come into their home with a wild story about a long-forgotten relative. The girl Kiku had indeed been Homma's aunt, an aunt whom he had never known. There was no mortuary tablet for her on the family shrine and young Jiro had never known about his great-aunt who had been born with only one ear.

Homma and his widowed daughter had taken Misako and the priest to meet Kiku's surviving sibling. She lived with her son's family. On the way, Homma warned them that the old lady didn't see or hear well.

"Don't expect her to remember much. Her sister left home a long time ago and recently she doesn't always know people. Last month she asked me who I was."

Still, Misako and Kensho wanted to meet Kiku's sister, even if it was just for a few minutes. Jiro ran ahead to arrange it.

The old woman sat on a *tatami* floor, wrapped in several layers of grey and brown wool kimono and shawls. She was very small, no bigger than a ten-year-old girl, with wisps of white hair tucked behind large ears. Homma introduced the guests, who sat stiffly before his old aunt. She smiled and bobbed her little monkey face, a face on which time and working in the sun had etched a myriad of lines.

Mr. Homma was loudly trying to explain to her who these people were and why they had come. The old lady smiled a toothless smile, her pink tongue popping over her lower lip as she repeated the sounds "*eh, eh, eh,*" in a mousy squeak. She was listening to him with eyes as empty as those of the doll that decorated the *tokonoma* alcove, until he said the name "Kiku."

317

"Who?" she asked screwing her little face up.

"Your long-lost sister, Kiku-*san*."

"We were four sisters," she said, putting out her fragile-looking hand and folding her thumb into her palm. It was a charmingly childlike gesture to indicate the number four with her fingers. "Four is an unlucky number," she said, making a squeaky attempt at a laugh.

"Do you remember your younger sister, Kiku?" the nephew asked with his face close to her ear.

"*Eh*, no ear," she said and touched the right side of her head. "No ear. She went away."

"We know, Auntie," Homma's daughter spoke into the other ear and patted the old woman's sleeve. "These people are from Shibata."

"*Eh*, Shibata." The old woman leaned forward, toward the hazy figures that were kneeling directly in front of her. "Do you know my sister?" she asked.

Misako smiled at the memory. When she returned Cleo and Coco were on her bed. She sat down and stroked their silky fur. They made her think of the fluffy three-coloured, bob-tailed cat the Hommas had in their house. The cat had rubbed against Misako when they were eating their lunch. Teishin had packed so much food that Misako had placed a variety of delicacies on a plate for the family to enjoy. The three-coloured cat wanted her share. Jiro tried to chase the cat away but Misako smiled and petted the animal saying, "Aren't you a pretty cat."

"She's a lucky cat," Mr. Homma said, grinning. "If I had a bigger boat, I would take her fishing with me. Three-coloured cats are lucky for boats."

"Such a nuisance!" his daughter said. "The cat is pregnant again. What are we to do with kittens? Neya is full of cats."

"I'll take a kitten," Misako said brightly. "The temple in Shibata should have a cat."

The woman laughed. "I would give you them all, gladly, but Shibata is far away."

"We have to come back," Misako said. "We have to bring back your aunt's ashes."

Uneasy glances were exchanged. "*Ah so ka!*" Mr. Homma said.

"It can be very simple," Misako said, seeing their discomfort. "We will come back again with the priest from my grandfather's temple, if you will allow it."

She didn't mention Kensho because it didn't seem right to commit his time. Her instinct had been right. On their journey back to Shibata, Kensho finally told her that he was going to California.

Misako put the cats aside and climbed under the quilt. She felt lonely just thinking about Kensho going so far away. Who would she turn to for advice? Misako sighed, closed her eyes and saw herself when she said goodbye to the priest. She was standing on the temple's kitchen step again, about to step down into her shoes. Kensho was standing on the ground when he turned to her. Their eyes were on the same level and they were both fighting back tears. Misako put her head on his shoulder, the way she had the day after her grandfather died. This time, Kensho put his arms around her and kissed her hair. For one eternal moment they held each other. "I'm going to miss you," he whispered.

"I'm going to miss you," she repeated and his lips slid to her forehead, her cheek and then paused over her trembling mouth. This was a moment of consequence. If he kissed her, both their lives would become complicated. Suddenly, he stepped back and bowed his head. "I must fulfill my obligation."

"*Hai*, I understand," Misako said and stepped down into her shoes. Without speaking, Kensho walked her to the car. They bowed to each other and said goodbye. Never had the word *sayonara* sounded so sad and final.

THIRTY-THREE
Summer 1966

*B*y the third week of June, the rainy season made the days warm and weepy. In Shibata, the temple grounds were so heavily shrouded in morning mist that Konein seemed to be swimming as he made his way to the bell tower. Even the bell's voice sounded muffled, like a singer wearing a gauze mask.

This was the growing season, and in the country little beams of electric light began to pop on at five in the morning, lighting up windows as the farmers started another busy day. By mid-afternoon, the rain would often stop and the sun would try to burn off the clouds. Everything would take on a twilight glow, the green of the fields turning to emerald and the roof tiles to patent-leather bright.

It was during one of these incandescent hours that Teishin rode his bicycle, zig-zagging down a country road. He was happily singing to himself, smiling, loving the way the rice paddies mirrored the patchwork sky and the breezes sent ripples across the flooded fields. He could see the bent backs of the farmers moving through the mud, tending their paddies. One man, wearing a straw coolie style hat, straightened up and waved to the priest. Teishin waved back and looked up at the sky in surprise as thunder growled off in the distance.

During three o'clock tea time, the rain was falling again with renewed vigour. Keiko looked out the office window, watching the little rivers run down the glass, and complained that the electric bill would be horrendous this month. "Only half the beds occupied, and because of the rain almost every light has to be on in the hospital."

"It can't be helped," her husband said. "The rain is good for the farmers, at least for those who still have workable paddies after last year's disaster. They will need a good harvest this year."

"That is true," Keiko sighed. *"Honto."*

❀ ❀ ❀

Misako was waiting outside her apartment building for a taxi and worrying about getting her new shoes wet; they were Italian and very expensive. That's what happened when she shopped with Sachiko—everything had to be European. Where were the taxicabs? The azalea bushes outside the apartment house were no longer splendid hills of rolling colour. She hadn't even noticed them dying off. There was a time when Misako had been aware of every phase of every season. Well, she sighed to herself, working for Sachiko takes all my brainpower. Nothing but business registers these days.

Suddenly the sky opened and big drops of rain bounced on the pavement. "My shoes!" Misako cried, and dashed back into the building's lobby. She would have to wait for the rain to let up. That would make her late, but she couldn't have the rain destroy her shoes; they had cost thirty five thousand yen. Looking down at her shoes made her think of the temple and feel guilty. They were beautiful shoes, but for only twice their price the temple in Shibata could have a new bathtub. Her date was going to have to wait. She wasn't particularly keen on this man anyway. He was another first son and Misako had vowed that if she ever did remarry, she would never again live with a mother-in-law. Yuri had brought the man to play tennis with them. Now she was going to have dinner with him, not because she wanted to but because Yuri and Sachiko kept nagging her to date and get on with her life. But as she waited for the rain to let up, she didn't feel right. Here she was dressed in expensive clothes, about to go to a smart restaurant with an attractive man, and instead of being excited, she was thinking about the temple's old, rotten bathtub.

❀ ❀ ❀

The rain slid over the roof of the Imai house, rushed down the drainpipe and made gurgling noises outside the downstairs *tatami* rooms. Mother Imai had turned off her light and stood in her sleeping kimono with her face pressed to the glass door leading out to the garden. She was trying to hear the muted *thump-thump* of the plums dropping off the old plum tree. The tree had been in the garden when she first came into the house as a bride. That first June she didn't know what the *thump-thump* in the garden was and asked her husband. She remembered how Papa had laughed, taken out his writing box and brushes and written the Chinese characters for "plum" and "rain." It read *tsuyu*, for the season when plums ripen and fall to the ground along with the rain, like heavy, bright droplets. It made her think of Fumiko resting upstairs, so big, so uncomfortable, so irritable and so ripe. If only she would drop her bounty as well.

Fumiko lay on her futon and listened to the rain drum on the roof over her head. She moved her hand over her large belly and moaned. Everything was ready. Her bag was packed and Mother Imai had tied all the sheets and towels she would need for the hospital in one large bundle. It was in the dining room, ready to go, if only it would be soon.

Tokyo's weather was hot and sticky. Fumiko wondered why it was taking Hideo so long to get her a cold drink. Her throat was dry, her back ached and her head was pounding. She closed her eyes, hoping for happy thoughts of her beautiful son, but thought instead of the nonsense that the old teacher had put in her head. Fumiko had asked her doctor about twins. He had laughed and asked her if she had been to another doctor. Fumiko felt ridiculous telling him that a *samisen* teacher had suggested it. He had smiled when he answered, "I can't hear or feel anything that would indicate that you are having twins."

That old woman made a fool of us, Fumiko said to herself. The baby is probably a big boy. His kicks are so strong that sometimes it hurts.

It was hurting now, really hurting, but a different kind of hurt. This was a really sharp pain! She gasped and started to breathe through her mouth. "THAT HURT!" she screamed.

"What's the matter?" Hideo asked as he came into their bedroom carrying a glass of cold barley tea.

"I'm not sure. Here, help me up, I think I have to go to the toilet." Her face was very pale as she leaned on his arm and walking down the hallway. Halfway down the stairs, Fumiko bent over in pain. The labour had started. They called the doctor and started timing the contractions. At three in the morning, Hideo took her to the hospital.

Fumiko's mother had told her what to expect. She said that it would hurt, but that it would be a pain that was forgotten as soon as the baby was born. But this baby was taking his time. After several hours without a delivery, Hideo had to leave her at the hospital. He had to get his sleep and be fresh for the office the next day. Uncle Buddha was being very hard on Hideo these days.

Fumiko's mother stayed the night with her, sitting by the bed, wiping her forehead and urging her daughter to be brave. Nurses came in and out the room, checking on their patient. Fumiko asked if they couldn't give her something to help her pain. They gave her small smiles and little reminders that pain in childbirth is natural. "Taking such medications is not the Japanese way," they told her.

During his lunch break, Hideo called the hospital, but Fumiko still had not given birth. At two in the afternoon, only an hour after her mother had gone home, a doctor examined Fumiko and said she was ready. The nurse told her to get out of bed and follow her down the hall. An exhausted, bedraggled Fumiko obeyed, dragging the bundle of linens that were needed for the delivery. The nurse gave her a chair to sit on, arranged the sheets and then helped Fumiko lift her bulk onto the delivery table. A bright, round light burned down on her face.

"Mother!" Fumiko cried out after a strong, pulling pain. "Please, where's my mother?"

"You have to be brave," the nurse said, but Fumiko was breathing fast and couldn't control the noises forming in back of her throat. The doctor's face appeared and Fumiko heard him say, "Everything is looking good. I can see the baby's head." Fumiko squeezed her eyes tight and pushed from her waist, down past her hips and out, out, out—out!

"*Ala-ala-ala-ahh*," the doctor mumbled, until Fumiko heard a cry that was not coming from her own throat.

"Happily, it's a baby boy!" the doctor said, "*Otokonoko de yokatta!*"

"I'm so glad. I'm so glad," Fumiko kept repeating through her tears. "*Yokatta!* I'm so glad." The relief was enormous. For months she had lived with the gnawing doubt that she had been mistaken. This baby is a boy! A baby boy! "*Yokatta!*" It was wonderful, exhilarating—she had done it—a boy. The nurse showed her the newborn boy. He didn't look as she had imagined. Fumiko had expected a big baby. This child was so small and red, and she still had pain.

"*Ala-ala* . . . What's this?" the doctor was poking at her. "*Ala-ala* . . . What have we here? Another baby?" He turned to the nurse and spoke sternly, "Hurry, call Dr. Fuji. I think I need help here."

Like most mothers, Fumiko would soon forget the pain of giving birth to her precious son, but she would never, never forget the fear, confusion and pain that came with the birth of her daughter. She slipped into a kind of hell, mostly because she did not understand what was happening. She heard a different doctor's voice. He was calling for forceps, and then he was hurting her. Fumiko wanted them to stop. The pain was unbearable. "Stop! Stop!" she howled.

She had her boy. She didn't want any more pain. She didn't want another baby. Suppose it is a girl?

"Ah, a little girl," the doctor said. No one in the room added the happy word *"yokatta."*

"Well," the doctor said with a little laugh, "you can't complain. You do have your boy."

The new mother was wheeled back to the room and put to bed in a state of extreme exhaustion. In a matter of only moments, Fumiko was in a deep sleep.

"She'll need a lot of care and rest," the doctor told Fumiko's mother. "She really had a very hard time with the second baby. The little girl was stubborn. Fire-horse girl, *ha, ha!*"

Both babies were small but healthy. The little girl was only four pounds, the boy one pound and three ounces heavier. Mother Imai burst out crying when she arrived at the hospital just minutes after the births. The emotions were too much for her and that was exactly why Hideo had insisted that she not be at the hospital while Fumiko was in labour. Now she wanted to talk to every nurse who passed by. She wanted to see Fumiko. She wanted to see the babies. But the poor new mother was exhausted and sleeping. The babies couldn't be seen at that moment.

"Have you called the father with the news?" a nurse asked. Mother Imai had been so excited that she hadn't thought of it. There was a red phone box in the lobby and she got out a ten-yen coin from her purse, but there were people all around. They would hear her talk about the twins, the double birth, and the fire-horse girl. She couldn't see Fumiko and the babies anyway. She decided to go home to make the call in private.

The fifteen-minute taxi ride seemed to take forever. Mother Imai was so excited, she had to tell someone. She told the taxi driver that she had just become a grandmother for the first time, a little boy.

"Ah so," the driver said, *"Otokonoko de yokatta!"*

She didn't mention the little girl.

"How's your daughter-in-law?" the driver asked.

"Just fine," Mother Imai said and sat back to think. Fumiko had had a terrible time but it was over now. She is a healthy young woman. She'll recover. Imagine a grandson and a granddaughter. Her teacher had been right!

I'll have to call *Sensei*, she thought. Imagine that old woman being right about twins. I'll have to call my sister as well. The thought made her wince. I know what that sister of mine will say just to be mean. She'll bring up that old superstition that boy and girl twins are bad luck. Some people say twins are the reincarnated spirits of star-crossed lovers who committed double suicide in another life. Stupid old wives' tale! Such nonsense! I'm not telling her anything. If she finds out that the little girl was a difficult birth, she'll say that the baby's fire-horse personality is already in place.

No, she had learned her lesson and wasn't going to call her sister. The first thing she had to do was call Hideo, which she did as soon as she opened the door to her home and removed her shoes. In her excited, high-pitched voice she told Hideo that he was the father of twins, a boy and a girl. She told him that Fumiko had had a very hard time and was exhausted. No, she hadn't seen Fumiko or the babies. Fumiko was sleeping.

Hideo hung up the phone and told his fellow workers that he had to leave for the hospital. "*Otokonoko de yokatta!*" he said as he grabbed his brief-case and rushed out the door, never mentioning his newborn daughter.

By the next afternoon, Fumiko was feeling better. She sat up in bed with her beautiful hair tied back in a ribbon, nursing her little son. Her little boy was at her breast sucking hard and hungrily. It was one of the most pleasurable experiences of Fumiko's life. She had been born for this!

Trying to feed the little girl was different. Fumiko couldn't help remembering how painful it was giving birth to this little thing. Besides, this baby was so small and the forceps had left frightening marks on her head. Why was she always crying and clenching her little fists? It was as if she was angry, crying until she was almost purple. When she was placed in Fumiko's arms, the new mother was so shocked that she felt a wave of revulsion. How could this ugly little creature be her daughter?

Fumiko was young and had little experience with newborn babies. Somehow she had expected her child to be born fat and laughing, or at least pretty, since she and Hideo were both very attractive people. The boy wasn't too bad. He was small and red with a little fringe of black hair, but the girl had those awful marks on her head from the forceps. Fumiko could hardly believe that such a scrawny little creature was her daughter.

"I've seen ducks hanging in the windows in Yokohama's Chinatown bigger than that," she told the shocked nurse. Still, it was her child and she had to try to nurse it. The strange thing was that the baby girl didn't seem to like her mother any more than her mother liked the baby girl. It was as if the infant felt the rejection and was fighting back. She wouldn't take her mother's nipple, just turned her cheek, pulled away and screamed louder. No matter how many times Fumiko tried, the tiny thing wanted no part of feeding at her mother's breast. It presented a great problem and the nurses were trying everything. Finally, they tried a bottle, but that was no better. Fumiko tried, the nurses tried, but the baby didn't seem to want to suck.

When Mother Imai witnessed this, her heart squeezed with pity. This child was not unlike the premature baby that she had given birth to long ago, the tiny girl who had lived only a few hours. How well she remembered the pain of losing that tiny daughter. Now she had a granddaughter who was screaming like a cat in agony.

"Please, let me try," she pleaded. Fumiko gladly handed her mother-in-law the child and bottle. Mother Imai cradled the little blanketed package and sat in a chair by the window. She rocked the child and hummed for a minute and then very gently rubbed the bottle's nipple around the crying baby's lips, humming all the time. It took several minutes, but the little mouth finally clutched the nipple and began to suck.

"Ah," a nurse commented, "it looks as if this little one likes you better than she likes her mother."

"From now on, it will be easy," the nurse told Fumiko. "Your mother-in-law got her started." But the next feeding time wasn't easy. The baby girl sucked for a second or two, pulled away and started to scream.

"What's the matter with her?" Fumiko's question was heavy with peevish irritation. The baby screamed louder. They tried again and again. By now the little face was purple with rage.

"You have to keep trying," the nurse told Fumiko. "You have to persevere. You have plenty of milk."

Again and again, Fumiko tried putting the little girl to her breast. The baby would nurse for as much as a few minutes and then start crying. Feeding time was always a struggle.

When the new mother and her babies arrived home, the infant boy fed greedily and slept well. The infant girl did not want to nurse and rarely stopped crying. Mother Imai got up in the night, went upstairs to Fumiko and Hideo's room and took the tiny girl down to her own futon. When the baby cried again, her grandmother was there to soothe her, to hum and rock and try to give the little twin her bottle. And that was how the routine developed.

Upstairs, the baby boy spent the nights in his mother's bed. Hideo would admire his son before going to his mother's old room to sleep. During the night, when the baby fussed, Fumiko simply pulled the boy twin to her breast. Both mother and son were happy.

Downstairs, the girl twin slept with her grandmother. When the baby fussed during the night, Mother Imai cuddled and cooed and got up to warm a bottle. The child would nurse a little and fall asleep but woke up minutes later crying. After one such feeding attempt, the baby's mouth found Mother Imai's breast and tried to suck through the light sleeping kimono.

Mother Imai began to cry. "Poor little thing. I have no milk. No matter how I try, your grandma will never be able to give you what you really need."

THIRTY-FOUR

*T*okyo turned into a gigantic sauna bath in July. Office ladies went to work wearing pretty cotton dresses and carried delicate folded fans in their purses. Men loosened their ties, carried their jackets over one shoulder and wiped the sweat from their faces with immaculate white handkerchiefs. Hotels decorated their rooftops with coloured lanterns and blasted Hawaiian music, creating a Japanese version of a beer garden where the city's harried citizens could snack, drink and try to catch a breath of air after work. Fans whirled everywhere and people greeted each other saying "It's hot!"

In Niigata, everything was growing as the tenderly courted land responded to the heat. The cuckoo birds had finished their wily arrangements for other birds to hatch their eggs and raise their young. Now they had the time to fly from one tall pine to another, filling the sun-blessed days with their giddy calls. Often the sweet notes of the Japanese thrush caused a farmer to stand still in his field to savour the beauty of the little bird's song. People sat at open windows at night, fanning themselves and falling asleep to the chorus of countless frogs in the rice paddies.

At nine o'clock, the priest Teishin hit the temple bell, sending lovely, lonely sounds floating through the warm night air. Dr. Ichimura and Keiko listened from the room overlooking their small garden. Their night was perfumed by the white lilies that Keiko had brought from an outing to the mountains and transplanted some years before. Husband and wife had just come from their bath and were relaxing in cotton kimonos, drinking *mugicha*. During such weather, almost every refrigerator in Japan contained a used whiskey bottle filled with this cold barley tea.

"I want to show you something," Keiko said and produced a photograph and two sheets of paper. Dr. Ichimura put on his glasses and leaned toward the lamp. The picture was of a pleasant-looking young woman wearing kimono, looking straight into the camera.

"Who is this?" he asked. "Someone we know?"

"No, but I want your opinion. I think she would be a good wife for Teishin-*san*. Read her resume. She is thirty-five years old, never married

328

and healthy. She is the daughter of the farmer who died recently. I have heard that she has a very sweet personality."

The doctor quickly perused the resume, looked at the picture again and grunted.

"Well? What do you think?" Keiko asked.

He handed his wife back the picture and resume and yawned. "It is not important what I think. What does Teishin-*san* think?"

"I haven't shown it to him yet. I intend to do that tomorrow."

"*Ah so*," the doctor said and turned back to face the garden.

"*Anata*," the endearment carried a hint of frustration. "You haven't told me what you think."

"What is the use, Keiko? No matter what I say, it won't stop you from going to the temple tomorrow with this picture."

Keiko frowned. "Maybe so, but I still want to know want to know what you think."

"I think you are about to cause Teishin-*san* a great deal of anguish. I think you should leave the man's personal life alone, and I think I am going to bed." Saying this he got up and left the room.

"*A-n-a-t-a!*" she said with a pout. "Men just don't understand!"

❀ ❀ ❀

No matter how hot it got, Sachiko always managed to look perfectly cool in her pale linen dresses and understated summer makeup. This July, however, she was anything but calm. She was overworked and stressed out. Ever since the charity ball, Sachiko Kimura had become the designer of choice for many of Tokyo's wealthiest women. They wanted special clothes for the autumn season and they wanted Sachiko to attend to them personally. It meant a great deal of work because this was an exciting new branch of clientele that she had to pursue. By the time Sachiko returned home at night, she didn't have enough energy to do anything but go to bed, alone. It was making her so nervous that she had almost started biting her nails again. It's not worth unattractive hands, she decided, and picked up the telephone.

During their Sunday breakfast ritual, Misako told Sachiko about the unpleasant dream she had had that morning. "I could feel Hideo in the room with me. I woke up when I heard the front door open. I assume your playmate is back again or is this a new mystery man?"

"Well, let's say a mystery man was here last night, I've been nervous enough without totally depriving myself of a little relaxation."

"Does not having regular sex really make you nervous?" Misako asked, looking into her coffee cup. She had been thinking of her own sexless life lately.

"I'm human, after all," Sachiko said, stroking her cat.

Misako was suffering a deep, pink blush. "Here I go asking personal questions again. I am not even sure why I am so curious."

"What has gotten into you this morning?" Sachiko stood up and stretched. "If the interrogation is over," she added with a yawn. "I think I'll get dressed."

Misako folded her arms and spoke down into her chest. "Do you know that the only sex I've ever had was with Hideo?"

That caught Sachiko's attention. "Was it at least good?"

"It was wonderful in the beginning," Misako said. "After we made love we would lie in bed and talk about having a sweet home and children."

Sachiko sighed. "You got the sweet home with an added bonus of a mother-in-law who listened at your bedroom door. I doubt if that happens now. Someone like Fumiko would never put up with it. She probably has the old snoop sleeping in another part of the house by now."

"Impossible!" Misako blurted out, her head spinning at the thought of it.

"From what you told me I'd say Mother Imai is no match for this Fumiko," Sachiko laughed. "I'll bet you a meal in a good restaurant that the grandmother got kicked downstairs." It was a pretty safe bet for Sachiko to make—she had learned a lot about the Imai household from last night's pillow talk with Hideo.

"I wish I knew," Misako said, biting her lip.

"If you really want to know, go and find out. You found out who Hideo's mistress was and I still don't know how you managed that."

"Just a stroke of luck," Misako murmured.

"Well, manage it again," Sachiko threw over her shoulder as she escaped to her room. It didn't seem wise to spend too much time with Misako this morning. Sometimes that uncanny way she had of picking up on things could get uncomfortable. It was getting dangerous now that Sachiko knew more about Hideo's life than Misako did. Sooner or later she might let something slip.

Anyway, Sachiko wanted to go back to bed. She was still tingling from a fantastic play session. Well, this new arrangement could work out very well. The beauty of it was that Hideo had to be discreet. He had too much to lose. He expressed some reservations about Misako being in the same apartment. For that reason, Sachiko had told him that Misako would be away all last night. It was a lie but the risk was worth it. Getting it on with Hideo while his prim little ex-wife was sleeping down the hall was a very big turn-on for Sachiko. The tension in this arrangement was just too delicious.

That afternoon Misako decided to go to her old neighbourhood and have her hair done. The little shops were almost always open on Sundays and with luck she wouldn't run into Fumiko or Mother Imai.

It was a great day for a walk. Misako dressed in a sundress and sandals and got off the bus at Shibuya Station. It was a strange feeling, walking through the sidestreets of the old neighbourhood she knew so well. As she got closer to the Imai house, her heart began to race. Suppose I come face to face with Hideo again? Suppose I meet Fumiko or Mother Imai? What will I say? Misako took a deep breath and tried to think how Sachiko would answer those questions. She would say the streets are public places and if you do see them, you don't have to even acknowledge them. You can have your hair done anywhere you want. Sachiko's imagined words made her braver, but she knew she could never be rude to Mother Imai.

The bell on the shop door tinkled as Misako entered the shop. The owner came out of the little room where she dressed women in kimono. That room flashed an unpleasant memory in Misako's mind. It was where she had found out for sure that Hideo was cheating on her.

"*Ala, maa*! Imai-*san*, how surprised I am to see you. It's been such a long time," the owner gushed.

Misako's face flushed and she for a moment hesitated. Suddenly, the adventure seemed a mistake. "Oh, I see you are busy. I was passing and thought my hair could use a wash and blow-dry. Don't worry, I'll come back another time," she said, and turned to go.

"No, no," the owner pleaded. "Please, I'll be finished in a few minutes. Can't you wait a few minutes?"

Misako sat down on one of the cheap plastic chairs near a large revolving fan. She checked her watch and thumbed through a magazine. It was an old magazine, the one with the article about Sachiko. Why would anyone want to write this drivel? The thought made her sigh. The owner heard her and put her head out of the little room. "Sorry, just another two minutes." It was actually five minutes by the time she rushed the kimono-clad girl out the door on a stream of compliments.

"You look beautiful, just the right figure for kimono, perfect shoulders!"

The owner adjusted her apron and pushed her hair back before turning to Misako. "*Maa*! You look lovely and cool. You are doing well, I hear."

Misako managed a laugh as she sat down in the shampoo chair and put her head back on the sink. She knew the owner knew she was here for information and she couldn't have fed her a better opening.

"Is that so?" Misako said merrily. "What exactly did you hear?"

The owner was rubbing shampoo into her hair; the water was only slightly warm. "Well, you know," the owner started, "your ex-mother-in-law is an emotional person. She told me you got lots of money in the divorce settlement. I say good for you! I know he was carrying on while you were married."

This wasn't what Misako had come to hear. The woman washed and rinsed her hair and then led her to the chair in front of a long mirror.

"You certainly have a good haircut. One of those expensive shops in Harajuku, I suppose."

"Yes," Misako said casually, "near my office."

"Ah yes. I heard you were working for that designer who was is getting famous. Good for her!"

"She's very talented, but tell me, how is my ex-mother-in-law these days?" As Misako spoke, she watched the woman's face in the mirror.

"She still has trouble with her knee. She told me she had to move her bedroom downstairs because the knee was too painful to go up and down the stairs to the toilet at night. She prefers the downstairs bedroom because of her knee."

"*Ah so*," Misako said, remembering her bet with Sachiko. "She's not getting any younger."

"That's true. Sometimes she looks tired because the baby keeps her up at night. She brought in her tiny granddaughter for me to see. I've never seen a grandmother so attached to a grandchild."

"*Ah so*," Misako said, "then Hideo's wife had a baby girl?"

"Oh, didn't you know?" the woman said with glee. "Twins! Imagine, a boy and a girl at one time! In the old days that would be considered bad luck, but in these modern times, no one believes that kind of superstition."

As she worked on Misako's hair, she told her a story about how boy and girl twins had been born into a noble family in the early years of the century. "The boy was allowed to become a prince, but the little girl was secretly taken away to a temple in Kyoto and raised to be a nun. She's an old lady now, the abbess of the temple, the image of her brother. I know a lady who says she saw her, but I'm not sure I believe her. Anyway, superstition can ruin lives. Even these days, many people believe that a fire-horse girl will grow up and kill her husband; that's why no man will marry a fire-horse girl. The Imai family may have their hands full with that little one some day, but now her grandmother is crazy about her. Do you know the little girl sleeps with her grandmother every night?"

"Is that so? How interesting," Misako said and checked the back of her hair with a hand mirror. "Thank you, you have done very well, very well indeed."

"Come again," the owner said, bowing. "I'm always happy to see an old customer."

THIRTY-FIVE

Since Teishin was no longer receptive to Keiko's motherly advice, she turned her attentions to the introverted young priest, Konein. It started when she noticed that the young man's acne was worse then ever. There was blood on his cheek. The sight of it moved her, and that evening she asked her husband if there wasn't a medication they could give him.

Dr. Ichimura gave her a lotion that could help dry up the eruptions. It meant that Konein had to wash his face with a special soap several times a day and apply the medication faithfully. It gave him a ghostly pale, powdered complexion. Keiko's interest and concern for the young priest was sincere, but it was also an excuse to go to the temple without her husband frowning and telling her to "give Teishin-*san* the space to do things his own way."

Keiko's kindness to Konein gradually cracked his protective reserve. He started to actually talk to her. Not much at first, only words of thanks spoken as dryly as if he were inhaling one of his cigarettes. Then slowly, as his face began to heal, he allowed small facts about himself to drop, simple things mostly, such as how he liked working alone, didn't mind routine, that he wanted anonymity. Once, over a relaxed cup of tea, Konein made mention of his fondness for mathematics and the abacus. Yes, she remem-bered Teishin telling her how helpful Konein had been with the temple accounts. The more they talked about it, the more impressed she became and began to see him in a different light. They were becoming friends and "abacus talk" became their common language.

Teishin was relieved to see Keiko's interest in Konein. It meant that he no longer had to fear another lecture from her. He greeted her warmly when she came into the kitchen entrance early on a hot July morning. He was in the middle of chopping cabbage for the pickled cabbage he loved to eat with his rice.

"Let's go inside where it is cooler," she said after greeting him. "I've something to show you."

Teishin wiped his hands and followed her into the sitting room where the *shoji* had been rolled away, opening the *tatami* room to view the bamboo trees that grew near the temple wall. A large bee flew in and out the room. Keiko sat on the *tatami* and removed an envelope from her large summer purse. Teishin's heart sank the instant he saw it. She had warned him some time ago that she was going to find him a wife. How he had hoped that her new interest in Konein had made her forget that project.

"I want you to take a good look at this picture. A nice-looking young woman, don't you think? Everyone says that she has a sweet personality, very kind. Like you, she was brought up on a farm. I think she would make you a good wife, a real asset to the temple."

Teishin still had the small towel he used while cooking draped around his neck. He wiped his sweating brow and hands with it before picking up the picture. He didn't want to appear ungrateful. "She looks like a nice lady," he said weakly, recognizing the recently deceased farmer's daughter who had been making excuses to visit the temple recently.

"I have checked the horoscopes," Keiko began with all the fervour of a high-powered salesperson. "Teishin-*san*, you were born in the year of the rabbit. This lady was born in the year of the dog. A dog woman would be a very good wife for a man born in the year of the rabbit. By every sign, a good match. You know that it is not easy to find a bride for a forty-year-old bachelor like yourself. You can't imagine how fortunate it is to find a nice woman who is still unmarried, born in the year of the dog and willing to consider you for a husband. Not many women are willing to marry a priest and embrace temple life."

Teishin touched his head to the *tatami* in a deep formal bow. "Really, I thank you very much for the trouble you have taken on my behalf."

"Yes, yes, but take a good look at the picture and tell me what you think? Shall I arrange a meeting?"

Teishin wiped his face again and blushed. "I hope you understand, Keiko-*san*, I don't want to think about marriage or any other life changes at this time. It would not be proper until the first anniversary of my master's death is over." Saying this, he slid the picture on the *tatami* floor back to Keiko. "Really, I am sorry."

Keiko frowned with disappointment and passed the picture back to Teishin. "Teishin-*san*, keep the picture for a while. Study it when you are alone and think about the advantages a wife would bring to your life. There need not be an engagement, or even a meeting, until late in the fall. Think about it, please."

The priest pushed the picture back across the *tatami* again. "Please forgive my rudeness, but I just cannot consider such a thing until the time of mourning for my master is past."

There wasn't any argument that Keiko could put up against his sincere, strong feelings. After all, he was talking about showing respect for her father's memory.

"*Hai*, I understand," Keiko said with a sigh, and put the picture back in the envelope, determined to try again after her father's first-year death anniversary.

The subject was gently changed. They talked a few more minutes and then Keiko went to find Konein. At least he was more receptive to her suggestions.

Teishin went back to the kitchen. He didn't know what he wanted to do about the wife Keiko and some of the elders were telling him he needed. He mumbled to himself as he fiercely chopped at the head of cabbage. Why do I need a wife? We get on very well at this temple without a woman. I don't mind making the meals. I like making the meals. Why do I have to get married? The woman they choose will probably put too much salt in the food.

Maybe he could put Keiko off for another few months, but once the anniversary was passed Teishin knew he would be pressured again. His dead master had often said that when his daughter put her mind to something, nothing could stop her. Suddenly he lost enthusiasm for making the pickles. He had more gratifying business to attend to.

He and Misako planned to return Kiku-*san*'s ashes to her family in August, before the three-day festival of the dead. To prepare for the trip to Neya, they had agreed that Mr. Saito should be informed about Teishin finding the identity of the unknown bones. Teishin had called the museum director and the meeting was to take place in the big house at Shimizuen garden at two o'clock that afternoon. He put on his second-best summer kimono, which a woman from the congregation had skilfully patched, and set out on his walk through Shibata's sunny streets.

The director was pleased to see the priest who had showed interest in his storehouse restoration. After the caretaker's wife had served cold towels to refresh their hands and face, and tall glasses of an iced fermented milk drink to cool their throats, Teishin began his story.

"Saito-*sama*, you will be pleased to know that we have found the identity of the girl whose bones were found in the pond."

Mr. Saito wasn't sure if he was pleased or not, but he was surprised. "Really? Is it true?"

"*Hai!*" Teishin said and lept right into all the details of how he accidentally got on the trail of the girl's identification.

The director was astounded. "And you say that your dead master's granddaughter has already visited this family in Neya?"

"Yes, sir, she has. She and the Zen priest from Kamakura went there and told the Homma family the story of their long-lost relative. They even met an old lady who is the dead girl's one surviving sister."

"Unbelievable! Unbelievable!" the director repeated several times.

Teishin smiled shyly. "My dead master's granddaughter plans to return the girl's ashes to Neya to be buried with her honourable ancestors. It has already been arranged. She and I will go on the tenth of August, three days before the festival of Obon. The Homma family is expecting us on that day."

"This is splendid news. Well done." Mr. Saito now realized that it was a good thing that this whole affair was at last coming to an end. The museum had suffered ever since the old rumour of a spirit in the garden had been revived. Requests for renting the teahouse had dropped off over the past year. Surely now, if there ever was a restless spirit in the garden, it will be gone. "Hopefully there will be no more incidents to fan more rumours," he said and smiled at the priest.

"All will be done as discreetly as possible," Teishin said.

"I would go to Neya with you if I had the time, but certainly I will send a gift with you for the Homma family. Will you be kind enough to take a gift for me? I'll send it around to the temple tomorrow."

Teishin bowed deeply and thanked the director. He felt the excitement building as he walked along the street. Now he had another positive report for Misako. Life was good! Amazingly, he seemed to be getting things right. A man of the museum director's high position had praised him today. Who said I need some farmer's daughter for a wife? I can't imagine what it would like to be married, anyway.

The words had barely formed in his mind when he remembered the tender moments with Misako in the hospital. The sudden flash in his mind surprised him so much that he put his head down and began to walk faster, hoping that no one would see his hot, red face.

❀ ❀ ❀

Obon, the Festival of the Dead, takes place in Tokyo over three days in mid-July. Sometimes called the Feast of Lanterns, it is the ancient Japanese tradition that honours ancestors. On the night of July thirteenth, it is the custom to light a fire or hang a bright lantern to guide the spirits home. Over the next few days, fresh fruit and other foods are placed on the family Buddhist altar. On the sixteenth, the spirits and their gifts are sent back to their own ethereal dimension, often in candle-lit, miniature boats launched on the river or sea. During these festival days, people gather to join in a folk dance, associated with this festival, called a *Bon-odori*.

In the Tokyo of the 1960s, many of these customs had been adapted to suit modern life. When Misako was married to Hideo, the Imai family shrine was cleaned with great care and adorned with fruits and flowers during *Obon*. Misako had hung bamboo curtains and two beautiful blue-and-white paper lanterns at the entrance to the room that held the shrine. It was more preparation than Mother Imai was accustomed to. People visiting the house said how nice it was that bride from Niigata still kept some of her charming old ways.

In rural Niigata, the *Obon* festival is held in August, according to the old calendar. In past years, Mother Imai didn't exactly prevent Misako from returning to Shibata during that time, but she did not encourage it either. This year, there was no question of not returning to her family roots. Misako no longer had an obligation to the Imai family. Considering how badly she had been treated, it was easy for Misako to imagine that even the dead ancestors had forgotten all the care she had given the Imai family shrine.

Even though Sachiko's heart secretly ached to honour the mother who had sacrificed so much for her, she had no intention of going to Niigata for *Obon*. The last time she had gone there, she had such a nasty shouting match with her aunt that Sachiko vowed never to return until the woman was dead. Her solution was to send money to the Zen Buddhist temple where her family worshipped, to ensure that prayers would be chanted at the Kimura family grave. Every year she felt less and less guilty about the arrangement.

This year she was going to the summer resort called Karuizawa to be with Auntie Kaz. As far as she was concerned, Auntie Kaz was her family. Besides, it would be lovely to be in the cool of the mountains in mid-August. All the best people had villas there. She might even play a game of golf and meet some of her Tokyo society clients. At least she and

Auntie Kaz could enjoy their scotch in the cool of the evenings and trot off to the elegant old Mompei Hotel for dinner.

When she told Misako about her plans, they were eating sandwiches at Misako's desk.

"I'm so glad for you," Misako said. She thought Sachiko was overworked and a vacation was just what she needed to improve her mood. It was a good time to mention her own plans since she had already bought a train ticket for Niigata on the ninth of August.

"I hope it doesn't inconvenience the office that I'm leaving a couple of days early. I want to be home for *Obon*. Actually, I have to attend another memorial ceremony on the tenth."

"I thought your grandfather's one-year memorial wasn't until October. Is this for someone else?"

"Yes, it is," Misako said and bit into her sandwich.

"Another dead relative?" Sachiko inquired.

"No," Misako said and wiped her lips with a napkin. "Not a relative, but attending this particular memorial is important to me. I have wanted to tell you about it."

"I don't want to hear it," Sachiko snapped. "All these memorial ceremonies are so damned morbid. I'm beginning to think it is foolish to allow the dead to make demands on modern, busy people. We have little enough time to ourselves these days. Instead of praying over a tomb-stone during the little free time you have, you should be enjoying a real vacation. Come with me to Auntie Kaz's place. Enjoy a week with friends your own age. Play tennis. You like to play tennis. There is no telling who you could meet. Even the Crown Prince found his true love on a tennis court in Karuizawa."

"I'd rather go home for *Obon*," Misako grinned. "I guess I am still an old-style Japanese who likes to visit graves and eat watermelon during *Obon*." Misako meant her answer to sound amusing, but Sachiko was testy.

"I don't have the time for quaint customs."

Sachiko's words cut. Misako took the remark personally. "What you call quaint customs, I call an honourable tradition."

Sachiko shrugged, put down her sandwich and went back to the glassed-in cubical. The delicate cup of friendship suffered another crack.

❀ ❀ ❀

On the tenth of August, Teishin and Misako left Shibata on their journey at eight in the morning, before the air grew heavy with heat. The sky was pale blue and cloudless except for one long lavender streak. It looked like a celestial road stretching across the heavens. The urn was now wrapped in a new white silk *furoshiki* and rested snug in a wicker basket on the car's back seat. Misako wore a simple black linen dress with a single strand of small pearls. She wanted to be proper and respectful but found it difficult to drive wearing kimono.

This time she didn't need directions; the roads were familiar. She knew how long it would take to get to Murakami, where to turn off onto the beach road and where to turn right to rejoin the mountain road. It was fortunate that she did because she no longer had a serious navigator at her side. Teishin was like a happy child on an outing. Although he was dressed formally in his summer robes, he was anything but solemn. This was a day of days for the priest, a day he had dreamed about, a day of great reward. He felt his dead master's smile on them and thought every beautiful thing that they saw was put there by spiritual arrangement: the emerald paddies heavy with their bounty, a crepe myrtle tree in pink bloom, the gentle mountains looming before them. When they turned off onto the beach road and a white crane flew above their car, Teishin put his head out the car window, saying, "Look, the spirit of the master is travelling with us."

Misako smiled like a patient parent with her five-year-old. Her first impulse was to tell him that it was just a bird, but when the beautiful white creature still hovered above them after five minutes, Misako waved and called out, "Hello, Grandfather!"

They stopped for a while to stand on a pebble beach at the foot of a great rock. It was beautiful watching the sun making the water sparkle.

"The sea looks so different from when Kensho-*san* and I took this drive," Misako observed. "The waves were dark and angry that day."

Teishin produced a chocolate bar from the sleeve of his kimono. Grinning sheepishly, he broke it and offered Misako half. "How far have we come?"

"I would say we are about halfway there. You will enjoy the ride through the mountains. It's very pretty."

"I know those mountains," he said. "I was born in the mountains near the Yamagata border. When I left home to become a priest there was no highway. We walked down the mountain path to where the buses ran, and then had to take a train."

"How long has it been since you were home?"

"Oh, many years," he said with a wistful smile. "My parents are dead. My older brother and his family live in the farmhouse. Toyoko, my older sister, still lives in that area."

"Then, by all means, you should go for a visit. I'll drive you sometime."

A great blush crept into the priest's face. "I couldn't expect you to go through that much trouble for me, Misako-*san*, besides, Shibata is my home now."

"It wouldn't be trouble, it would be a pleasure. I like spending time with you, Teishin-*san*."

"Really?"

"Really!" Misako laughed and stepped gingerly on the rocks to the water's edge where she bent to wet her handkerchief. Teishin was aghast as Misako came near to him and started to wipe his face.

"Chocolate!" she said. "You can't be a dignified priest with chocolate on your face. There, that's better." She stood back, smiling at him. "My mother is right. You do need a wife."

"Thank you," he said nervously, and backed up a little. "It's too bad Kensho-*san* couldn't be with us today," he added, trying to change the subject.

"*Hai*," Misako said and took in a deep breath of the salty air, "but Kensho-*san* has a new life in far-off America and Grandfather is gone. It is up to us to bring this business to a proper end. You and me." As she said the word "you," she touched the priest's chest. When she said "me," she pointed to her own nose.

"You and me? You and me," Teishin repeated her words softly as if they were a whispered prayer.

It was almost eleven-thirty when they found the narrow road that led down a sandy slope to the ancient fishing hamlet of Neya. The news of their coming had spread and some neighbours had gathered outside the Hommas' house. Women and children and a few old men bowed as Misako and the priest left the car. Teishin, now with the colourful priestly brocade on his shoulder, walked slowly, clutching his prayer beads and the little metal gong he would ring during the memorial service. Misako followed with her eyes downcast, carrying the white silk-wrapped urn. A murmur hummed from the small crowd. It was a miracle that a long-lost daughter was returning to the humble fisherman's house perched on the sandy lip of a capricious sea.

Mr. Homma waited at the entrance and his daughter and grandson knelt on the inside step that led into the house. When Misako and Teishin removed their footwear, the Homma family members led them into the main room of the small house. The windows that had been blocked out by wooden shutters when Misako was here before were now open and hung with bamboo blinds that fluttered with the sea's breath. A fresh, salty smell mingled with the perfume of the incense sticks burning on a low, narrow table that served as an altar. The little old woman who had remembered her long-dead sister bowed when they entered the room. She was sitting between her son and an old man named Endo. He claimed to have childhood memories of the girl who had only one ear.

Misako walked slowly across the worn *tatami*, bowed and carefully placed the urn containing the long-lost girl's ashes on the altar. Then she turned and bowed her greetings to the small group gathered for the memorial service. Everyone bowed back. Mr. Homma formally thanked Misako and the priest for bringing his aunt's ashes home. Teishin produced a beautiful white folded-paper envelope, tied in black rice-paper cord, which was the gift of money sent by the museum director, Mr. Saito. Mr. Homma thanked the priest and suppressed a gasp when he saw the money amount discreetly written on the back—fifty thousand yen. He blinked and looked again at this priest and young woman, seeing another dimension to his aunt's adventures. His daughter and grandson arrived with tea and cakes. Thirty minutes later, the service began.

Everyone knelt facing the altar, knowing exactly what they were to do. This daughter of the long-past Meiji era was hardly known to the present Homma family, but still, she was *shinseki*, a blood relative, born in this house, an honourable ancestor. Today her spirit would be welcomed home. After a few days, their own priest would commit her ashes to the family grave.

Teishin took a deep breath, making the same kind of headback gesture that his old master had made before starting the invocation. He hit the small gong and began: "*Ki myo mu ryo ju ny rai . . .*"

Misako immediately felt icy hands compressing her heart. She remembered her grandfather chanting these very words in the big garden less than a year ago. She closed her eyes and bowed her head, telling herself that this time it was different. Her experience today would not be like it was the day her grandfather died; she would not let it. Nothing must happen to dear Teishin. And why would it? They know the identity of the girl. This ceremony is more of a celebration, the fulfillment of a long journey. There was nothing more she had to know for closure, but something was happening that she could not control.

A vague sense of familiarity was emerging in her mind, changing the look and feel of her surroundings. Something internal was slowly flowering, spreading its great petals to softly cover Misako's own essence. Her hearing had changed, as if someone had stuffed her right ear with cotton wadding. Teishin's voice had become faint, somehow channelled to the left half of the room. A strong breeze flipped the bamboo curtain and for an instant Misako had a flash view of waves rushing toward the beach, a fishing boat overturned on the sand and lines of bamboo poles covered with drying seaweed.

A strong fishy smell filled the air and the room became smaller. She seemed to be viewing the room from a small hole, a tear in a paper wall. Twisting her head to peek with her left eye, with her left ear pressed against the *shoji*, she could see a man who wore nothing but a loincloth. His body was sun-bronzed, thin and muscular. He was swaying from drink. She knew the man was Kiku's father. He was standing in a threatening pose over his kneeling wife. Kiku's mother was sobbing, begging for mercy. The man was shouting: "Only another mouth to feed! Not even good enough to sell to a brothel!"

Time had washed backwards. Misako had become the girl behind the torn paper *shoji* watching as her parents decided her fate. The horrific moment filled her body with a great sense of sadness. She bowed her head and covered her face with her hands. "Please!" the woman was pleading. Kiku's mother was always pleading, defending her, protecting her from her father's wrath. At the moment of Kiku's birth, she had to fight to keep the infant from being smothered. The mother's instinct was as fierce as a tiger's. The moment was so interwoven with past and present and dreams that Misako could not untangle them. She only knew it was a moment of pain that she, herself, was now feeling. She was falling into a deep, dark well of pain. Despair, loneliness the likes of which Misako had never known, was slowly engulfing her entire self, mind and body. Her shoulders slumped as the deep despondency gripped her heart.

The gong was hit and the sound tilted Misako's head to the left. The pain was subsiding and the soft petals were folding back into themselves and fading away. "*Namu amida butsu, namu amida butsu,*" Teishin's voice burrowed into her right ear. His prayer was lifting her head, pulling Misako back to her own body, her own time. Tears filled her eyes as she repeated the holy words. And as she did, Misako began to understand that she had lived one of many terrible moments in the unfortunate Kiku's life. For a period of time, perhaps only seconds, her body had been the vessel in which a miserable, long-dead emotion had flared one last time, like a match in the dark, and then burned away forever.

Teishin turned from the altar and faced the room, bowing deeply. He smiled and thanked everyone for attending the ceremony. Jiro and his mother got up and left the room. Homma made a little speech to express his thanks and invited everyone to relax and enjoy refreshments. Mother and son returned with trays laden with small dishes, glasses and bottles. Orange soda, beer and sake were poured and cigarettes lit as the woman of the house went back to the kitchen to fetch the food.

The host was now making a point to especially thank Misako and the priest for all they had done to make this day possible. He said that the spirits of his grandparents must surely feel peaceful now that the remains of their lost daughter had been returned.

"What is he saying?" the child-sized remaining sister asked.

Her son spoke into the old woman's ear and her face broke into a pink-tongued smile. She moved her head up and down in approval.

"Kiku-*chan*," she said in a rasping whisper, "*Ii ko deshita*. She was a good child."

What did it matter if more than seventy years had passed, wasn't she remembering her sister more clearly every day? She turned and pointed a wrinkled, shaking hand at the open window.

"We used to run and play on the beach out there. We had good times."

Because her voice was so weak, her son repeated what she had said. Everyone in the room smiled, pleased that she had such memories.

The flapping of the bamboo blinds caught Misako's attention. She was still feeling weak from the experience of the vision. It was difficult to keep her head up, but she could hear the distant laughter of the children on the beach. The sea breeze was growing stronger, flipping the blinds higher and faster. Through them, Misako caught glimpses of two sun-browned little girls running along the water's edge.

"How interesting to hear such a memory. *Arigato gozaimasu*," Teishin said with a little bow. "In those days, I wonder how a young girl would travel as far as Shibata. How would she have gotten over the mountain?"

A sudden surge of excitement was restoring Misako's strength. Teishin was asking an unexpected, important question. It was becoming clear to her how he had been able to gather the information that had led to the identification of the unknown girl. He didn't just stumble into lucky bits of information. He had a talent for zooming in on an important point.

The question hung in the room and people looked at each other for a moment. Then the old man, Endo-*san*, piped up in a surprisingly strong voice for his age and size.

"In the old days, fishing boats were going up and down the coast all the time. I suppose someone could have taken her most of the way by boat."

"But," Teishin said, rubbing his bald head, "how could she make her way to Shibata from whatever beach or town the fishing boat would leave her? A young girl alone, it could be dangerous."

"She must have carried a letter of instructions," the old woman's son offered. "Perhaps the priest from the temple wrote it."

Teishin carried on: "A letter couldn't guarantee her safety. Perhaps she travelled with someone the family knew."

"A priest," the old woman said. "My mother gave my sister to a priest who was travelling with pilgrims. They were returning home to Shibata, walking over the mountain, stopping at temples. My mother wanted to send Kiku-*chan* to her sister in Shibata."

"*Ah so desu ka?*" Teishin said, shaking his head with pity. "That makes sense, but the poor girl must have been bewildered."

Misako spoke up, "She did reach her destination because we know she went to live with her aunt in Shibata. Perhaps the priest on the pilgrimage was my great-grandfather. He would have taken her to his temple to stay with his family until they could locate her aunt."

"*Horr,*" Endo-*san* said. "Imagine!"

"*Maa!* That is something hard to believe," the lady of the house commented as she passed around a bowl of deep-fried squid.

Misako turned her chopsticks around to transfer a morsel from the bowl to her plate. It was obvious that the woman did not think much of the theory.

"*Ah so da,*" the old sister's son said as he got up to fetch something from the entranceway. He returned with a little cloth package. Sitting back down on the *tatami*, he pulled away the cloth and produced a roll of paper. "My mother wanted to show you this. It is a picture that was done long ago by her sister Kiku. My mother said her sister often stayed at the temple on the beach, just up the road here. The nun there taught her things. My mother kept the picture all these years."

He turned to his mother and said in a loud voice, "This is your sister's picture?"

"*Hai*," the old lady said, showing her pink tongue. "*Hai, Kiku*-chan *no e*."

The son spread the black and white brush-painted picture out on the *tatami* for Misako to examine. It was a beach scene with a fishing boat and some racks of seaweed drying in the sun. For a child's work, it was very good. There were unexpected little details like the spray jumping up from the surf. One could catch the feel of the waves rolling in toward the shore.

"Very good," Misako said. "This is very, very good." Her voice caught when she noticed the little flower on the lower right-hand side. It was identical to the flower on the temple picture in her great-grandmother's box. "What kind of flower is this?" The question almost caught in her throat.

The old woman's son put on his glasses and leaned over the picture. "I think it is a chrysanthemum . . . like her name, Kiku."

Misako looked up from the painting. Her face was full of emotion. "Thank you for showing this to me. There is a similar picture at our temple in Shibata. I found it recently in a box that had belonged to my great-grandmother. She too liked to make pictures."

A moment of silence followed her pronouncement. "*Ehh?*" the old woman, Kiku's last surviving sister, pulled at her son's sleeve, asking him to repeat Misako's words in her ear.

There was no doubt now. Kiku had travelled to Shibata with Misako's great-grandfather and his small group of pilgrims. The child must have found safe shelter at the temple while her Shibata relatives were located. Misako's great-grandmother could have taken Kiku under her wing and have discovered the child's artistic talent. Perhaps they worked together. If only those stern faces that looked down from the walls in her grandfather's old room could talk.

A new thought came to Misako. Kiku may have arrived at the temple when her grandfather was a boy. They could have played together. That would explain the old man's obsession with the girl's ashes, a stirring in his heart of something long forgotten. Even her own protective feeling toward the unknown girl's remains could have been a result of some memory ancestral, the tiniest speck of recollection, enclosed in an inherited gene from her great-grandmother. She must have been fond of the child. Why else would she have kept her picture in the box with her own? The thought made her shiver.

Misako wanted to see where the old temple had stood. Mr. Homma took her and the priest for a walk down the beach. There was little there to tell the tale after all these years. Misako walked around the area, stopping to collect some sand from the beach. She placed it with two beach stones in her handkerchief.

"I remember hearing about the old nun who lived here once," Mr. Homma said. "She was a holy woman. People came for the medicines she made with herbs. I heard she had come from a high-ranking samurai family. When I was a kid, I once found a broken writing brush in the rubble around here. My mother said it must have belonged to the nun because the bristles were fox hair."

*I*t was September when Misako returned from work on day and found
a second fat letter from Kensho. The envelope was long and decorated
with red and blue airline symbols, along with many colourful American
stamps. The letter inside was written carefully, filled with wonderful
descriptions of fantastic scenes. As she read, she could hear his voice: "I
thought California would be like Kyshu, but even in August the hills here
are burnt golden and the city winds can be cold as Hokkaido. "

He wrote about the students, the American monks, their temple, his
struggle with the culture shock, the food and his frustrations over not
understanding English well enough. He described a different world and
ended the letter with a plea for news from home, "Please tell me more
about taking Kiku's remains back to her home."

Misako did her best in her reply. She wrote a report of the trip to Neya
with Teishin, telling him how Neya had looked on that hot summer day.
She even enclosed a small tissue-wrapped packet of sand from the beach.
She told him who was in the room, what had been said, how she felt
and the incredible experience of losing the hearing in her right ear during
the ceremony. Such was his regret over missing the second trip to Neya,
however, that his reply to her letter asked still more questions.

"After all has been said and done, what do you imagine the girl's story
really was?"

Misako took in his question and pondered. How could she make Kiku
as real to him as she had become to her? Then, late one night, when she
and the cats were fast asleep, the answer came. It made her leave her bed,
sit at the desk and start to write. Without hesitation, she took her calligraphy pen and filled several pages with beautiful flowing characters. She
told her friend her innermost beliefs in the form of a simple folk tale.

Mukashi, mukashi. Once upon a time, in the reign
of the great Emperor Meiji, a tiny girl was born in a poor
fishing hamlet at the very tip of the prefecture of Niigata,

on the Japan Sea. At the time of the birth, the fisherman father was on a boat in the waters that washed the shores of Siberia. Moments after the birth, the mother was glad that her husband was far away. At least he had been spared the disappointment of knowing that his second child was just another daughter. For a little while, he was also spared the sad knowledge of the child's deformity.

The otherwise perfect little creature had only one small ear on the left side of her head. The right side was as smooth as an egg. No one in the hamlet had ever seen anything like it. No one had ever heard of such a deformity before. It seemed a bad omen. Poor families had been known to smother an unwanted infant daughter. No one would have blamed the unfortunate mother.

But killing the child was not possible because the young mother felt an overwhelming love for the pitiful little creature. She ignored the advice of the woman who helped her birth, the advice of her own mother; she wanted to hold this child and protect it always. Under their disapproving eyes, she suckled the babe as tenderly as she had done her other daughter.

Everyone warned the mother that her husband would not allow her to keep the child. He was a man of extreme mood swings. His wife worried. She knew that one day his face would turn purple with rage and the child's life would be in danger.

In desperation, she took the child to the ancient temple that stood on the outskirts of the hamlet. It was not a place of comfort. It was a poor temple, partly in ruins, standing lopsided on a sandy rise, snug among weathered rocks and old bent pines. Inside there were dark, incense-perfumed beams and an altar with a statue of the holy Buddha. Surely there would be compassion in a place like this.

And there was great compassion, in the person of an old nun. No one knew where the nun had come from or why, but they respected her because she could write and paint holy pictures very well.

In those days, it was usual for an older man, even one of distinction and rank, to leave his worldly goods behind

349

and seek a penitent's life before the consummate luxury of death. Perhaps it was in that spirit that the woman had left all luxury behind, save her writing box and paper, to enter into the austere, mystical life of prayer.

To the people of the hamlet, she was a holy woman, with a shaven head and patched robes. The priest and his family allowed her to live in the back room of the temple. In return, she opened the gates in the morning, closed them at night, swept the rooms of sand and chanted sutras. During the afternoons she spent her time making pictures or gathering useful things. She gathered shells, seaweed and fish bones from the beach; roots, wild herbs and mushrooms from the wooded areas. All of these treasures she turned into soups and pickles and medicines.

The holy woman touched the earless side of the child's head and listened to the young mother's fears. She herself could not care for an infant but she could shelter the child when danger loomed. And that is why the child Kiku came to spend periods of time in the back room of the old temple by the sea. When her father's eyes glowed with the first hints of rage, Kiku's mother would bundle her up and run along the beach to the temple. When the child reached five and six, she knew from one terrified look what she was to do. She would scamper off, mostly in the dead of night, to the protecting arms of the old nun. There in the back room she would hide in the big cupboard filled with smells from the sea and forest.

Over the years, the question floated between mother and nun protector: What to do when the child got older? The mother had a sister who had married a metalworker and now lived in the castle town of Shibata in Niigata. Surely, if they could get the child to her sister, Kiku could earn her keep by helping with the house and children. At least she would be safe from her father's rages.

Because of the nun's healing powers, the old temple was becoming known outside of the area. From time to time, pilgrims came to the temple, seeking small bags of healing herbs or salves for burns. One such group stopped there to spend the night the year that Kiku was turning eleven. The pilgrims were both men and women, led by a kindly priest. When the nun heard that they were on their way back to a place called Shibata, she rushed off to Kiku's home.

The fisherman father was away. The good nun said this was a God-sent chance and urged Kiku's mother to send the child to Shibata with the pilgrims. She had already spoken to the pilgrim priest. He promised to keep the child safe at his temple until her relatives were found.

All that night, the nun and mother worked to prepare what Kiku would need for the journey, packed in a cloth package small enough to sling around a child's shoulders. The nun wrapped one of her precious fox-hair brushes in some rice paper as a farewell gift. When the sun began to break the black shield of night, the pilgrims were on their way; this time with a child. The mother and the nun stood by the gate of the temple enclosure. No words were spoken. The farewell was said in bows. Oh, the weight of that silent grief, the mother knowing she was never to see her child again.

"The priest kept his promise. Kiku lived at his temple for the weeks that it took to find her aunt. This temple home, too, smelled of incense and rang with chants. This home, too, had a protective mother that gave smiles. When this woman saw Kiku owned a writing brush and paper, she took out her own such treasures to share and teach. She encouraged the child to write on a slate and sometimes let her rub the ink stone and paint the images of her new world.

One day Kiku was taken to her new home. The aunt was kind, although there was no longer time nor paper to make pictures. Now she cleaned the house and cared for her cousins. The years passed and Kiku tried to do her best, until she began to have spells of falling moods. Sometimes she felt so heavy she could hardly lift her head from her pillow. Her young face had echoes of her father's dark days. She began to suffer from feeling homesick, from the strangeness of this place, the hard work and the cruel teasing about her ear. She missed her mother, her sisters and brothers, even

351

her father. She missed the old temple, the good nun and the salty smells of the sea. She wanted to go home but it had been such a long, hard walk from her native village to this place. It had taken the little party many days to cross the mountains, to go to one temple after another, ringing their bell and begging a night's shelter. Kiku had walked with the women behind the men. Every evening someone would try to mend her straw sandals. How could she ever do it alone? How would she ever find her way back to her mother?

Then one night the heritage of the childhood fears that still hung to her like an aura finally pulled her into a deep melancholy. It was while in the grip of that dark depth that Kiku understood that she would never make the trip home. At least not her body, but perhaps her spirit could. A spirit did not need sandals or balls of rice for a long journey. A spirit could ride anywhere on the wind. She imagined her spirit-self flying along the beach at her mother's shoulder, or floating through the cracks in the old temple.

On a moonless night she crept from her bed and stealthily made her way through the dark streets to the great garden in the centre of the town. No one saw the slight teenager squeeze past the thick wall of bamboo. Like an animal she crept on all fours, as quietly as she could, so as not to alert the night watchman. On the bridge she spread the square of fabric she had brought with her. She made several crawling trips to the edge of the pond to gather rocks to place in the middle of the square. When the heavy package was made, she hoisted it onto her back, tied the two ends across her chest, knelt on the stone bridge and tumbled into the black water. It took seventy years for her remains to make the journey home, but that is for another time to tell.

When the priest Kensho read the story, he wept. He wept for the child Kiku, for himself and for Misako. He wept for the beauty of the nightingale's song.

❀ ❀ ❀

How could everything have changed so drastically in one short month? It was a terrible moment when Sachiko sat on the white sofa and ad-mitted to Misako that her creativity had ebbed. Here it was the end of September and she had been back to work for weeks, yet she had not be able to produce one good idea. Orders were coming in but nothing seemed to excite her. The week before, the popular actress, Etsuko Sasaki, invited Sachiko to lunch. She wanted a dress for a television special she was hosting in early October. It had to be as exciting as Madam Pearl's dress, another masterpiece.

Considering the fame of the actress, everyone at the atelier was excited. They expected their boss to go to work immediately, producing sketches and ordering fabrics, as the dress had to be ready in less than a month. Days passed and none of that happened.

"I just can't get into it," Sachiko confessed. "It's as if my flow of inspiration has run dry."

All Misako could say was, "Please, Sachi. Give it more time."

It was hard to advise Sachiko these days. Things had not really been the same between the old friends since their heated argument in August. They were getting on well enough, but subtle changes were taking place. Misako was feeling a lot of resentment toward her friend, a feeling she couldn't justify. And Sachiko was sometimes short with Misako for no apparent reason. The friendship had become fragile.

Sachiko shrugged. "Time is running out. Etsuko is the most famous television actress in Japan. Can you imagine how many people are going to be watching that show?"

Misako studied her friend for a few seconds. "Maybe you are going through some sort of change. Maybe we both are entering into a new life cycle."

For the first time in a month, Misako had managed to say some-thing that amused Sachiko. "Are we old enough for that? You mean like menopause?"

Misako's words may have been flip, but they raced around Sachiko's head all night. At six in the morning an agitated Sachiko ran a hot bath. Immersed in sweet-smelling bubbles and steam, she thought about how much she liked the idea of a new life cycle. A person's third life cycle wasn't supposed to happen until their thirty-sixth year. Sachiko had six more years to go for that. Still, it had a certain optimistic ring; it was better than admitting to being burned out. Negative thoughts were counterproductive.

Sachiko had been through other life cycles and survived. Why not create my own new life cycle? she asked herself.

That thought put Sachiko in a dreamy state. She slid deeper into the tub, until the bubbles touched her chin. My business has really grown, she thought. Even if I lose my touch and have to sell out at this stage, I'll be fine. Auntie Kaz and I own the building my business is in and I own this apartment outright. She and I are iron butterflies.

"Oh, of course! Butterfly wings!" she said into the sweet-smelling, steamy air. Etsuko's dress should be as beautiful and as delicate as an exotic butterfly's wings. The answer had just popped into her head. That was it! She would use that fabulous bolt of filmy, gossamer silk that she had been saving all these years. It had all the rich metallic blues of the giant Morpho butterflies of tropical South America. Papa had bought her the entire fifteen yards during their first trip to Paris together. When he saw how lovingly she touched the delicate stuff, he had insisted she have it. *Morpho Menelaus*, Sachiko had learned the Latin name for the butterfly that had inspired the masterwork. She had wrapped it in handmade, acid-free paper and stored it in her bedroom. It was one of her treasures and now was the time to part with it.

The dress, she decided, should be strapless, with an empire waist, draped in the front so the skirt floats with every movement. I'll suggest that Etsuko make her entrance almost running down a staircase, quickly, lightly, with her hands raised above her head, holding a long delicate scarf of the butterfly-wing fabric that will float above and behind her. Audrey Hepburn had come down a staircase like that in a movie with Fred Astaire. Etsuko would remember.

While Sachiko was sorting out her life that morning, Misako was waking up filled with a sense of danger. The cats were being very vocal. Coco was on her chest meowing. Cleo was at the door. Just as this disturbing fact registered, the bed started to heave and the hardware on the dresser began to rattle. Things were sliding off the shelves; books and trinkets tumbled onto the desk and the geisha doll crashed to the floor, sending up a shower of glass as the case smashed. Misako opened the door and dashed out. The cats ran under the white sofa.

Sachiko's bathtub felt like a ship at sea: the water slopped over the sides of the tub. "Earthquake!" she screamed and grabbed her robe. Misako was banging on the bathroom door. "Sachie! *Jishin!* Hurry!"

Together they ran to the apartment door and threw it open.

"The cats!" Sachiko said, heading back into the apartment. Misako caught her arm. "They are under the sofa. They are safer there than we are."

The rattling slowly began to subside. Frightened people were coming out of the other four apartments on the same floor, worried if this was the big one they all feared. The next-door neighbour's nine-year-old daughter was holding onto her mother, screaming. The foreign couple that lived across the hall were hugging each other and talking in rapid German. Everyone was frightened, waiting for the second shock, holding their breath. Two minutes passed before a man called out: "I think that's it this time. Is everyone all right? Better keep your doors open for a while, there might be an aftershock. No one wants to be trapped in their apartment."

"It's finished. It is all over now," the mother told her child. "Now stop crying."

Slowly people went back to their apartments. Misako and Sachiko did the same, but left the door open. Misako picked up a bowl of flowers that had fallen from the foyer table onto the white rug. Her hands were shaking.

Sachiko's collection of Japanese prints was all askew on the walls and the kitchen floor was littered with broken crockery. They were trying to shrug off their fear as they went through the apartment to check the damage. A mirror built into the bathroom wall was cracked and a bottle of perfume had tumbled into the sink. It hadn't broken but it was leaking the fragrance of Chanel No. 5. Misako put it back in its place and closed the door. She had to pee and try to recover.

Small possessions had fallen down everywhere. Sachiko was in her room checking on her precious butterfly fabric and picking up the incense burner that had tumbled off her dresser.

"Let's pick up what we can and leave the rest for the maid," Sachiko said, "but first I need a cigarette." They both flopped down on the white coach. Sachiko retrieved the cigarettes from the rug and searched around for the ashtray.

Misako put her head in her hands. She was close to tears. "Oh, that was frightening. That earthquake was probably only a five, but it felt much stronger at this height. One of these days there will be a major earthquake in Tokyo and I don't want to be on the eighth floor when it comes."

Sachiko lit her cigarette and blew the smoke toward the ceiling. Misako remembered the cats and got down on the rug, trying to see under the sofa.

"They won't appear for hours," Sachiko said. "They don't trust the world."

Misako could understand that feeling. She no longer trusted the world around her. There was something very uncomfortable growing in this apartment, something very unhealthy. She sometimes woke up in the morning feeling betrayed and threatened. It made her very insecure and unhappy, the kind of feelings that brought on her visions.

Misako shuddered. "I don't trust Tokyo's world. There are no bamboo groves close by, not enough safe places."

Sachiko frowned and blew out more smoke. "There may be bamboo groves in Niigata but no opportunities. What would you do in Niigata? Run errands for your mother at the hospital? Make tea for the nurses?"

Misako tilted her head to one side in thought. "I could start a business of my own. Someday I might even marry again."

"Who would you marry in Shibata? A priest or a farmer?" Sachiko said, stubbing out her cigarette and standing up.

"I could do worse," Misako grinned, trying to lighten up their exchange.

Sachiko closed her eyes and put her hand on her forehead as if she had a headache. "Oh, I give up. I introduced you to a new world, but you've never tried to fit in."

"I don't like your Tokyo lifestyle," Misako said. "Why should I try to fit in?"

"Because without me, you have *no* lifestyle!" Sachiko almost screamed.

"That's not fair!" Misako yelled back. Their angry voices shocked them both into silence. Misako bit her lip and a tear ran down her cheek.

Sachiko took a wad of tissues from her robe pocket. "Here," she said, "wipe your eyes and let's stop this. You are right. That wasn't fair and I do think my way is best. I'm sorry, but that's the way I am."

All Misako could do was sigh. The earthquake had broken more than glass and pottery.

The earthquake had hit on a Friday morning. That afternoon Misako left the atelier early to catch the five o'clock train to Niigata. "I'll be back on Sunday evening," she announced to Sachiko at the office.

"You didn't mention going home for the weekend this morning."

"I didn't know this morning. I only decided at lunchtime."

"I thought you were taking time off next month for your grandfather's memorial."

"It's the weekend. I'm just leaving a little early on Friday. I'll be back Sunday night."

"*Ah so*," Sachiko said coldly, her face stormy.

"Don't be angry, Sachie. I just want to go home to be with my family for the weekend. My mother said the harvest is in and you know there is nothing more delicious than Niigata's new rice. I'll bring back a kilo of it, if you like."

Sachiko had no recourse other than to swallow the clouds and smile back. "Yes, please, that will be a treat."

It was almost ten o'clock that night when Misako arrived at her parents' home. Considering how early she had been shaken out of bed that morning, she was surprised to find that she wasn't tired at all. In fact, there was a new energy bubbling inside her. She couldn't go to bed. She and Keiko had their tea and it was already eleven o'clock. Dr. Ichimura was working late. Misako decided to go over to the hospital to see him.

That is what she told her mother, but she felt drawn to the hospital for another reason. She wanted to go to the upstairs room where she and Teishin had shared a dream and long conversations. It had to do with her mother telling her that real love was a comfortable air that developed slowly, and flowed naturally between two people. When she was alone in Sachiko's apartment, she found herself looking out the living room window into the night, thinking about the whispered talks she had shared with Teishin that night.

As she came through the door, Dr. Ichimura was coming out of the delivery room. "Ah, Misako, come make me a cup of tea, please. Would you believe no births for a week and now three in one day? You see, not everyone is superstitious about a fire horse year."

They sat in his office, on either side of his desk, sipping their tea. "Papa, I want to talk to you about something important, but I'm not ready to discuss this with Mother yet."

"Oh," he said with a smile, "it sounds serious."

"I'm thinking about moving back to Shibata but I want to have my thoughts clear before I talk to her. You have always had good sense."

"Getting tired of life in Tokyo?" he guessed.

"*Umm.*"

"We can find you a job here, you know, but it won't be as well-paying or as exciting as Tokyo."

"If I do come back, I think I would like to teach calligraphy. I have the certification and I know I would love to work with children."

"That's a fine idea, Misako." The news made him grin. "After-school classes are very popular these days."

"I have money of my own. I could rent a small house to live in and hold my classes there."

"Or you could at live home and hold your classes at the temple. That place could use some new life within its walls."

"Now that," Misako said, "is a fine idea!"

"Could be a problem though," the doctor continued, "since your mother wants Teishin married. I suppose you know she has the woman chosen and has been annoying the poor fellow with her picture."

"No, I did not know," Misako said, frowning. "What did Teishin say?"

"He managed to put her off by saying he doesn't want to think about it until after Grandfather's one-year memorial. Knowing Mother, she will be back at the temple with the picture before the memorial incense burns down."

"Oh," Misako said, trying not to let on how upset his words were making her. "Teishin will never agree to that kind of marriage."

"I don't know how the poor fellow can avoid it," the doctor said, shaking his head. "You know your mother, and now she has the elders behind her."

THIRTY-SEVEN

With a little help from three strategically placed electric fans, the butterfly dress was a sensation. When Etsuko almost danced down the wide, white staircase, the audience at the television studio broke into applause. The camera kept the actress framed perfectly until she made a full turn at the bottom of the stairs, still holding the scarf over her head. That was when the camera zoomed in for the close-up of the billowing length of silk, making people watching all over Japan think of an exotic, giant blue butterfly.

At that moment six seamstresses and Misako jumped up and down on the white rug and cheered. Misako had invited them to the apartment to watch the show, eat Chinese food and celebrate their shared success. Like a fine kimono, every stitch on the cloud-like fabric had to be sewn by hand. Nabuko, the sewing-room supervisor, told the story of how she had come into the sewing room one morning and found Sachiko working on the butterfly dress herself.

"She must have been sitting in the corner of that small room sewing for hours. Her stitches are the finest in the entire dress."

Sachiko and Auntie Kaz were spending the evening at the French Embassy. They and six other guests were having a quiet dinner with the ambassador and his wife. At eight o'clock, during cocktails, they all went into the den to see the dress that Sachiko had talked so passionately about. Etsuko's entrance was particularly wonderful on the embassy's large television screen. The colour was brilliant and Sachiko's heart raced as she watched Etsuko descend the stairs with the grace of a ballet dancer. It was exactly as Sachiko had envisioned, right down to the close-up.

"Wherever did you get that amazing fabric?" the ambassador's wife asked.

"In Paris, of course," Sachiko smiled and lifted her glass as if she was proposing a toast.

"You know, there is something very familiar about the way that girl came down those stairs," the ambassador said. "It reminds me of a movie with that famous American actress. Do you know who I mean? I can't remember her name."

"Audrey Hepburn," Auntie Kaz laughed. "It was very similar to a scene from one of her movies. But then, I don't doubt that the ambassador knows only too well that we Japanese have no reservations about copying things we admire."

"*Oui*, Madam, I know only too well," the ambassador sighed.

✦ ✦ ✦

Ordinarily, Hideo would have slipped away to another room while his mother and Fumiko watched anything like a big, well-publicized television special. This time he sat at the dining-room table sipping his whisky all through Etsuko's show. His inside information made him smirk when Fumiko and his mother raved over the spectacular butterfly dress. Certainly they would have changed channels if they had known who created the dress. Now his only problem was how to leave home quietly after everyone had fallen asleep. Sachiko had sounded very wired on the telephone when she called his office this morning. She wanted to play tonight and she wouldn't take no for an answer.

The well-tipped night clerk at the apartment house hardly looked up from the desk when Hideo headed for the elevator. Removing his shoes, he quietly turned the key, slowly opened the door and crept down the hallway to Sachiko's room. He was unaware that he was passing the room in which his ex-wife was sleeping.

The sewing girls had left the apartment about ten o'clock. Misako had gone straight to bed and slept soundly. When she woke up at about five o'clock in the morning she thought she was dreaming. There was something that looked like a black-and-white movie being projected onto the ceiling over her bed. She rubbed her eyes and opened them wide. What she was watching was a startling performance of a nude couple in the midst of a torrid sex act. The woman's head was thrown back over the side of the bed. Misako could see the expression of pure ecstasy on her face, her red lips open and showing perfect white teeth. Sachiko's teeth! It was Sachiko and Hideo making love. Misako sat up and the picture faded, leaving every nerve in her body wide awake and her senses heightened. Her now supersensitive ears picked up the small sounds coming from the room down the hall, and there was a slight scent of a familiar hair tonic.

Misako was too weak to do anything but lie back down in bed and try to understand. Sachiko and Hideo! Now she knew why the vibrations in the apartment had been so negative of late, why she felt depressed. It was a cruel game the thrill-seeking, amoral Sachiko was playing. Hideo was her new mystery man and having his ex-wife in the apartment must have added an extra kick to the sex. Misako closed her eyes in disgust, trying to block out the pink glow in her bedroom. Her mind raced on for more than an hour. A noise coming from the hallway pulled her out of it. She jumped from her bed, threw the door open and came face to face with Hideo and Sachiko.

"Misako, go back into your room," Sachiko commanded. "This is none of your business." Hideo put his head down and walked on. Misako stepped back, closed the door and fell on the bed feeling ill.

It was almost eight o'clock in the morning before she emerged. Sachiko was in the living room, dressed for the office. There was a tray of coffee and thick buttered toast on the coffee table.

"You are not dressed," she said, looking up at Misako. "You'll be late for work."

Misako almost laughed. "Do you really expect me to continue working for you?"

"If you want to resign, that's your privilege, only do it properly. We don't want to lose face and cause gossip. Make sure you don't leave loose ends at the office. You owe me that."

Misako sat down in her usual place. "All right," she said, "I'll do it your way, but I am definitely leaving."

Sachiko handed her a cup of coffee. "I suppose it won't help to say I'm sorry. It wasn't about hurting you. It was a caprice gone wrong."

Misako shoulders went up and down in the gesture she had learned from Misako. "This is your apartment. Hideo is no longer my husband. I shouldn't have been living here this long. As you said, it was none of my business."

Sachiko's frowned. "I really am sorry. I went too far this time."

Misako sighed. "It doesn't matter anymore. I am going back to live in Niigata as soon as possible. I no longer have any doubts about where I belong."

"I understand," Sachiko said as she passed Misako a plate of toast.

Both women understood that their friendship had been smashed beyond repair, but they managed to appear on good terms until Misako left town. It was Hideo who was having major problems with his nerves. Why had

361

he given in to the temptation and gotten involved with Sachiko? Now he was petrified that Misako would call his mother and tell all. If that was to happen, his home could explode into a war-zone. It would be the last straw for Uncle Buddha. He surely would be kicked out of the company in disgrace. Every time the telephone rang at home, Hideo held his breath and broke into a cold sweat.

❁ ❁ ❁

During those first days back home, Misako unpacked and had long conversations with her parents. They discussed her step-brothers, the hospital and especially the temple. Finding Teishin a wife came up in conversation one morning as she and her mother chatted at breakfast. Misako expressed interest and asked her mother if she could see the woman's picture and resume. Keiko raised her eyebrows. "*Maa!* Aren't you the curious one?"

"That could be something I inherited from my mother. You are not the only one capable of minding other people's business."

Keiko handed over the envelope before she went out the door. "Put it back on the bookcase when you are finished looking at it. I'll be interested in what you think, since I can't get an opinion out of Papa."

Alone in the house, Misako sat frowning as she studied the picture. The woman was thin and pleasant-looking, wearing a kimono, sitting in a chair with her hands folded like a schoolgirl. The picture had obviously been taken in a photographer's studio.

Still looking at the picture, Misako dialled the temple's number. A strange voice answered and identified herself as a member of the congregation who was watching the temple. "No, both priests are out. Yes, I will tell them. Who? Misako-*san*. They are expected back after three o'clock. *Hai*, I understand."

Misako hung up wondering if the woman watching the temple was the very one whose picture she was still studying. Maybe Teishin was already spending time with her. Biting her lip, she found a pen and paper, sat down at the *kotatsu* and started to write.

That afternoon, Keiko had to drive the doctor into Niigata City. At about three o'clock, it started to rain; by four o'clock it was pouring down. Misako was getting tired of waiting for Teishin to call. Her head was bursting with plans and possibilities. The water was cascading off the roof into the garden. It didn't matter. She found a long hooded raincoat and her mother's rubber boots and started out for the temple on her bicycle.

When she rolled back the temple's kitchen door, Teishin was standing at the table in his baggy working clothes, cooling a pot of rice. When he saw her standing in the entrance looking like she had just come out of the river, he dropped the bamboo fan and rushed to help her.

"*A la la*! Misako-*san*! Oh, why did you ride your bicycle in this weather? I thought you would drive. You'll catch cold. Konein-*san*, bring a towel!" he shouted. "Here, take these slippers."

"Don't worry. I'll be fine."

Konein arrived with a towel in one hand and the three-coloured kitten in the other.

Misako wiped her face and reached for the kitten. "How big he is getting. How cute. What have you named him?"

"Tama," Konein blushed. "I had a cat named Tama when I was young."

"We all did," Misako laughed, cuddling the cat. "Oh, Teishin-*san*, what are you making?"

"Vegetable sushi," Teishin said. "I thought you would be hungry."

"I am, but how did you know I was coming?"

"I got your message. The lady that watched the temple today said you would be here after three."

"*Ah so*," Misako smiled. She put the kitten down and took the big, old kettle to the sink and filled it.

"I'll do that," Konein said.

"Oh, let me," she pleaded. "I used to live here, you know."

The two priests and Misako ate the vegetable sushi sitting around the table in the little room where she so often had shared food and tea with her grandfather. The rain beat down on the roof. The kitten went over to investigate the pail that was in the corner of the room catching a leak. Misako looked distressed when she saw it.

Teishin noticed her expression. "It will be fixed soon. I don't want any changes until after next month's memorial service."

Around seven that evening, Keiko called the temple looking for Misako. "I thought you might be there. Why would you go out in such weather? Stay there. I'll drive over to pick you up in about thirty minutes."

It was now or never, Misako thought. They were sitting alone on the sitting room's *tatami*. Misako put aside their tea cups and told Teishin she had something to show him before she went home. The priest looked pleased until he saw her pull a familiar large envelope from her handbag. She placed the envelope on the floor between them.

"Teishin-*san*, everyone is saying that you have to find a wife within the next year. With that in mind, I wish you to consider marriage to the woman whose picture and resume I have brought you. My mother is more skilful at the go-between procedure, but I beg your patience with my lack of experience." She slid the envelope toward him and bowed.

Teishin inwardly groaned. He had gone through all this with her mother and it was disappointing to think that Misako was giving her approval to this arrangement. He returned her bow and explained that her mother had already presented him with this very envelope and he had told her that he could not consider it. "Please, please understand, I do not want to make any such decision until after next month's memorial," he said.

Looking totally miserable, he slowly pushed the envelope back toward Misako and sighed. "I can speak more frankly with you than I could with your mother. I have seen this picture. I don't want to look at this picture again. I don't want to marry this lady, ever."

"But this is a different lady," she said, passing it back, her face serious and unsmiling. "Please do look this picture over. No one needs talk of marriage until after the memorial. I just want you to look at the picture."

"No, thank you," he said, showing his stubborn streak. "I still won't be interested."

"Teishin-*san*! I have made this trip here in the teeming rain mainly to show you this picture. Don't be so rude."

The tone of her voice startled him. With shock written all over his face, he reached out and picked up the envelope. He opened it, removed the picture and stared blankly at it for a few seconds before it registered. He was looking at a picture of Misako, an ordinary snapshot of her standing next to her bicycle. With disbelief, he slowly looked up.

"This woman has many flaws," she said. "This woman has been divorced. Under such circumstances, your congregation may not allow it. This woman also has many strange characteristics. She has a troublesome imagination, and sometimes she even believes that she has visions. But, since this woman would like to spend the rest of her life at your side, I thought you might possibly consider her for your wife, in spite of her faults."

With a heart almost bursting in his chest and tears in his eyes, Teishin bowed deeply and could only say, "Misako. *Arigato gozaimasu.*"

Reluctantly, Keiko agreed that Misako and Teishin had the right to marry. Dr. Ichimura assured her that they would make a splendid couple and be very happy.

"Think how comforting it will be having Misako living so close to us. This time there could even be a grandchild."

"A grandchild? I'm not sure Misako can have children."

"The last doctor who examined her found nothing physically wrong. There are a number of reasons why a couple don't have children. Sometimes a man's sperm is not compatible with the woman's chemistry, or maybe they aren't performing the sex act right."

"Oh," Keiko moaned. "I wonder if Teishin has had any sexual experience. Will he know what to do?"

Dr. Ichimura laughed. "If he doesn't, I imagine he'll learn fast enough."

It was agreed between Misako and Teishin that they would not announce their engagement until after her grandfather's one-year memorial. Her parents were the only ones who knew, and they too thought it better to wait. Keiko hoped that the delay would give Misako time to think it over and maybe change her mind. She liked Teishin and gave him credit for making great strides over the past year. Still, in the back of her mind there lingered the shadow of her mother's hard life. Being the wife of a Buddhist priest was not easy.

"Times have changed," her husband assured her when she expressed her concern. "The local farmers are getting rich with the government protecting the rice prices. If the farmers can send their children off to college, they can certainly support their temple. Some of them are having the priests come to their homes every month now to chant sutras at their family altars. And there will be extra income from Misako's and Konein's classes. Considering how much Misako loves the temple, and how well she and Teishin get on, it all seems very positive to me."

The very next day, an envelope arrived from Sachiko. There was no note inside, only a forwarded letter from Kensho. Misako smiled at the American stamps and familiar writing. In sweet anticipation she made a cup of tea to take out into the small garden where she could read the letter in the warmth of the autumn sun.

Dear Misako-san,

Thank you for Kiku's story. I will treasure it always. It helped me put myself with you at the service at the Homma home in Neya. I felt as if I had been truly there, praying with you and Teishin-san. Although the experience during the ceremony must have been difficult to bear, it would be comforting to believe that, once again, your sensitivity and generosity allowed that lost spirit to express the misery she knew in life. Just as you described her pain, so too did you describe a wonderful sense of peace. If this came from Kiku-san's lingering energy, or entirely from your own self, it no longer matters. What matters is that those of us who have been touched by what we perceived as a sad wandering soul can be content that her spirit must finally be at peace. Your grandfather's quest has been accomplished. I congratulate you and Teishin-san for your excellent efforts.

May you both be blessed.

> *As always,*
> *Your friend,*
> *Kensho*
> *October 1966, San Francisco, California*

❀ ❀ ❀

The ancient custom of holding memorial services for the dead was traditionally held on the first, third, seventh, thirteenth, twenty-third, twenty-seventh, thirty-third, thirty-seventh, fiftieth and one-hundredth anniversaries of the death. Many people gave up having these services when no one living had any particular memory of the deceased. Often the services merely meant that family members gathered and a priest came to the house to pray, followed by some sort of a meal. More traditional families, such as a priest's family, were likely to hold a more elaborate affair, especially for a first anniversary.

The old master's one-year memorial ceremony was planned with a certain amount of joy. Two days before, Teishin and a group of farm women journeyed by bus to the hot spring area near Deyu to gather mushrooms that the old man dearly loved. They could be found under the red pine trees that grew on the side of the mountain. It took them many hours of running their hands through the pine needles under the trees to find enough of the prized *matsutake* to fill a basket.

These mushrooms are difficult to find and very expensive to buy, but Teishin had been the son of a mountain farmer and he seemed to be able to smell where the mushrooms were hiding. Happily, it was going to be possible for the memorial luncheon feast to feature *matsutake gohan*, the pine-mushroom rice dish that everyone knew was most loved by the old master himself. Without a doubt, Teishin was the hero of the day. The farm women praised his skill and joked to themselves about the phallic shape and size of the mushrooms. In fits of giggles, they covered their mostly silver teeth with their hands and speculated about whether the dead master's daughter, Keiko, would ever find the priest a bride.

On the day of the ceremony, the women of the congregation arrived early to prepare the luncheon. Most of the food was cooked that morning, to be served cold, with the exception of the warm *matsutake gohan* and miso soup. By the time the memorial service began at ten o'clock, many layers of smells permeated the temple. Incense smoke hung in a perfumed haze about the smells of radish pickles and fish.

Teishin and Konein chanted the sutras before the altar that held the picture of the departed priest and the memorial tablet on which his death name had been written. By now, most of the congregation were confident that Teishin would be a very good priest. Besides, he had never looked so well and happy as he did today; he was absolutely glowing.

There seemed to be little sense of mourning, either during the ceremony or when they went to pay their respects at the temple's gravesite. When Dr. Ichimura and a dozen senior members of the congregation sat down for their luncheon, the mood lightened even further. Keiko and Misako worked along with the other women serving the food. When that was done, they went around pouring drinks and personally thanking the guests for attending. Halfway through this ritual, Keiko was called to the telephone and Teishin left his cushion to take her place next to Misako. For almost ten minutes, Teishin and Misako moved from guest to guest together, talking, bowing and pouring sake. One or two of the smarter older ladies looked at each other, raised their eyebrows and smiled.

When it was all over and the guests gone home, Keiko joined her daughter to sit a while at the *kotatsu*. A storm was blowing up and the warmth felt good.

Keiko looked past the glass doors into the garden and fell silent as she watched a gust of wind send a shower of small red maple leaves flying.

"I never thought about you and Teishin-*san* as a couple. When did it start? Whoever put such an idea in your head?"

Misako smiled. "It was you, Mother. Don't you remember the night you told Papa and me that Grandfather had hoped I would marry a priest?"

"*Maa!*" she said. "Did I say that? I don't remember that at all."

THIRTY-EIGHT

Kensho-sama,

The weather was beautiful yesterday for Grandfather's one-year memorial. Your presence was very much missed. I thought about you all during the ceremony and several members of the congregation asked about you. Even my mother said that she will always be grateful for the help you gave so willingly during that sad time. Was it only a year? It seems longer.

You will be glad to know that Teishin is well and the temple is running smoothly. He and the elders are making plans for all manner of improvements to be made to the old building. The roof repair is first on the list.

I have just returned from Shimizuen garden and wish that you could have shared today's experience with me. It started yesterday when Mr. Saito came to the temple to pay his respect to Grandfather's memory. After the ceremony, he asked me about our trip to Neya. He seemed very glad that the girl's ashes had finally been returned to her home. It was then that I asked his permission to drop the small amount of sand that I brought from Neya into the pond where Kiku-san drowned. He told me to bring the sand to the garden tomorrow, early in the afternoon. Since the garden is closed to the public every Monday, it would be the best time to do it quietly.

When I arrived there today about one o'clock, the caretaker was in the office and allowed me to go through to the garden. As I walked to the back of the pond, I met Mr. Saito coming out of the tea house. I showed him the handful of sand which I had wrapped in a handkerchief along with two beach stones. He was most agreeable to my plan. He also invited me to take a cup of ceremonial tea before I left for home.

You can imagine my emotions as I walked slowly to the bridge. The autumn colours were exactly as I had remembered them to be last year. One difference was that the pond water seemed darker. I knelt and tried to meditate on the meaning of this small act. Then, recalling all the moments of that fatal day, I put my hand as far as possible into the pond and released the little package. It sank quickly, releasing a few bubbles. In time, I suppose, the linen handkerchief will come apart and the sand will rest on the bottom of the pond, perhaps near the remaining bones. When it was done I was filled with the sweetest sense of calm that I have ever known. It seemed to be in the air, in my body and in my soul. I went to the tea house feeling serene.

You must know that there can be moments in our lives when time and space seem to dissolve. And so it was during the quiet tea ritual, gracefully performed to the healing whispers of kettle, water and tea whisk. When Mr. Saito placed the tea bowl before me, I received it with a reverence that, I believe, Christians feel for sacramental wine.

Do you remember seeing the sazanka tree that was in bloom in that garden on that fateful day last year? Today I stopped to enjoy its beauty when I was leaving the garden. It is indeed a different kind of tree, heavy with calm white flowers when other trees are throwing off their bright leaves.

And now my life is about to take a different road. Kensho-san, perhaps you will not be too surprised to learn that Teishin-san and I are going to be married in December. It will be a quiet affair with only immediate family and some senior members of the congregation.

There are some who may well think of Teishin and me as an unlikely couple. I understand it took the committee of temple elders hours to agree to the marriage. The fact that I was divorced was not as serious an issue as our horoscopes were, I being born in the year of the rat and Teishin-san in the year of the rabbit. It seems that for a rabbit man, a rat woman would be the worst possible wife. I intend to work hard at proving that horoscope wrong.

I am sure that you will be happy for us. There is no
longer any doubt in my mind that this is the correct path
to follow for myself, for Teishin-san and for the temple.
Even my mother has to agree that Grandfather would have
approved. As you know, it was he who made the first turn of
the wheel that led to this ummei.

Best wishes for your good health and we pray that your
life in America is happy and rewarding. We look forward to
your return to Japan and your visit to Shibata.

Your friend,
Misako
Shibata, Niigata Japan
October 12, 1966

❀ ❀ ❀

On December tenth, a calendar day of good luck, Misako and Teishin were married in the main altar room of the temple by the priest Konein. Misako wore the same formal kimono and *obi* that she had worn to the wedding of Hideo's cousin. The temple smelled of fresh, new *tatami*, befitting the home of a new bride.

During the ceremony, Misako kept her eyes down in the traditionally demure manner that is expected of a Japanese bride. Only once did she look up to give her new husband a reassuring smile. That was when Teishin's nerves made his stomach rumble and face turn scarlet. Dr. Ichimura's mouth hinted at a smile but Keiko kept her mask intact. It was about this time that Tama the cat caused a slight distraction by strolling into the room.

The reception afterward was formal, for family and the most senior members of the congregation. Many more parish members were working in the kitchen, serving and finding all manner of chores to busy themselves at the temple that day. Everyone came into the room when the speeches began. All were given cups of sake for the toast. When that was over, the bride and groom knelt in the middle of the room and bowed with their heads touching the new *tatami*, in a formal expression of their thanks. Everyone responded by applauding.

Kensho wrote a warm letter of congratulations from California and arranged, through a nearby Zen temple, for a young *sazanka* tree to be sent to the temple garden as his wedding gift. Misako had it planted where it could be viewed from the space that they were converting into a school room for the abacus and calligraphy classes.

As a wedding gift, Sachiko sent a *haori* kimono coat that was a superb example of Japanese tie-dying, called *shibori*. It was frightfully expensive and a work of art.

"Look at this wonderful gift from Sachiko," Misako said when she showed her mother the coat.

"*Maa!* A shame to waste it," Keiko said. "It's too grand for a priest's wife. If you wear that at the temple, people will talk behind your back and say you are putting on airs."

"No they won't. I will wear it proudly on special occasions and tell people the truth. That it was a gift from a very generous woman who had helped me during a very painful time of my life. Everyone will be happy for my good fortune."

Misako's wedding gift to herself and her husband was a small car. Teishin arranged to attend a local driving school, but not until after they returned from a short trip. As a mini-honeymoon, they spent the night in a hot-spring hotel not far from the beach where they had stopped on their way to Neya. The next day the happy newlyweds drove further north through a light snow, to Teishin's family's home.

Life in such an old farm house was a new experience for Misako. They sat with his brother's family around an open fire-pit and filled their bowls from a great pot of country stew. The pot was hung over the fire from a rope and a hook fastened to the smoke-darkened ceiling beams; it felt like taking a step back in time. Misako looked up at the ceiling beams and thought that she could feel the great surges of energy left by the lives of many generations.

Her brother-in-law noticed Misako looking up at the high, dark ceiling. "There could be spirits lingering in those dark places," he teased. "I hope you are not afraid to sleep in such an old house."

"No, not at all," she said. "I find the presence of ancesteral spirits very comforting."

Her new family laughed at this surprising answer, and so did Misako.

That night, the newlyweds slept in a room under the stairway that led to a second floor where the family raised silkworms as a winter occupation. The house was pleasantly filled with the constant rustle of the little creatures in their mulberry leaves.

Teishin was not a man who could ever tell his wife that he loved her. Instead, he held Misako close and whispered, "I must have done something very good in my past life to have this happiness."

❀ ❀ ❀

In the spring of 1967, the priest Kensho walked along the street in the Japan Town area of San Francisco. He was missing Japan and chided himself for feeling low, for not being at his best. As he walked along, he noticed several large, white Japanese chrysanthemums in a florist's window. They were both shaggy and beautiful. He stood on the street admiring them for several minutes. The flowers brought the remembered joy of wonderful talks and heart-stopping moments. He stood there recalling an autumn garden, shared rice balls on a train and a farewell almost-kiss.

On an impulse he went inside the store and bought one flower. The woman behind the counter was a second-generation Japanese. She wrapped the flower carefully and instructed him to carry the flower upside down to keep it fresh, and to strip off the bottom leaves before he put it in water. When he returned to his room, he placed it in a tall glass of water. He tenderly touched the petals and breathed in its scent. Every time he looked at it that day, he smiled.

Before he went to bed that night, he took out his paper and brush and wrote:

> *Remembered joy*
> *Lives in its beauty and scent*
> *One chrysanthemum.*

ACKNOWLEDGEMENTS

For over twenty years, this novel has lived in bits and pieces on my bookshelves. The finished product wouldn't have happened without a great deal of help.

A very big thanks goes to my husband David for invaluable help, patience and cheerful encouragement.

I want to thank the terrific team of Frances and Bill Hanna who worked so hard to make it all come together.

Big thanks to my publishers Ruth Linka and Lee Shedden for their help in the publication of this novel. I am grateful for their excellent editing and their faith in my work.

Huge kudos to Dr. David Greig, otolaryngologist, Dr. Steven Richie, orthopedic surgeon and Barbara Richie RN. All three of these friends and neighbours helped guide me through the medical scenes.

I send thanks to Japan to Mrs. Shigeko Kazama for years of friendship and for contributing her skill in calligraphy for the cover of this book. I also thank Martha Ichiyanagi for answering my e-mailed questions from her home in Yamagata. And to Victoria Yoshimura of the Shonenji Temple in Kyushu for information about Japanese temple life and Buddhism.

Hugs and thanks to my Brantford friends, Nancy and Jamie Westaway, for reading the book in the early stages. Nancy took great trouble helping me find an agent. Thanks goes to dear friend Susan Malcolm and to Pat and David Clemons for reading and correcting.

The Global Women's Writers group, an offshoot of the Association of Foreign Wives of Japanese, deserves thanks for their support.

Loving thanks to Natacha Hochman, Jackie Dunphy and Betty Calder-Fuiks for their constant encouragement and countless talks about our mutual experiences in Japan. And a deep bow to the late, dear, Jack Fuiks, who generously offered me professional advice and his infectious enthusiasm.

If I have left anyone out of this acknowledgment, I hope they will forgive me.

JOAN ITOH BURK was born in New York City and became totally immersed into Japanese society when she married the first son of a large land-owning family in Japan. For the thirteen years of that marriage, she lived in an enormous Meiji era house on the rice plains in Niigata. During the 1970s, Joan Itoh wrote a weekly column for *The Japan Times* called "Rice Paddy Gourmet." A collection of her half-diary, half-recipe essays evolved into the popular *Rice Paddy Gourmet* book. Of this book, James Clavell wrote to her: "It's a lovely book and you're a lovely writer."

One Chrysanthemum is Burk's first novel, inspired by her love of Japan and the Japanese culture. For the last twenty-five years, she has been living with her Canadian husband in southwestern Ontario.